Praise For Julie Anne Long's Previous Novels

BEAUTY AND THE SPY

"Serves up a perfect blend of romance and adventure with thoroughly engaging characters and sparkling dialogue. I highly recommend *Beauty and the Spy* for its fine story-telling, excellent romance, charming wit, and memorable characters."

—*Romance Reviews Today*

"TOP PICK! Four-and-a-half stars! There's enough action, romance, passion, wit, and historical details in Long's latest . . . to have readers sighing with delight. This top-notch new voice gets better with each book!"

—*Romantic Times BOOKclub Magazine*

"Four stars! Wonderful tale! Loved it! Long's best story yet and I can't wait to read the rest of the series."

—*RomanceReviewsMag.com*

"A lovely romance . . . filled with surprising compatibility and an extraordinary amount of luck . . . Long has created an excellent blend of mystery and romance that's perfect reading . . . It isn't your typical romance."

—*FreshFiction.com*

"A delightful historical tale."

Baryon Magazine

more . . .

TO LOVE A THIEF

"A wonderful story."

—Midwest Book Review

"A delightful read. The characters and their repartee sparkle with humor and charm."

—Rendezvous

"What an amazing book! I love a good romance story, but I love a book even more when it is well written. *To Love a Thief* may be one of the most wonderful Pygmalion stories yet to come out of the romance genre."

—Rakehell.com

"A perfect blend of romance and humor . . . magical and engaging, a treat for anyone who believes that fairy tales can come true."

—TheMysticCastle.com

"Compelling and highly entertaining . . . *To Love a Thief* is extremely well written, fast-paced, and entirely enjoyable."

—RoadtoRomance.com

"Lily is a wonderful heroine, and *To Love a Thief* is a fun read."

—Bookloons.com

"An excellent historical novel . . . the relationship between Lily and Gideon is the very substance of every young woman's romantic dreams."

—*RomanceJunkies.com*

THE RUNAWAY DUKE

"Wonderful and charming . . . at the top of my list for best romance of the year . . . It is a delight in every way."

—LikesBooks.com

"Julie Anne Long is an author who shines with a promising and noteworthy talent."

—RomanceReaderatHeart.com

"Thoroughly enjoyable . . . A charming love story brimming with intrigue, witty dialogue, and warmth."

—*Rendezvous*

"Hilarious, heartrending, and tender . . . ample suspense . . . A guaranteed winner."

—CurledUp.com

"A must-read . . . Combining the ideal amount of romance, suspense, and mystery, Long gives us a marvelous and dazzling debut that overflows with intelligence, wit, and warmth."

—*Romantic Times BOOKclub Magazine*

"Two fantastic lead protagonists . . . Fans will want to run away with this delightful pair."

—*Midwest Book Review*

ALSO BY
JULIE ANNE LONG

Beauty and the Spy
To Love a Thief
The Runaway Duke

WAYS TO BE WICKED

Julie Anne Long

NEW YORK   BOSTON

Copyright © 2006 by Julie Anne Long
Excerpt from *The Secret to Seduction* copyright © 2006 by Julie Anne Long. All rights reserved. No part of this book may be reproduced in any form or by any electronic or mechanical means, including information storage and retrieval systems, without permission in writing from the publisher, except by a reviewer who may quote brief passages in a review.

Warner Forever and the Warner Forever logo are trademarks of Time Warner Inc. or an affiliated company. Used under license by Hachette Book Group, which is not affiliated with Time Warner Inc.

Cover design by Diane Luger
Book design by Stratford Publishing Services

Warner Books
Hachette Book Group USA
1271 Avenue of the Americas
New York, NY 10020
Visit our Website at www.HachetteBookGroupUSA.com

Printed in the United States of America

First Printing: October 2006

10 9 8 7 6 5 4 3 2 1

This one's for you, Melis.

ACKNOWLEDGMENTS

My gratitude to the Fog City Divas
for perspective, support and laughter,
to Melanie Murray for patience and insightful editing,
and to Steve Axelrod, for being the fount
from which all wisdom and sanity springs these days—
and for cheerfully grousing about bad coffee
by a hotel elevator in Reno.

WAYS TO BE WICKED

CHAPTER ONE

IRONIC, SYLVIE THOUGHT, that the pitching and rolling of that wretched wooden ship should set up a corresponding pitching and rolling in her stomach, given that motion was more native to her than stillness. She in fact leaped, stretched, and pirouetted every day, achieving semiflight with no ill effects apart from sore muscles and the perversely gratifying jealousy of all of the other dancers in Monsieur Favre's corps de ballet. Sylvie Lamoreux was, in fact, the darling of the Paris Opera, object of desire and envy, the personification of beauty and grace—not accustomed, in other words, to losing the contents of her stomach over the side of a ship.

She supposed it had a little something to do with control. When she danced, *she* commanded her body. Well, and Monsieur Favre had a bit of a say in it, too: "I said, like a *butterfly,* Sylvie, not a cow. Look at you! I want to moo!" Or "Your arms, Sylvie, they are like timber. Lift them like so—ah yes, that is it, *mon ange,* you are like a dream. I suspected you could dance." Monsieur Favre was a trifle prone to exaggeration, but if she was his best dancer, he had helped make her so, and confidence was marvelous armor against sarcasm.

She'd rather be at Monsieur Favre's mercy any day than that of a bloody wooden ship, heaving this way and that over the choppy waters of the Channel.

He would not be pleased to find her gone.

The letter in her reticule said very little. But what it did say had launched her like a cannonball across the Channel to England for the first time in her life. For two weeks, Sylvie had furtively planned her journey, hurt and fury, poignant hope and a great inner flame of curiosity propelling her. She hadn't told a single soul of her plans. This seemed only fitting, given the magnitude of the things that had been kept from her.

Odd to think that a few mere sentences of English could do this. The letter had begun with an apology for bothering Claude yet again. *Yet again*—a little flame of anger licked up every time Sylvie thought of these words. It was not the first such letter sent, in other words. Or even the second, it would appear. And then, in the next sentence, it begged information about a young woman named Sylvie. *For I believe she might be my sister.*

The signature at the bottom said, "Susannah Whitelaw, Lady Grantham."

My sister. Sylvie had never before thought or said those two words together in her life.

To Sylvie the letter meant a past she'd never known, a future she'd never dreamed, and a store of secrets she'd only half suspected. Her parents were dead, Claude had told her, God rest their souls; Claude had raised Sylvie as her own. And if not for the fact that Claude had decided to holiday in the South as she did every year at this time, with a kiss on both cheeks for Sylvie and instructions to mind her parrot, Guillaume, Sylvie might never have seen the letter at all.

Sylvie had left Guillaume the parrot in the care of Claude's housekeeper. He would be in danger of nothing but boredom, as he spoke two more languages than the housekeeper, which was two fewer than Etienne.

Etienne. Sylvie's thoughts immediately flew from him as though scorched. And then flew back again, guiltily.

He was generous, Etienne, with ardor and gifts. He flirted as only one descended from centuries of courtiers could flirt; he moved through the world with the confident magnanimity of someone who had never been denied anything. He made heady promises she hardly dared believe, promises that would give her the life she had worked to acquire, that she had dreamed of.

But his temper . . . Sylvie would never understand it. Her own was a starburst—quick, spectacular, gone. His was cold and patient, implacable. It waited; he planned. And his retaliations always came with chilling finality and a sense of righteousness.

She'd last seen Etienne a week ago in the mauve predawn light, an arm flung over his head, his bare back turned to her as he slept. She'd placed the letter on her pillow, telling him only that she was sorry, but that she would see him again soon.

He loved her. But he used the word so easily.

But just as she knew Etienne would have tried to dissuade her from leaving Paris, she knew he would try to find her. And his temper would have been waiting all the while, too.

She did not want to be found until she'd learned what she'd come to learn.

The ship had released the passengers, and at last Sylvie's feet pressed against England. She allowed herself a giddy surge of triumph. She'd made it this far, entirely on her own. But she could still feel the sea inside her stomach, and color and movement and noise came at her in waves: men swarming to unload the ship, the early morning sun ricocheting hard between smooth sea and blue sky, gulls wheeling in arcs of silver and white. No clouds floated above to cut the glare or soften the heat. Sylvie took her first deep breath of truly English air. It was hot and clotted with dock odors, and made matters inside her stomach worse instead of better.

So be it. She would *will* her stomach into obedience. To date, there had been nothing Sylvie could not make her body do if she willed it.

She nodded to the man who shouldered her trunk for her and briskly turned to find the mail coach that would take her to London. She had never before traveled alone, but she had contrived the perfect disguise, her English was passably good, and she was not a child needing coddling or protection from a man. Besides, after Paris, a city as intricate, beautiful, and difficult as the ballet itself, no city could intimidate her. Great cities, at their hearts, were all the same.

She glanced up then and saw just the back of him, through the crowd, the broad shoulders, the way he stood. The sight of Etienne slammed hard, sending a cold wave of shock through her confidence. *It couldn't be. Not yet. Not so soon.*

But it was not a risk she was prepared to take. She swiveled her head, saw the mail coach, and made her decision.

ঞ ঞ ঞ

Tom Shaughnessy was alone in the stage coach mulling another failed trip to Kent, when a woman flung herself into his lap, wrapped her arms around his neck, and burrowed in, crushing her face against his.

"*What* in the name of—" he hissed. He lifted his arms to try to pry hers from about his neck.

"Hush," she whispered urgently. "*Please*."

A man's head peered into the coach.

"I beg your pardon." He jerked his head hurriedly back, and vanished from view.

The woman in his lap had gone completely rigid, apart from her rapid breathing. And for a moment neither of them moved. Tom had an impression of rustling dark fabric, a lithe form, and the scent of spice and vanilla and roses and . . . well, female. This last made his head swim a little.

Startling, granted. But not precisely unpleasant.

Apparently deciding a safe interval had elapsed, she took her arms from about his neck and slid from his lap into the seat a distance away from him.

"And just when I was growing accustomed to you, Madame," he said wryly. He touched her arm gently. "Allow me to intro—*ow!*"

He jerked his hand back. What the *devil*—?

His eyes followed a glint to her lap.

Poking up from her neatly folded gloved hands was a . . . was that a *knitting* needle?

It was! She'd jabbed him with a damned *knitting needle*. Not hard enough to wound anything other than his pride. But certainly hard enough to make her . . . er . . . point.

"I regret inserting you, sir, but I cannot permit you to touch me again." Her voice was soft and grave, refined; it trembled just a bit. And, absurdly, she did sound genuinely regretful.

Tom glared at her, baffled. "You regret inser—Oh! You mean 'stabbing.' You regret . . . *stabbing* me?"

"Yes!" She said almost gratefully, as though he'd given her a verb she considered useful and fully intended to employ again in the future. "I regret *stabbing* you. I regret sitting upon you, also. But I cannot permit you to touch me again. I am not . . ." She made a futile gesture with her hand, as if she could snatch the elusive word from the air with it.

She was not . . . what? Sane?

But he could hear it now—she was French. Which accounted for the way her syllables subtly leaped and dipped in the wrong places, not to mention her unusual vocabulary choices, and perhaps even the knitting needle, because God only knew what a Frenchwomen was capable of. And apart from that tremble in her voice he would have assumed she was preternaturally self-possessed. But she was clearly afraid of something, or someone, and he suspected it was the man who had just peered into the coach.

He looked at her hard, but she kept her head angled slightly away from him. She was wearing mourning; he could see this now that she wasn't precisely on top of him. Her hat and veil revealed only a hint of delicate jaw and gleaming hair, which seemed to be a red shade, though this might perhaps be wishful thinking on his part. Her neck was long; her spine as elegantly erect as a Doric column. She was slim, but the gown she wore gave away very little of the shape of the woman inside it. The gown itself was beautifully made, but it fit her ill. Borrowed, he decided. He was accustomed to judging the fit of female clothing, after all, and this dress was not only too large; it had been made for someone else entirely.

Since he had done nothing but gape for nearly a minute, she seemed satisfied he didn't intend to reach for her again and slid the needle back up into her sleeve. For all the world like a woman tucking a basket of mending under a chair.

"Who is pursuing you, Madame?" he asked softly.

Her shoulders stiffened almost imperceptibly. Interesting. A further ripple in that self-possession.

"Je ne comprende pas, monsieur." Delivered with a pretty little French lift of one shoulder.

Balderdash. She understood him perfectly well.

"Au contraire, I believe you do *comprende* my question," he contradicted politely. His own French was actually quite good. All the very best courtesans were French, after all. Many of the dancers who passed through the White Lily were as well, which is why he knew all about the caprices of Frenchwomen.

The veil fluttered; she was breathing a little more quickly now.

"If you tell me, I might be able to help you," he pressed gently. Why he should offer to help someone who'd leaped into his lap, then poked him with a knitting needle eluded him at the moment. Curiosity, he supposed. And that delicate jaw.

The veil fluttered once, twice, as she mulled her next words. "Oh, but you already *have* helped me, monsieur."

And the faint but unmistakable self-deprecating humor and—dare he think it?—*flirtation*—in her words perversely charmed him to his marrow.

He opened his mouth to say something else, but she turned decisively toward the window, and an instant later seemed to have shed her awareness of him as neatly as a shawl or hat.

Damned if he wasn't fascinated.

He wanted desperately to gain her attention again, but if he spoke she would ignore him, he sensed; he suspected that if he so much as brushed the sleeve of her gown his hand would be swiftly "inserted" as neatly as a naturalist's butterfly to the mail coach seat.

He was watching her so intently he was startled when the coach bucked on its springs, taking on the weight of more passengers: a duenna ushering two young ladies, both pretty and diffident; a young couple glowing with contentment, as though the institution of marriage was their own marvelous, private discovery; a young man who looked very much like a curate; a plump prosperous merchant of some sort. Tom made his judgments of them by their clothing and the way they held themselves. At one time, each and every one of them, or someone of their ilk, had passed through his life, or he through theirs.

The little Frenchwoman widow might as well have been a shadow of one of the other passengers; with her slight build and dark clothing, she all but vanished against the seat. No one would trouble her or engage her in conversation if she appeared not to welcome it; she was a widow, and ostensibly still inside a bubble of grief.

Tom doubted it. He knew a costume when he saw one.

People wedged aboard the coach until it fair burst with heat and a veritable cornucopia of human smells, and the widow finally disappeared completely from Tom's view. When they were full, the coach lurched forward to London.

And as Tom was a busy man, his thoughts inevitably lurched toward London along with the coach: his meeting with investors regarding The Gentleman's Emporium was one line of thought. How he was going to tell Daisy Jones that she would *not* be playing Venus in the White Lily's latest production was another.

Ah, *Venus*. The concept was so inspired, so brilliant, such a delicious challenge for his partner's formidable talents that The General had very nearly entirely forgiven Tom for promising a particular earl a production involving damsels and castles . . . inside a week. A frenzy of choreography, carpentry and epithets had resulted in a production comprised of a brilliantly constructed little castle, scantily clothed damsels, and an inspired, prurient song regarding lances. It had been a roaring success, and The General had all but refused to speak to Tom for weeks afterward.

Tom had known the damsels would be a success. The inspirations that dropped into his mind suddenly and whole, like a bright coin flipped into a deep well, invariably were. The production had since become one of the staples of the White Lily's nightly offerings. But the reason audiences returned to the theater again and again was because they could count on Tom Shaughnessy to surprise them, to feed their ceaseless appetite for novelty, and Tom knew he would soon need another small surprise to keep his audiences from becoming restless.

But Venus . . . Venus hadn't been a coin-dropped-in-the-well sort of inspiration. The theater itself had given it to him, just the other night: Tom had swept his eyes across the gods and goddesses who gamboled across the murals covering the theater walls . . . and the image of Botticelli's Venus, rising from her shell, had risen up in his mind. Venus would be a *tour de force,* a masterpiece, and the enormous profits he anticipated, along with the backing of a few key investors, would make his dream of The Gentleman's Emporium a reality.

Now all that remained was the delicate task of informing Daisy Jones that she would not be the one rising from the shell.

Tom smiled at the thought and glanced up; the curate sitting across from him gave him a tentative little smile in return. Very much like a small dog rolling over to show its belly to a larger, more dazzling dog.

"Exceedingly warm for this time of year," the curate ventured.

"Indeed. And if it's this warm near the sea, imagine how warm it will be in London," Tom answered politely.

Ah, weather. A topic that bridged social classes the world over. Whatever would they do without it?

And so the passengers passed a tolerable few hours sweating and smelling each other and exchanging pleasant banalities as the coach wheels ate up the road, and there was seldom a lull in conversation. And for two hours, Tom heard not a single word of French-accented English in the jumble of words around him.

When the curate stopped chatting for a moment, Tom slipped a hand into his pocket and snapped open his watch; in an hour or so, he knew, they would reach a coaching inn on the road to Westerly in time for a bad luncheon; he hoped to be back to London in time for supper, to meet with investors, to supervise the latest show at the White Lily. And then, perhaps, enjoy late-night entertainments at the Velvet Glove in the company of the most-accommodating Bettina.

And then in the lull a pistol shot cracked and echoed, and the coach bucked to a stop, sending passengers tumbling over each other.

Highwaymen. *Bloody hell.*

Tom gently sat the curate back into his seat and brushed off his coat, then brushed off his own.

Brazen coves, these highwaymen were, to stop the coach in broad daylight. But this stretch of road was all but deserted, and they'd been known to stop the occasional coach run. A full coach was essentially fish-in-a-barrel for highwaymen. Which meant there must be many of them, all armed, if they were bold enough to stop a loaded coach.

Tom swiftly tucked his watch into his boot and retrieved a pistol at the same time; he saw the curate's eyes bulge and watched him rear back a little in alarm. *Good God. No man should be afraid to shoot if necessary,* Tom thought with some impatience. He tugged the sleeve of his coat down to cover his weapon; one glimpse of it might inspire a nervous highwayman to waste a bullet on him.

"Take off your rings and put them in your shoes," he ordered the newlyweds quietly. Hands shaking like sheets pinned to a line, they obeyed him, as no one else was issuing orders in this extraordinary situation.

Tom knew he had only a ghost of a chance of doing

something to deter the highwaymen, no matter their numbers. Still, it never occurred to him not to try. It wasn't as though Tom had never taken anything; when he was young and living in the rookeries, he'd taken food, handkerchiefs, anything small he could fence. But he had ultimately chosen to work for everything he owned; he found it satisfied a need for permanence, a need for . . . legacy. And damned if he was going to allow someone to take anything he'd earned if he could possibly avoid it. Even if it was only a few pounds and a watch.

"Out, everybody," a gravelly voice demanded. "'Ands up, now where I can see 'em, now."

And out of the dark coach stumbled the passengers, blinking and pale in the sunlight, one of whom was nearly swooning, if her buckling knees were any indication, and needed to be fanned by her panicking husband.

The air fair shimmered with heat; only a few wan trees interrupted the vista of parched grass and cracked road. Tom took in the group of highwaymen with a glance: five men, armed with muskets and pistols. Clothing dull with grime, kerchiefs covering their faces, hair long and lank and unevenly sawed, as though trimmed with their own daggers. One of them, the one who appeared to be in charge, gripped a knife between his teeth. Tom almost smiled grimly. *A showman.* Excessive, perhaps, but it certainly lent him a dramatic flair the others lacked.

Tom's innate curiosity about any showman made him peer more closely at the man. There was something about him . . .

"Now see here . . ." the merchant blustered indignantly, and promptly had five pistols and a knife turned on him. He blanched, clapped his mouth shut audibly. Clearly new to being robbed at gunpoint, he didn't know that etiquette required one to be quiet, lest one get shot.

And then Tom knew. Almost a decade ago, during a few difficult but unforgettable months of work in a dockside tavern, Tom had spent time with a man who drank the hardest liquor, told the most ribald jokes, tipped most generously, and advised young Tom which whores to avoid and which to court and imparted other unique forms of wisdom.

"Biggsy?" Tom ventured.

The highwayman swiveled, glowering, and stared at Tom.

Then he reached up and plucked the knife from between teeth brown as aged fenced posts, and his face transformed.

"*Tom?* Tommy *Shaughnessy?*"

"'Tis I, in the flesh, Biggs."

"Well, Tommy, as I live and breathe!" Big Biggsy shifted his pistol into his other hand and seized Tom's hand to pump it with genuine enthusiasm. "'Avena seen you since those days at Bloody Joe's! Still a pretty bugger, ain't ye?" Biggsy laughed a richly phlegmy laugh and gave Tom a frisky punch on the shoulder. "Ye've gone respectable, 'ave ye, Tommy? Looka tha' fine coat!"

Tom felt the passenger's eyes slide toward him like so many billiard balls rolling toward a pocket, and then slide back again; he could virtually feel them cringing away from him. He wondered if it was because he was on a Christian-name basis with an armed highwayman, or because he had "*gone* respectable," implying he had been anything but at one time.

"Respectable might perhaps be overstating it, Biggsy, but yes, you could say I haven't done too badly."

" 'Avena done 'alf bad meself," Biggsy announced proudly, gesturing at the characters surrounding him as though they were a grand new suite of furniture.

Tom thought it wisest not to disagree or request further clarification. He decided upon nodding sagely.

" 'Tis proud I be, of ye, Tommy," Biggsy added sentimentally.

"That means the world to me," Tom assured him solemnly.

"And Daisy?" Biggsy prodded. "D'yer see 'er since the Green Apple days?"

"Oh, yes. She's in fine form, fine form."

"She's a grand woman," the highwayman said mistily.

"She is at that." Grand, and the largest thorn in his side, and no doubt responsible for a good portion of his fortune. Bless the brazen, irritating, glorious Daisy Jones.

Tom gave Biggsy his patented crooked, coaxing grin. "Now, Biggsy, can I persuade you to allow our coach to go on? You've my word of honor not a one shall pursue you."

"Ye've a word of honor now, Tommy?" Biggsy reared back in faux astonishment, then laughed again. Tom, not being a fool, laughed, too, and gave his thigh a little slap for good measure.

Biggsy wiped his eyes and stared at Tom for a moment longer, then took his bottom lip between his dark teeth to worry it a bit as he mulled the circumstances. And then he sighed and lowered his pistol; and with a jerk of his chin ordered the rest of the armed and mounted men accompanying him to do the same.

"Fer the sake of old times, then, Tommy. Fer the sake of Daisy, and Bloody Joe, rest 'is soul. But I canna leave everythin', you ken 'ow it is—we mun eat, ye ken."

"I ken," Tom repeated, commiserating.

"I'll leave the trunks, and jus' 'ave what blunt the lot of ye be carryin' in yer pockets."

"Big of you, Biggsy, big of you," Tom murmured.

"And then I'll 'ave a kiss from one of these young ladies, and we'll be off."

Clunk. Down went the wobbly new missus, dragging her husband down after her; he hadn't time to stop her fall completely. Never a pleasant sound, the sound of a body hitting the ground.

Biggsy eyed them for a moment in mild contempt. Then he looked back at Tom and shook his head slowly, as if to say, *what a pair of ninnies.*

"All right then. Who will it be?" Biggsy asked brightly. He scanned the row of lovely young ladies hopefully.

Tom thought he should have known his own formidable charm would get him only so far with a highwayman.

The crowd, which not a moment before had been mentally inching away from him, now swiveled their heads beseechingly toward him. Tom wasn't particularly savoring the irony of this at the moment. He wasn't quite sure how to rescue them from this particular request.

"Now, Biggs," Tom tried for a hail-fellow-well-met cajoling tone, "these are innocent young ladies. If you come to London, I'll introduce you to ladies who'll be happy to—"

"I willna leave without a kiss from one of *these* young ladies," Biggsy insisted stubbornly. "Look a' me, Tom.

D'yer think I'm kissed verra often? Let alone by a young thing wi' all of 'er teeth or 'er maidenhe—"

"Biggsy," Tom interjected hurriedly.

"I want a *kiss*."

At the tone, the men behind Biggs put their hands back upon on their pistols, sensing a shift in intent.

Tom's eyes remained locked with Biggsy's, his expression studiedly neutral and pleasant, while his mind did cartwheels. *Bloody, bloody hell. Perhaps I should ask the young ladies to draw straws. Perhaps I should kiss him myself. Perhaps we—*

"I will kiss him."

Everyone, highwaymen included, pivoted, startled, when the little French widow stepped forward. "You will allow the coach to go on if I do?" she asked.

Ze coach, Tom thought absently, is what it sounded like when she said it. Her voice was bell-clear and strong and she sounded very nearly impatient; but Tom caught the hint of a tremble in it again, which he found oddly reassuring. If there had been no tremble, he might have worried again about her sanity and what she might do with a knitting needle.

"My word of honor," Biggsy said almost humbly. He seemed almost taken aback.

Tom was torn between wanting to stop her and perverse curiosity to see if she intended to go through with it. She hadn't the bearing or voice of a doxie. *I am not . . .* she had struggled to tell him. She was not someone who suffered the attention of gentlemen lightly, he was certain she meant to say. Not someone who was generally in the habit of leaping into the laps of strangers unless she had a very good reason to do so.

He hoped, *hoped* she didn't intend to attempt anything foolish with a knitting needle.

Biggsy recovered himself. "I'll take that, shall I?" He reached out and adroitly took her reticule from her. He heard her intake of breath, the beginning of a protest, but wisely stopped herself. Ah, she'd good judgment, too.

Tom saw her shoulders square, as though she was preparing herself for a launch upward. She drew in a deep breath.

And then she stood on her toes, lifted her veil, and kissed Biggsy Biggens full on the mouth.

And a moment later, Biggsy Biggens looked for all the world as blessed as a bridegroom.

CHAPTER TWO

THE CONFIGURATION INSIDE THE COACH on the way to the coaching inn was this: Tom at one end; the other passengers all but knotted together for protection.

And then the widow.

All was silence. He and the widow might be the hero and heroine of the hour, but no one wanted to acknowledge it, no one wanted to *touch* them, and certainly no one wanted to know either of them.

Once all of the passengers tumbled out of the coach in the inn yard, where they would be served a dreadful lunch before continuing on to London, Tom saw the widow glance furtively about.

And rather than follow the rest of the travelers inside, she made her way surreptitiously, but very purposefully toward the stables. She rounded the corner and disappeared from view; he picked up his pace and stopped when he saw her snug against the side of the building, half in shadow, her shoulders slightly hunched.

A wrench of sympathy and respect for her privacy made him pause. She was attempting to discreetly retch. He'd been within whiffing distance of Biggsy's breath;

he could only imagine what it must have been like to taste it.

She whirled suddenly, sensing him there, swiping the back of her hand across her mouth; he took a step back, safely out of knitting-needle range. She stood very still and regarded him through that veil.

Wordlessly, cautiously, he reached into his coat, produced a flask, and held it out to her.

She looked down at the flask, then up at him. Two cool movements of her head. But she made no move to accept it from him.

"Or perhaps you prefer the taste of highwayman in your mouth . . . Mademoiselle."

Her chin jerked up a little at that.

After a moment, with a sense of subtle ceremony, she slowly, slowly lifted her veil with her gloved hands. *Ah, a woman confident of her charms.* This heightened Tom's sense of anticipation, which surprised and amused him. He wasn't precisely jaded, but surprise when it came to a woman was something he felt so rarely anymore. *Veils,* he noted to himself silently. *Must use more veils at the White Lily Theater. Perhaps a harem act . . .*

Still, nothing could have prepared him for the shock of her face when she finally tilted her head up to look at him.

He felt her beauty physically, a sweet hot burst low in his gut. A jaw both stubborn and elegant in its angularity, lifted now in pride or arrogance or defense; an achingly soft-looking mouth, the bottom lip a full curve, the one above it shorter, both the palest pink. Eyes very bright in her too-white face. They were pale green, her eyes, intelligent and very alive, with flecks of other colors floating in the irises. Two fine, straight chestnut brows slanted over them.

Her eyes met his, and with great satisfaction, he saw that impossible-to-disguise swift flare of her pupil. It was always a good moment, a delicious moment, the recognition of mutual attraction that passed between two beautiful people. Tom smiled at her, acknowledging it, confident and inclusive, inviting her, daring her to share it.

But she turned her head away from him slowly—too casually—as though the pigeons listlessly poking about in the stableyard were of much more interest to her than the man standing before her with a flask outstretched.

When she returned her gaze to his she reached out her hand for the proffered flask, as though the pigeons had cemented her decision. She lifted it fastidiously up to those soft lips and took a sip.

Her eyes widened. He grinned.

"I wonder what you were expecting, Mademoiselle. Whiskey? Do I strike you as the whiskey sort? It's French—the wine, is. Go ahead and swallow it. It wasn't cheap."

She held it in her mouth for an instant; at last, he saw her swallow hard.

He bowed, then, and it was a low, elegant thing, all grace and respect. "Mr. Tom Shaughnessy at your service. And you are Mademoiselle . . . ?"

"Madame," she corrected curtly.

"Oh, but I think not . . . For I have splendid *intuition*." He used the French pronunciation. The word was spelled just the same in English and in French, and meant precisely the same thing: a very good guess. "And *I* think you are a mademoiselle."

"You presume a good deal, Mr. Shaughnessy."

"I've always had luck with being presumptuous. One might even say I make my living being presumptuous."

She scanned him, a swift flick of her green eyes, up and down, drawing conclusions about him from his face and clothes and adding those conclusions, no doubt, to the impressions she'd already gleaned from his acquaintance with the highwayman. He saw those green eyes go guarded and cynical. But oddly . . . not afraid. Yes, this was a mademoiselle, perhaps. But not an innocent one, either, if she could draw a cynical conclusion about the sort of man he was. It implied she knew rather a range of men.

"It was brave, what you did," he said.

"Yes," she agreed.

He smiled at that. He could have sworn she almost did, too.

"Do you have any money?" he asked. A blunt question.

Again, that stiff spine. "I do not believe this is business of yours, Mr. Shaughnessy."

"A knitting needle and widow's weeds are all very well and good, but money, Mademoiselle, is everything. Have you enough to continue on to your destination? The highwayman took your reticule, did he not?"

"Yes, your *friend*, Mr. Biggsy, took my reticule. I might not have been so brave had I known the price of my bravery."

"Were you perhaps clever enough to sew your money into your hem?" He pressed. "Or into your sleeve, along with your weaponry? If one travels unaccompanied by a maid, one best be resourceful in other ways."

She was silent. And then: "Why are you interested in my money, Mr. Shaughnessy?"

"Perhaps, as a gentleman, I'm merely concerned for your welfare."

"Oh, I think not, Mr. Shaughnessy. For you see, I, too, have *intuition*. And I do not believe you *are* a gentleman."

As dry and tart as the wine he'd just passed to her. And just as bracing. Perhaps even—and this surprised him—a little stinging.

"All right then: Perhaps I'm concerned because you are beautiful and intriguing."

She waited a beat, studying him with her head tilted again.

" 'Perhaps'?" She repeated. And up went one of those delicate chestnut brows, along with the corners of her mouth. As though she had struggled against her nature, and her nature had won.

A little thrill of pleasure traced his spine. Ah, there *was* a coquette in there; he had sensed it. But it was like viewing her through a fogged windowpane; he wanted somehow to rub away the fear and mistrust to bring the real woman, the vibrant, no doubt interesting woman, into view.

Her color looked better now; there was a healthier flush in her cheeks. Then again, good French wine will do that for a person.

"I can help you," he said swiftly.

"I thank you for your . . . *concern* . . . Mr. Shaughnessy," she all but drew quotation marks around the word, "but I do not wish assistance from . . . you."

As in, *you would be the last man in the world I would turn to, Mr. Shaughnessy.*

And given the circumstances, he could hardly blame her. He respected her wisdom in deciding not to trust him—this was not a foolish woman, despite the fact that she'd kept her money in her damned reticule—even as he felt the disappointment of it keenly. For she was right, of course. Gallantry played a role in his offer to help her. But it wasn't the primary role by far. And Tom was certain he wouldn't trust himself if *he* was a woman. In particular, not after he'd exchanged warm reminiscences with a gun- and knife-wielding highwayman.

"Very well, then. Let me just say that I do not 'regret' the fact that you . . . 'inserted' me, Mademoiselle. Or . . . 'sat upon me.'"

She studied him for a moment, head tilted slightly.

"Do you mock my English, Mr. Shaughnessy?" She sounded mildly curious.

"Why, yes, I believe I do. A little. *Un peu.*" He was surprised to feel a little bit of his temper in the words.

To his astonishment, she smiled then. A full and brilliant smile, a genuine smile, which scrunched her eyes and made them brilliant, too, dazzling as lamps. It was the kind of smile that made him believe she laughed often and easily, in other circumstances, the kind of smile he felt physically again, as a swift and strangely sweet twist in his gut.

He was suddenly desperate to make her do it often.

But finding himself uncharacteristically speechless, he bowed and left her.

His mind oddly both full and jumbled, following the rest of the decidedly less-interesting guests into the inn for luncheon.

ॐ   ॐ   ॐ

If not for the fortifying dose of surprisingly good French wine provided by Mr. Tom Shaughnessy, Sylvie would still be trembling now. All of her money was gone, the letter from her sister was gone, and a sort of delayed fear had overtaken her at lunch. She'd been able to push it away the way she did any sort of discomfort in order to take her through her encounter with the highwayman.

But now she could scarcely choke down the watery soup and indifferent bread and tough grayish meat. *Peh.* The English knew nothing of cooking, that was certain, if luncheon was any indication.

She peeked up from her silent meal—no one attempted to engage her in conversation, nor did she feel equal to making an attempt of her own. Mr. Shaughnessy seemed to have thawed the curate and the married couple, and the four of them appeared to be laughing together over some English witticism.

She jerked her head away from them, focused again on her gray meat.

She could not recall the last time she'd needed to look away from a man to recover her composure. Certainly Etienne was handsome, admired and swooned over by all the other dancers in the *corps de ballet.* Desired by all of them. But the sight of Etienne had never stopped her breathing.

And when she had seen Tom Shaughnessy, it was as though someone had taken a tight little fist and rapped it between her lungs.

In the full sunlight, Tom Shaughnessy's eyes had seemed nearly clear, like a pair of windows. Silver, she would have called them. His face could only be described as beautiful, but it wasn't soft: it was too defined; there were too many strong lines and corners and interesting hollows, and there was a hint of something pagan about it. His surname and his wavy red-gold hair implied Irish ancestors, but his complexion, a pale gold, suggested that something a bit more exotic also swam in his veins: Spanish blood, perhaps. Or Gypsy. This last would not have surprised her in the least.

And then there was that smile. It blinded, the smile. She considered that perhaps that was its purpose; he used it as a weapon to scramble wits and take advantage of a moment. It made a dimple near the corner of his mouth. A tiny crescent moon.

And his clothes—a soft green coat no doubt chosen for its unorthodox color, a dazzling waistcoat, polished boots and brilliant buttons—all might have looked just shy of vulgar on someone else. On him they seemed somehow as native as wings to Mercury's ankles.

And she'd seen as they had all stood in the hot sunlight next to the mail coach a glint in his sleeve, and looked more closely. He'd tucked a pistol in his sleeve, had cupped the barrel of it in his fingers, prepared to slide it out and use it. Somehow she had no doubt he knew precisely *how* to use it.

And every other man in that clearing had seemed prepared to allow the highwaymen to have their way with them.

He was armed in too many ways, it seemed, Mr. Shaughnessy—with those looks, and a charm that won and disarmed too easily, and clothing that was just a little too fine and a little too deliberately new, and with a hidden pistol, with dangerous friends. If a man was thusly prepared for danger, he could only be dangerous in some way himself.

But she *should* have choked down more food. She didn't know where she'd next acquire another meal, and even if she didn't feel hungry now, she was human, and her body, accustomed to rigorous activity, would no doubt eventually expect a good meal and begin demanding it with growls and aches.

In her trunk there were things she could sell if necessary, a few pieces of fine clothing, gloves and shoes, she supposed. She wouldn't know where or how to sell them, but she would discover how to do it if she needed to. She had always done what she needed to do.

She wondered whether anyone in England would find a use for ballet slippers.

When the mail coach finally lurched to its stop at its London destination, all the passengers hurriedly dispersed into the arms of waiting loved ones or into other coaches as quickly as ants fleeing a magnifying glass, without turning back. Shedding the dread of their earlier experience, and filled with a tale to tell. Sylvie imagined she would be the topic of conversation over dinner tables throughout London tonight.

The thought made her feel just a little lonely. But only a little. She truly didn't know what it was like to sit at a table with a large family and talk of the day, and it was difficult to miss what one has never truly known.

Though it had never been difficult to imagine it. Or, on occasion, to long for the things she'd imagined, when the life she shared with Claude, who was kind, was so small and careful and often fearful, as money had always been scarce.

She had memories of being shuttled away in the dead of night in a coach, bundled with other little girls. A strange man, a kind man with a kind voice, had attempted to soothe and hush them. She remembered she'd been crying. And then she had thought she should not cry so that she could hold the hands of the little girls with her, to keep them from crying and from being afraid.

And so she had stopped crying.

She had seldom cried since that evening.

My sisters, she thought. *They were my sisters.* They must have been. And yet the memory of that evening, and all that had passed before it, and the people in them, had become indistinct, wearing away in patches, it seemed, until she had begun to believe she had dreamed them.

And Claude had never done anything to discourage the idea. Sylvie could scarcely remember now how it had happened, but she had gone to live with Claude. And Claude had told her only that there had been an accident, and that her mother would not be coming home. She never mentioned sisters, which had made it easier to believe the other girls might have been just a dream.

Sylvie put her hand over her heart. She had suspended the miniature of her mother from a ribbon, and it hung there beneath her dress now, where it was both protected and, in a way, protection, a talisman. And soon, hopefully, it would be proof to Susannah, Lady Grantham, that they indeed shared a mother.

Sylvie stood next to her own trunk in the inn yard now, a little island of dark clothing amidst a swarm of people going purposely about their business. *So this is London.*

To be fair, one could tell very little of the city from the yards of coaching inns, she knew. It rather looked like any large city, cobblestones and storefronts; when she craned her head, she could see the tall masts of ships at harbor through the gaps in the buildings. The smells were city smells, the smells of thousands of lives lived close together: food spoiling or being cooked, coal smoke rising, the warm beasty odors of horses and other animals.

Despite herself, a little excitement cut through the trepidation. She'd done it. She was standing in London, she'd managed to cross the Channel entirely on her own, and soon, perhaps, she would learn what she'd come to learn.

"If you crane your head about like that, Mademoiselle, it will become obvious to the less savory among us that you're new to London, and no doubt someone will attempt to rob you—or perhaps kiss you—again."

She started and turned to find Mr. Shaughnessy before her, hat in hand. He bowed low. "Is someone meeting you?" he asked, when he was upright again.

"Yes," she said swiftly.

Up went one of his brows, betraying his doubt of this. "Very well, then. But you should *always* appear as though you know precisely where you are going, Mademoiselle. And if you do find yourself longing for my company, you can find me at the White Lily."

A grin flashed, and then he was gone before she could say another word, melting confidently into the crowd as he jammed a hat down on his bright head.

ঞ   ঞ   ঞ

Sylvie glanced about; her eyes met the eyes of a portly fellow standing near a hackney, the driver. She saw him assess her, her clothing and bearing, and make a decision in her favor.

"Need a coach, Madame?"

He said it politely enough, and there was nothing prurient or predatory in his gaze. Regardless, she was armed with a knitting needle and extraordinary reflexes, should the need to defend herself arise. And she hadn't really a choice.

"Yes, please. To . . . Grosvenor Square."

His eyes flared swiftly, almost imperceptibly. "Shilling," he said shortly.

Quick thinking was clearly necessary. "My sister is Lady Grantham. She will give the shilling to you when we arrive."

The man's expression changed then . . . but peculiarly. Not into the sort of expression someone of his station typically donned when the aristocracy was mentioned. No. Gradually, before Sylvie's puzzled eyes, it became harder. Then sharply curious. And then finally, inexplicably . . .

Amused?

"Your sister is Lady Grantham?"

"Yes." She frowned.

"Lady Grantham is your sister, is she?"

"I believe I said 'yes.' " She'd clenched her jaw to steady her nerves.

He paused and appraised her again. "An' look, ye've a trunk and everythin'," he said it almost admiringly. He shook his head to and fro in apparent wonder.

Sylvie knew her English was quite good, but perhaps an entirely different dialect was spoken in the heart of London, the way those who lived in Venice spoke their own version of Italian. Perhaps this London dialect was one in which the inflections meant entirely the opposite of what one might expect.

"An' she'll pay me when we arrive, like?" he said,

sounding amused. For all the world as though he was humoring a madwoman. "Lady Grantham?"

"Again . . . yes." Regal now, and cold.

He regarded her a moment longer. And then shrugged good-humoredly and smiled, as though he'd resigned himself to some odd fate.

"All right. Let's go see your *sister,* Lady Grantham, shall we?"

And still, despite his acquiescence, his tone could not be construed as anything other than ironic.

CHAPTER THREE

Grosvenor Square turned out to be comprised of rows of imposing edifices, homes several stories high built snugly together, as if symbolically to prevent interlopers such as herself from wedging between them.

"Go on, now. Go see to your sister. Shall I bring your trunk up?"

"Perhaps not just yet," she said.

"Of *course* not," he said.

More irony. *Oh,* but the man was grating.

Sylvie ascended the steps, not faltering, but conscious of the curtains at windows along the row of houses parting, then dropping when she turned her head swiftly at the movement.

Though the temptation arose, she knew turning on her heel and fleeing was no longer an option. Her journey *must* end here.

On the imposing door, a snarling brass lion held a loop of metal in its teeth; Sylvie took a deep breath for confidence, took the knocker in her hands, and rapped hard twice.

Her breath came short now. What if the woman who lived in this house had nothing at all to do with her?

Would she be kind? Would she be stunned to discover her sister was a ballerina, someone who had occupied a twilight world where she was admired and envied by women like herself—but only from a distance? And, not infrequently, courted and pursued by their husbands?

But Etienne had promised to buy her a home. He owned many homes, homes she had never seen, homes, she was certain, many times the size of this one.

Moments later, the door opened; a butler stared at her. His face was bland, as impassive as the walls of the home itself, his hair and skin were a matching shade of gray-white, no doubt the result of a life spent indoors.

"May I be of some assistance to you, Madame?" A neutral sort of politeness, the sort at which servants excelled, and he'd employed it because he hadn't the faintest idea who she was and to which social stratum she belonged. She saw his eyes flick up, note the hackney at the foot of the steps. Flick back to her. Searching for clues as to whether he should warm the temperature of his voice.

He doesn't know who I am, Sylvie reminded herself. *Doesn't know I'm a dancer, with a lover, who fled across the Channel.*

"Is Lady Grantham at home, please?" She tried not to sound defensive. She also tried not to sound French, but this was virtually impossible.

The impassive expression changed not a fraction. "The viscount and Lady Grantham are away, Madame. Would you care to leave your card?"

"A-away?" Perhaps he meant they'd . . . gone to the shops or for a stroll, she thought desperately. Though, somehow, given the tenor of her journey thus far, she suspected this was optimistic bordering on the delusional.

"By *away*, I mean they've gone to France, Madame." Something that might have been the beginnings of a frown shadowed the place between his eyes.

Suddenly the ramifications of the viscount and Lady Grantham going to France struck.

"Did they perhaps go to visit . . . Lady Grantham's sister?"

"'Sister,' Madame?" It was almost sharply said.

And then his face, in a heartbeat, went from bland to cynical and wary.

"I am Lady Grantham's sister," Sylvie said with some dignity.

She heard the sound of a cleared throat eloquently from the street. The hackney driver.

"Of *course* you are, Madame." Sylvie blinked; his words were all but chiseled from scorn. "You and every other opportunistic female on the Continent. Ever since the trial. It's not an original idea, though I must admit your widow's weeds are a new approach."

"T-trial?" "Trial" was seldom a good word in any language.

"Come now, Miss. Mr. Morley's trial. What a sordid business it was, what with him involved in the murder of Richard Lockwood, and Anna Holt blamed for it, and out it came that Lady Grantham—the wife of a *very* wealthy viscount, mind you—had two sisters who disappeared when she was very young, and she doesn't know what became of them. Oh my, the letters we've received, the young ladies who've appeared on the doorstep . . . the story seems to have inspired every opportunist on the

Continent. You're not the first to think of it, Madame. Quite a nuisance, it's been, the flocks of young ladies and the pleading letters. Posing as a widow, however, is a novel approach, I will say that for you, Madame. And you've shown a certain amount of daring—or would it be stupidity?—in telling such a story when my employers have begun to prosecute the transgressors. They are, in fact, offering a rather large reward for the apprehension of them."

Sylvie's hands were now clammy inside her gloves, and despite the sun beating at the back of her neck, the black of her gown soaking in every ray of it, a sick, icy feeling suddenly made her even more aware of how empty her stomach was.

"But . . . I had a letter. From Lady Grantham. Susannah. I brought it with me, you see, but the highwayman . . . the highwayman . . . he took it . . ."

She trailed off when the butler's expression grew more and more incredulous. "Lady Grantham's sister is in France," he said sternly. "Lady Grantham has gone to France in search of her."

"I have come from France. *I* am French," Sylvie said indignantly.

"So are thousands and thousands of other people, more's the pity."

Sylvie's patience slipped and her hand darted into her bodice, fishing for her miniature.

The butler's eyes bulged like hen's eggs when she did, and then he flung an arm over his face. "Madame, I assure you that exposing yourself won't convince me to—"

She finally retrieved the miniature on its little black ribbon. "Please look." She said struggling for calm.

The butler kept his arm up over his eyes.

"I have a miniature," she coaxed softly.

There was a silence. From the foot of the stairs, the bloody hackney driver began to whistle a mocking little tune.

"A miniature *what*?" the butler ventured nervously. Only his lips moved from beneath his arm.

It would have been a simple enough thing to say, "a miniature of my mother, Anna, whom I suspect is also Lady Grantham's mother." But the devil in Sylvie was stronger, as was the coquette. "Why don't you have a look, monsieur?"

Ah, so he was a man after all. He slowly pulled his arm away from his eyes. And he looked. She bit back a smile.

He recovered his composure quickly enough when he saw the miniature she held out on its ribbon.

And then, after his first quick glance, his posture stiffened, and he stared at it.

Sylvie allowed this stranger to study her mother's sweet face: those pale eyes tilted with laughter, the fair hair, the finely drawn bones, the image she had cherished her entire life. The only reminder of the family she had lost. Apart from Claude, Sylvie had never shared this image with anyone until this man who looked at it with wary eyes.

But then the butler's expression transformed. As gradually as winter melts into spring and spring into summer, she saw speculation become uncertainty and—and her breath caught at what this might mean—at last she saw a glimmer of sympathy.

He cleared his throat. Good God, she was surrounded by men who cleared their throats. "May I hold the min—"

"No," Sylvie said the word tersely, but then again, her patience and nerves were frayed. "I hope you understand," she added, conciliatorily. "It is precious to me."

"I suppose I do understand," he said, sounding abstracted now. "May I ask how you came to own this miniature, Mrs. . . ."

"My name is Sylvie Lamoreux. I've had it always. I'm told it's my mother, Mr. . . ."

"Bale. My name is Mr. Bale."

He fell quiet. At the curb, the hackney driver cleared his throat.

"*Mon dieu,* have *patience,*" Sylvie snapped over her shoulder.

She turned back to Bale, just in time to see the corner of his mouth twitch. He still seemed thoughtful; he said nothing. She turned the miniature over. "And see, there are words."

"*To Sylvie Hope of her mother Anna,*" Bale read slowly aloud, half to himself. Wonderingly.

Sylvie allowed him to absorb this information. Then she tucked the miniature into her bodice once more while he averted his eyes. Ah, so prim for a man.

"Did the other young ladies who arrived on your doorstep present miniatures, Mr. Bale?" Her tone was lightly acerbic.

The butler looked pensive. "I know nothing of any miniatures of Anna Holt, Mrs. Lamoreux."

"Holt?" Sylvie pounced eagerly on the name. "My mother's name was Anna *Holt*? Sir, I know nothing of her. All my life I have wanted to know . . ."

Mr. Bale said nothing. His lips worried over each other, folding in, folding out, as he thought.

"Can you tell me please whether Lady Grantham and her husband intended to call upon someone named Claude Lamoreux in Paris?"

The butler was an edifice of silence. As seemingly immovable as the walls of the house he attended.

He was merely being dutiful, Sylvie knew, protecting the privacy of his employers, but at the moment his silence felt unspeakably cruel. But his silence at least spoke of doubt, and the doubt had mercifully eliminated his dreadful patronizing for the moment.

"When will they return? Lady Grantham and her husband?"

"I cannot say, Miss Lamoreux." Flawless, his pronunciation of her name was.

"But can you tell me, *please,* Mr. Bale, does Lady Grantham resemble me?"

"I cannot say."

"Cannot, or *will* not?" she demanded desperately, with growing impatience.

But all at once she comprehended the expression on his face earlier, the source of what appeared to be dawning sympathy.

"She looks like my mother," Sylvie breathed. "Susannah, Lady Grantham . . . perhaps *I* do not resemble her, but she *does* resemble the woman in the miniature, yes?"

Sylvie saw the answer in his face, saw him look at her now, as if inventorying her features, trying to draw conclusions. Hope dizzied her.

"Please, Mr. Bale. All of my life, I have wanted to know something of my family. I've had none, you see, and I was told . . ." She stumbled. "I was told things that I think are not true."

"Miss Lamoreux. I cannot stress enough the significance of the trouble this has caused Lady Grantham. The viscount has in fact arranged for one interloper to be arrested, and has offered a reward to anyone who assists in apprehending impostors. Do you understand my position, Mrs. Lamoreux? I implore you to abandon your charade if you *have* embarked upon a charade."

Do you understand my position? I am alone and penniless and hundreds of miles away from home because I am a headstrong fool.

A silent stalemate ensued.

She imagined saying, "It is *not* a charade," which seemed unproductive. So she tried hauteur instead.

"Will Lady Grantham be angry with you, Mr. Bale, if she discovers you turned her true sister away?"

It worked. He glared at her, clearly torn, frustrated, and wishing she hadn't arrived on *his* doorstep.

"Where will you be staying, Mrs. Lamoreux, while you are in London?" he asked finally, with some resignation.

"I don't know, Mr. Bale," she said bitterly. He deserved the punishment of wondering whether he had done the right thing, she decided unfairly. "Perhaps you should look at the White Lily."

She caught a glimpse of his eyes going wide again as she turned her back and marched down the steps. No royal army had ever retreated more proudly than Sylvie Lamoreux.

"You knew," she accused the hackney driver. "Why did you say nothing?"

"Say nothing? I thought ye knew what ye were about, Miss, and I thought ye'd the look of someone who might verra well 'ave a plan. I mean, ye've a costume, a trunk—ye'd given it all some thought, seemed to me. Thought ye deserved a chance."

He smiled, a hatefully amused gap-toothed smile. "So where shall we go? To visit another relation? To see if the king is in?"

She thought about it for an instant; arrived, suddenly, at what appeared to be her only option. "To the White Lily, please."

The driver's eyebrows shot skyward. "Did you say . . . the White Lily, Miss?"

"Yes." She wasn't certain how to interpret the surprise. "Mr. Tom Shaughnessy will pay my fare." She hoped this was true. Her mind veered to more inventive options she might employ to earn money and immediately batted them away.

"Shaughnessy? *Tommy* Shaughnessy?" All warmth and genuine grins now.

Good God, did *everyone* know Tom Shaughnessy? Perhaps she should have asked the butler whether he knew Tom Shaughnessy to gain an entrée into the viscount's home.

"Mr. Shaughnessy! Well, then! Looking for honest work now then, are ye? The sort of work fer a miss like yerself? Given up the impostor business 'ave ye now?"

"I am *not* a fraud, Mr. . . . ."

"Me name's Mick," he said simply.

"I am not looking for 'honest work,' Mr. Mick. Mr. Shaughnessy is . . . is my relation."

The hackney driver's eyes flew open wide. "Your relation?" he said flatly.

"Yes." This man was growing more and more tiresome.

"Tom Shaughnessy is your relation," he repeated. His mouth began to tremble then, and his eyes grew pink at the rims, and then began watering. Sylvie took a single nervous step backward.

And then as though a dam burst, as though he'd been storing it up all day, he exploded into great gusts of body-buckling laughter.

"Your *relation*!" He howled, and slapped his thigh resoundingly a few times, sending the flesh of it wobbling to and fro in his trousers. "Yer related to everyone in London, are ye now? To viscounts *and* to the likes o' Tom?"

The likes o' Tom? This hardly sounded promising. No doubt, given the luck she was experiencing thus far today, Tom Shaughnessy was a flamboyant criminal of some sort. But she couldn't now ask the hackney driver what the White Lily might be, or who Tom might be, because she imagined it would make him howl even louder, and she didn't think she could bear that.

The storm of laughter finally stuttered out into scattered hiccups, then ended in a deep, satisfied sigh. The hackney driver wiped his eyes, which Sylvie found excessive.

"Oh, all right, Miss. I'll go 'ome poor today, but 'tis your lucky day, as I'm in th' mood fer a lark. Come aboard then."

CHAPTER FOUR

THE DURATION OF THE COACH ride merely seemed to emphasize the societal gulf between Grosvenor Square and whatever the White Lily might turn out to be. Through her coach window, Sylvie watched the scenery gradually become darker, narrower, dirtier: well-dressed Englishmen and -women promenading through grand, tailored squares gave way to labyrinthine streets lined with vendors, filthy children crowding them the way mosquitoes swarmed over split fruit. She saw several clearly inebriated people propped against walls, heads lolling.

The great lurid flower swinging on a board over the White Lily's entrance didn't clarify matters for her. Was it a brothel? A tavern? It looked rather like a theater. She doubted a brothel would advertise itself quite so proudly, but then considered she might know less of big cities than she originally thought, and perhaps London was a little different after all.

Perhaps it was a theater. Which would be tremendously ironic, given that nearly her entire life to date had been spent in theaters of some sort, and that she had worked her entire life to avoid spending her days in the sort of theater she suspected this one was.

"Go on, then," the hackney driver coaxed, grinning, still maddeningly amused.

Sylvie was not accustomed to being considered a comedienne. She gave her head a toss and pushed on the door of the White Lily; it gave, and she took a deep breath and stepped inside.

It was empty of people and dim at the moment, but an impression of exaggerated luxury rushed at her, an almost caricature of classicism. Red, the ruby sort, was the predominant theme, seen in the plush carpet and upholstery and the great heavy curtain of velvet that swept across the front of the stage and pooled on the floor of it. There was a pianoforte centered before the stage and room for more musicians on either side of it. Rows of seats sloped upward from where she stood; above them, balconies and tiers traced with gilt and ornate carved plaster gleamed dully, and a few boxes featuring curtains to ensure the occupant's anonymity swelled out from the walls nearest the stage. She tilted her head back and noticed an enormous chandelier—twined brass supporting row upon row of dangling crystal—presided over the subtly domed ceiling. And when she lowered her gaze once again, slowly, she noticed that not a single inch of the walls was bare: murals of gods and goddesses clad—well, "clad" was perhaps too emphatic a word for what they were— diaphanously, chasing and being chased by each other, as was the wont of gods and goddesses.

The place was unabashedly, cheerfully lurid; it was a celebration of sex, the way a man no doubt saw it— necessary, pleasurable, a game perhaps—and made no apologies for it.

"Couldn't stay away, Mademoiselle?" The soft words came from the left of her.

She jumped and turned to find Tom Shaughnessy.

And for a moment she couldn't speak, for the man's face was a fresh shock. It seemed the sort of face that one would always find something new in, its assemblage of angles and shadows. His pale eyes were bright in the dim theater.

When he bent that broad-shouldered frame into a low bow so elegant it nearly mocked, it occurred to her that she hadn't yet spoken, had only gaped, which no doubt gratified the man's vanity.

"Says yer a relation, Tommy." The hackney driver had poked his head in the door. "Ye've a lot of bloody relations, if ye' ask me. All female. But there must 'ave been a male in the lot somewhere t' 'ave spawned all these females."

Tom laughed. "What can I say, Mick? The Shaughnessys must be exceptionally . . . fertile."

Mick, the hackney driver, laughed with him. Sylvie suppressed a gusty sigh. If one more man took amusement at her expense, she might very well need to throw something.

And then, and this was the last thing she expected him to say, Tom turned to her and asked, "Are you hungry? Would you like something to eat?"

Sylvie was weary and light-headed and wondered what sort of compensation he intended to extract from her in exchange for paying the hackney driver, and hoped he would say and do nothing untoward, as she wasn't certain she had it in her to employ her knitting needle again when his face was sheer poetry. But no. Though her stomach was empty, it twisted, rebelling at the idea of more food of the sort she'd been given at the coaching inn today.

"No," she said. "I am not hungry, that is. Thank you."

"You ate very little at the inn."

He'd been watching her? Perhaps as aware of her as she'd been aware of him? Difficult to know with one such as he. In her profession, she had known flirts very nearly as skillful as Tom Shaughnessy. It was a skill they shared generously with nearly every woman, a means to keep it honed.

"Perhaps I require very little, Mr. Shaughnessy."

This made him smile slowly, his way of turning her words into an innuendo. "Oh, I doubt that, Mademoiselle. I expect you require rather a good deal."

She felt the corners of her mouth start to tug up in response, an accomplished flirt's reflexive response to another accomplished flirt; it couldn't quite completely become a smile, however. She was too weary. Too wary. Too angry at herself for leaving herself no other options.

And, though she hated to confess it even to herself . . . simply, quietly afraid.

The hackney driver cleared his throat.

Tom swiveled in his direction. "Oh, of course, Mick. My apologies." Tom fished about in his pockets, came up with a handful of coins, pressed them on Mick. The hackney driver disappeared for a moment and reappeared with her trunk, which he deposited unceremoniously on the floor of the theater. *Clunk.*

"Thank you for looking after her, Mick," he said somberly. "I . . . have her now."

Mick tipped his hat to the two of them; the door swung shut, and suddenly all was silence.

I have her now, Sylvie thought.

"Now . . . I believe you are now in my debt. Shall we discuss how you should repay me?"

Her heart began to trip. She was as interested in the dance of flirtation as in the art of ballet, but her nerves were frayed, and at the moment she felt like a mouse between the paws of a well-dressed cat. He wasn't to know it, however.

"I believe we both know I am now in your debt, Mr. Shaughnessy. Please speak your intent."

Eyebrows up, amused. "All right, then. First, please tell me your name."

"Miss Sylvie . . ." she hesitated. And then she remembered the butler's warning about the prosecution of those pretending to be Lady Grantham's sister, and considered that someone in London might very well know her name, and thought it best she remain, on the whole anonymous. "Cha . . . Chapeau."

"Miss Sylvie Chapeau." He repeated flatly.

She nodded weakly.

"You are Miss Sylvie . . . Hat." He said it almost warningly, as if giving her an opportunity to choose a less ridiculous name.

"Yes," she said, chin hiked.

He nodded thoughtfully. "And you are from . . ."

"Paris."

"And you are in London because . . ." he coaxed.

"Because I wished to see it." She wasn't anxious to watch his handsome face become as cynical as the hackney driver's or the butler's when she told him she was, in fact, the sister of Lady Grantham.

He laughed. "Oh, and we were doing so *well* with

honesty, Miss Chapeau! Allow me to rephrase my question. Whom precisely are you running from?"

"I am not running from anyone." It was an effort to keep her voice even.

"Running *to,* then," he corrected blithely.

"I believe we were discussing repayment, Mr. Shaughnessy, and not the reasons for my journey." Temper licked at the edges of her words.

"Perhaps I require information about you as payment of your debt."

This seemed reasonable if ungentlemanly, so she remained silent, and began to seethe a little.

"Your English seems improved," he mused suddenly.

"Perhaps because I am no longer . . ." *Nervous,* she thought, though she reconsidered the wisdom of confessing this to him.

"Running from someone?" he supplied helpfully.

She turned on her heel and made as if to leave. He didn't yet know she had no other place to go, and she suspected he would attempt to lure her back, but it did seem an excellent way to make her point.

"Quite right," he said hurriedly, laughter in his voice. "My apologies for indulging again my curiosity, Miss Chapeau. Very well, I shall ask only questions relevant to your debt. How long do you intend to stay in our fair city?"

She hesitated. "I do not know."

"And do you have any money at all?"

She paused again.

"It's really a simple question, Miss Chapeau." He was beginning to sound impatient. "A 'yes' or 'no' will answer it. You are either here at the White Lily because you have no money and no other options, or because you found me so irresistible that—"

"No," she said quickly.

He grinned, the bloody man. He'd all but cornered her into an admission of her greatest vulnerability: She was currently penniless. It would be wise not to assume she was cleverer than he, despite his too-bright smile and too-bright clothes and this lurid theater. His friends included hackney drivers and highwaymen and only God knew whom else.

"You've no money," he repeated musingly, regarding her unblinkingly. His eyes were so clear it seemed a little unfair, almost, that she could not read the thoughts passing behind them.

The man did have disconcertingly broad shoulders, she noticed absently.

"And do you need a place to stay?"

At this, after another brief hesitation, she merely nodded.

"Do you think you can dance, Miss Chapeau?"

"Of course." The answer was startled from her.

"I didn't mean the waltz."

"Nor did I."

He was quiet a moment, and then, peculiarly, Sylvie thought she saw something like regret darken, just briefly, his face. "How fortunate for you, then, that I, as the owner of this theater, am in a position to employ and lodge you. Your timing could not be better. Come with me."

He pivoted and walked to the back of the theater. Sylvie looked toward the door through which she had entered the White Lily. Outside, it was daylight and an unfamiliar London.

She turned her head back to the theater, where Tom Shaughnessy's broad back and shining head were rapidly moving away from her.

She knew which void she preferred to leap into.

Sylvie scrambled to follow him.

ↀ   ↀ   ↀ

Tom stopped before a door and tapped on it. Behind it she heard giggles and the sound of rustling fabric, familiar sounds to her; the sounds any roomful of women was bound to make, unless they were in mourning. And even then, she'd known a few—

The door swung open to reveal a startlingly lovely woman.

"Good day, Mr. Shaughnessy," she said breathlessly. She dropped a curtsy.

"Good day, Lizzie. May we come in? Are the lot of you fully clothed?" He asked it playfully.

"Would it matter, Mr. Shaughnessy?" She lowered her head and peered up at him through her lashes.

He gave a laugh, which in fact sounded more polite than flirtatious to Sylvie's ears. And he waited, with a sort of calm authority. As he was the man in charge, after all, the girl stepped aside to allow Tom in, Sylvie behind him.

Sylvie found herself plunged into a veritable nest of girls. The room was windowless but aglow from dozens of small lamps and littered with mirrors and dressing tables and well-worn wooden chairs, and it smelled powerfully, provocatively of female—powder and a stew of different perfumes and soap and stage makeup, kohl and rouge. It was a scent familiar to Sylvie, as she'd dressed in rooms just like this before performances many times before.

A glance over the girls. One was dark-haired and sloe-eyed, another had marble-fair skin and silver-blond hair, another had cheeks warm as hothouse peaches. Each unique but for one shared characteristic: they were all lushly rounded—arms, breasts, hips—in the ways that mattered to men. Sylvie could imagine the flocks of men arriving at the theater night after night for the pleasure of watching—or pursuing, if they had the money to do the pursuing properly—their favorite.

She wondered if Tom Shaughnessy partook of these young ladies as one would a box of sweets.

To a woman, the box of sweets returned her perusal.

"*What* is *that?*" One of the lovelies murmured under her breath, her eyes fixed on Sylvie. A chorus of hushed giggles followed.

Tom either didn't hear the question, or pretended not to hear it, and Sylvie would have wagered the latter.

"Good afternoon. Molly, Rose, Lizzie, Jenny, Sally . . ."

Sylvie lost track of all the English names and studied the girls instead. Pretty, all of them, some startlingly so.

"Allow me to introduce Miss Sylvie Chapeau, ladies. She will be joining you onstage. Please make her welcome. I trust you will extend the appropriate hospitality? As you know, The General expects you for rehearsal very shortly. I apologize that I cannot remain longer, Miss Chapeau, to assist with your orientation, but I have an important engagement."

Sylvie glanced at Tom Shaughnessy; his eyes were glinting in fiendish merriment. The silent message in them was: *See if a knitting needle will help you now.*

And then he gave a crisp bow and left Sylvie to the mercy of the girls.

All those pretty eyes, brown and blue and gray, continued to stare at her. Sylvie had seen more hospitality reflected in a row of icicles.

"It's a chicken," the one called Molly mused thoughtfully, answering her own earlier question. "Plucked. With great staring eyes."

Giggles, musical as strummed harp strings and malevolent as cholera, rustled through the room.

Chin up, Sylvie let the giggles wash over her. For her, jealousy was like ants at a picnic . . . a tiny annoyance that merely confirmed the grandness of the main event.

And Sylvie, of course, was accustomed to being considered the main event.

"Does it 'urt very much?" Molly asked when the giggles had faded away, her brow furrowed in sympathy. Chestnut ringlets, eyes fluffy-lashed spheres of blue, lips a pillow of pink—that was Molly.

Sylvie knew she was clearly being led into a trap of some sort, but apart from feigning deafness, which no dancer could convincingly do, she saw no other option but to respond. She thought she'd try politeness first.

"Forgive me, but does what hurt, Mademoiselle?"

"The rod up your arse. Does it 'urt very much?"

Another rustle of giggles. With a taut little anticipatory edge, now.

"Oh, not so much as jealousy," Sylvie said mildly. "Or so I'm told."

A shocked silence.

And then: *"Oooohhhh,"* one of the dancers breathed in

either admiration or terror of what Molly might do, perhaps both.

Scarlet rushed over Molly's smooth face. Sylvie saw the girl's fingers curl a little more tightly around the handle of her hairbrush.

"*Does* jealousy 'urt?" the girl called Rose whispered, sounding genuinely curious. The girl next to her elbowed her hard.

"Why should I be jealous of a plucked chicken?" Molly turned, saw with fresh satisfaction her own incomparable reflection—slightly redder in the face than it had been moments ago, granted. Her shoulders relaxed, confidence restored. She dragged the brush once through her shining length of hair, a little self-caress of reassurance.

Sylvie had just opened her mouth to respond to the chicken remark when a small man—a *very* small man—burst into the room in a blur of brilliant tailoring, and everyone jumped.

"It's five minutes past the hour," he barked. "What the devil are you females—" He saw Sylvie, stopped abruptly, and glared up at her, thick brows knitting into one brow for a moment. "Who are *you*?"

Ah, the White Lily's version of Monsieur Favre, no doubt. "Miss Sylvie Chapeau." She curtsied.

The man didn't bow or introduce himself. He continued frowning and staring as if her presence was so incongruous he could never hope to decipher her purpose here.

"Mr. Shaughnessy hired me," she clarified finally.

"Ah," the little man said. It seemed to Sylvie a more cynical syllable had never been uttered.

His eyes traveled over her shoulders, her torso, returned to her arms, lingered on her face. The scrutiny wasn't entirely without appreciation, but it was more the sort one applied to a potential investment, to a carriage or heifer or silver salver, rather than to a woman. Sylvie was accustomed to being scrutinized dispassionately, as she was a vehicle for the dance in her own way, and a certain amount of dispassion was expected.

Still, this little man didn't know her, and she didn't know him, and she began to feel a little pique.

She gazed evenly back at him—or rather, down at him—and felt her spine go just a little straighter.

And then he reached some sort of conclusion; she saw it in his face, a peculiar sort of guarded thoughtfulness.

"I'll . . . have a word with Mr. Shaughnessy." He sounded ironic. "Until then, Miss Chapeau, please wait here. Girls, you know what to do. I will join you shortly."

The girls stood and followed The General out of the room, gazes trailing past Sylvie on their way out of the door, sharp as fingernails.

             ❧   ❧   ❧

Tom didn't even jump when The General burst into his office, but his papers fluttered up. He patted them down just in time.

"She's a dancer, Tom."

"I know that, Gen. I hired her. Go tell her what to do."

Tom was feeling a trifle impatient. His sleeves were rolled up, and the stack of correspondence—bills, invitations, accounting of expenditures and profits and bribes to Crumstead, the king's man, for looking the other way with regards to the bawdier productions of the White Lily, letters from females pleading for an assignation—

awaiting his attention seemed dauntingly tall this morning. Some day he would hire someone to do this—sorting, ordering, responding—for him. In fact, in just an hour or so he would attempt to enthrall a crowd of investors with the plans that might very well make this possible. And once the The Gentleman's Emporium was thriving—

Tom looked up, surprised at The General's assessment. And, quite frankly, at his tone. Warning and ire mixed with a sort of . . . well, he might have called it *yearning,* if he was of a poetic bent. He was not.

"Did she actually tell you she was a ballerina?"

"No," The General said shortly. And said nothing more.

Tom studied his friend for a bemused moment. He didn't doubt the truth of what The General said. They had been partners for years now, but much of The General's own story remained untold, bits of it came out every now and again. Tom had learned to be patient and not to pry; he rather enjoyed the gradual unfolding of the tale.

"What makes a ballerina a 'real' dancer, Gen?" He said it somewhat irritably. "And there's no money in it. Only the bloody king wants to watch it. And women."

"She'll be trouble, mark my words. It's in that spine of hers," The General said cryptically.

And then Tom couldn't help it: He let a smile take over his face, little by little. "And in everything else of hers, too, I'd warrant."

The General was speechless for a moment. "God, Tommy." His voice cracked. "Tell me you didn't . . . *smile* at this woman." Tom's smile invariably led to trouble.

"Smiling doesn't work on her, Gen." Tom heard the wistful note in his own voice. "Nothing seems to."

The General squeezed his eyes closed, appeared to count to five, then opened them again. "So that's why you *hired* her? To practice upon her until you find the thing that does work?"

"Oh, for heaven's sake." Tom leaned back in his chair. "Rest easy, Gen. She's a pretty woman. She came looking for a job. I gave her one. And I do not, as you know . . . er . . . trouble the dancers. You know I have a very strict policy in that regard."

"That's not a pretty woman, Tom. That's a *beautiful* woman. Even worse, possibly an *interesting* woman. Who clearly thinks quite highly of herself. And she hasn't an ounce of spare flesh on her. What on earth will the audience *look* at? If she has breasts at all, I'd be—"

"She'll be different, Gen," Tom said mildly. "And our crowd likes a novelty."

"She'll be trouble," The General said grimly. "She's already trouble. I found the other dancers staring at her like a pack of hounds ready to descend upon a fox."

Tom smiled faintly at this. "I wager she'll hold her own."

"Molly was scarlet, as a matter of fact." The General sounded indignant.

"Was she?" Tom said with genuine interest, wondering what on earth the self-possessed Miss Chapeau might have said to cause Molly, a woman who was soft as a peach on the surface and hard as a cobblestone underneath, to turn colors.

Still, he realized that he had, very likely, quite selfishly and uncharacteristically and utterly on a whim, complicated The General's life, having introduced a rogue element into their little cadre of dancers, thus requiring dances to be rethought, costumes resewn, alliances reshuffled. Usually everyone had plenty of warning before such an event took place, for these very reasons. A new show was planned, discussed, rehearsed. Just the right girl was located and hired after thought and consideration, as the sheer number of girls vying for jobs at the White Lily was boggling. Tom did feel a bit of chagrin.

In truth he'd deliberately installed Sylvie with the dancers, safely out of his own reach. She'd appeared, and buffeted by myriad conflicting and confusing sensations, he'd reacted reflexively, for all the world as though dodging a musket ball or a comet. He wasn't proud of doing it, necessarily; but it was done, and as he was stubborn, he wasn't about to undo it simply to please The General.

"I'm sure you'll cope splendidly, as always, Gen."

And at this, Tom watched with interest as his friend's chest inflated with a deep inhale; then shrank again with an exhale of exaggerated patience that fluttered his cravat as well as the papers stacked on the corner of Tom's desk, as he wasn't very much taller than the desk. Tom patted a hand down over them just in time. He reminded himself to get a paperweight.

"I built a damned castle for you Tom, in a week. I didn't complain. I made sure we had costumes for a bunch of bloody damsels. I didn't complain. And now you've gone and—"

"And they loved it, didn't they? Our audience? The damsels in distress? The song about lances?"

The silence was a concession.

"And you love the sound of coins jingling in your pocket, Gen, am I right?"

"No, I like quiet pockets, Tom."

Tom grinned at this. Such a temper, The General had. Such a gift for sarcasm. But his tone had gone from irate to ironic, and would soon give way to resignation, he knew. So Tom said nothing, just waited for it. Tom could simply exhaust with charm if he so chose.

"You should have consulted me before you hired her, Tom. You usually do."

"I should have," Tom allowed gently. "And I apologize. But by now, I thought you might have learned to trust my instincts."

"Your instincts as a man of business are impeccable, Tom. Your instincts as a *man* get you into duels. And will one day, no doubt, get you killed."

The General stared at him with defiance, and when it was clear that Tom could think of nothing glib to say, the defiance metamorphosed into a sort of satisfaction that had nothing of triumph in it.

"It's a quarter past the hour, Gen," Tom said finally. Cruel, he knew, but it was his only remaining line of defense.

The General jumped and swore and all but bolted from the office.

Tom sighed, half-smiling, then reached back into his stack of mail.

He frowned when he touched one letter.

And then he slowly picked it up, stared down at it. Saw the address upon it, and went very still. Little Swathing, Kent.

He slit it open.

We should be pleased to receive you should you call again.

Cold, formal, polite. But it spoke of pride swallowed,

or reservations breached at last, by his own insistent campaign.

He'd made the journey once a week for months now. But today he'd found the occupants of the little cottage in Kent not at home. And now this.

Tom held the letter, staring down at it, not unaware of this irony.

Now that he'd been granted the thing he'd sought out of sheer stubbornness for weeks, he wasn't certain whether in truth he really wanted it.

૪૪   ૪૪   ૪૪

Sylvie had been waiting alone in the dressing room a mere ten minutes or so when the girl called Rose appeared, and Sylvie almost smiled. *So Rose was the least thorny of the flowers in this particular theater,* and like the tactician he no doubt was, The General had decided not to leave Sylvie alone with someone significantly more . . . challenging, such as Molly, or her sort just yet.

Rose looked at Sylvie with no particular emotion other than a sort of bemused curiosity, which Sylvie suspected was Rose's default expression. It was a pity, because Rose had the sort of beauty that could drop men's jaws—hair and eyes glossy and dark as a crow's wing, a soft natural flush in her ivory cheeks—but she lacked the sort of fire or self-awareness that would fascinate a man to the exclusion of all else. Someday, no doubt, she would be endlessly indulged by a wealthy elderly man seeking an undemanding mistress.

Rose wore her beauty as nonchalantly as her costume,

as though she knew this, knew it was only temporary, only part of the show.

"Yer French, then?" Rose asked with barely an inflection to indicate she'd just asked a question, and flung open a large wooden wardrobe. "Truly?"

Yes. No. Maybe. "Yes." It was the simplest answer.

"Well, I suppose The General wants ye to be a fairy today, same as the rest of us, soooo . . . ye'll need a wand . . ." When Rose rooted about in the wardrobe, a number of things came tumbling out; a wooden wand topped by a painted star clunked to the floor. Rose plucked it up, set it aside. "It was Kitty's, ye know. Kitty was the girl before ye."

If she stopped to think about it, it would dizzy her, the fact that she was about to dress as a fairy in order to earn her keep. Sylvie decided to ask questions instead.

"The girl before me?"

"The one who left, ye see. A few months ago. They say what Mr. Shaughnessy turned 'er off. Got 'erself in a right . . . *bind.*" Rose whispered the last word meaningfully and cupped her hands meaningfully below her belly."

"So he . . . 'turned 'er off'?" Sylvie repeated, aghast. She was fairly certain she knew what this particular English turn of phrase meant, given that the girl had gotten herself into a *bind:* He'd sent her away.

"Canna verra well put 'er onstage when she gets big like, can 'e?" Rose observed pragmatically, extending her arms out as though she was encircling an invisible pumpkin. "She was 'ere one day, cryin' and the like, told Molly she'd gone to speak to Mr. Shaughnessy about 'er troubles. An' she was gone the next day. 'Avena seen 'er since."

Rose turned and studied Sylvie for a moment, apparently considering whether to tell Sylvie something that, judging from Rose's expression, was clearly going to be interesting. "Molly says what Mr. Shaughnessy is the papa."

A thrill of horror coiled in Sylvie's stomach.

And Rose nodded once, gratified by the expression on Sylvie's face. "But then, Molly says a *lot*," Rose added in mild wonder. As though she could scarcely fathom why anyone would want to say more than was necessary.

"You do not believe it?"

Rose hesitated, then shrugged. "Mr. Shaughnessy . . . well, I dinna think 'e would touch a girl what works fer 'im."

"How do you know this?" Sylvie found herself asking. *And whom does he touch instead?*

"We've all 'ad a go at it, ye see." Rose grinned at this. "Water off a duck's back, to Mr. Shaughnessy. 'E brooks nooooo nonsense when it comes to the White Lily and those girls what work 'ere. 'E jus' smiles until we give up."

Interesting, given that the man seemed inclined to both frivolity and danger.

"So why would Molly say such a thing?"

"Because 'e willna touch *'er,* though she's tried and tried, and *she* thinks it's because of Kitty. She says Kitty was Mr. Shaughnessy's favorite. We *all* thought Kitty was Mr. Shaughnessy's favorite. 'E *did* seem to like 'er best. 'E . . . laughed wi' 'er, ye see. An' 'e 'asna 'ired a new girl until . . . today. It's been months. An' Molly wants 'im—Mr. Shaughnessy—fer 'erself. Well, and dinna we all?"

No. Yes. Maybe.

Sylvie tactfully ignored the question, which seemed to be rhetorical anyway. And so cheerfully and matter-of-factly said, as if Mr. Shaughnessy's appeal was universal and could be understood and appreciated by any female.

"But Mr. Shaughnessy . . . ever since Kitty left, ye see . . . once a week or so he goes to Kent, I 'eard 'im say t' The General once. But no one knows why. Not even The General. Not even 'Er Majesty."

" 'Her Majesty?' " She had been under the impression that the English were ruled by a king. Perhaps this was another honorary title, like The General.

"Daisy," Rose said laconically, as if this clarified anything. "She's 'er own room to dress in and entertain guests and the like. She doesna share wi' the likes of us. Ye'll see 'er soon enough, no doubt. But she willna speak to the likes of ye."

Ah, a diva. Sylvie was familiar with the sort. As she was something of the sort herself.

"But ladies, they do come to look for Mr. Shaughnessy," Rose hurried to assure Sylvie, as if the fact that he didn't touch his dancers would call his manhood into question. "Cryin' an' beggin' to see 'im, in fact. An' 'usbands are forever callin' 'im out, our Mr. Shaughnessy. Even though 'es not a gentleman, like. It's because 'es such a verra good shot."

"Duels? He fights *duels?*"

"Best shot in London. Shoots the 'eart right out o' the target each time."

Sylvie felt faint. She wondered if duels were any more legal in London than they were in Paris, and doubted it. She remembered the glint of the pistol in Tom Shaughnessy's sleeve as they stood in the clearing among those highwaymen.

"He kills people?"

"Kills?" Rose sounded faintly appalled. Only faintly. Sylvie wondered whether Rose experienced any emotion rather strongly, and given the tempests of her own various passions, felt a slight twinge of envy, wondering what it might be like to drift comfortably through life's dramas.

"Oh, no. They shoot at each other, but everyone seems to miss."

Tom Shaughnessy routinely shot and allowed other people to shoot at him? *Over other men's wives?*

"And The General—he is . . ." Sylvie paused to think of the word. "In charge of the dancing?"

"'E is, an 'e invents the shows, like, but even 'e answers to Mr. Shaughnessy, an' 'tis Mr. Shaughnessy, oo 'as the *big* ideas. One show a night, every night save Sunday, three acts at least, six or eight songs, usually. Mr. Shaughnessy likes to jumble it up a bit, an 'e seems t'ave a new idea every week. Keeps us busy, 'e does. We've rehearsal every day for as long as The General says. It's a right bit o' work, but it's good pay, and Mr. Shaughnessy, 'e looks after us."

Right bit of work? Sylvie wondered what on earth the dances entailed.

"Do you live here at the theater, Rose?"

"At the theater?" Rose's eyes widened with astonishment. "I've me own rooms up the street. Mr. Shaughnessy pays right well. We all do—'ave our own rooms. The girls, and Poe and Stark, the men what guard the stage door outside, an' Jack, 'oo guards the dressing-room door, an' the boys who work for The General. But there *are* rooms 'ere at the White Lily, up the stairs. Was a grand 'ouse once. Where d'yer live, Sylvie?"

Sylvie didn't know how to respond to that question.

She was spared from answering when the top half of Rose disappeared into the wardrobe and she began fishing about inside it.

She emerged with a gown, a gossamer thing, pale pink over some silvery fabric. It would provide about as much flesh coverage as mist, though in dimmed lights one couldn't *precisely* see through it. Sylvie eyed it askance.

" 'Ere. We've five minutes before The General 'as a fit. I'll 'elp wi' yer laces."

Sylvie was accustomed to dressing in front of other girls; modesty was frivolous when one was a dancer preparing to perform. But Sylvie was suddenly profoundly aware of how slight she was, a willow twig compared to these vivid blossoms of girls. It was as if anything superfluous to ballet had melted away from her body, leaving behind only what was necessary to fulfill Monsieur Favre's commands—elegant muscle.

She turned around and presented her back to Rose, and Rose worked the laces on her mourning gown for her. She watched with frank curiosity as Sylvie slipped into the dress.

The dress was too large, hung on her frame loosely, exposing an expanse of chest, stopping just shy of revealing her bosom altogether. And the ribbon from which her miniature hung. Sylvie put her hand up, disguising it.

"The General, 'e won't want ye to wear stays, but ye've not much of a bosom, 'ave ye?"

How on earth did one respond to such a question? Ironically, Sylvie decided. "No, I suppose not."

"Mmm. Stays *will* 'elp wi' the—" Rose covered her own round bosoms with both hands and gave them an illustrative push upward. "Make ye look like ye've a bit more."

Sylvie appreciated that Rose was trying to be helpful, but bosoms had always been about as helpful as ballast in Sylvie's line of work; they got in the way, in other words. She felt herself growing warm in indignation.

And when Rose handed her the big wooden wand, and she turned and got a look at herself in the mirror, the indignity was complete.

But wait. Rose was still rummaging about in the wardrobe, and plucked out a pair of wings, sheer, luminous fabric ingeniously stretched over a frame of wires, fitted with straps. An admirable bit of construction, admittedly. She would admire it more if she weren't required to wear them.

But Rose held them out to her, and Sylvie resignedly took them. She saw loops in the center for her arms. She pushed her slim arms through them. *Voilà!* She was a fairy.

The wings, she had to admit, *were* pretty. They would have done justice to the costumers at the Paris Opera, where some of the finest and most ingenious seamstresses were employed.

"Why did Mr. Shaughnessy take ye on?" Rose wanted to know.

Now that Rose was satisfied that her body was not the typical White Lily body, she apparently could not resist the question.

Sylvie decided that building her own mystique would be a marvelous strategic defense during her stay at the theater.

"Mr. Shaughnessy and I shared a mail coach, which was robbed, and when I kissed a highwayman, they agreed to let us go on."

Rose's dark eyes stared. And then: "*Cor!*" she breathed.

In short, if Sylvie would kiss a highwayman, what *else* might she be capable of?

Sylvie felt absurdly gratified. She might be skinny and dressed inadequately as a fairy, but she could still impress.

"What's funny, it was sudden-like, and 'e always takes 'is time findin' a new girl. Tells us all about it. We thought 'ed never replace Kitty. So ye're a surprise."

I imagine I am.

CHAPTER FIVE

The General regarded Sylvie dispassionately: the big dress, the wand, the studiedly stoic expression on her face.

"The costumes will need ... significant ... altering. How are your skills with a needle, Sylvie?"

"I believe you mean 'Miss Chapeau,'" she said almost reflexively. Perhaps it was a mistake, but she was a tad irritated, as her dignity felt chafed by her costume and by Rose's assessment of her bosom. "My skills with a needle are adequate."

"You may have noticed that we don't stand on ceremony here, Sylvie. Now girls, places please. Sylvie, because of your height, you can stand between *Molly* and *Jenny*—"

"What is *your* name?" Sylvie considered perhaps she should have eaten something when Mr. Shaughnessy offered, as she knew her temper was easier to rouse when her stomach was empty, and it was tempting her now to take risks.

He fixed her with a gaze meant to intimidate, no doubt. "The General," he said evenly. "The. General." He gazed at her with those sharp dark eyes. "Now Josephine, if you'd begin—"

"Your given name is 'The'?" Sylvie said mildly.

Sylvie heard what sounded like a collected sucking of breath. The other girls had done it.

The General turned very slowly and stared up at her wonderingly.

"Then I may call you 'The'?" she pressed on, calmly. Taking a certain perverse, reckless pleasure in it.

"Oh, my, oh my, oh my, oh my," Rose whispered gleefully.

"Don't don't don't don't don't," another girl hissed.

The General muttered something, and Sylvie could have sworn he was taking the name of Tom Shaughnessy in vain. He took in a deep breath, appeared to be counting.

And then he beamed at Sylvie. "Yes. Please do call me 'The.' Or call me cuddlecakes. Call me that 'gorgeous bastard.' I suppose it doesn't matter what you call me when you have need of calling me, as I will more likely need to call *you,* Sylvie. And now, if you would please stand between Molly and Jenny. I assume you can . . . move to music?"

The last three words were given a special frisson of irony, which puzzled Sylvie just a bit.

"I shall certainly do my very best," she said solemnly.

"Josephine," The General barked.

Josephine, a fair-haired woman who looked astonishingly ordinary in contrast to the rest of the denizens of the theater—as round and pleasant-faced and wholesome as the wife of a country squire—gave a start and landed on the pianoforte, her fingers finding and playing a song with a waltz pattern, tinkling and saucy.

The girls onstage began to sway, arcing their wands to and fro gracefully above their heads.

This presented little challenge; Sylvie managed to master the swaying motion quickly enough.

She noticed The General's eyes on her, and she could have sworn he looked a little amused.

But the swaying motion was pretty in its way, harmless enough, despite the wands and shamelessly gossamer gowns and her pair of wings. She could even imagine how pleasing they all might look beyond the footlights during a performance, all shimmer and beauty.

"Smiles, girls!" The General bellowed.

Rows of pretty teeth were instantly bared. Sylvie suspected hers more closely resembled a grimace, from the feel of things. Still, she curled her lips back.

The music tinkled on for a bar or so, at which point the girls rotated in a circle until their backs faced the audience, all the while twirling their wands in tight circles over their heads. And then they linked arms, a motion Sylvie managed to follow smoothly enough. Sylvie wasn't particularly anxious to touch Molly, but she did it anyhow, and took Jenny's arm, too, and continued to sway to and fro.

This was child's play; she could probably do this and nap at the same time. In fact, a nap was sound—

The row of girls bent double and pushed their fannies up into the air and sang out *"Wheee!"* dragging a startled Sylvie abruptly down with them.

And then they were upright and gently swaying again.

"More derriere next time, Jenny! Get it up there high!" The General ordered, as if commanding troop maneuvers.

They swayed for a bar, twirling their wands, and then, Dear God—

"Wheee!"

They did it again, chins to their knees, derrieres in the air, dragging Sylvie down with them.

When she was upright this time, Sylvie's eyes were wide and nearly watering with horror.

"Ye've scarcely an arse, Sylvie. See the seamstress straightaway and get that dress altered," The General barked over the music. "And the word is *'wheee!'* I want to hear it. *One,* two, three, *one,* two, three, *one,* two, three . . ."

And suddenly, abruptly, Sylvie unhooked her arm from Molly's and Lizzie's and almost blindly fled down the little stairs of the stage, reflexively fleeing what seemed to her the things she'd devoted her entire life to avoid becoming.

ᕕᖇ   ᕕᖇ   ᕕᖇ

She wasn't quite certain where she was heading, but "away" seemed a sufficient destination at the moment, and her general direction appeared to be the White Lily's door.

She nearly ran headlong into the wall of a linen-clad chest, stopped abruptly and looked up into Tom Shaughnessy's face.

"Tired of dancing so soon, Miss Chapeau?"

"Derrieres . . . bending . . . *wheee!*" Sylvie stammered furiously, hands flailing helplessly, unable to convey the horror of it all. "That is *not* dancing, Mr. Shaughnessy."

"You stand there, move about, smile." He was obviously confused. "Of course it's dancing. Audiences pay good money for derrieres and *'whee,'* Miss Chapeau.

Does 'dance' mean something else now in French?" And then he frowned in comprehension. "Oh! I believe I see what you are driving at. But I'm afraid no one will pay to see"—Tom paused, as if to give the word a wide mental berth from his other words, and said it gingerly. "*Ballet.* If that's what you're asking. There isn't any money in it."

Sylvie went still for a moment. How on earth would he have known about—

She took a deep breath. "Is there something else I might do to assist here at the theater?" she managed to ask in a steadier voice. "In order to earn my keep."

She hoped, hoped, hoped he wouldn't interpret this question pruriently.

She needn't have worried. "Perhaps you sing?" he asked, his mind clearly ticking away.

"Well—" Sylvie could carry a tune, but more often than not, the tune carried her. It was her body, not her voice, which understood music so well. "Yes." Which was merely a short version of the truth.

"Do you sing . . . well?" He sounded troubled by the very idea. "You see, we don't want to frighten the audience with . . . exquisite singing. Most of these men can hear a soprano in any drawing room, you see. They come here to get *away* from sopranos in the drawing room. Sopranos remind them of long evenings with their wives."

"No one will ever invite me to sing in a drawing room," Sylvie told him quite truthfully.

"Would you be willing to sing a bawdy song then?"

She blinked. "A baw—" The words began as a choked laugh and stopped when she noticed there was absolutely nothing of humor in his face. It had been a flat question.

He was a businessman deciding how to deploy an asset, and she was the asset.

"A bawdy song," he reiterated impatiently. "Such as . . ." Tom paused in thought, and then tilted his head back and in a surprisingly decent tenor sang:

"Nell was a young woman so young and so fair
Who cherished her virtue 'til she met Lord Adair
Who took her for a ride in the warm summer air
And gave her a necklace of baubles to wear
Of baubles, of baubles, of baubles to wear,
Oh!
He gave her a necklace of baubles to wear!

He looked at her. "A bawdy song," he concluded briskly.

And now the expression on his face was so distinctly at odds with the content of his song that incredulity warred with hilarity as she decided what to say next.

"Pretty song," she finally said, solemnly. "Perhaps *you* should sing it, instead."

"Oh, I would," Tom assured her in all seriousness, "if I thought anyone would pay to see *me* rouged, or in a shift."

"And are you certain no one would?"

The words were out before she could stop them, because it was precisely the thing any accomplished coquette would have been unable to resist saying in similar circumstances. She regretted them for an instant.

In the next instant, she was surprised to find herself rather breathlessly looking forward to what Tom Shaughnessy might say.

Nothing, as it turned out—for a time, anyway. He regarded her instead, eyes aglow in pure pleasure—he was utterly pleased with *her*—the corner of his mouth quirked upward speculatively, as if deciding what to say next.

"I can sing the French version, too," he said suddenly. "My friend Henri taught the words to me. Would you like to hear it?"

"Have I a choice?"

He ignored her question, and squeezed his eyes closed for a moment in thought, apparently scanning his memory for the lyrics.

At last he opened his eyes, and opened his mouth, and—

Well, the language he used was certainly French.

But the song suddenly had nothing at all to do with Nell and Lord Adair.

Instead, it was all about what a certain man would like to do to a certain woman and what position he'd like to do it *in,* and how certain he was that the woman would enjoy it. Baubles *did* play a role—though they were called something else entirely in this version of the song, as this was French—and the chorus was sung just as enthusiastically.

Perhaps most shockingly, it all rhymed beautifully.

And as he sang: heat. In her cheeks, in the pit of her stomach, sweeping up her arms. *Everywhere* as he sang, the song creating the most specific pictures in her head.

She was certain the bloody man had made the lyrics up on the spot.

For heaven's sake, she'd danced for kings; she couldn't recall the last time she'd conjured a genuine blush. But this man had sent her composure scattering as surely as a cue dashed into a triangle of billiard balls.

When he was done, silence dropped with the ceremony

of that great heavy velvet curtain. Tom's face was solemn as a vicar's, but his eyes glinted like the very devil's. He clasped his hands behind his back and waited with wide eyes for her to comment.

Sylvie could not recall words ever deserting her; the traitors, they were doing it now.

"That . . ." Her voice was a little hoarse. She cleared her throat. "That wasn't the same song, Mr. Shaughnessy."

"No? Wasn't it?" All innocence. "Bother. Henri must have misled me. I'll have a word with him. Perhaps my French is not quite so good as I thought."

She paused. "No," she agreed slowly. "'Good' is not the word I would have chosen to describe your French, Mr. Shaughnessy." She waited, and her heart beat just a little more quickly in anticipation.

"Wicked, then?" he suggested quickly. "Would you perhaps use 'wicked,' instead?" He sounded as earnest as a schoolboy making a guess at an arithmetic problem.

She couldn't help it; it burbled out of her, a vein of humor struck. She laughed. He'd said precisely what he should have said next in the dance of flirtation, and it delighted her more than it should have, made her breathless the way a well-executed *pas de deux* did.

The laughter, of course, only encouraged him; the wicked grin flashed. "Which part of the song did you like best, Miss Chapeau?"

"The ending," she said quickly, recovering.

He looked at her again, speculatively. "Mmmm," he said, considering this. "That might very well be true, but"—he reached out one finger and dragged it lightly along her flaming jaw—"you should see how attractively pink the *rest* of the song has made you."

She froze. Of all the bold, presumptuous—

He took his hand away and glanced down at it briefly; confusion flickered, his brows dived a little.

And even as outrage flamed in her eyes, even after he took his finger away, his touch echoed through her unnervingly.

An odd silence followed.

"A thought-provoking song, nevertheless, wouldn't you say, Miss Chapeau?" he said, finally.

"It provoked only a longing to hear a *good* tenor, Mr. Shaughnessy." A tart and scrambling effort to impose a distance and gather the shreds of her composure.

Up went his brows. "Did it? My apologies." He sounded genuinely disappointed. "I thought perhaps you understood the lyrics. Clearly you did not, and I have misjudged you, and you are a mere innocent after all."

"I'm not a *mere*—"

White teeth and that crescent-shaped dimple came into view again. "Yes?"

She realized too late how ludicrous it was to defend her honor by declaring she was *not* innocent. Funny, but it had been the word "mere" her temper had reared up against. Sylvie had never been "mere" in any way.

And as she wasn't certain how to ease her way out of this particular corner, she remained silent.

"Mmm. I didn't think you were, somehow," he said idly, and dipped a hand into his pocket and retrieved a watch; it glowed like a tiny planet in the dim theater. He nudged it open with his thumb, and when he saw the time, everything about him became brisk.

"To the subject at hand, Miss Chapeau. I do not operate a charity."

She blinked. It was as though he'd finished a quick afternoon snack and was now pushing himself away from the table to get on with the rest of his day.

"I beg your pardon?" she said.

"It's simple, you see. You may sing a bawdy song of my choosing, or you may dance with the other girls, or you may leave. Those are your choices. And yes, you are passing fair, but you may have noticed beauty is not a rarity, but a requirement, here at the White Lily. Had you been any plainer, I would have sent you packing much earlier. As I said, I cannot afford to offer charity."

Sylvie was speechless. *Passing fair?* When earlier she had been "beautiful"?

"It's called work, Miss Chapeau. *Travailler,* I believe they call it in your language. Or perhaps you're unfamiliar with the concept?"

The weight of the accusation landed full force on her chest, made what felt like a veritable crater in it; indignation and anger sizzled up out of it, robbing her of breath.

Everything she valued in her life—the soft bed she rose from in the morning, the sound of hands put together in applause, the flowers brought to her each night at the end of a performance, the barbs of the girls in the dressing room born of awe and envy, and the quiet adulation of most of Paris and the devotion of a man like Etienne, *everything*—had been forged from discipline and commitment and grim determination. In other words: from work. What could this . . . this . . . gilded *street ruffian* possibly know of the sort of sweat and pain required to make people forget themselves as they watched you, to make them soar inside when you danced for them?

She—of the quicksilver, hand-waving, shooting-star temper—was nearly paralyzed by fury.

"You know nothing of me, Mr. Shaughnessy." Her voice was low and taut.

"And whose fault is that, Miss Chapeau?" Pleasantly said. As though the waves of righteous indignation pouring from her were naught but a summer breeze.

She remained incredulously silent.

"Does that mean you *do* know how to work?" He said it patiently, into her silent green glare.

"Yes, Mr. Shaughnessy," she managed ironically. "I warrant I could teach *you* a bit about work."

He gave a short laugh then. "Oh, I'm certain you're quite correct, Miss Chapeau. Consider my work, for instance. It's no trouble at all to order lovely girls about. Mere child's play, in fact. I shall look forward to my lesson about *work* from you. Now: you need to wear what The General tells you to wear, do what he tells you to do, smile, and play nicely with the other girls. Do you think you can manage to do that, or will you be leaving now?"

She listened to his words, but for some reason the words "passing fair" were the ones that scraped away in her mind like a trapped thistle.

Funny, of all the things this man had said, this one for some reason bothered most.

She wondered if he would truly send her packing if she refused; she sensed he wasn't as indifferent to her as he purported to be, and it was tempting to take that risk, to call his bluff.

Passing fair, indeed.

Then again, perhaps he was the sort who trifled idly with novelty and tired of it quickly. A man with his face, even bereft of his . . . *singular* . . . charm would certainly be able to view women as offerings on the groaning sideboard of life. Tom Shaughnessy was like a mirror in which the world was reflected backward, different, brand-new, infuriating. Invigorating as a bolted glass of whiskey, and probably just as dangerous and addictive.

All right. So she cherished her pride.

But she *needed* money.

"When will I be paid?"

Was it just the changing light of the day passing through the theater? Or did relief soften his expression briefly?

"When you've performed onstage for our audience, Miss Chapeau. Until then you are an apprentice, and living upon the charity of the White Lily. Will you be staying, then?"

Sylvie Lamoreux, an *apprentice,* living upon *charity?*

"Will you be staying?" There was a faint note of urgency in his voice now. She wondered whether it was concern about her imminent departure or about whatever appointment it seemed she was keeping him from meeting, judging from his one impatient glance at his watch. Perhaps he financed these theaters with the highwaymen's spoils, and he was on his way to meet Biggsy Biggens to sort through his take.

"I shall stay. I shall"—she took a deep breath, and still she couldn't deliver the word with anything other than irony—"dance."

There was a beat of silence before he spoke. Her vanity decided to interpret it as relief.

"Very well, then. And when you return to rehearsal, you may wish to apologize to The General. He predicted that you would be trouble. Perhaps you'll be able to convince him otherwise."

His tone, and the quick grin that accompanied his words, told her he had no confidence whatsoever in her ability to do so.

She didn't disabuse him of that notion.

"And when you are done, Sylvie, please ask Josephine to show you to your room. I've asked her to see that you get something to eat. I won't have you starving."

She stared at him. He stared back at her patiently.

"Thank you," she managed at last with some dignity, and pirouetted neatly to bravely rejoin the hostile little flock of females.

She couldn't help it. She glanced back just once, to see if he was admiring her exit.

But he wasn't. Oddly, he was looking down at his fingers again, and she could have sworn his expression was haunted.

CHAPTER SIX

COMBINED, THEY COULD HAVE FINANCED the English army twice over, yet there was only a title or two among them: Lord Cambry, a baron; George Pinkerton-Knowles, who'd amassed a fortune in shipbuilding; Major William Gordon, Viscount Howath, a few others. They'd inherited the money, or they'd earned it, or they'd all but stolen it through some legal means. But all that mattered to Tom was that they had it, enough of it to ensure that they were often bored and restless and in search of novelty. Enough of it to ensure they had power and status and connections, should it become necessary to call in a few markers in order to achieve his grand goal. And they'd backed him before, taken a risk on the White Lily, perhaps as a lark, and Tom had earned their investment back for them more than three times over. And since he'd done this once, naturally they were interested to hear if he might do it for them again. Tom had been invited to meet with them at Major Gordon's club. From there they would go on to their dinners, and then, very likely, to the White Lily.

Good brandy and better cigars had created the sort of bonhomie necessary for them to loosen their purse strings; the smoke in the air wreathed lamps and full, flushed faces.

Pinkerton-Knowles had in fact unbuttoned his coat, and his unfettered belly rested comfortably on his lap. "Talk to us, Shaughnessy," he urged.

It had never occurred to Tom to feel intimidated by any of them. It had never occurred to Tom to want to *be* any of them, which was precisely why they more or less liked him, and more than one of them fancied they wanted to be *him.* He didn't try to be anything he wasn't, and he clearly took such great pleasure in who he was—part Irish, rumored part Gypsy, unapologetically a bastard—that they envied him and enjoyed his company.

He wouldn't be welcome to court their *daughters,* but they envied him and enjoyed his company.

"Gentlemen." Tom rose. Slimmer than all of them, taller than all of them, and far, far better-looking than all of them, their heads craned up. "Thank you for agreeing to meet me today."

"No, thank *you,* Shaughnessy, for my Melinda. And Melinda sends her thanks, as well," the major called out. A chorus of laughter rose up. Melinda had spent some time in the employ of the White Lily before she'd been persuaded to become the major's much-coddled mistress.

Thoughts of Melinda and the major's particular brand of happiness made Tom's thoughts veer to a seemingly innocuous moment at the White Lily, and Miss Sylvie Chapeau. It had been barely a touch, something he'd done out of flirtation so many times before, so easily, so casually. He hadn't expected to find the texture of her skin so . . . well, *achingly* fine. She'd seemed all pride and steel and fire and wit; perhaps that was why the discovery that her skin was vulnerably soft had been so startling. But the discovery, for some reason, had made him feel strangely awkward and uncertain—which irritated him, as he couldn't recall the last time he'd felt awkward or uncertain about anything.

"Give my regards to the fair Melinda," Tom said with mock solemnity, and reached for his glass to lift. "I'm delighted I could contribute to the happiness of two such fine people."

"To Melinda and the major!" the group roared in unison, and tossed back the balance of their glasses. A series of *thunks* followed, glasses landing on the table again.

"To the business at hand, then," Tom intoned formally. "Gentlemen, I believe it's safe to say that the White Lily has greatly contributed to our collective . . ." he paused for effect, ". . . *happiness* and well-being over the past few years. And in light of his earlier confidences, I believe the major, in particular, would concur."

Much rumbled laughter and muttering. "Hear, hear!" the major said with feeling.

"Fine job of it, Shaughnessy. Earned my money back twice over. You've a gift for this sort of thing."

More concurring rumbles.

Tom accepted their tributes with a modest nod. "And no man could ask for better partners in business than yourselves, gentleman. Which is why I've invited you here this evening. I'd very much like for you to be the first to hear of . . ." he paused strategically, and lowered his voice a fraction, ". . . an exclusive opportunity."

Pinkerton-Knowles delicately stifled a belch with a palm. "Opportunity, Shaughnessy? What sort of opportunity?"

"Why, simply an opportunity to participate in one of the boldest, surest, most lucrative endeavors you'll no doubt encounter in your lifetime," he said mildly. "Shall I go on?"

They were silent now and as attentive as hunting dogs, all bonhomie quenched in favor of the businessman and adventurer in each of them.

"Gentlemen, I give you the"—Tom, a showman to his bones, whisked aside the fringed velvet curtains at the window, and light flooded in, revealing his beautifully rendered sketch propped upon an easel there—" 'Gentleman's Emporium.' A theater, a gentleman's club, a gaming *heaven*, special entertainments . . . all housed on several floors in one elegant building. Imagine, if you will, if the White Lily were wed to White's, if White's were grafted to Gentleman Jackson's, and—if one is an exclusive, private member—where one may dine privately with beautiful women after an evening's entertainment."

"Only 'dine'?" someone repeated, sounding disappointed. A few hoots rose up.

"Only dine." Tom sounded sympathetic. "What you manage to persuade her to do *after* you dine is another thing entirely, of course"—he paused while laughter and teasing jests rippled around the room—"and you will need to find other accommodations for such things, as the Gentleman's Emporium's current plans do not include them."

A diplomatic way of saying, No, he was not opening a brothel.

"Wish I had *your* powers of 'persuasion,' Shaughnessy."

"And *I'm* glad that you do not," Tom shot back.

More laughter. Which then died away, leaving a thoughtful silence as they considered what Tom had just said.

"And the property?" the major barked. "Build or buy?"

A little thrill of excitement spiked in Tom. Specific questions such as these indicated genuine interest. "Buy, renovate, *and* build. I know just the property. Needs a fair amount of work, but behind me"—Tom motioned to the artist's rendering—"you can see how it will look. I invite you to inspect it more closely."

They gathered around the illustration, spent some time in solemn silence, perusing it, then fired questions at him. About location, and licenses, and time lines, and sopranos (no: no sopranos). He answered them deftly.

And then, when the questions ebbed to a trickle, they resumed their seats, gazing at the drawing, considering. Tom looked levelly at them, patiently awaiting the next and most important question, because if someone asked it, it meant the interest had gone beyond idle; it had taken root. If *he* brought it up, it placed him in a position of vulnerability.

It was the major who spoke. "I might as well be the one to ask it, Shaughnessy. How much do you want from each of us?"

Bravely, Tom told them.

The silence that followed was the sort that follows a kidney punch.

"Good God, Shaughnessy," the major rasped when he'd recovered. "It's a brilliant idea, granted. If anyone can make a go of it, I think it's you. But you don't need to buy a barouche for your wife or send a boy to Eton, or to Oxford, and I do. And the *money* . . ."

"Your boy is but five years old, is he not, Major?" Tom asked smoothly. "I imagine your investment will have doubled itself by the time he's of Oxford age."

A laugh rose up, amused and gently mocking the major

for his lack of fiscal nerve. *Good.* They were beginning to recover from their shock, beginning to hear the faint siren song of a good gamble. And no doubt would be amenable to negotiating now.

"But Tom's boy wouldn't be going to Eton or Oxford even then, would he? You're a lucky bastard, Tommy, no offense. Have to give them a decent start in life, you know, but children are bloody expensive."

More laughter.

Tom was far too comfortable with who he was and what he'd accomplished to care much what anyone said about him, and it *was* absurd to think that the son of an Irish-Gyspy hybrid bastard might go to Eton and Oxford and muck about with the sons of proper gentlemen.

So he did laugh; a showman, he knew what was necessary to sell his proposal and was willing to do what the moment required. But though it was true, had always been true, he was distantly amused to find that suddenly nothing about the comment amused him.

It was time to seize control of the situation once more, which was part of his strategy. He strode to the curtain, pulled it closed, symbolically and abruptly cutting off the vision of potential riches and pleasant masculine «mayhem.

"Gentleman, thank you for joining me today. I'm looking for a very small and select group of investors, men of vision whom I trust, and naturally I thought first of you. Nothing would please me more than to continue to contribute to your wealth and happiness . . . not to mention add to my own."

Appreciative laughter.

"But the owner of the property in question shall require

an answer from me within a fortnight, as he has others interested in purchasing it. Please do give it some thought, ask any questions you wish—you know where to find me—"

"Follow the trail of women!" someone who'd had a little too much brandy blurted.

"Or look in the arms of Bettina at the Velvet Glove at midnight!"

Tom grinned. "And if I don't hear from you within a fortnight, I'll assume you've decided to invest your money elsewhere. Hope to see you at the White Lily tonight, and"—he lowered his voice—"I'd like you, my friends, to be the first to know that we have the most *extraordinary future* production planned."

In unison, the men leaned forward, grown men all, eager as children.

"Tell, Tommy!"

"I'll give you a hint, gentlemen. Just one word, so remember it." They waited, leaning forward more steeply. He waited a strategic moment, then leaned forward, mouthed it *sotto voce*.

"*Venus.*"

"Veeenusss," someone repeated slowly, sounding awed.

"Spread the word," Tom said. "You've never seen anything like it, and you'll never forget it."

ᏉᎵ   ᏉᎵ   ᏉᎵ

Apart from inventing and singing a naughty French song to Miss Sylvie Chapeau, the day had been one of unrelieved strategic challenges. The moment he returned from his meeting with investors, Tom decided he ought to talk to Daisy, just to get it over with. She often took her supper in her own dressing room before the evening's entertainments—she never joined the girls for rehearsal—so that's where he headed.

How should he approach this? Somberly? Sternly? Brightly? It would be a delicate task, no matter how he went about it, as Daisy was as canny as she was buxom, and they knew each other almost too well. Long years of familiarity, contempt, triumph, and tragedy had created the fabric of their friendship, which was worn and warm as a quilt. Frayed and well used, nibbled about the edges by moths perhaps, but useful and cherished in its way.

"I want to be Venus, Tom." Daisy said it very calmly the moment he set foot in the room.

Damnation. Who on earth would have gotten to her so quickly? How did she *know*? It could not have been The General. He considered the men in that smoky room he'd exited a mere hour ago and cursed all of them, for clearly one of them had somehow communicated with Daisy. Daisy was shrewd enough to know that the very fact that the show hadn't been mentioned to her meant Tom and The General had something else in mind.

"Oh, now, Daize, don't you think you should give the other girls a chance to shine?"

"Why?" she asked flatly.

The answer to this, as Daisy well knew, was that she was getting older. The flesh beneath her chin was loosening, her posterior was more than a shade wider than ample, her costumes required letting out on a regular basis now, and her majestic bosom was succumbing a little more each day to the tug of gravity. She knew it, Tom knew it, The General knew it, and Daisy, cruelly, wanted Tom to spell it out for her and knew he never, ever would.

Bloody woman.

"Because I need to keep them employed, Daisy, and if I give one or two of them an opportunity to shine, it helps to keep the peace."

This was at least partially true, and Daisy knew this, too. He saw amusement and wry admiration flicker in her eyes.

"Which girl, then? That Molly chit? She 'asn't the *presence* for it."

"Presence"? When had Daisy begun using words like "presence"?

It was time to be stern. "Daisy, the White Lily thrives on novelty, you know that as well as I, and quite simply, using a different girl is a business decision. And should the show fail—"

"It can't fail, Tom," Daisy interrupted firmly. "Which is why I want to be Venus. It's a marvelous idea, and The General is a gen . . ."

She stopped herself suddenly and swung about to face the mirror, completing a circle of rouge on one cheek, her fingers fussing in her hair, which trailed down over one shoulder.

"The General is what, Daisy?" Tom asked innocently.

"A jester looking for a court."

"Mmm. Odd, I could have sworn you were about to call him a 'genius.' "

"I would no sooner call that wee tyrant a genius than you'd turn Quaker, Tommy."

"Quaker is about the only thing I haven't been, Daisy. I'm thinking of giving it a go."

She smirked at him in the mirror. "Don't change the

subject, Tommy. You know I'm perfect for the role of Venus."

Tom knew nothing of the sort. He looked at Daisy and tried to imagine a great oyster shell creaking open to reveal a plump pearl of a dyed redhead instead of the lithe creature Botticelli had painted and that he and The General envisioned. There was no getting around it, really. He couldn't allow it to happen. The fortunes of the theater depended greatly upon it; his own fortunes, and his dream of The Gentleman's Emporium rode greatly upon it.

And besides, he'd promised The General, who doubtless had something tastefully titillating in mind, and only a lithe girl would do.

"Daisy—" he began diplomatically.

"Now listen to me, ye beautiful sod." She whirled on him and wagged her hairbrush at him. Mother-of-pearl-handled, the thing was, had cost a small fortune, as had everything in this room, the plush pink furniture, the soft rugs, the grand gilt mirror, all to please her, to reward her. "Do I need to remind ye of the reason this theater stands 'ere at all?"

"Because I had the good sense to take advantage of your talents?" He gave her a winning smile.

She tried to scowl, but it was clear she couldn't quite force herself to do it in the face of that smile. So she sighed instead. "Come 'ere, Tommy, ye've a thread." She beckoned with a hand and he inched forward obediently; she reached out and wrapped a loose thread hanging from one of his coat buttons around her finger and gave it a yank to snap it. She smoothed his coat down with absent affection.

"Wouldn't want a thing to mar yer perfection now,

now, would we, Tommy?" A faint tang of bitterness in her tone now.

He wasn't certain how to deal with this fear and bitterness and pride. He remained silent, and knew she would interpret his silence as sympathy, and would hate it. But Daisy had become a bit comfortable in her diva role, avoiding the other girls or treating them with coolness, arriving late for rehearsals, holding court like a buxom empress in these dressing rooms after the show. Tom was just as familiar with her origins as he was with his own; perhaps, he thought, this was her way of continuing to distance herself from her past, the way owning grand theaters and producing bawdy spectacles and accumulating money was his.

But *he'd* provided a place and the throne for Daisy to blossom into divahood. She'd never abandoned her gutter accent, nor even attempted it, the way he had buffed his own methodically out of existence through listening to gentlemen talk and imitating their inflections, learning their words phonetically, discovering through any means possible what the words meant. Swallowing pride and asking; charming people into teaching him to read. It simply hadn't been necessary for Daisy to make the effort when one possessed a bosom as unforgettable and profitable as hers.

"Ye'll get old, too, Tommy, ye bugger," she said softly. It wasn't an accusation or a threat; it was more like a plea. It made him desperately uncomfortable.

He decided to change the subject. "You'll never guess who I saw, Daisy. Biggsy Biggens."

"Biggsy!" Daisy's eyes widened in surprise. "Good Lord! Where'd yer see 'im? Swingin' 't the end of a rope?" She said it only half-jokingly.

"He was robbing the coach I was aboard, actually."

Daisy snorted. "A good 'eart, but precious little imagination, Biggsy always had. 'E'll come to a bad end yet."

"He asked after you, Daize."

"Yes, well, ye see, Tommy, because even after all of these years, I leave *quite* an impression." She addressed this to the mirror, but her eyes met and held Tom's, pride and defiance . . . and nervousness. He hated the nervousness; Daisy was a peacock, a diva, it was out of place. And it made him feel a cad; he slid his eyes casually away from hers, toward the brandy decanter, then decided he'd already had enough at his investor meeting.

" 'E didna shoot ye, apparently? Biggsy?"

"I managed to persuade him not to, for the sake of old times. He required a kiss from one of our passengers, however, as the price of leaving with most of our belongings."

Daisy smiled at this. "I take back what I said about 'is imagination. Did 'e get one?"

Tom paused. "He did. Someone . . . volunteered." Tom saw the image in his mind, Sylvie's slim body, shoulders squared, standing on her toes to reach the highwayman's mouth, Biggsy's near-humble acceptance of the favor proffered, the awe and gratitude lighting the ugly man's face. Tom felt a sharp twinge of something, a pang of indefinable emotion, intriguing but uncomfortable.

Restlessness surged. This conversation with Daisy was taking too long; he decided it was time to be firm. "Daisy, I'd like another girl to play the part of Venus. I haven't decided who it should be. But I have also hired a new girl."

She looked up sharply. "Ye've 'ired a new girl? When?"

"Today."

"Does The General know?"

Ah, but Daisy was shrewd. Tom smiled faintly. "He does now."

Daisy thoughtfully regarded him in the mirror. "'Oo is this girl? She's the replacement for Kitty?"

"She's not a 'replacement' for anyone, Daisy," Tom said sharply. "She's the one from whom Biggsy extracted a kiss."

Daisy's mouth set; however, she looked reluctantly intrigued. "Ye took 'er on out o' pity? Seems unlikely, Tom." She said it dryly.

Tom knew a moment of pique; Daisy perhaps more than anyone had benefited from his pragmatism and good business sense, and he was not without a heart, and she knew it. He ascribed it to her wounded pride, and let it go, and knew the fact that he had let it go would hurt her pride even more. It could not be helped.

"I took her on an impulse." Somehow he thought she would find this a more acceptable answer. He smiled crookedly. "She also jabbed me with a knitting needle when I touched her arm."

Daisy gave a short, surprised laugh, a reluctant little sound. She was intrigued, too. "She's pretty?"

"No, I thought it would be a nice change of pace to hire a homely girl, Daisy."

She snorted at this. "Jus' makin' certain yer still possessed of yer faculties, Tommy. This girl . . ." She faltered momentarily. "Ye think she's yer Venus?"

Yes. Oh, yes. No. Perhaps.

"I haven't yet decided, Daisy."

"But ye've decided it willna be *me*."

"I'm glad you understand, Daisy," he said briskly.

He saw her jaw drop nearly to her collarbone as he left

the room, but wisely, she said nothing, having known Tom long enough to know when enough was enough.

⁀ ⁀ ⁀

The General drilled them for three hours, and the seemingly tireless Josephine played the same several tunes again and again. It might have driven another person mad; but Sylvie understood the need for it, having danced over and over to the same tunes for much of her life, having repeated the same motions again and again until they were flawless.

The demands on her body were minor. The demands on her dignity, however, were rigorous.

The other girls did the dances cheerfully, or at least willingly enough, taking it on as matter-of-factly as pushing a broom about the floor, smiling, twirling, hopping, twitching hips, showing a saucy bit of ankle. But Sylvie would never, never, never become accustomed to throwing her derriere up in the air and singing out "whee!"

Molly even sang a bawdy song while the other girls sang a chorus behind her and suggestively wielded their wands—Sylvie now understood the eloquence of that particular prop—and patted their own behinds.

And then, to Sylvie's dismay, they turned to pat the behinds of the girls in front of them.

As it turned out, it was *her* destiny to pat Molly's comfortably plush behind. A rump like a pair of pillows, Molly had.

Good God.

Sylvie became adept rather quickly, as none of it really required the grace or precision of a *grand jeté,* and after the first hour The General only shouted at her once or twice per song. "Get it up there, Sylvie! And don't make that face when you pat Molly! She's a very fine arse! Consider it an honor!"

I can't grow an arse in only three hours, Sylvie felt like grousing to him. *This is all the arse I have.*

Good God. Only three hours and she already sounded like an English street urchin in her thoughts. What sort of word was "*arse*"?

Sylvie had begun to see spots before her eyes from hunger, when rehearsal came to a close with a hearty "Thank you, ladies!" from The General.

The girls drifted away, down the stairs of the stage, filing toward their dressing room to change from fairies into girls again. Sylvie hovered, wondering whether she should follow, then looked up at a touch on her arm. It was Josephine, a bit red-faced and mussed from her energetic turn at the keyboard.

"Mr. Shaughnessy asked me to see to ye, Sylvie, and I think we need to get some food into ye now—ye've gone right peaky. Come wi' me."

She followed Josephine through a narrow corridor, past the dressing room where giggles and squeals came from behind the door, and it occurred to Sylvie that perhaps she should change out of her big fairy dress and put her wand away, and she almost felt excluded from the merriment. She wondered if they would receive her more warmly now that she'd bent and patted derrieres all afternoon.

But then, even in Paris, her status as Prima Ballerina set her apart from the other girls, and there were those who fawned and wanted to be her, and those who plotted and were cold and wanted to be her, or those who were overtly jealous and wanted to be her.

It left her rather as she had been in the mail coach today, with an invisible wall of sorts about her.

She reached her hand up to cover her heart, touched the miniature of her mother lightly through her fairy dress. Thought of Susannah, Lady Grantham. *Perhaps this is someone with whom I belong*. She wondered how she would go about learning when or how Susannah had returned from France.

Josephine saw her glance at the dressing-room door. "Food first, I think, m'dear. Mr. Shaughnessy willna be pleased if ye faint away, like. Sets a bad example fer the other girls." She smiled to show she was teasing. "And I'll show you where ye'll be sleeping."

They traveled the corridor; behind a set of wide doors, much like those that opened onto a ballroom, Sylvie heard the sounds of hammers and saws; something dropped with a deafening clatter, someone swore colorfully, a string of English phrases. She could have sworn it was The General.

"They're building sets," Josephine confided in a low voice. "For Venus." She said the word "Venus" with a hushed sort of reverence.

What on earth was *Venus*?

ॐ   ॐ   ॐ

Josephine took Sylvie up a steep flight of stairs, like the servants' passage, to another corridor lined with rooms, long and narrow, lit by a small window at the far end; candles were tucked into simple sconces along the walls. The wicks were cleanly trimmed; none of them seemed to have been lit recently.

"The White Lily was a bit of a wreck when Mr. Shaughnessy bought it. Turned it into a right beautiful theater," Josephine said as proudly as if he was her own son.

She stopped at the third door from the left in the corridor. " 'Ere's your room, luv. The girls usually take dinner on their own before the show. We'd the 'ousekeeper bring up summat t' eat."

On the little dressing table Sylvie saw a tray covered by a cloth; she tentatively plucked at the corner of the cloth and peeked beneath, afraid of the English food she might find. She discovered thickly sliced brown bread, and a yeasty scent still rose from it, so no doubt it was somewhat fresh. Feeling more confident now, she tugged the cloth all the way off and saw slices of cheese—she was a bit worried abut English cheese, too, but this was pungent and sharp-smelling and sliced in generous slabs, at least; there were two small rosy apples and a few slices of what appeared to be cold breast of fowl roasted in herbs, if the golden, crusty edge of the meat was any indication. She tugged at a roll of white linen; it proved to be a napkin, and a shiny knife and fork tumbled out. A tiny pot of tea and a cup and saucer completed the setting.

Hunger suddenly took Sylvie so violently her stomach nearly turned in upon itself, and she almost retched. She realized she hadn't slept for nearly a day. And suddenly she was thoroughly weary, so weary she didn't think she could form a sentence or do anything besides satisfy the needs of her body.

She looked around the little room and saw a rectangle of a hooked rug on the swept wood floor, a narrow iron bed made up with white sheets and a coverlet was pushed against the wall, a blue blanket was folded into a rectangle at the foot of it, and at the head two snowy pillows looked almost obscenely plump and welcoming. A wooden stand in the corner held a pitcher and a washbasin. There was no window or fireplace, but there was a small dressing table, and a small oval of a mirror hanging from a ribbon looped over a nail.

It was nothing at all like Claude's small, dark, cluttered apartments in Paris. And it was a world—or at least a continent—away from what she knew her life with Etienne would be, gilded, marbled, gleaming, vast. But something about its size and clean simplicity was soothing in the way she imagined a nun's cell might seem soothing.

And this thought made her nearly laugh aloud. Hunger was making her delusional. Thanks to Etienne, she was most certainly not a nun.

"Chamber pot under the bed," Josephine said matter-of-factly. "Come down to the kitchen later, if ye like. Mrs. Pool is making a tart. Just follow the smell down the stairs. There's some what live 'ere, at the theater. Meself and the 'ousekeeper, Mrs. Pool, and the maids, and there's Mr. Shaughnessy—"

"Mr. Shaughnessy lives here? At the theater?" This surprised Sylvie. She thought for certain he'd have a suite of rooms of his own in London, or a grand town house, rooms as glittering as his appearance.

But then again, she'd met the man in a mail coach. Perhaps his budget was apportioned to silver buttons on his coat.

"Mr. Shaughnessy is a practical man," Josephine said

approvingly. " 'E lives where 'e works. 'E knows the meaning of economy."

But not, Sylvie thought, *the meaning of restraint.* It was an interesting juxtaposition.

"The General, 'e 'as rooms in town," Josephine volunteered. "And if ye've skill wi' a needle, Sylvie, I've need of some 'elp wi' the costumes for all of it, so when ye're not rehearsin' . . ." Josephine looked hopeful. "It's Mr. Shaughnessy, ye see, and 'is ideas. Always wi' the ideas, and 'e always wants 'em straightaway. So we can sew in the mornings, rehearse in the afternoon, and do a show at night."

Sylvie wondered whether she would be offered any additional money for sewing, then wondered what on earth she might do with the rest of her time here at the White Lily, and decided she might as well sew. She found herself nodding, agreeing.

"*Quelle heure*—" she began, in her fatigue finding the French words easier to recall than the English. "That is, what is the time now, Josephine, please?"

"Why, time for you to eat m'dear. I'll come and fetch ye before the show, about eight o'clock."

"For the show?" To watch?

"Ye'll be in the show tonight, me dear. Mr. Shaughnessy *did* 'ire ye for that reason. We'll pin yer dress t' fit and alter it tomorrow. The work never ends 'ere a' the White Lily."

She smiled and closed the door, leaving Sylvie to her little feast.

Sylvie was torn between the attractive little heap of food and the soft heap of pillows on the bed.

A moment later, she dived into the food, ignoring the

fork, making little shameless moaning sounds as the savory meat and cheese and bread met her tongue. She swallowed, felt it fill her stomach, began to feel human again.

And it probably wasn't wise to sleep on a full stomach, but her body was giving her no choice. She dabbed the corners of her mouth with the napkin and sank backward onto the bed, shifted up until her head found the pillows, sighed, and slept.

CHAPTER SEVEN

THE TAP ON THE DOOR woke Sylvie with a start, and when she shifted a bit, she realized she was still in her fairy dress, and her legs were tangled in its folds. She gave a few little kicks to free herself; she rolled sleepily over and blinked: A wooden wand was on the pillow next to her.

Ah, so it hadn't been a nightmare induced by coaching inn food, then.

"Sylvie? Time to prepare for the show, m'dear." Josephine's cheery voice came through the door.

Sylvie snatched up her wand, rolled over, fighting a bit with her dress in the attempt, and went for the door.

Josephine eyed her with critical concern.

"Well, there's rouge," she finally said, resignedly, as though the rest of it could not be helped. "And we'll pin yer dress, like, and yer 'air will be down. Ye'll be pretty enough." She sounded as though she'd cheered herself some, if not Sylvie. "Come along wi' me, then."

⚜ ⚜ ⚜

And so Josephine led Sylvie from her little nun's room back to what surely must be the opposite of little nun's rooms everywhere—the dressing room full of buxom girls, giggling in their shifts, rummaging through cupboards for props and costumes, exclaiming over the shiny gifts sent by admirers that littered the little dressing tables. The lamplight burnished their bare arms pale gold and gleamed on glossy hair and fairy wings.

Lizzie held up a pair of earbobs for all to admire.

"Ooo! Garnets, Lizzie!" Molly peered at them expertly. "They're meant to dangle."

"Like the bloke 'oo sent 'em," Lizzie said sadly. "'E does naught but dangle, no matter *wot* I do." She demonstrated by holding her fairy wand perpendicular to her body for an instant, then dropping it sadly so that the star pointed at the floor.

An explosion of wicked giggles followed.

And then Molly opened a box and went very still.

"What d'yer 'ave there, Molly?" Lizzie asked.

Molly lifted up a painted ivory-and-silk fan, an exquisite and nearly excruciatingly tasteful thing and probably worth a dozen pairs of garnet earrings in cost. She held it almost gingerly. Instantly everyone hovered about her to gasp over it.

"New bloke," Molly said shortly. She was reaching for nonchalance but fell short of the mark. "'E asked Poe to send it in to the . . . loveliest . . . girl 'ere." She faltered over the adjective as though it was not a word she typically included in her vocabulary, as though she wasn't certain she had a right to it. But triumph edged her voice. Perhaps it was confirmation of something she'd long suspected.

Even from the doorway Sylvie could see the fan was a remarkable little thing. Almost . . . pointedly singular. A gift calculated to intrigue and flatter and disarm, and these three things were the first step in seduction, she knew. A wealthy man might send in jewels to a girl such as Molly—Sylvie had been sent more than her share of jewels by admirers—but only a man of breeding and intelligence would have chosen this strategic little fan. Sylvie knew this, because it rather reminded her of the sort of gifts Etienne had sent to her when his wooing had begun. Fine little glittering snowflakes of gifts, which had gradually accustomed her to his attentions, then eased her into expecting them.

Sylvie suddenly felt a peculiar weight in her chest, as though a hand pressed there, limiting her breath. She inhaled deeply, then exhaled, just to prove to herself that she could do it.

Perhaps it was simply because it had been days since she'd danced, days since she'd felt that delicious hard hammering of her heart in her chest from the exertion of it, since she'd worked until a fine sheen of sweat coated her exhausted, exhilarated body. She suspected her body craved the stretch and release of it.

She wondered, a little desperately, when she would have an opportunity to dance again. Ballet, that was. Not . . . well, whatever it was they did here at the White Lily.

"'Ave ye seen 'im, Molly? Yer new bloke. 'Is 'e 'andsome?" Lizzie asked eagerly.

"I'll know if 'e's 'andsome tonight after the show," Molly said slyly. "'E'll send a carriage fer me after the show. Po told me 'e would."

"Ye've so many admirers," Rose said somewhat resignedly, but without obvious rancor. "'Ope *yer* new one doesna . . . dangle."

More giggles.

"Willna Belstow and Lassiter and all of the rest of yer admirers be jealous, now, Molly?"

Molly shrugged with one shoulder. "I told Belstow I canna give 'im more of the time until 'e 'as more of his papa's money, and what Lassiter doesna know willna trouble 'im." She hadn't moved her eyes from the fan.

Molly at last looked up from the fan then and noticed Sylvie and Josephine in the doorway. "Miss Chicken 'as arrived," she said grandly.

"Oh, ye're to be a fairy as soon as tonight, then, Sylvie?" Rose's voice was mildly pleased. "Perhaps ye'll learn to be a damsel tomorrow."

"D'yer really kiss an 'ighwayman, Sylvie?" Jenny, big-eyed, wanted to know. "Rosie said ye did."

"I did," Sylvie confirmed. "He wanted a kiss in exchange for not robbing our coach. And so I kissed him."

"*Ooooh!*" Awed attention swiveled toward Sylvie. But Molly's chestnut head had turned away and was now fixed on a mirror. She was smoothing rouge onto a fair cheek, desperately trying not to look interested.

Sylvie shrugged nonchalantly. She deliberately omitted, "and then the highwayman took all my money and the letter from my sister, forcing me to cast my lot in with the lot of you." She thought perhaps remaining enigmatic might be useful. She shifted her wand into her other hand as Josephine reached beneath her arm.

"Be still now, Sylvie, whilst I pin yer dress." Josephine's mouth was bristling with pins; her large deft hands were plucking at Sylvie's skirt, pinning it closer to her body.

Sylvie dutifully remained motionless until Josephine nudged her this way and that to reach other parts of her dress.

"An' so Mr. Shaughnessy 'ired ye because ye were brave?" Lizzie wanted to know.

Oddly, Sylvie was a little insulted. *No, because I am beautiful.*

But why *did* he hire her? Surely that *was* the reason.

"I do not know," she answered, more or less honestly. With another inscrutable little French shrug. "I needed to work."

"No shrugging," Josephine ordered, plucking a pin from her mouth and poking it into the dress.

And then the door burst open, flinging hard against the wall. The girls shrieked and jumped.

A man stood there: young, handsome but already going to fat, red in the face with fury, breathing as though he'd run for miles. His fists were balled and white with tension, and they were raised, poised to launch.

Sylvie knew danger when she saw it. Her heart raced into her throat. "Get help," she mouthed to Lizzie, who was closest to the door.

Lizzie sidled against the wall behind him and bolted out of the room.

His head swiveled, found Molly. "You," he said flatly, contemptuously. He snatched at the bodice of her dress with one hand and yanked her out of her chair. "Who is he?" he demanded.

"Belstow, I—"

"Tell me who he is!" the man snarled. "Who are you giving your favors to now, you little whore?"

And then, to Sylvie's horror, he struck Molly with the flat of his hand across the face.

A horrible sound, that smack of flesh. Molly cried out.

And when the man lifted his hand over Molly again, Sylvie lunged for him.

ঞ   ঞ   ঞ

Before every performance, while the girls dressed for the show, Tom and The General convened to discuss the particulars of the White Lily's business, and the room they did it in was a snug male fantasy of comfort. Plush chairs sprawled about a hearth like a pride of lazy, sated beasts, and the crackling fire threw light up onto vivid murals, smaller, slightly more lurid versions of the ones that decorated the interior of the theater: satyrs and nymphs, gods and goddesses cavorted in the leaping light of the flames. Ever since he'd learned to read, Tom had loved the unabashed, joyous carnality of Greek myths, the violence and playfulness, the magic and the lessons in them.

There was one character from mythology, however, who never made it up onto the murals: Chiron, the wounded healer. Not an erotic character, Chiron. He lived with pain every day and grew the wiser for it. A teacher, Chiron was. Noble cove.

Tom knew *he* was not a noble cove, and doubted he ever would be. This knowledge did not cost him sleep.

Tom fished a little moon of gold from his pocket, snapped it open, reviewed the time. He could hear through the walls the low cheerful rumble of the gathering crowd of men who nightly enjoyed the entertainments he provided. It was one of his favorite sounds, along with the jingle of shillings and the sounds a woman made in the throes of pleasure.

A pleasant hitch of breath accompanied that last thought,

which led to thoughts of one woman in particular. "So how did the new girl fare today, Gen?"

The General pulled a cigar from his mouth and admired the glowing tip. "She has no arse, she's proud and impudent, and I do believe half the girls are wildly jealous of her, thanks to you, and the way you just foisted her upon our cozy little group. How did you think she'd fare, Tom?"

Tom grinned, relishing the description. "But can she dance?"

"She'll do," The General growled.

"Good, then. I'll have a look myself tomorrow, during rehearsals."

"And you . . . broke the news to Daisy about Venus?" The General ventured gingerly.

"Yes," Tom said grimly.

"I expect she took it gracefully?" More stock-in-trade irony from The General.

"Would you *ever* describe Daisy as graceful, Gen?"

There was a curious pause. The General turned away from Tom and studied his cigar again, as though the answer to this question could be found there. "Not the first word that comes to mind," The General finally allowed. Tom would have sworn the words were almost wistful.

Tom studied his friend in bemusement for a moment, frowning slightly.

"I've already had notes from the Major and Lord Cambry. They're in. They want to be a part of The Gentleman's Emporium." His voice was quiet, but triumph infused every note of it.

"Mmm." The General made a little sound of appreciation. "Do you need the whole of that group involved before you go forward with it?"

"If I get at least commitments from all of them this week, I'll buy the property with the capital I have and sign agreements with the builders. You're in, Gen?"

"You need to ask? I want my share in this, too, Tommy. You've all but guaranteed me a prosperous dotage."

"Can you see it now? We'll have—"

Sudden frantic pounding on the door had Tom in his feet in an instant. He flung the door open.

Lizzie stood before him, wild-eyed, breathing hard. "The dressing room—Molly—Mr. Belstow—ye best come—*oh please*—"

დ   დ   დ

Tom took in the scene in the dressing room with a glance: Molly, one arm raised to shield her face; four other girls in various stages of undress cowering in the corner; Belstow standing over Molly, arm lifted, either to protect himself or to strike again.

And next to Belstow Sylvie Chapeau, a starless shard of a wooden wand in her hand, hand raised as if to administer another blow.

Quickly and gently, Tom closed his hand over Sylvie's other arm and tugged her behind him, keeping his fingers closed around her. She resisted him a little, almost reflexively, still bristling with her own anger.

"Where would you like it, Mr. Belstow?" Tom's voice was low and taut. Deceptively polite.

Belstow whirled, startled, frowned in surprise; his hand froze midair.

"'It'?" he repeated. And for a moment, the bastard

looked almost hopeful. As though Tom had come bearing a selection of gifts.

"The knife," Tom clarified slowly. An almost cheery deadliness in his voice. "Through your gullet, across your throat, perhaps . . . ?" Tom gestured casually to his own throat, then swept his coat back idly, just a little, as though it was merely in his way.

Everyone saw the knife tucked there in its sheath at the top of his trousers.

Belstow's face spasmed in disbelief. "You wouldn't *dare*, Shaughnessy. I caught this little whore with another—"

Tom's hand snapped out and seized a fistful of Belstow's shirt and cravat, yanking it taut as a noose, pulling him to the balls of his feet. Belstow teetered on his toes within inches of Tom's face.

"Test me." Tom measured each word out tonelessly, as though nothing in his life had ever bored him more than the man dangling from his fist.

Tom held him a moment longer, allowing the message in his eyes to penetrate fully.

When Belstow's face went ashen, Tom knew he'd succeeded.

He released him abruptly.

Belstow dropped to his knees, his legs too weak to hold him. And then everyone watched, and no one helped, as Belstow struggled awkwardly, shakily to his feet. He rubbed at his throat.

"When my father hears of this, Shaughnessy—"

"I know your father, Mr. Belstow. I assure you, when I tell him what you've done, you'll be sorry I didn't gut you. I wonder if your father approves of hitting women?"

It was a bluff. Tom didn't know the senior Mr. Belstow from Adam, really; he'd seen him but twice at the theater. But he struck him as a good sort, and Tom's instincts along these lines were typically sharp enough.

His instincts were borne out. Belstow's ashen face took on a lovely undertone of green. Ah. Most weak young men *were* afraid of their fathers.

"I don't think I need to tell you that you're no longer welcome here," Tom added politely. "And I'll leave you to imagine what might happen to you if you *do* choose to show your face here again. Can you leave under your own locomotion, Mr. Belstow, or will you require further assistance?" Tom was all mock solicitousness now.

Belstow's mouth opened and closed. He glared at Tom in quiet fury for another moment.

Tom met his gaze unblinkingly.

Belstow turned, unable to hold the gaze. A moment later, he turned and stalked out the door, without saying another word.

Tom turned and kicked the door closed behind the man. Breathed in and out, letting air sift through the rage that made it difficult to breathe. He was aware of how quiet the little room was, the way the chatter of birds ceases when a cat is spotted.

Tom turned to Molly. "There now," he said softly. "Come, show it to me."

Molly raised her head up tentatively, keeping one hand shaded over her eye, ashamed, still trembling. Tom gently lifted her hand, and beneath it, her eye was red. It could very well turn a panoply of colors over the next few days. He'd seen enough—too many—blackened eyes on both men and women over the years.

"I . . . I need the work, Mr. Shaughnessy."

Molly's voice shook, and for good reason. She knew Tom couldn't put a bruised girl onstage—bad for business. She also knew dozens of pretty girls clamored for a job like hers, a job that paid enough for a decent room and clothes and opportunities to meet dozens of wealthy admirers, and required little more of her than following instructions and a willingness to dress in what amounted to little more than her shift.

She was as replaceable as the lamps that lit the room.

Tom looked down at Molly. He still felt the spiky heat of rage on his skin. Diplomacy with Belstow would no doubt have been wiser—he was wealthy, Belstow, in his own right, and connected through that fine webbing of connections the wealthy and privileged enjoyed, and Tom knew both the value and danger of connections.

But he despised cowards who hit women. He'd seen much of that sort of misery when he'd lived in the rookeries, fury and violence brewed by gin and hopelessness. And in the rookeries, one could almost comprehend the source.

But again—Belstow was privileged and wealthy.

Tom felt one of his hands curl into a fist.

"How did he get back here?" he asked everyone in the room curtly. "Where's Jack? Why wasn't he watching the door?"

Silence.

And Tom knew defeat. Knew Jack had probably found the lure of gin more appealing than the lure of a few more bob from Tom Shaughnessy and had left his post for that reason.

Tom didn't look at The General. His own guilt was strong enough without seeing it reflected in The General's face.

Tom dropped his hand from Molly's face, took a deep breath. He supposed there was something to be said for learning sense and caution and judgment the hard way; it was the way he'd learned the most valuable lessons in his own life. Still, the beauty of the White Lily was that Tom had been able to protect any number of people from learning things the hard way, or from learning any more lessons than necessary.

And then suddenly, looking down at Molly, inspiration struck, which was the capricious way of inspiration in general.

"Well, the news is not all bad, Molly. We've decided to introduce a . . . piratical theme into the show next week. The General will build a ship and we'll have a pirate dance, a song or two. We'll have you in an eye patch if your eye shows a bruise. I wager you'll make a pretty pirate, eh?"

Tom didn't dare look at The General, who would now be required to build some sort of pirate ship and create a dance involving scantily clad female pirates inside a week.

Molly sniffed and gave a tentative little laugh, comforted by the note of flirtation. All around him, he could see shoulders dropping in relief, as the other girls could feel Tom restoring things to order.

But . . . well, now that Tom thought about it . . . cutlasses and female pirates . . .

It was still more genius, frankly. And precisely what

they needed to keep the audiences satisfied while the grand work of Venus was under way.

At this conclusion, Tom risked a sideways glance at The General.

The General was glaring incredulous daggers at him.

"Th-thank you, Mr. Shaughnessy." Molly was calmer now.

He looked back at Sylvie. She still held a pointed shard of a wand; he saw the star that belonged on top of it, fallen, severed from its stem, shining on the floor at her feet. She was just as pale as the other girls, but with a difference: Two spots of hectic color sat high on her cheeks, and her eyes were glittery as jewels.

She was furious.

"Every time I see you there's something pointed in your hand," he said to her softly. A jest to ease her temper. She was such a fierce little thing.

And she did smile a little at that. She took her own deep breath.

"Did you hit him?" Tom asked her, gently.

"Not hard enough," she told him fervently.

He couldn't help but smile. "Will he have a bruise in the shape of a star?"

"I hope so."

And then a thought occurred to him. "Did he touch you?" He said it curtly.

" 'T'was just a push."

He looked down at her, small and slight; she would come to Belstow's shoulder, and felt a cold kernel of horror in the pit of his gut when he thought of what might have happened to her or to Molly had he not entered the room. She would not retreat, this one, whether or not it was sensible. Her response had been to leap into the fray rather than cower, sensibly, away from it.

Emotion always lit her eyes, he'd noticed during their short acquaintance. She might remain circumspect about the details of her life, but her eyes gave away the woman inside her, what she felt, and they were still hot with a righteous anger. Her hair was unbound, and a few strands of it clung to her flushed face, the rest spilling over her slim shoulders, and she was pinned into her fairy dress. The pale blush color of it suited the high color in her cheeks.

All rose and fire, softness and heat. His fingers gave a little twitch at his side. Having once touched her skin, it seemed they wanted to know if her hair could compete for fineness.

And yet here he stood in a room surrounded by visions of softness.

"He just . . . hit her." Sylvie said it with a sort of helpless, wondering fury. Quietly. As though the words were only for him.

"I know," Tom said gently. "I won't allow it to ever happen again."

He realized then he'd been looking into her eyes, and she'd been looking back for quite some time, and he jerked his head up. The rest of the girls were watching him, their own faces pale, pinched with worry, waiting to hear what he wanted them to do next, trusting him to take care of them as he always had.

Odd for an instant, a dizzying instant, he'd all but forgotten anyone else was in the room.

"E would 'ave 'it Molly again, Mr. Shaughnessy, but Sylvie came at 'im wi' 'er wand," Rose informed him proudly. Doing her part to build Sylvie's legend. "And then ye came into the room."

Tom released Sylvie's arm.

"Cool water and a rag for the eye, a little brandy for the nerves, Molly. Poe and Stark or someone else will watch the door at all hours from now on. Sylvie, you can take her to our room in the back; get her settled, then come back and finish dressing. Do you think you can dance tonight?"

"Yes," Molly told him quickly.

He glanced at Sylvie, whose face had darkened somewhat. She was watching him strangely. Almost in reproach.

"As for the rest of you . . . come now, we've a show to do." He made it a cheery command. "Don't sit about staring. Where are your wings, girls? Get them on!"

The best way to return everything to normal was to make everything appear as though it had never been anything but normal, he knew.

Happy to be told what to do, everyone scrambled into their wings, plucked up their wands, and prepared to file to the back of the stage.

CHAPTER EIGHT

MINUTES LATER, Sylvie was standing backstage in a darkened theater pinned into a gossamer dress, holding a hastily-mended wooden fairy wand in preparation for patting the fannies of similarly dressed girls. All while a great crowd of enthusiastic men looked on. All in the name of a temporary roof over her head.

She teetered between a moment of panic and ironic humor. Her entire life she'd worked to ensure her life was nothing like Claude's, and yet here she was all the same. As though having been raised by an opera dancer, vulgar performance was a drain toward which she must inevitably flow.

She knew another brief moment of dizzying unreality: Everything in her life to date had been planned so carefully. And once Monsieur Favre had discovered a spark of talent in plain Claude Lamoreux's beautiful little girl, Sylvie had given herself to the dance entirely, knowing, perhaps, it was her only chance to be anything other than ordinary. And as she danced, she told herself that every *grand jeté*, every pirouette, every precise and stinging criticism from Monsieur Favre took her further away from sharing the same ultimate fate as Claude Lamoreux: poor, lonely, struggling, with scarcely the energy to be properly bitter. Dance had given Sylvie purpose, and then fame . . . and then Etienne. And every bit of this had been planned.

This—this cheerful audience at the White Lily, the patting of derrieres—was clearly her reward for a moment of rashness.

But there was still something about the sound of a theater before a performance, regardless of the *nature* of the performance that thrilled her blood. The excited murmur of voices, the squeak of chairs as people shifted their bodies into them, the dimming of lamps, all fed her anticipation, and she couldn't find it within herself to dread it totally. Odd to think it had been nearly two weeks now since she'd danced for an audience. She knew a whimsical urge to *grand jeté* out onto the stage, which no doubt this particular audience would find more shocking than any song about baubles.

And then she simply longed, wistfully, to do anything at all that resembled ballet. She wondered how long it would be before she could dance—truly dance—again.

She peeped out from behind the curtain. A group of other musicians, a violinist, a cellist and, startlingly, someone who appeared to be holding a trumpet that winked a regal gold in the theater lights, had joined Josephine, who sat at the pianoforte, dressed for the occasion in scarlet velvet exposing a grand expanse of chest. Sylvie glanced up, toward those exclusive boxes; she saw the curtains enclosing one of them sway a bit, and knew an extremely wealthy man had come for an evening's entertainment, too. Perhaps Molly's new admirer.

At the top of the aisle near the theater entrance, so close to where she stood on stage she could almost touch them, stood Tom and The General, for all the world like a pair of vivid dukes receiving ball guests. They were dressed in brilliantly striped waistcoats and billowing cravats, and the silver buttons on Tom's coat glinted, bright as a row of eyes inspecting the arriving patrons. Together they were a tableau: Sylvie might have called them *Elegantly Tall and Elegantly Small.*

The audience entered through the wide doors near the stage, then proceeded to their seats. Sylvie took up a nook behind the curtain and watched, listened as Tom warmly greeted nearly every man by name as if he hadn't just threatened to gut someone in a dressing room.

"Good evening, Mr. Pettigrew." Pettigrew: medium build, large comfortable stomach preceding him into the room, conservative evening clothes. *No doubt his wife chooses them,* Sylvie thought. *Wonder if she knows where he is this evening?*

"Shaughnessy, my good man! Sorry I've been away for a few days. My wife insisted upon being entertained as well, and so I've endured a few sopranos for her sake. What do you have for us this evening?"

"If I told you what I had in store for you, Pettigrew, it wouldn't be a surprise then, would it? Don't you care for surprises?" Tom feigned shock.

"I like surprises of the sort *you* provide, Shaughnessy, of course! Those are my very favorite. Very well, I shall prepare to be surprised, then."

". . . and the flowers are for?" Pettigrew was holding a paper-wrapped bouquet of vibrant blooms, fresh from a hothouse, from the looks of things. Tom took them.

The man looked a little bashful. "Rose. You'll put in a good word for me, Shaughnessy?" he asked anxiously.

"Of course I'll put in a good word for you," Tom assured Mr. Pettigrew, who, his face now relaxed and lit with hope, went on to find his seat. Tom handed the roses to The General, who handed them to a boy whose job it was to scurry away with the bouquets and bring them to the dressing room to vie for attention with all the other flowers.

Tom waited until Pettigrew was several feet away. ". . . for him, and for Johnstone, and Mortimer, and Carrick, and Bond, and . . ." he said to The General.

"Lassiter, too, I think," The General added. "I think you promised to put in a good word for Lassiter."

"I believe Lassiter has transferred his affections to Molly," Tom mused.

"Ah," The General said, as if making a note of it. "I believe Molly is now firmly in the lead in terms of 'good words,' then. Perhaps even beyond Daisy now."

Sylvie turned and whispered to Rose. "You've an admirer. A Mr. Pettigrew. He brought flowers."

"Oh, I've lots of admirers," Rose replied in her own whisper, without a trace of conceit. "But nothing like what Molly 'as."

Molly's eyes caught Sylvie's. She tossed her head and turned away.

She seemed a bit subdued. She hadn't thanked Sylvie for coming to her defense, but perhaps she felt ashamed; no doubt her pride was a bit singed. Sylvie contemplated asking her whether she felt equal to dancing, whether her eye was aching, and then decided Molly wouldn't welcome the question.

Sylvie jerked her head back toward Tom when she heard a bit of a commotion. She peered out, riveted.

A handsome young man, wild-eyed and blond and young enough to have a red spot on his chin, had planted himself in front of Tom and was shouting up at him.

"Name your seconds, Shaughnessy!"

"Now, Tammany—"

"It's my *wife,* damn you, Shaughnessy! My wife! She called your name out in a . . . in a . . ." Tammany faltered and lowered his voice almost to a mumble. ". . . certain moment."

The faltering and mumbling unfortunately rather diminished the injured gravity of his outburst.

"She called out . . . 'Tom Shaughnessy' . . . in a certain moment?" Tom sounded genuinely puzzled. "It seems rather a lot to get out in that *particular* moment. And there are quite a few Toms in the world, are there not?" He turned to The General for confirmation.

"At least a dozen," The General confirmed solemnly.

"She cried out *'Tom!'*" young Tammany clarified indignantly. "'*Tom,*' I tell you! More specifically, '*Oh, Tom!*' I knew it was you she meant. She cannot stop *talking* about you. Thinks you're the most charming bugger this side of . . . of . . . *Byron.* What have you *done* to her? I demand satisfaction!"

There was a pause.

"Have I met his wife?" Tom lowered his voice and said this to The General.

"*Yes,* you damned scoundrel!" Tammany bellowed. Tom winced. "At the shop that sells wooden toys on Bond Street just last week. You met the two of us, and bowed, and said something—"

"Very well." Tom became quickly, resignedly matter-of-fact. "If it means that much to you, The General here will act as one of my seconds as usual and shall we meet—well, why don't we meet at dawn, two days hence? I'll shoot you, and then I suppose I'll console your wife as a favor to you, as she'll no doubt miss you when you're dead. As will I, as you're one of my best patrons, Tammany. One of my very favorites, and truly, I do not exaggerate. Meanwhile, why I would be honored if you took a seat and enjoyed our show one last time. In remembrance of the former warmth of our friendship."

Tom smiled, managing to make it look both warm and gently regretful.

Sylvie, from where she watched through the curtains, put a hand over her mouth in awe. It was frankly an astonishing performance.

Tammany suddenly looked a little less certain about his grievance. "You can just *apologize,* Shaughnessy, and be done with it," he said huffily.

"I would apologize, Mr. Tammany," Tom said gently, "if I thought I'd done anything requiring an apology."

It struck Sylvie that Tom might be genuinely amused by all of this. There wasn't a shred of fear in his expression, or bearing. He didn't even appear to feel threatened.

Such light talk about shooting one another. She gave an involuntary little shudder. She remembered Rose's words, *Best shot in London.*

Tammany simply glared at Tom, beyond words. And practical considerations—Tom's reputedly extraordinary aim among them—were clearly warring with his pride.

Bateson, the man Tom had deliberately missed just a night earlier, chose that moment to come strolling up the aisle, refreshments in hand, oblivious to the drama taking place.

"Tammany, my good man. You really must ask Mr. Shaughnessy for some pointers at Manton's. He can shoot the heart right out of a target every time!" he volunteered cheerfully. "He's giving me lessons!" He playfully pointed his thumb and forefinger at Tom and strolled on by, and Tom did likewise.

"Boom!" Tom said cheerfully.

"Bateson pulls left," Tom explained solemnly to Tammany. "I nearly shot him last night." Tammany had gone several shades paler. The red spot on his chin now glowed indignantly.

"It's a good show tonight, truly, and we've a new girl. You might wish to cheer her on," Tom coaxed. "She's very pretty, but a bit meek."

Sylvie could have sworn this was for her benefit. She thought she saw Tom Shaughnessy's mouth twitch a little, subtly, as if he knew very well she was listening.

Tammany did some more glaring, but it became less focused as the crowd milled around them, mindless of the little drama, or used to it. Men greeted each other with cheerful familiarity.

"Ho, Tammany!" someone called, and gave a cheery little wave. "Ho, Shaughnessy!"

Tammany managed to curl his lip in response to the greeting.

"Oh, *come* now, Tammany. We've got the girls as fairies tonight," Tom added by way of persuasion. "I know you like the fairies. And you'll *never* believe what we'll have in a week or so."

Tammany glared at him for another few moments, but Tom refused to be anything other than cheerful. So the glare had no place to lock, and thus deprived Tammany of fuel for his ire.

Tammany spun on his heel and stalked up the aisle toward the seats.

Then stopped abruptly, spun about, and stalked back to Tom. "*What* are you having next week?"

Tom dropped an arm over Tammany's shoulder and said it low, making it seem a confidence meant just for Tammany. "*Pirates.*"

Tammany's eyes went wide, then slowly glazed with anticipated pleasures. "And Daisy?" Tammany asked, sounding as though he hardly dared hope.

"Captain of the ship," Tom confirmed with a grin.

Tammany's face finally softened and brightened into a blazing grin. "How do you *think* of these things, Shaughnessy?"

Tom shrugged modestly.

And Tammany, whose stride was now considerably less belligerent—it in fact, had a bit of a spring to it—made his way to a seat.

"Don't worry, Gen. He'll want to be alive for the pirates. See? Now aren't you glad I thought of them?"

The General ignored this. "What did you do to his wife, Tom?"

"Hmmm. I honestly don't know. I believe I merely smiled, and she . . ."

"There's no 'merely' about how you smile at women, Tom. There never is."

Tom smiled at this, remembering. "She *was* pretty, now that I recall. And I rarely do more than smile at actual wives. That's why God invented the Velvet Glove."

"I'm not certain it was *God* who invented the Velvet Glove, Tom."

"Mmmm. If not, his name is certainly *invoked* often enough there."

"What is the Velvet Glove?" Sylvie turned to ask Rose in a whisper.

"Brothel," was Rose's laconic reply.

Sylvie nearly sucked in a breath, torn between horror and hilarity.

"You're going to get yourself killed one day, Tom, if you keep toying with these hotheaded lads."

"Can I help it if I'm obliged to defend my honor?" Tom feigned injury.

"If I'm not mistaken, you believe honor is a notion for the rich and bored.

"Oh, it is. I've no use for it. Survival seldom has anything to do with honor. But I consider it my mission in life to entertain the rich and bored."

The General sighed. "Here's another question, Tom: What were you doing in a shop that sells wooden toys?"

"Tammany was mistaken about that bit," Tom said absently. "I must have been introduced to her elsewhere."

The General was silent, but his skepticism was nearly deafening.

"Like church?" he finally said.

"I didn't touch her, Gen, I swear it." Tom sounded defensive.

"Some men settle down with *just one* woman," The General said meaningfully. "They settle down, and they don't continually smile at other people's wives, or get into duels."

"How selfish of you, Gen. I know you think only of

your own peace of mind when you say that, and not my happiness." Tom flipped open his watch. "It's time for the show."

ঞ   ঞ   ঞ

A few minutes later, in front of a crowd of enthusiastic men, Sylvie Lamoreux linked arms with a half dozen pretty girls, bent over, thrust her bottom into the air and shouted "whee!"

It was over quickly enough, thankfully. Though no doubt she'd relive it again and again, the way one was haunted by bad meals.

And the response to the show—which, Rose and the other girls had assured her they had already performed dozens of times before—was so warm, appreciative, and boisterous that Sylvie began to wonder why she worked so hard to perfect her own art when it was clearly much easier to please an audience—an audience of men, at least—than she'd ever dreamed.

Though of course pleasing an audience was truly only a small part of why she did what she did.

When it was over, and Molly had sung her own bawdy song—which involved much suggestive wielding of her wand—to rapturous applause, a crew of boys scrambled to push a long, low, carved structure onto the stage, carved in ripples, painted a rich dark green. Seaweed, apparently.

And then Sylvie learned what the trumpet was for.

It sounded, a noble golden peal over the theater, and a hush fell.

Sylvie heard a creaking noise, and looked up. A great, silk-flower-bedecked swing, suspended on a pair of chains, was being lowered from the stage rafters by two sweaty boys. There was an urgent scuffling noise from the wings, and Sylvie saw, to her astonishment, a woman, eye-poppingly buxom, curved, as a matter of fact, as extravagantly as an hourglass, waddling because the bottom half of her was tightly wrapped in a resplendent, sparkly purple mermaid tail. Her hair was long, brilliant with henna, and sparkles no doubt fashioned of paste and streamers of something no doubt meant to be seaweed clung to it.

" 'Er Majesty," Rose whispered.

"If she gains even 'alf a stone, that swing will snap like kindling," Molly muttered bitterly.

Ah, so this was Daisy Jones.

Sylvie watched with fascination as they quickly got her settled into her swing—it did make a subtle, if ominous, groaning sound when her posterior was centered on it—and her hands, shiny in gloves that reached her elbows, gripped the chains. The boys then raced to get behind her, scrabbled frantically and in vain for a moment to get enough traction to push her into motion, and then Daisy, rapping out a soft and colorful epithet by way of encouragement, finally gave them a little assist by flapping her tail. The three of them got the swing going to and fro, the chains creaking musically, the trumpet sounded again, and the red velvet curtain swooshed up.

"DAISY!" The crowd bellowed in gleeful greeting.

Daisy waved with regal cheer and blew kisses from her fingertips to them, a number of whom pretended to catch them on their own fingers, apply them to their own mouths, and swoon. She gave her tail some vigorous flaps, and soon the swing was soaring above them, and men were trying to get a look underneath it for a glimpse of her magnificent posterior. Daisy's long, dyed-red hair was affixed to the front of her, and her torso was draped in some sort of clever sheer fabric. Her hair flew up tantalizingly, but remained within the bounds of the legal.

Oh, come all ye laddies who e'er set sail and
gather round fer a glimpse of me beautiful tail . . .

And Daisy's voice, though it reached handily to the rafters, would never be mistaken for "exquisite."

"A mermaid on a swing?" Sylvie said quietly to Rose.

"It's an underwater world, Miss Chapeau." Tom Shaughnessy's voice was a low murmur behind her, and somehow it managed to travel along her spine as though a finger had been dragged lightly there. She felt the gooseflesh rise on the back of her neck. "We create fantasy here at the White Lily. It's a dream, if you will—mermaids playing beneath the waves on swings." He looked out at the crowd, and a satisfied smile curved his mouth. "A *lucrative* dream."

He met her eyes for a moment, then slowly took his gaze away from hers and watched the proceedings—Daisy sailing through the air on a swing that was indeed looking just a bit taxed by her girth—as intently as a scientist or a judge. He glanced below at the audience, his brow crinkling a little, as if wondering how many men would be flattened beneath Daisy should the swing give way.

"Or a nightmare," Sylvie murmured.

Tom turned his head sharply toward her then. And his face became studiously expressionless.

"I suppose it's all in how you view it, Miss Chapeau," he said evenly. "You've earned your wages for tonight. You may collect them from me tomorrow, if you wish."

Once again she saw the gleam of his watch in his hand, and he slipped away to oversee some other aspect of the show.

The show was over, the crowd was gone, and the theater was nearly quiet again. Sylvie watched, as one by one, the girls filtered out the back door of the theater into the night dressed in their own clothes, fairy costumes, wands and wings tucked away in the wardrobes for the evening.

At the side door of the theater, where a small crowd of admirers waited, Sylvie peeped out.

Flanking the door were two enormous men, one missing an eye and not bothering with the formality of a patch; judging from the rest of his attire, perhaps he'd feel overdressed in one. The other man was as wide as he was tall, his mouth pulled up into a permanent half grin by a scar ironically in the shape of a smile itself. Instead of a left hand, he sported a hook, which he lifted in farewell to the girls as they wandered away in pairs, a steely little twin of the slice of moon curving above.

From inside the door, Sylvie watched Molly helped by a footman into a very fine unmarked carriage, saw her slim stocking-covered ankle flash, heard her laugh almost shyly, then she vanished inside to meet the sender of the little fan.

Watching Molly board the fine coach was almost disorienting; Sylvie could almost see herself as she'd been a year ago, when Etienne had begun his pursuit—beautiful, flush with the triumph of that beauty. A fine carriage waiting for her outside the theater, inside it an unimaginably wealthy and important man bearing gifts just for her.

"G'night, Sylvie!" Rose raised her hand in farewell,

turned away to trudge off through the streets of London to her own rooms.

"Can I escort ye safely anywhere, Miss?" The man with the shiny curved hand bowed politely. "Ye mus' be the new girl Tommy 'ired." He smiled; the few teeth still embedded in his gums gleamed like skulls in a cave. "Me name's Poe. An' this is Stark."

Stark, the man missing an eye, bowed, too, and said nothing. Sylvie wondered if perhaps Tom had deliberately advertised for men who were missing parts of their bodies.

"Th-thank you, Mr. Poe, but no." She smiled politely, hoping it wasn't impolite to show her full complement of teeth to a man with so few of them, and backed into the theater again.

And into utter silence.

Sylvie availed herself of a candle, but as she began to make her way up the long flights of stairs to the top of the theater, she saw a light burning softly in Tom Shaughnessy's office, which seemed to be a library of sorts; she saw shelves lining the walls. She stopped to peer from the shadows. Through the space made by the open door she was surprised to see Tom, shirtsleeves rolled up, quill in hand, head bent, writing something so slowly and painstakingly he reminded Sylvie of a schoolboy practicing his letters. He glanced up, turned his head to the side in thought, and she watched him massage the fingers of one hand with the other, kneading them methodically, thoughtfully, stretching and fanning the fingers, a half smile on his face at something he'd perhaps been thinking.

She took a moment then to boldly admire the line of his profile, not like Etienne's, which was clean, elegant, refined by centuries of his flawless bloodline the way the sea polishes stones to smoothness. Tom's profile was more difficult to interpret; it offered more interesting places for the eye to land. And despite Tom Shaughnessy's own version of polish, his clothing that bordered on gaudy, she noticed now that he radiated . . . calm. He glittered: his eyes, his smile, those coat buttons . . . but at the core of it was this quiet sort of . . . certainty.

Or perhaps it was ruthlessness.

And then he pressed his palms against his eyes, briefly, and took up his quill once more, dipped it, continued to diligently write. As though he'd given himself an assignment requiring completion tonight.

His memoirs, perhaps, she thought, half-amused. Like *Don Juan,* or *Casanova.* But the tableau, Tom bent over his desk, struck her as odd. Surely London was filled with gaming hells and pubs and places where men like Tom Shaughnessy could find entertainment and feminine company and more women over whom to fight duels. The contrast between the coarse, merry mayhem of hours earlier, the swift violence in the dressing room before the show, and this quiet Tom bending over the desk was incongruous.

She wondered about his mistress. She didn't wonder whether he *had* one; there was no question in her mind that he did. He must. Sylvie wondered who she was. A titled widow? A professional courtesan? Who would appeal to Tom Shaughnessy?

Was he in love with Kitty, the dancer who had disappeared? Or did he really "turn 'er off" for being pregnant to set an example for the other girls? Did he make her pregnant and keep her in Kent, and dutifully visit?

Men like Tom Shaughnessy. She realized, suddenly, that she wasn't certain what this meant.

She'd been too busy to be afraid today, and yet, when she gave it some thought: this was a man who had known highwaymen, whose theater was run by a surly dwarf, whose dancers had no doubt been plucked virtually from the street. Who had, with lightning speed, snatched a burly man up by the cravat and calmly threatened to kill him earlier this evening.

In the moment, Sylvie had believed he would do it. And in the moment, in the flames of her temper, she had to admit that she'd almost hoped he would.

When she'd seen Belstow's hand rise for a blow, as if it had simply been his *right* to strike Molly . . .

Standing in the White Lily's cheerful faux grandeur, she began to wonder whether it had truly been Etienne she'd seen standing at the harbor, or whether her own guilt and nerves had conjured him from some other vision of a tall, broad-shouldered man. Whether it truly had been Etienne's voice she'd heard saying, "I beg your pardon" as he peered into the coach. Had he followed her through Paris to London, somehow?

In the dark of this odd theater, she could almost believe she had imagined him, that it had been some other man entirely, and that only the events inside the White Lily were real.

A dream, Mr. Shaughnessy said. A *lucrative* dream.

Of nearly all of the places she could have landed in Paris, she imagined Etienne was least likely to look for her in an establishment such as this. Etienne's taste in entertainments ran to the rarefied and refined, to the very best of everything. Which had perhaps naturally led him to Sylvie Lamoreux, for she embodied all that was finest of beauty and grace.

It was difficult to believe that she might have hurt Etienne by leaving suddenly. Sylvie wondered whether one truly longed for someone, could truly love, when nothing had ever been denied.

And whether it mattered at all.

Weariness tugged at Sylvie's limbs, her eyelids. She would sleep hard tonight.

And so she climbed the quiet stairs again, counted the doors in the darkened hallway, and thus found her room again.

She knew a moment of gratitude for the place to sleep and the lock on the door, a moment of nervousness about her unusual environment, which strangely had begun to feel more comfortable than she'd almost prefer it to; then, her body, in its wisdom, took her to sleep.

CHAPTER NINE

Tom was enjoying the feel of cool morning air—there was mercifully still some damp in it at this hour, some freshness—and the horse he'd hired was a splendidly game animal, taking the road quickly in long smooth strides. Hiring a horse cut the time of the journey to Little Swathing in Kent in half; he wasn't eager to board a mail coach again anytime soon.

Someday he would keep his own carriage. He knew just the one he wanted, just the horses he would choose. Not gray to match the typical English weather, as so many of the titled chose, but something bright, something with a bit of flash: a quartet of bays, perhaps. Or four black geldings, white stars between their eyes or white stockings round their forelegs. He'd even been to Tattersall's, to plan and dream.

He could buy the horses and carriage now and keep them if he chose, for there was a mews behind the White Lily, but Tom was selective about his expenditures. He had decided sometime ago that this particular expenditure could wait, that his journeys about London could take place in hired hackneys and horses and carriages sent by friends. His capital was needed for other things: to pay his employees, for example. To build pirate ships.

To hire beautiful Frenchwomen on a whim.

He half smiled to himself at the thought, but the sudden image of green eyes and flushed cheeks tensed the muscles in his stomach in a way that surprised him. The thought brought a difficult-to-define, distracting pleasure; it carried with it more of an edge than thoughts of beautiful women usually did. He'd watched her last night, smiling and bending and swaying in time with the other girls, and though he could find no fault with her performance, he could not take his eyes from her. She seemed wrong, and yet unimaginably right at the same time.

Odd to think that two such dramatically new things should drop into his life on the same day. Both, in their way, had thrown him ever-so-slightly off course, leaving him, for the first time in years, feeling uncertain of his footing; but both, were perhaps, temporary.

He shook the thought of Sylvie Chapeau away as the cottage came into view. He tethered the horse and pushed open the little white gate, took the flagstones up to the door, to the other new thing.

He'd decided, at last, he should come, at least once, and to do it at once. To ascertain whether in fact it was true.

Mrs. May greeted him at the door. He offered a tense bow to her, and she offered a swift, nearly begrudging, curtsy in return, and polite, stiff words of welcome. Tom imagined there wasn't a good deal written in etiquette books about such occasions, and so he defaulted to quiet politeness for the moment.

Mr. May hovered at the ready, should the infamous Mr. Shaughnessy do anything untoward; Tom saw him out of the corner of his eye, then heard him moving about in another part of the house, making purposeful sounds, picking things up, putting them down, to make his presence known. Somewhere else in the house he heard the voices of older children.

It had taken some very determined coaxing to earn his way over the threshold of this cottage. He'd had the door shut in his face more than once. Mr. May had halfheartedly threatened him with a musket, but Tom had stood his ground; he'd recognized the musket's vintage; it probably had more kick than it did firepower; it would probably harm the shooter more than the target.

And then Tom had come literally hat in hand; he'd come bearing gifts; roses and sweets, and once, in a stroke of originality, a ham.

And then he'd begged.

And really, in the end, very few could withstand a full charm assault from Tom Shaughnessy, which no doubt explained yesterday's letter. Certainly the Mays' pretty daughter Maribeth had scarcely even tried; she'd developed a taste for adventure, a man or two before she landed beneath Tom, and had finally run off with another man entirely. He'd all but forgotten about Maribeth until her letter had arrived a few weeks ago.

"He's yours. You've only to look at him. The hair gives it away."

Ah, romance, Tom thought now, in retrospect.

And when he'd read the letter . . . he'd gone cold. The blood had left his hands and rushed into his face to heat it.

He was tempted just to crumple it and get on with the business of building a bawdy empire.

He did crumple it in fact. Squeezed it in his fist. Where it all but pulsed, the damn thing, as though he'd crushed in his hand a heart.

And so he'd smoothed it out again and stared at it, darkly angry. The anger was strangely unspecific. With himself? With Maribeth? With fate, for casting something in his path that had nothing at all to do with the plans he'd forged from persistence and work and danger and sheer cleverness?

Maribeth had left the boy—Jamie, she'd said his name was—with her parents, who had despaired of their daughter long ago. Her parents were considerably more respectable and conservative than their daughter, if impoverished. They lived in a small cottage in Kent with their other children.

So he'd thought about it. And as a formality, perhaps, Tom sent a letter—polite, formal—requesting to see the boy.

He'd been coldly rebuffed. *"Given your occupation, we think it best for him that you don't see him,"* was the essence of the reply the Mays had sent.

Which is why, in the way of Tom Shaughnessy, seeing Jamie had become a quest.

And in the way of all of Tom's quests to date, he'd been successful.

૭ﻻ૭   ૭ﻻ૭   ૭ﻻ૭

Mrs. May brought the boy to him in their sitting room, leading him by the hand.

His name was James; he was not yet two years old, Tom had been told. His hair was a silky sheet of copper, his baby-colored eyes already turning gray.

Silver, Jamie's Grammy Shaughnessy would have called them, had she lived to see her grandchild.

Tom, for an instant, couldn't breathe. He could see it. The child looked like him. Just like him, so much smaller, and yet . . . would grow to be an *entire person* who would look just like him.

The little boy stood and stared back at Tom with bald, unblinking amazement, as surely as though Tom was a dancing bear or a firework. It was both a little flattering and disconcerting, though Tom imagined that everything new that entered Jamie's world was treated to the same stare.

And then Mrs. May released the boy's little hand, and took a seat on one of the two settees that faced each other, each worn, and nearly as curved as a smile from years of being sat upon.

A judge presiding, Tom thought, mordantly amused.

Awkwardly, he remained standing, hat in hand. He couldn't very well *bow* to the child. Or shake his hand. He was . . . miniature. Everything about him was miniature, the tiny hands and feet, the little ears, that round, delicate head.

So Tom sat down stiffly on the settee, for all the world as if he'd come courting.

What on earth did one *do* with a toddler? And why on earth was he here, after all? The Mays seemed to have it all in hand, and from the sounds heard in the rest of the house, had managed to keep other children alive and fed.

Jamie toddled toward Tom, unable to resist the newness of him.

There was a ball on the braided rug near Tom's feet, a little thing made of leather, a toy. Tentatively, Tom leaned over and rolled it across to the boy.

"Ball!" Jamie bellowed, looking shocked and delighted. He fumbled at it with plump little starfish hands; when he managed to pick it up, a smile scrunched his face nearly in half, as though joy had split it right open.

Jamie tottered over to Tom and generously held out the ball.

After a moment's hesitation, Tom took it. "Why thank you, my good man."

Jamie patted his hands together, pleased to have given a gift. *"Ball!"* he reiterated on a piercing squeal. Tom fought a wince, certain the sound had drilled through his eardrum, fought the impulse to twist one finger in his ear to check.

"Yes, and an *excellent* ball it is, too," Tom agreed. He knew the language of babies, he just wasn't about to speak it, and he wasn't convinced that babies wanted to hear it from adults, either. He admired his gift for a moment, to Jamie's wide-eyed pleasure, then rolled the ball gently across the room for Jamie to wobble after.

Two, three steps, then—oh no!—*splat.* Down he went.

Jamie didn't burst into tears, though he did look surprised, as though he fully hadn't expected his legs to betray him. And then, hands on the floor for leverage, round bottom in the air, he pushed himself upright again and continued his pursuit.

He gets that from me, Tom thought. *Single-minded determination.*

The very thought that anyone—let alone an entire, tiny human being—would have gotten anything at all from him stunned him breathless again.

He watched the boy. *My son,* he thought, trying out the words in his mind to see how they felt. *My son.* Foreign, as it turned out. Two little words, but immense in their implication, like a great mountain he couldn't see around.

He turned suddenly, to find Mrs. May watching him.

It was perhaps even more disconcerting to see the faintest hint of compassion softening her cool, stern vigilance.

This was when he quickly stood again.

"Well, thank you, Mrs. May. I'll just be off then."

He bowed, and left the two of them before she could even rise to her feet, as surely as though hounds were on his heels.

      ॐ   ॐ   ॐ

After a breakfast of very good bread and hot tea in the kitchen with Josephine and Mrs. Pool, Sylvie was led back upstairs to a very handsome sitting room. Soft shades of cream and blue were everywhere in the worn but tasteful furniture and the decent rugs and heavy curtains. There was even a little hearth, dark now as the weather was warm and the east-facing window allowed in a good deal of morning sun. Sylvie had abandoned her widow's weeds and was wearing muslin, elegantly cut, subtly striped in a soft shade of willow. A narrow band of lace edged the neckline.

She saw Josephine's eyes widen a bit when she took in the dress. No doubt she had a sense of its cost. But she said nothing; she merely settled Sylvie into the chair across from her and handed across a basket full of snipped-out segments of black flannel.

"Pirate hats," she said matter-of-factly, brandishing one she'd finished with a flourish, to show Sylvie how they should look. "Next we'll do the sashes and pantaloons and cunning little shirts, and dresses for the sea nymphs. Though *those* willna be much more than togas, and I'm thankful fer that, fer Mr. Shaughnessy, 'e does 'ave 'is ideas, one right after t'other, an 'e wants everything done straightaway. First the costumes and song and the sets—and that's The General's bailiwick, ye see, the sets are—and then the lot of ye'll be in rehearsals in two shakes of a lamb's tail. And Mr. Shaughnessy, 'is 'and is in all of it, ye ken. Not that I'm complaining, mind ye," she added hurriedly, "but I'm 'appy fer yer 'elp. And we'll take in all of yer costumes as well, as they're too big for ye."

"Pantaloons?" Sylvie almost breathed the word. "There will be pantaloons?" Even in Paris, pantaloons for women were scandalous.

"They will look like skirts," Josephine said with some relish, "but we'll sew 'em together so that we can 'ave a leg in one side and a leg in the other. They *will* be pantaloons. Mr. Shaughnessy does have 'is ideas," she reiterated admiringly. "And then we'll write a song."

"'We'll'?" Sylvie repeated.

"Mr. Shaughnessy and I," Josephine clarified benignly, deftly stitching a pirate hat into shape.

Sylvie stared wonderingly at Josephine, who could very well pass for the wife of a curate, with her round cheeks and mild eyes.

Josephine looked up, noticed Sylvie's astonished

perusal, and smiled sweetly. "Oh, me 'usband, 'e dinna mind. 'E's known Tom fer simply years, which is 'ow I came into Tom's employ. First wi' the sewing bits, mind ye. Then 'e discovered I'd a bit of a musical flair."

She bent her head again to her sewing, then glanced sideways through her lashes at Sylvie, and said in a humble hush, as though confiding a secret, "and 'tisn't difficult, ye ken, to rhyme things with lance, or joust. It all jus' . . . comes to me, like. 'Tis a gift."

ঞ্চ   ঞ্চ   ঞ্চ

Tom was relieved to be back again in the White Lily, in his office, among plans of his own making. He knew the way forward from this room—how to make shows, hire and discharge employees. He knew how to talk to a man with a hook for a hand or to a beautiful woman or to a rich investor or to a man threatening to shoot him at dawn.

But he hadn't the faintest idea what to do with the miniature version of himself.

He would write to Mrs. May and thank her for her time, then send money quarterly until the boy was grown, and this would dispatch his duties in this particular situation. Doubtless it wasn't unusual; he was certain more than one man had found himself in similar circumstances.

Somewhat relieved at how tidy this solution felt, Tom turned to his stack of correspondence gratefully. Mrs. Pool had anticipated his return, and a tray of strong tea, which she had clearly only recently brewed judging from the heat and aroma of it, waited for him. He poured a cup of it as he sorted through his mail, and found wonderful news:

Viscount Howath would be pleased to invest in the Gentleman's Emporium.

And that completed his group of investors. They were all in.

He leaned back in his chair and took a sip of tea, rolling it about in his mouth as if it were the taste of victory itself, and the sweet heat and enormity of triumph swelled in him and momentarily overtook every other concern. He knew a moment of awe: Tom Shaughnessy, former street urchin, would soon own one of the largest buildings in London, and the wealthiest men in London would flock to it in order to be entertained.

Tom allowed himself a moment to dream, to allow the dream to spiral outward to when the building was renovated and alive with entertainments, each floor a fantasy of escape and pleasure.

And then he reined his dreams back into the needs of the present, which included the creation of a song for female pirates. And he ought to see The General, who no doubt was in the workshop, begrudgingly supervising the frantic creation of a pirate ship and a great oyster for Venus to rise up out of, and swearing and hammering things.

Tom thought it would do him a world of good to hammer and swear at things for a bit. He would see The General, he decided, then visit Josephine.

☙ ☙ ☙

The little pile of pirate hats had quickly grown. Josephine wasn't stringent about the needlework; she required only that Sylvie be swift. They set to work on the pantaloons next, cutting from measurements taken from each girl and refreshed each time a new show was created.

The work was soothing; Josephine wasn't one for talking, and Sylvie felt lulled by the soft sun coming in through the window and the rhythm of her needle passing in and out of the fabric. It had been a very long time since she'd done anything quite so ordinary, and oddly, she found it refreshing. They might be a curate's wife and a curate's daughter, apart from the fact that they were sewing pirate hats and pantaloons.

"Josephine! I'd hoped to find you . . ."

Sylvie and Josephine looked up abruptly at the voice. Tom Shaughnessy had trailed off when he saw Sylvie perched on a chair opposite Josephine, a basket of sewing demurely on her lap. He looked bemused for an instant, and met her eyes so Sylvie could see it. It was as though he somehow suspected that this version of her, the quiet version dressed in a muslin gown and demurely stitching things, was somehow as wrong as a derriere-patting fairy.

He recovered from his bemusement, but remained in the doorway.

"Oh, so you've given Miss Chapeau something sharp to wield, have you, Josephine? I shall stand over here, Miss Chapeau, at a safe distance, lest your passions become inflamed, and you become tempted to insert me with a needle."

"Should you continue to stand at a . . . safe distance . . . Mr. Shaughnessy . . . I shall not complain," Sylvie replied evenly.

Suspecting that no distance from this man was in truth safe.

This made him laugh, and he came all the way into the room. Fawn trousers today, tall boots, emphasizing those long, long legs. Boots so shiny the light bounced from them as he walked. A coat in a fine mahogany-colored wool. Red-gold hair mussed, falling in loose waves over his brow, as if the wind had just artfully tossed it. The waistcoat was fawn-colored, too, striped in cream, and the buttons on it were, it seemed, brass. Surely they couldn't be gold?

He wandered to where the two ladies sat, then paused when he saw the growing mound of pirate hats. He gazed down at them a moment, then plucked up one of them, fingering it idly, almost delicately, a moment, his expression abstracted.

And then he abruptly put it down again and strode toward the pianoforte.

"Speaking of inflaming passions, Josephine . . ." Tom struck three or four random keys. "We'll need a new tune for our pirate theme, and we'll need it straightaway, of course. I thought perhaps something to do with . . . swords?" It was a serious query. "Seems the obvious choice, anyhow."

Josephine became brisk. She abandoned her hats to the chair, a little spill of black felt, and bustled over to Tom to take a seat at the pianoforte.

"I've just the tune, Mr. Shaughnessy." She clasped her fingers together and stretched them out, then positioned them over the keys and struck a hearty, seafaring chantey-like melody.

"Me 'usband was a sailor," she explained over her shoulder to Sylvie. "And when I 'eard about the pirates, I thought to meself, I can jus' '*ear* it now . . .'"

She played a few bars of it while Tom listened attentively.

"Yes, I do think that will do. *Now* all we must do is compose a song that every man who leaves the theater will want to launch into when they're drunk. Perhaps something to do with . . . *thrusting* swords?" Tom suggested, rubbing his chin in thought.

Josephine tilted her head. " 'Ow about . . ."

*Now thrust yer sword laddie, now thrust yer
sword . . .*

She paused and looked up at Tom for approval.

"Good, good," he murmured. "It's a beginning." He tilted his head up, searching the ceiling for the next line. "Lord? Bored?"

"Toward?" Josephine suggested, wrinkling her nose to indicate her opinion of her own inspiration. "Snored? Roared?"

"Reward," Sylvie murmured under her breath.

Josephine and Tom swiveled toward her.

There was a brief charged moment of silence.

"What did you say, Miss Chapeau?" Tom asked mildly.

But she'd known this man long enough now to hear the suppressed glee in his voice.

Oh, no. Sylvie kept her face down, jabbing the needle through the flannel, then into her own fingers, and she was forced to bite her lip to keep from squeaking from the pain.

"Come now, dear, do share," Josephine encouraged, as gently as anyone's mother.

Sylvie cleared her throat. "Reward," she said, more loudly this time.

And this time looked Tom evenly in the eye. It was outrageously invigorating to flirt subtly with this man. Still, she could feel heat in her face. Her eyes darted toward the hearth, as though she was tempted to blame it. Deuced thing was dark.

"And, pray tell, how would you use 'reward' in the song?" Tom asked the question with wide-eyed innocence. And then he held up a hand. "I've an idea. Josephine, begin playing the song, if you would. Miss Sylvie Chapeau will complete the line for us at the appropriate time."

"I—" Sylvie began to protest.

But Josephine had already begun playing, her large capable hands jumping over the keys to make the tune spring out.

"Come now, dear!" she urged supportively. "Let's 'ear it!"

And Josephine sang:

Now thrust yer sword, laddie, thrust yer sword

She turned her head over her shoulder to peer at Sylvie, wagging her eyebrows upward encouragingly, her hands bouncing their way through several bars of the tune.

Sylvie flicked a glance at Tom. His eyes had nearly vanished with amusement.

Dear God. Josephine looked so enthusiastic and hopeful, head turned over her shoulder, those encouraging brows uplifted, that Sylvie found she simply could not disappoint her.

So she squeezed her eyes closed and sang, resignedly:

Send me, send me to my reward.

For that, God help her, was precisely what she had been thinking.

Josephine jangled to a halt.

Tom stared at her speechlessly.

Sylvie forced herself to stare back at them with all apparent innocence.

"Your . . . 'reward'?" Tom repeated, finally, in a voice entirely lacking inflection.

Sylvie nodded gingerly.

He wasn't smiling. But still, somehow, his entire face was positively fulsome with unholy, triumphant mirth. It was as if laughter could not possibly do adequate justice to her contribution to the song.

"Hmmm." He paced to and fro before the hearth. "Thrust your sword, laddie, *thrust* your sword." He gave the words a *To be, or not to be* gravity. "Send me, send me to my—" He spun and all but purred the word to her. "—*reward.*"

She suspected her flaming cheeks rather defeated the purpose of her cool stare, which was to make him believe she was entirely unaffected.

Where on earth had the word *come* from? It had just popped right out of her.

Who knew that bawdy songs were contagious?

"Well, I must confess, I think it's bloody brilliant," he said, shaking his head. "It really is. And I do believe I now have the rest, as a result. Josephine? If you would begin again, and we'll sing it together?"

And so Josephine played and sang:

Thrust yer sword, laddie, now thrust yer sword
Send me, send me to my reward,
Whether it takes one thrust or a few
I beg you to

Josephine and Tom completed the last line together, their voices blending skillfully:

Thrust . . . yer . . . sword!

"Well then," Tom said crisply, when they were done. "We can have the girls swooning at the 'reward' portion of the song, and clasping their hands in entreaty at the 'I beg you' portion, and at the 'thrust your sword,' part, well—we'll have them thrusting swords." He grinned. "Another fine day's work here at the White Lily, ladies. I'll share the song with Daisy and ask her and The General to come visit you here, Josephine, to learn it. And don't forget, we'll need a song or two for Venus. Think of the possibilities inherent in the word 'pearl.' And I do believe you've earned your keep for the day, Miss Chapeau."

In a quick motion Sylvie was growing to associate with him, he reviewed the time and turned to move toward the door. But then he paused as surely as though something invisible had tugged him gently back, and wandered back to where Sylvie sat, his tall frame blocking the sunlight from the window.

She looked up at him, felt again that familiar, inconvenient shortness of breath, that needle-sharp spike of awareness that accompanied his closeness.

But he wasn't looking at her. He instead picked up one of the completed pirate hats again and turned the cunning little item about in his hands, shifting it this way and that, his expression oddly reflective, unreadable.

He lowered it back to the chair, slowly, thoughtfully this time. "Do you suppose . . ." he began. And then he turned to Josephine and continued with a more decisive air. "Do you suppose you could make a very small pirate hat?" He held his hands up and apart, then studied them, and adjusted the space between them to the size of a small melon. "About . . . this size? By . . . tomorrow?"

Josephine looked a little puzzled. "Certainly, Mr. Shaughnessy."

"Thank you." He turned to leave. "And I shall see you downstairs in the theater in an hour or so, Miss Chapeau. The General and I have an announcement to make. After rehearsal, do come to see me. Perhaps we can then discuss your . . . reward."

A grin flashed at them, he bowed once, a gorgeous flourish of a bow, and was gone.

ঞ ঞ ঞ

Summoned for Mr. Shaughnessy's special announcement, seven lovely women stood on stage—five young and plush, one young and slender, and one from whom the bloom had fled several seasons earlier, leaving behind a fully blown rose: a lived-in face, hennaed hair, and a rump that many Englishmen insisted that visitors to London should make a point of viewing with deference and awe, the way one viewed the Tower of London or Whitehall. A national treasure, was Daisy Jones's arse, they declared.

Daisy Jones herself stood several feet removed from

the lovelies, as if aware of the contrast, or not wanting to dilute her queenly status by breathing the same air as the other girls.

"Jus' look at 'Er Majesty. None too pleased to rub elbows wi' the likes of us," Lizzie murmured.

"'Er bosom is down around 'er elbows, now, anyhow. Wouldna want t' find meself rubbin' *that* by accident, anyway." This was Molly.

An explosion of giggles. High, incensed color rose in Daisy's cheeks, but she neither turned her head nor moved an inch.

"Ladies, you may have heard, thanks to your *many admirers* who cannot seem to stay quiet . . ." Tom said it teasingly, and the girls giggled. ". . . of the new production I've planned. It will be a *tour de force,* a thing of beauty and sensu*a*lity . . ." he gave each syllable the loving, thorough attention of a seducer, weakening the knees of more than one girl on stage. "And it will require just the right girl to make it a success. We are calling it—" Tom paused.

"Venus," all the girls said with a sigh.

Everyone, that is, but Daisy, who remained silent and dark as a thunderhead.

"Quite right. And The General and I will be watching over the next few days to see which of you we believe will personify Venus."

The General whipped his head around at this, seized Tom's arm, and yanked him backward out of earshot of the girls.

"Are you *mad,* Shaughnessy?" he said, his voice low and furious. "They're all going to be *impossible* if they think they're in competition with each other. I thought we discussed that Molly would be Venus."

"Or . . . they'll outdo themselves, behave beautifully, perform outrageously onstage, and we'll have crowds in here up to the rafters night after night this week, at which point we'll disclose who our Venus will be, a decision that you and I will make together."

The General glared at Tom.

Tom waited patiently.

"Or . . . a bit of both," The General conceded, slowly, reluctantly, seeing the potential brilliance of the tactic.

Tom grinned. There was a pause.

"Probably Molly," Tom said briskly. The businessman in Tom said this in a lowered voice. The dreamer in him saw an entirely different Venus rising up from the sea: a lithe one, with crackling green eyes and a shard of a wand in her hand, daring the audience.

"Probably Molly," The General agreed just as briskly, in the same lowered voice.

This was based more on the size and number of bouquets sent to her than on anything else at the moment. They were practical men, and it was a fiscal, not an aesthetic decision. More men at the moment would probably want to see Molly rising up out of the sea scantily clad in the shell. She hadn't Daisy's vocal range, but her voice was clear and her interpretation of the lyrics was more than convincing; she was fresh, and had a following of sorts as well as a beautiful bosom. She was Venus from St. Giles, Molly was.

Whereas Venus of Paris was up there looking uncomfortable in that row of dancers, stoic, proud, staring back at him, again looking faintly wrong in a damsel costume that required altering. A bit like a real princess disguised as a princess.

Tom gave The General an encouraging pat on the back. "Good luck! You *are* giving cutlasses to them, are you not?" He said it almost innocently.

"Cutlasses," The General repeated slowly. "Brilliant! Of course, Tommy. I'll get the crew to work on them today."

"Wait until you hear what I think they should be doing with their *hands* and cutlasses while they sing."

The General grinned, too. "I can already picture it."

"And we've a wonderful new song. Involving swords, of course."

"Good work, Shaughnessy."

Tom grinned. "And now I'm off to see a man about a building, Gen. They're in. They're all in. We'll have our Gentleman's Emporium by next spring. I'll return before rehearsal is over."

∽   ∽   ∽

Once Mr. Shaughnessy had made his announcement and left them again, The General sent all of them to finish dressing like damsels, which involved the addition of pointed hats and flowing sheer capes trimmed with jewels, which would gleam and twinkle when softly lit, and which apparently were to be flourished provocatively.

Everything was to be done provocatively at the White Lily, Sylvie now knew.

A great wooden castle, complete with turrets and a drawbridge that appeared capable of opening and closing, was pushed onto the stage by the seemingly ever-present crew of young boys. It occurred to Sylvie then that Tom Shaughnessy employed rather a lot of people and kept all of them hopping.

The castle seemed outrageously heavy; the boys were cherry-colored in the face and throwing all of their weight behind it, and the rest of the damsel-clad girls filed onto the stage, Sylvie among them, her body engulfed by the dress and cape. She glanced down glumly. She would need to alter these, too.

"Daisy!" The General bellowed toward the back of the theater. "Get your galleon-sized arse out here or I'll—"

There was an ominous creaking sound; everyone spun.

The boys were slowly lowering the drawbridge of the castle, and it thunked to the floor of the stage, sending up a tiny cloud of dust. The girls coughed and waved at the air.

And there stood Daisy at the entrance of the castle. She struck a pose, arms up and braced in the castle doorway, bosom outthrust, long red tresses tumbling across her shoulders, and waited until she was certain every eye in the place was upon her. The General watched her in smoldering silence as she sashayed across the drawbridge, then Sylvie watched his chin slowly lower until his gaze landed in the vicinity of Daisy's hips and stayed there, as surely as though her hips were the tool of a mesmerist.

There was no denying that Daisy Jones knew how to make an unforgettable entrance. Sylvie suspected that this, for some reason, had been Daisy's point.

She reached the end of the gangplank and paused.

"She gave me a penny to do it!" One of the boys squeaked by way of explanation before dashing offstage, apparently unable to decide who was more fearsome, Daisy or The General.

The General gazed at Daisy at length, inscrutable, no longer glowering. She gazed back at him, faintly defiant, but clearly pleased with herself. The rest of the girls looked on in resentful silence, perhaps knowing they could only dream of making an entrance as majestic.

At last the General cleared his throat. "Josephine—if you would? Sylvie, please, as you did yesterday, just follow along. You're a clever girl. I'm sure you'll catch on."

Again, that frisson of irony. As though something about her privately amused The General.

Josephine clasped her fingers together and stretched them out, then landed them on the pianoforte keyboard. A tune with a faint medieval lilt spilled out.

Daisy plaintively sang, in that voice that reached the rafters, but would never soothe the angels in heaven:

> *"Kind sir, kind sir, we damsels fair*
> *are begging for release*
> *Please wield your lance*
> *Or we've no chance*
> *Of ever finding peace . . .*

The girls swayed, raised the flat of swooning hands to foreheads, linked arms and . . . God help her . . .

Bent double and waved their derrieres in the air.

Again. And Sylvie, sighing inwardly, followed along.

"Get it up there, Sylvie! And if you would *please* not roll your eyes!"

And this, naturally, made Sylvie roll her eyes.

When they'd run through the song a good half dozen times, it seemed, and were upright and turned around to face the audience again, Sylvie saw Tom Shaughnessy at the head of the aisle, his bright eyes fixed rather emphatically on her, walking stick in hand, marking off time almost absently. The expression he wore was strangely . . . confused. A faint frown hovered between his eyes, as though she was a puzzle he was very close to deciphering.

So he'd returned, then, from whatever business had drawn him briefly away.

Sylvie felt unaccountably, absurdly glad, both at his return, and at the fact that he was clearly watching only her.

When her eyes met his, his faint frown tilted up at the corner and became that smile of acknowledgment, and wicked amusement lit his eyes as surely as if a light had caught them. Reflexively, her own lips turned up slightly, and something else inside her lifted, too.

"Oh!" Pain sliced through her as someone came down hard on the inside of her foot, nearly taking her slipper entirely off. Sylvie teetered briefly, one knee buckling. She righted herself quickly enough, as did the other girls, and danced and smiled through the pain, as she was accustomed to dancing and smiling through pain.

Both The General and Tom Shaughnessy were wearing genuine frowns now, and they were both directed at her. Tom's was puzzled. The General's was censorious.

"Goodness. *So* sorry," Molly murmured to her. Her smile remained in place, her face fixed forward. But her eyes, when Sylvie glanced sideways, her eyes glinted, glass-hard and satisfied.

ცმ   ცმ   ცმ

He'd told her to find him in his library after rehearsal for her reward, and she knew precisely where this was as she'd seen the light pouring from it last night. As she had essentially spied on him very briefly last night.

She paused in the doorway. Tom Shaughnessy wasn't looking at her, he was sifting a hand through things on his desk, pushing them this way and that, as though he was looking for something in particular. A smile was curving his lips, as though he found the mess immensely satisfying.

Suddenly he froze and his face went dark and taut. With a swift motion he lifted one hand and pressed the thumb of his other hand hard against his palm, sucking in a short, harsh breath.

Sylvie's stomach contracted involuntarily in sympathy. She knew pain when she saw it.

He glanced up, noticing her at last, and his expression shifted instantly, light flooding into it. "Old wound," he explained glibly, lifting up his hand, fanning it out. She saw the scars, white, pulling tightly between thumb and forefinger. "Now and again it sends a humbling reminder through my nerves. Have you come for your . . . *reward* then, Miss Chapeau?"

She went very still. It was the way he'd said the word. It seemed to have . . . *dimensions,* the way he'd said it. He'd given it rich levels of innuendo, all of which implied he'd decades of experience rewarding women. He wasn't smiling, but the corners of his mouth were quivering, ready to laugh if she gave him a reason.

Tom Shaughnessy could very likely effortlessly outstrip her in the game of flirtation, she conceded. *She* felt obliged to a certain amount of decorum. Whereas he seemed fearless. And very nearly shameless. Though thankfully, so far, he seemed to be using his fearlessness and shamelessness somewhat judiciously.

"I am here as you requested, Mr. Shaughnessy. Did I earn more for contributing a bit of verse to your . . . production?" She couldn't resist a bit of irony.

The humor faded from his eyes. "Ah," he said, matching her irony. "I gather you feel our little *productions* lack a certain artistry. But I will tell you this, Miss Chapeau: There's great freedom in not feeling obliged toward respectability."

"I imagine you would know, Mr. Shaughnessy."

It was meant as a jest, albeit a tart one.

He went briefly very still again. His expression was difficult to read, and she considered whether she might have offended him, though it was difficult to see why this would be.

And then he opened up a small wooden box, reached in, and produced a stack of coins, which he settled on the corner of the desk: her wages. An eloquent but silent point made about the rewards of not feeling obliged to respectability.

Sylvie scooped them into her palm. Handed one back to him. "For my room and board."

He handed it back to her. "For the line of verse." They exchanged swift smiles. Tension eased a bit.

"Tell me: Do *you* aspire to respectability, Miss Chapeau?" He asked it idly.

She recognized it for what it was: a gauntlet thrown down, and still she could not resist snapping. "I do not *aspire* to respectability, Mr. Shaughnessy."

"Ah. I see. It is yours already." He was laughing silently at her. "And it was merely the cruel whims of fate that somehow led you to our little den of iniquity. I'm curious then: How does a respectable woman know about . . . rewards?"

"One can be respectable and know about . . . rewards, Mr. Shaughnessy." She heard how absurd the words sounded even as she said them.

"Can one?" he asked mildly. "I suppose that could be true if one is French. I suspect one wouldn't *blurt* the word out with such relish, however."

"I didn't—it wasn't—"

"And as 'respectable' so often means the same thing as 'married,'" he continued, as if she hadn't stammered at all, "and I do not think you are, or have been married, I must conclude that someone's *sword* has been sending you, or has in the past sent you, to your *reward.* So who sends you to your reward, Miss Chapeau? Did you leave a lover behind in France?"

The cutthroat boldness of the question wiped her mind of thought, and for an instant, she froze, unable to react at all. So much for judicious use of fearlessness and shamelessness.

She managed, finally, to produce a disapproving frown. And said nothing.

But this only made him smile, slowly, to demonstrate to her: *I have won this round, Miss Chapeau.*

Sylvie glanced around the room, an attempt to recover her composure. She supposed at one time it might have been used as a small library or sitting room, when the theater, as Josephine had told her, had been a great house; shelves were built into one wall. There were books on them now, which surprised her a little, as Tom Shaughnessy did not strike her as the academic sort—or even, necessarily, the reading sort, though he was certainly well-spoken enough—and all the books looked well thumbed through, too.

On closer inspection, she saw they weren't the sort usually proudly displayed in libraries, philosophical tomes and the like, the kind that are spotless and meant to impress guests. These were novels, for the most part. *Robinson Crusoe* was one of them, the ultimate male adventure. A few horrid novels, it seemed; she recognized them, as she secretly enjoyed them, too, and had read more than one in English. A collection of Greek myths, a large book that she was virtually certain was extravagantly illustrated given the theme of the theater's murals. She imagined they would appeal to his sense of drama and fantasy and whimsy.

But something tucked behind the books surprised her the most: a small wooden horse, a toy. It had a bristly mane and tail, wheels on its feet. She wondered if it had belonged to Tom as a boy, and why on earth such a thing would be tucked into a niche at the White Lily Theater.

And then she remembered the accusation of the man who had called him out: "*At that shop that sells toys.*"

Tom had denied being in any such place.

This was intriguing.

She glanced up to meet his eyes on her. He'd been silently watching her peruse his office. Momentarily disconcerted, she glanced down, and saw, unfurled on his desk, a beautiful drawing of a grand building.

"Plans," he said shortly. "For another theater."

"It looks very grand." It did. The building was downright stately, vast; rows of large windows marched across it, a columned entrance greeted guests.

"It will be bloody fantastic," he stated as firmly as if it

were already an established fact. "A floor for entertainments, a floor for dining, a floor for . . ." He trailed off, perhaps imagining it as he recited. And then he looked up at her. "We need a good deal of capital to make it a reality, but we should have the Gentleman's Emporium by next spring. I commissioned this drawing, and I'm working on the plans now." She heard the pride and conviction in his voice as he motioned to the papers spread over his desk. "It will be much like the White Lily . . . only much more so."

"But why . . . this sort of thing at all, Mr. Shaughnessy?" She gestured to the theater surrounding them with a wave of her hand. "Why the White Lily?"

He looked surprised at the question, then pretended to mull it quite seriously, head tilted back to look at the ceiling. And then he said suddenly, as though the answer had just then occurred to him: "Sex."

The word hung and pulsed in the air, all soft and crisp consonants, as lurid as the sign that swung over the White Lily's entrance. Long enough for both of them to picture once again what the word meant to each of them.

Long enough for Sylvie to feel distinctly light-headed.

"Very dramatic, Mr. Shaughnessy, but that word won't get any more or less alarming the longer you leave it there. You might as well continue to explain." She was aware that her voice was just a little bit frayed, and hoped that he wouldn't notice.

He threw back his head and laughed, delightedly. "Oh, very well then. It's simple, Miss Chapeau. I began my life with nothing. I wanted much much more than that. I knew a little bit about theater. I know a good deal about men and women, having encountered many kinds of both throughout my life. I followed the momentum of my talents and experience, and here we are. And where's the harm in it?"

"It's . . ." She waved a hand. *Appalling,* she thought. *Embarrassing. Overt.*

"Fun," he completed with a grin. "Lucrative. Everyone has a wonderful time."

"Including Molly?" she said, perhaps too quickly and sharply.

The grin faded when she said this; he studied her in silence for a moment. And then he inhaled deeply and sat down in his chair, leaned back and continued to study her, as if deciding whether to explain something to a child.

"Do you know what Molly would be doing if I didn't employ her?" he finally asked.

Sylvie was silent as she contemplated this. She could very well guess.

"Do you think she'd make a wonderful governess? Do you think she'd make a splendid scullery maid? Do you think her life would be any better then? Do you want to know where she was living before she came to the theater? What she was doing?"

"I take your point Mr. Shaughnessy. You are a veritable Samaritan."

He grunted a humorless laugh. "Hardly. But I do hire people that many employers would never dream of hiring, people who haven't a prayer of ever working at anything else. People I've encountered throughout my life. It isn't merely charity, Miss Chapeau. Usually I'm richly repaid in loyalty and commitment. But there are times . . ." he trailed off. "Well, I hired an old friend to watch the dressing-room door. Jack. And it seems"—he twisted his quill distractedly in his hand—"that Molly has paid for my mistake."

He was struggling to disguise the strain in his voice. The admission, and the event, and the harm to Molly, had cost him, greatly, Sylvie realized.

She was tempted to apologize. But then he became restless, glancing down at the work littering his desk. "Perhaps you'd understand, Miss Chapeau, if you had not been pampered your entire life."

A deliberate torch touched to the kindling of her temper. It leaped up instantly.

"I've *never* been—"

"Yes?" He looked up swiftly. His grin was small and triumphant.

She made it all too easy for him, she realized. But then everything she felt and thought seemed amplified and very near the surface when she was near him. As though it was rushing to be closer to him.

She supposed it was wiser, then, *not* to be near him.

"Do you know a little of work, then?" he pressed. "You did say you might be able to teach me a thing or two. You might even find me a willing pupil." Another wicked little grin.

"Yes, I know much about work, and a little about 'nothing,' Mr. Shaughnessy," she said quietly. "And I, too, intend to never have *nothing* again. I have worked all my life to make certain of it."

"So you're an ambitious woman, Miss Chapeau?"

"Aren't all women to some degree? Does life not require it of us?" She thought she heard a trace of bitterness in her voice.

He fell silent again.

And then he looked down, ran a light hand over the drawing of the grand building, smoothing it thoughtfully, proprietarily.

"What happened to Molly . . . what happened to Molly won't happen again. I always learn from my mistakes," he said suddenly, looking up at her again. Holding her eyes. Almost as though he was trying to persuade her of the truth of this. "One might in fact, even say the White Lily originated from a mistake." He grinned swiftly, ruefully, and held up his scarred hand, as if illustrating his point.

"I was ten years old, and I was stealing cheese. The vendor objected and came at me with a knife because boys like me were forever infesting his stalls like little vermin. I fought back, but he got me," Tom said nearly cheerily. "It became septic, and I very nearly died, but an apothecary took pity on me. He made sure I was healthy again, and he knew someone at a tavern at the docks who needed help, and they gave me a job, and that job led to another job at a theater, and . . ."

He paused, and his eyes lit with some amusement. "I've always just been lucky, I suppose. Particularly in my friends."

Lucky? Sylvie's head spun for a moment with the graphic images; her lungs tightened at the thought of a large man coming at a boy with a knife. Pictured Tom Shaughnessy as small and terrified and wounded and hungry and ill, even dying. It seemed impossible. He seemed . . .

As though he'd *never* been afraid.

And now she understood that the calm she'd sensed in him had been *earned* . . . through knowing he could survive the very worst life could conjure.

Sylvie frowned a little. "But your parents—"

"Were dead at the time. I never knew my father."

His smile became faintly cynical when he saw her expression. "Oh, there were thousands of boys just like me, Miss Chapeau. I *was* lucky. It's as simple as that."

She wasn't certain what to say. She wanted to say: *I doubt there were thousands of boys like you. It's impossible to imagine even one other like you.*

"I never knew my parents, either," she found herself saying, instead.

His face changed to something like surprise, whether at the nature of the confession or the fact that she had in fact confessed it, she wasn't certain. He studied her, too, as if adding this information to whatever judgments he'd made of her in his mind.

Sylvie thought she understood something now. The White Lily was the thing Tom Shaughnessy had built to separate him from his old life, in the way ballet was the thing that had lifted her up out of the ordinary.

They were perhaps more alike than different. This she found strangely disturbing.

"Was it yours, when you were a boy?" She said it lightly, and pointed at the horse on the shelf when the silence had shifted into something more intimate, much less familiar to her. And therefore perhaps more dangerous.

He looked at the horse. "It's mine for the moment, anyhow." An answer and not an answer. Ah, inscrutability from Tom Shaughnessy. "I always did want one when I was small."

It was difficult to know whether or not he was serious; the words were glib.

"I always wanted a . . . *boîte à musique*," she faltered,

almost to herself. She remembered it now; the memory of it returned swiftly, the yearning strangely stirred.

"A music box?" he repeated. He sounded curious. Encouraging, almost.

She fell abruptly silent and straightened her spine, as if pushing away the memory and the moment. There had scarcely been enough money when she was young for what they needed, for Claude never made very much money; there had certainly never been enough for something quite so frivolous as a music box.

Tom Shaughnessy's watch came out then, perhaps inevitably. "I've a builder to see, Miss Chapeau. I've given your wages to you today, as your employment is only temporary. The other girls are paid weekly. If you intend to stay on, I'll rearrange our budget accordingly. But perhaps we should see how things are . . . day by day."

"Day by day, if that suits you," she found herself saying.

"It suits me," he said softly. He somehow managed to make the words sound like a promise.

Her face grew warm, and she dipped a curtsy and left his office abruptly, her payment for throwing her derriere in the air clutched in her palm.

CHAPTER TEN

"I F YOU KEEP SWIVELING your head about like that, it will fly right off and go careening into those pigeons like a *bocci* ball." Kit Whitelaw, Viscount Grantham, gestured to the little cluster of iridescent birds jostling each other for crumbs near a fountain spraying skyward.

"We're in Paris, not Italy," Susannah reminded him. "I do believe you're as nervous about this as I am."

"Nervous?" Kit scoffed at the very idea. "When I spent a good portion of the war spying upon the enemy, dodging bullets—"

Susannah jerked her arm from his and put her hands over her ears. Trudged on in silence.

Abashed, he walked quietly by her side for a moment, allowing her to make her point.

And then, by way of apology, he gently took her hand from her ear, kissed her palm, and tucked her hand back into her arm, covering it with his own. A silent, symbolic promise: *I will keep you safe always.* It had been thoughtless of him to remind her of the dangers he had survived, on behalf of his country, and on her own behalf not too very long ago. He bore the scars. She'd once jested about those very dangers, about the number of times someone had tried to kill her, and he'd found it intolerable to hear.

"You're forgiven," she said magnanimously, finally.

He smiled.

And then he brought the two of them to a halt and looked up at the window of a flat; bright but wilting flowers trailing out of the window box. The high afternoon sun tinted the walls of the house a soft peach. Unassuming, pleasant, not at all dramatic enough for what it appeared it might be.

"This is the place, Susannah."

Tracking down Claude Lamoreux had proved challenging, but Kit was dogged and experienced and delighted once more to use the skills he'd acquired in service of the crown. The investigation hardly posed the sorts of dangers he'd experienced before—he and Susannah had mostly made the acquaintance of a number of aging former opera dancers, and not one of them had lunged with a knife or pointed a pistol—but the trail had finally led them here, to these apartments on the outskirts of Paris. A little narrow stone staircase led up to them.

It was indeed the same address to which Susannah had directed her letters. What remained for them to discover now was why no one had responded to them.

He could feel her fingers curling a little more tightly into his arm, and she was right. He was nervous on her behalf. They had come so far, and been through so much. He very much wanted Susannah to have the thing she'd dreamed about for so long: a family.

ॐ   ॐ   ॐ

The door was flung open by a housekeeper: gray hair spiraling anarchically out from beneath her cap, a little boomerang of a French nose, tiny, shrewd dark eyes.

An instant later, from behind the housekeeper, from inside the house, a raspy voice said something unspeakably filthy in German.

Susannah had seen Kit's eyes pop, then saw the telltale quivering at the corners of his mouth.

"What did he say?" she hissed.

"I will tell you later," he murmured back. "When you are naked."

That both quieted her and turned her scarlet and completely eradicated her nervousness, which Kit had always been able to do.

"*Pardonnez-moi,* but Guillaume, he over and over says these words, and I know not what it means. I think he is angry." The housekeeper was wringing her hands. "He is making me crazy."

The housekeeper was right. The filthy German words, sounding even more vehement now, were repeated. As if Guillaume were desperate to make a point.

"He is lonely, Guillaume, I think, for Madame Claude."

Kit really had no business knowing, but part of him wanted to meet the person who had such an unabashedly colorful vocabulary. "And who is Guillaume?"

"Guillaume is the parrot of Madame Claude."

This was somehow both disappointing and even better than if Guillaume had been a person.

"So Madame Claude is not at home? We have come from England and hoped to meet her. We believe we have a mutual friend."

"Madame Claude is away. Also Mademoiselle Sylvie. She left me alone here . . . with Guillaume," the housekeeper said with dark despair.

The German words wafted toward them again. This time they were a sad, low mutter, sounding nearly as despairing as Madame Gabon did.

"Mademoiselle Sylvie?" Susannah repeated, her voice faint with excitement and hardly dared hope.

Kit took her elbow to steady her, and spoke. "Tell me, Madame"—Kit paused, to allow her to complete the phrase.

"Gabon."

"I am Viscount Grantham, and this is my wife, Lady Grantham. Tell me, Madame Gabon, does Mademoiselle Sylvie look at all like Susannah? Does she resemble Susannah?"

If Madame Gabon thought this was an unusual question, nothing about her betrayed it. She seemed to welcome the little challenge. Madame Gabon peered at Susannah. "You are close in age to Mademoiselle Sylvie, I think, Lady Grantham. I think perhaps your hair?"

"Does Sylvie look like . . . like this woman?" Susannah opened her hand, extended the miniature of her mother, and Madame Gabon squinted at it. Susannah lifted it up a bit higher so the woman could focus upon it more closely.

"Oh no, Mademoiselle. Not so much. Not Sylvie." She looked up. "But you do!" She added hopefully, hating perhaps to disappoint this English nobleman and his wife.

"And Mademoiselle Sylvie is not at home?"

"No. Mademoiselle Sylvie, she left a note for Madame Claude. She is angry, Mademoiselle Sylvie, in the note she is. And they come to see her, Etienne, Monsieur Favre—all angry."

Susannah glanced sideways at Kit. This parade of angry men arriving to see Mademoiselle Sylvie did not sound promising.

"Who is Monsieur Favre?" Kit asked, deciding to begin with that name.

"Mademoiselle Sylvie, she dances for Monsieur Favre. She is very pretty," she added. "Famous. She is famous."

This was better. Or perhaps worse. It was increasingly difficult to know.

"Did Mademoiselle Sylvie travel to the south as well?"

"No, no. To England, the note says. It says . . ." The housekeeper frowned forbiddingly, as it to narrate the tone of the note. "Dear Claude: I have gone to England, and I believe you know why.'"

The housekeeper shrugged then. "*I* know not why, but perhaps Madame Claude, she does. But she is in the South. She is expected to return in two days."

When Guillaume muttered again, it was clear that as far as he was concerned, Madame Claude could not return soon enough.

"Do you know who Mademoiselle Sylvie might have gone to visit in England?" Though Kit suspected he knew the answer. Sylvie's reason was standing right before Madame Gabon at the moment, being gripped by the elbow by Kit.

"I know not. But Madame Claude knows only of a Mrs. Daisy Jones in England. Perhaps it is that Mademoiselle Sylvie is acquainted with her, too. But I do not know, Monsieur, Madame Viscount. But there were letters, too, from England."

"Letters?" Susannah repeated eagerly.

"Only very recently, Madame. Madame Claude burned them when they arrived. All but one, for it arrived but a week ago. Mademoiselle Sylvie, she read the letter. And then *poof*! She is gone to England."

Claude no doubt had burned them to protect Sylvie from the truth of her past; Claude could not possibly have known that all was safe at last. Susannah had not told the entire tale in the letter; she had only sought to know if Claude was indeed the Claude Lamoreux who had adopted one of Anna Holt's daughters.

Anna Holt, accused murderess.

Eagerly: "When did Sylvie leave? Was she alone?"

"Alone? I know not, Madame. I know that Monsieur Etienne did not accompany her. I told him that Sylvie might have gone to see Madame Daisy Jones, for what else might I say?"

"Who is Monsieur Etienne?"

"He is her lover," Madame Gabon said very seriously. "He is a prince. And, *mon dieu*, he is angry."

There was an eloquent pause as Kit and Susannah stood in the Parisian sun and allowed this little bit of information to sink in.

"Your family is proving to be so much more interesting than mine," Kit said enviously.

ৰ্চ ৰ্চ ৰ্চ

It was exceptionally early. An hour at which Tom Shaughnessy would have, more typically, been returning from the Velvet Glove to catch an hour or so of uninterrupted sleep in his own cozy room before embarking on the busi-

ness of his day. Early enough so that damp still clung to
the vines tangling the little picket fence, so that sun was
seen in the wan gold that touched the flowers and flagstones, but seemed to have gathered no heat yet.

He'd hired a horse again to make the journey quickly,
and to be able to return to London quickly, and he tethered the beast at the gate.

The door was already open, for of course the Mays
would have seen and heard the hoofbeats of his arrival.
Mrs. May stood in the entry, an apron still tied over the
well-worn striped muslin of her dress. Her gray-threaded
russet hair was scraped back away from her face, and a
dot of what appeared to be flour was high on her cheek-
bone. She'd been at her morning chores then.

"Mr. Shaughnessy."

It was all the greeting she offered, but she didn't sound
surprised. Tom bowed; she dipped a shallow curtsy and
stepped aside, allowing him into the house, and held out
her hands for his hat and coat. Her face, a worn reminder
of Maribeth's, had been all but impassive until she took
these things into her hands; her movements slowed, she
lingered a bit, as perhaps any woman would, over the
fineness of the fabric. He noticed it. He wondered what
she thought.

His *behavior* had so far been all that was gentlemanly,
glossy appearance notwithstanding. There remained,
however, the little matter of his reputation, which followed him like an invisible army into the house each time,
he was certain. And he was certain Mrs. May had ideas
about what a man of his reputation might do at any
minute, and was braced for all of his reprehensibility to
come spilling out of him.

"Thank you for allowing me to visit, Mrs. May."

"You're welcome, Mr. Shaughnessy. Have you brought ham, today?"

Tom paused. He could have sworn her eyes sparked for an instant. Then again, it might have been a reflection of the morning light.

So he smiled, to encourage further thawing, if thawing indeed was taking place.

"No, I am afraid not. I brought only . . . these." He held up his hands; in one was the tiny pirate hat; in the other, the wooden horse.

She peered at them for a moment.

"Even better," she said.

ॐ   ॐ   ॐ

Tiny as the hat was, it still engulfed Jamie's head, but it made him laugh mad, gurgly, contagious laughs and flail his arms about. There passed an hour or so in which they played some combination of pirate and peekaboo, which Tom found surprisingly diverting, and during which Tom taught him to growl "aye, matie!" and to say "Tom!" Jamie was quick, a veritable little parrot, and Tom found it strangely gratifying.

And then Tom got down on his hands and knees and showed Jamie how to pull the horse along. Jamie dragged it briefly, then picked it up by its string and dangled it.

"'Orse!" he told Tom.

Tom looked at Jamie and felt—well, nearly as though a celestial chorus had just sounded.

"Bloody hell—that is—by *God,* it certainly *is* a horse!"

"Buddy hell!" Jamie repeated happily.

Tom felt a little chill of horror. "Oh bloo—" Tom clapped his mouth shut just in time. "Christ. That is—"

"CHRIST!" Jamie bellowed, and grasped the horse by one of its legs and held it up to him.

Mrs. May appeared in the doorway with a tray in her hands. "I thought you might enjoy some—"

"*Christ!*" Jamie roared happily, clutching at the horse with one hand to show her. He toddled over to her and curled one fist into her skirt, looking up at her, offering the horse.

Mrs. Mays had gone utterly still. Her eyes bugged out briefly.

Jamie apparently thought Mrs. May's bulging eyes were funny, because he laughed his gurgly laugh. *"Buddy hell!"* he shouted gleefully, hopping up and down, the horse bouncing in his hand.

Tom squeezed his eyes closed briefly. Apparently "Aye, matie!" wasn't funny enough to repeat to Mrs. May. It certainly didn't make the eyes of adults bulge in that amusing manner. And the child possessed the most re-markable volume. *Everything* became an announcement.

But then again, when almost everything in your world is new, Tom supposed enthusiastic announcements were not untoward.

Mrs. May slowly lifted her head up from Jamie and met Tom's eyes. Tom held her gaze bravely.

There passed an incongruous moment during which little Jamie gleefully hopped about the rug, singing out "buddy hell!" at intervals, while the two adults regarded each other warily.

And then, before Tom's disbelieving eyes, Mrs. May actually, slowly . . .

Well, it was almost a smile. But whatever it was, it changed her face completely, softening and lightening it, and Tom could see the glimmers of Maribeth there.

"They're a challenge, Mr. Shaughnessy. Particularly boys. They hear—and repeat—everything."

Tom cleared his throat. "I fear he most definitely takes after me."

His way of apologizing, and a bit of a risk as far as jests were concerned, since as far as Mrs. May was concerned, he was about as disreputable as they came.

But Mrs. May smiled in earnest at that.

And so Tom knew several milestones had been reached. Jamie had added significantly to his vocabulary, and Tom and Mrs. May had made progress in the warmth of their relationship.

Jamie hopped over to Tom. " 'Orse!" he said, and lifted the toy up to him.

Now *he says horse,* Tom thought grimly.

But then, having caught on: "Horse!" Tom echoed delightedly. And made a point of bugging out his eyes.

Jamie clapped his hands. "Aye, matie!"

∽   ∽   ∽

Tom still didn't know why he had come. He only knew that when he had returned to London, it was as though he brought with him a little invisible strand that bound him to Kent and tugged at him like a string on a bow, pulling him back again.

∽   ∽   ∽

While Tom was visiting Jamie, Sylvie was learning how to be a pirate. The bawdy female kind, that was.

Josephine and Sylvie and a small crew of hastily recruited seamstresses had been very busy, and now all the girls stood before The General outfitted in pantaloons. Voluminous, nearly skirts, dark in color but sheer in weight, and, if one peered closely, or happened to catch a fortunate glimpse of them in just the right light—and it would be certain that the White Lily and The General would contrive to show them in the right light—deeply scandalous. They wore sashes and grand, ruffled white shirts, and miniature wooden cutlasses hung from their hips. The splendid little pirate hats topped their heads.

And then the results of the hammering and swearing Sylvie had heard behind doors were wheeled out onto the stage, a magnificent, miniature, rather convincing pirate ship, complete with sails of stretched sheets, a flag of skull and crossbones, and a gangplank. A hatch was carved in the hollow middle from which Captain Daisy would burst and sing the bawdy pirate chantey while the girls danced nearby.

Despite the context in which he employed his gifts, Sylvie could not deny that The General was indeed gifted if he had overseen this little masterpiece.

"Ye'll 'ave to make it bigger than that," Molly sniggered, when she saw the hatch.

"Where the bloody hell is Daisy?" The General bellowed.

The woman in question was just now emerging from the long hall that led to her dressing room, bedecked in her own significantly larger version of the pirate clothes, her commanding behind swinging behind her.

"Thank you for gracing us with your presence, Daisy." The General said it mildly, but somehow managed to engrave the sentence in sarcasm.

"Yer welcome, General," she said sweetly.

She swaggered her way up onto the stage, strode up the gangplank, and began to lower herself into the hatch. She was in up to her hips when, for some reason, she stopped lowering.

Daisy went still; her eyes widened in surprise. She twisted to the left. She twisted to the right. Stopped again. Looked confused.

Then alarmed.

"She's wearin' the ship," Molly whispered loud enough for everyone to hear.

A rustle of evil little giggles.

Daisy, a little panicked now, twisted rapidly to the left and right again, and then again, a great redheaded windmill. But she couldn't screw her body any farther into the hold of the small pirate ship.

"*Stuck* . . . Daisy?" The General asked idly.

Daisy jerked her head violently toward him. Her glare could have melted the windows of the theater.

It *did* rather look as though she were wearing a ship for a skirt, Sylvie noted.

"Jenny, Lizzie, if you would give Miss Jones a hand." The General sounded bored.

Lizzie and Jenny scrambled up the gangplank and knelt to push on Daisy's shoulders. Daisy sank a *bit* lower into the hatch, but her bosom effectively prevented her from going any farther. It lay on the deck in front of her and billowed up around her chin. She peered out from it, eyes bulging and glaring, cheeks scarlet.

"The hatch was cut to the measurements you gave to Josephine last week, Miss Jones," The General informed her.

Daisy's vehement response was muffled by her bosom. She tried to give her head a toss; it was all but immobilized between the pillows of her breasts. So she settled for flapping her arms and a making a rude hand gesture.

"One more good push should do it, girls," The General said, and Sylvie could have sworn his eyes had an unholy glint. "Tamp her down in there."

Daisy flailed her arms in vehement objection.

"On second thought, girls, we'd best pull her far enough up again so she can at least sing." the General allowed. "We've lost enough time out of the schedule as it is."

He reviewed his watch while Jenny and Lizzie tugged on Daisy's arms until her entire torso was visible again.

"All right, then! All aboard, maties," The General called, as though the wedging of Daisy was a minor inconvenience. "And I shall demonstrate the dance for you." He brandished a small cutlass. "It's a simple one. It requires a bit of this"—he made an unmistakable gesture with his hand and his sample cutlass, causing giggles—"and a bit of . . . Swordplay." And at this he winked.

More giggles.

Oh, dear God. Sylvie whirled about as though looking for an escape. *I can't do it. I can't,* can't *rub my cutlass like that. I'll sleep on the street.* Surely, please God, she wouldn't be required to—

"Daisy, when the girls have mastered the dance somewhat, *then* we'll do the song.

Just then Sylvie remembered she'd contributed a line of verse to the song. And . . .

Well, damned if there wasn't a small part—a *very* small part—of her that wanted to hear Daisy sing it.

Daisy, a fuming torso popping up from the deck of the ship, would be forced to wait her turn to perform. Sylvie half suspected The General had done this purposely.

"Josephine—the song please," The General ordered.

Josephine lowered her hands, and the merry burst of music sprang through the theater. The General clambered up onstage with the girls, and demonstrated with his own cutlass.

"And a one, and two, and *thrust* your sword and slide, slide, and turn and clash swords with your neighbor and *again* . . ."

And in this way he and Josephine took them through the song and dance five times. At last he decided to allow them to do it alone. He took a seat and called out the steps from the audience.

"Step, step, and *thrust* your sword—"

Molly thrust her sword right into Sylvie's rear. Sylvie jumped.

"Sorry!" Molly said *sotto voce,* eyes wide and contrite. "So sorry!"

Sylvie gave a shallow, cool nod, and kept up with The General's commands.

"Look lively, girls! And one, two, and turn and *thrust* and—"

Molly poked Sylvie sharply in the arse again, sending Sylvie nearly straight up in the air.

". . . one and two and I never said anything about hopping, Sylvie, and *slide* and four . . ."

"Lud, I *am* sorry!" Molly murmured. "I'll be more careful."

"I. Would. Be. Grateful," Sylvie murmured through a clenched jaw, as she thrust and slid.

"And turn, slide, and *rub* your cutlass, *rub* your cutlass, turn, turn, *thrust*—"

Molly thrust into Sylvie again. "Oh, I'm sor—"

Sylvie whirled around and clubbed Molly across the behind.

Molly shrieked and stumbled forward briefly, then regained her balance and swung her cutlass wildly at Sylvie. But Sylvie was quicker and smaller, and she dodged, bent, took calculated aim at Molly's ankles, and much to her satisfaction, down Molly went.

But Molly proved surprisingly nimble for one so plush. She was upright again in an instant, shrieking her outrage like a scalded parrot and wielding her cutlass like a club, and Sylvie parried expertly. The other girls flocked around them squealing encouragement and wagers.

But with one final parry and a clever and possibly unfair hook of her leg behind Molly's knees, Sylvie had Molly flat on her back and a wooden cutlass pointed at her throat.

They were both breathing like bellows.

"*Cor!*" Rose breathed.

Josephine had stopped playing the pianoforte long ago. All there was now was silence.

Which stretched as The General regarded the two heaving girls almost curiously, as if they were animals in a menagerie.

"Sylvie," The General drawled, finally. "May I have a word with you, please? Girls, the rest of you are dismissed for now."

Sylvie lifted the tip of her cutlass from Molly's throat and, with a small flourish, tucked it back into its tiny little sewn sheath. With dignity, all eyes upon her, she glided across the stage, trod lightly down the short flight of steps to the floor of the theater, and approached, chin up as if she was in fact the queen granting him an audience.

"Sack her." These were words disguised as a cough, and they came from the stage.

JP   JP   JP

Sylvie followed The General without protest into a room she hadn't seen before, and he closed the door decisively behind the two of them. It was another profoundly masculine room, the theme of the theater condensed in plush overlarge furniture, cigar-and-woodsmoke-permeated air, and lurid murals featuring explicit images of gamboling satyrs and nymphs.

The General halted and turned to her. "Let me begin by saying that I think Tom was dead wrong to hire you."

Sylvie stiffened immediately. "Are you going to . . ." What was the English term she had just heard? "Sack me?"

"'Sack you'?" He repeated, darkly amused. "No. That's not for me to do, Sylvie, as Mr. Shaughnessy hired you, and we *all* answer to Tom, ultimately. And he no doubt had his reasons; Tom has flights of brilliance, and flights of insanity, and fortunately the former typically outnumber the latter. I shall reserve judgment on which flight *you* happen to be though I do have my opinion. But you should know, Sylvie, that I'm on to you."

"'On to me'?" All the casual English expressions were making her more irritable, and were doing nothing to cause her cursed temper to curl up in a quiet corner. She wished the little man would come to his point.

He turned suddenly and paced almost restlessly across the room, a distance away from her. He stopped and idly fingered a tassel on a curtain.

Then spun about so quickly the tails of his coat whipped his legs.

"The Paris Opera, *Le Cygne Noir*." He said it as though accusing her of murder.

Sylvie's heart nearly stopped.

His face went slowly rueful, a little abstracted with awe. "You were magnificent."

Sylvie looked down the mile or so it seemed she needed to see into The General's face, and wondered distantly that there was never anything comic about this man, despite his near-miniature proportions. He never commanded anything other than respect.

She gave a short nod finally, acknowledging his compliment. She knew when she was magnificent, and when she was not, and she knew she *had* been magnificent in the performance he cited. A "thank you" would have sounded condescending, and The General seemed to know it, because he gave his own short nod.

"So what are you doing *here*?" he demanded.

"I came to London in search of a relative. I found them not at home. I hadn't any money or a place to stay. I needed to work."

"Why the false name, Miss Hat? Are you in trouble with the law? Are you running away from someone?"

She remained stubbornly silent.

He studied her a moment longer. "This"—he gestured, apparently to the White Lily, and everything about it—"is not a joke. I believe you greatly underestimate Tom Shaughnessy. He built this—*all* of this—from nothing. He couldn't even *read* when I met him, and he managed to accomplish this. I don't know if you could ever comprehend the kind of nothing Tom came from, but I assure you, what you see here amounts to very nearly a miracle. And if that's a joke, Miss Hat, then it's the sort of joke that keeps a roof over your pretty head and food in your stomach at the moment, isn't it?"

The General was succeeding in making her feel ashamed. He was right. She might not have indulged her temper, she might have tried a little harder to rein it in, she might not have whacked Molly with a cutlass, if he were Monsieur Favre conducting a ballet at the Paris Opera, and not an autocratic dwarf in control of a bawdy theater.

The General didn't seem to require a response from her, regardless. He clearly saw the answer he wanted in her face.

"A theater like this treads a fine line with the authorities; it's a delicate balance. If you endanger it in any way, or call undue attention to it . . . I shall see that you pay for it."

She looked at him, this man whose head barely reached the pit of her arm, knew a brief moment of indignation and the impulse to protest.

And then she could not help but respect his loyalty and admire it. She nodded shortly, accepting the threat.

"Do you think you can settle your differences with Molly in some fashion other than swordplay and in some other location than the stage during rehearsal?"

Damned if the man wasn't making her cheeks flame in precisely the same way Monsieur Favre was able to. She smiled, a way of collecting her own dignity.

"Mr. Shaughnessy says he is lucky in his friends." An attempt to disarm him.

The General wasn't to be disarmed. "Tom Shaughnessy's friends are lucky in him," he said curtly.

A respectful, if not warm, quiet ensued.

"What were you doing in Paris?" she asked suddenly.

"Drinking," he said grimly.

"Why are *you* here?"

"I like watching pretty girls dancing in very little clothing."

And then he grinned at her, a grin so Tom-like in nature she nearly grinned in response. "And I enjoy making audiences full of wealthy men happy, because it makes *me* wealthy," he added. "There's an art to that, too, Miss Lamoreux, whether or not you believe it."

She fought to keep her eyebrows from dashing upward in rank skepticism.

"There's a room at the top of the theater. Attic room. Spiders and dust in it, no doubt. I'll find a broom for you. And if you should . . ." He cleared his throat. "If you should care to . . . use the room when you are not required to rehearse . . . I shouldn't tell Tom. He would not approve of the waste of your time, as there's no money in it, Miss Lamoreux, and you are his employee. This theater does belong to him, and your time belongs to him as well, at least during the day."

The General was offering her a place to dance, should she care to use it.

He might simply have offered it as an attempt to rein in

her artistic temperament and thus make his own life more peaceful.

But she smiled softly at him anyway.

The General, she realized, did not precisely like her. But at his very soul, she suspected he was an artist. He probably understood what this would mean to her.

"Thank you, Mr. . . ."

"General," he said. "The. General."

ᗐ   ᗐ   ᗐ

Tom returned to the White Lily a little later than he would have preferred; still, the sun wasn't entirely high overhead. He expected to find the rehearsal of the pirate show in motion and to add his wisdom to the proceedings, should it be required.

All was silence.

He *did* see the pirate ship on the stage. The General had done a fine job, as usual. It was a magnificent little thing, cobbled together in a tearing hurry though it had been.

And suddenly he pictured, for an instant, what it might be like for a small boy to climb about the rigging and bound about the deck with a small wooden cutlass. How delightful it would be for a *crew* of small boys to—

What a startling thought. A foreign and *unprofitable* thought, and his mind seldom had room for those sorts of thoughts. He dodged it and moved briskly toward his office, when . . .

Wait. He peered more closely at the pirate ship.

There seemed to be a torso poking up out of the deck of the ship.

An *unmistakable* torso.

"Daisy?" he questioned tentatively.

"Tommy? Yer back, are ye then? They just . . . *left* me here, Tommy," she said plaintively. "Get me ou' of 'ere!"

He struggled not to laugh. "Are you . . . *stuck,* Daisy? In the hatch? What *happened*?"

She glared ferocious dark brown daggers at him. Her face was a dangerous shade of pink. "No, it's me new costume, Tommy," she said nastily. "The ship is. Now, ye bugger, get me out of 'ere!"

"Where's The General? Are you being punished? Were you naughty, Daisy? You can tell me." He was laughing silently now.

Then he had a horrible thought. "How long have you *been* there?" He realized any length of time like that would have been too long, so hilarity gave way to sympathy, and he loped up to the stage and took her by her arms, and pulled. Nothing happened, except that she squeaked when he tugged.

"Daisy, luv, I believe you've swelled up a bit. I don't want to hurt you, so we're going to have to cut you out. I'll go fetch a saw. Where's The General?"

"Scolding the new girl. She pinned Molly to the floor with a cutlass."

"*Did* she now?" Tom felt that increasingly familiar, marvelously slow, Sylvie-inspired grin spread across his face. "She can't be trusted with sharp things, you know. I imagine it was provoked."

"Oh, it was. I saw it all. Molly poked 'er in the arse with a cutlass. On purpose, now, mind ye. She 'ad it comin, that Molly did. There was quite a little battle." And Daisy, for the first time in an hour, smiled a bit.

Tom made a quiet mental note to himself; he was probably going to need to apologize to The General for the idea of a competition for Venus. Ah, well.

Wait: A *battle!* A pirate battle! A *female* pirate battle!

The audience would all but swoon for it.

Inspiration *did* arrive in the most unusual ways.

"*I* see the light in yer eyes, Tommy. Ye'd like there to be a battle up onstage." Daisy was watching him. She'd propped her elbows on deck, and propped her face in her hands. "Ye'd be askin' fer trouble, especially with this lot of females."

"You may have a point, but you must admit, Daize, it's a pretty splendid idea. I refuse to abandon it entirely. Now let me fetch a saw to get you out of here. Where have all the boys gone?"

"They scattered, too. Forgot all about me."

Those last four words, the very idea that anyone would forget all about her, Tom knew, was what terrified Daisy the most about the future. He still didn't know precisely how to reassure her; still, he knew reassuring her was tantamount to acknowledging a future without adulation. He gave her a brisk pat on one of her round arms and pushed himself to his feet. "I'll return in a moment, Daize. I promise I shan't forget you."

He leaped down from the ship into the aisle, which is when The General emerged from backstage then, Miss Sylvie Chapeau at his side.

Tom slowed, then stopped, and his eyes . . . feasted. She was dressed like a pirate, a blouse, a sash, those clever, just-shy-of-erotic pantaloons, a warm pink in her cheeks. The flush of the freshly scolded, perhaps. Or perhaps a flush fresh from a vigorous battle with wooden cutlasses.

The General saw Daisy still wedged in the pirate ship, stopped, and stared back at her.

"Happy, ye wee bugger?" she called to him, almost resignedly.

"It suits your eyes, Daisy," The General called in all seriousness. "The ship does. The brown. You should wear it more often."

If Tom was not mistaken . . . a blush crept in under Daisy's rouge.

"*You*"—The General whirled suddenly on Tom—"owe me an apology for your brilliant idea, Shaughnessy. *This*"—he gestured to Sylvie—"is what results from making Venus a *competition*. Cutlass battles."

"Can't be brilliant all of the time!" Tom confessed cheerfully. "It was worth a try, you must admit."

The General didn't appear to be in the mood to admit anything of the sort.

Tom turned away from the little man's glower and addressed Sylvie instead, as he much preferred to look at her.

"I turn my back for one moment, Miss Chapeau, and what do I hear? You've been brandishing sharp objects yet again." It was meant to be teasing, a crisp scold. He was surprised to hear his own voice emerge as nearly husky.

Sylvie looked swiftly up at him, read his eyes. Responded to what they saw there.

"I shall endeavor to be good, Mr. Shaughnessy." Her tone solemn, her eyes brilliant, her breath held in seeming anticipation.

"I imagine being good will be . . . a bit of a stretch for you." Never had a sentence been so redolent of innuendo.

And she laughed, a full-throated and feminine laugh, head thrown back.

The laugh splashed over Tom like a sudden burst of sunlight, washed all other thought from his mind. Tom was motionless for a moment. He just watched her with a faint wondering smile on his own face, and felt peculiarly breathless. Peculiarly light.

They both knew he'd not said anything particularly funny.

And then a silence followed that neither Tom nor Sylvie seemed to notice, as they were watching each other.

But The General and Daisy watched the two of them for a moment and then exchanged speaking looks with each other.

"I'll fetch a saw, Tom," The General said firmly. It sounded like a warning.

"A saw?" Tom repeated absently, turning his head with apparent difficulty toward his friend.

Sylvie Chapeau had turned her own head away at last and was now studying the murals, forehead slightly furrowed, as though she was trying to place precisely which gods were which, or was counting them.

"A *saw,* Tom. To free Daisy?" The General repeated patiently. "I'll fetch it. You might wish to know a message arrived for you whilst you were out. You'll find it in your office. And Miss Chapeau, will you please collect the rest of the girls so that we may conclude our rehearsals? That is, if *you've* no objections . . . Tom?"

More irony from The General.

"No objections," Tom said, cheerily enough.

Without another word, Miss Sylvie Chapeau turned to go. Tom watched her go, those sweetly narrow hips moving beneath her pirate trousers, those slim, elegant shoulders almost militantly squared, the little cutlass thunking at her side.

And when Tom turned for his office, he sang softly under his breath all the way there.

"Thrust your sword laddie, now thrust your sword . . ."

       ॐ   *ॐ*   *ॐ*

When Sylvie opened the door to the dressing room, a Tom-Shaughnessy-induced smile still faint on her lips, she saw all the other girls clustered together as if for protection, motionless and utterly silent. At first thought it was because of her, and she was tempted to hold her hands up over her head to show them she was unarmed and came in peace.

But then she noticed they were staring at something on Molly's dressing table, eyes fixed and bulging as if a wild animal had all cornered them in the room. Sylvie stood on her tiptoes to see what it might be. And saw . . .

Well, they had all received their share of flowers, ranging from flawless hothouse bouquets to sorry clumps purloined from flower boxes in drunken inspiration on the way to the theater. But these were . . .

Daunting flowers.

Immense roses, red as actual hearts and nearly as large, so vivid they nearly seemed to pulse, twined with lilies and ivy. Standing as high in their vase as a two-year-old child. Drowning the room in scent, as if their intent was to drug all the room's occupants.

"*Cor,* Molly!"

"There's a box! A little box with it!"

Molly snatched it up, slid a small triumphant glance and a matching smile toward Sylvie. Sylvie's dressing table was bare, whereas all the other girls' tables sported at least a trinket or two.

They all crowded snugly around Molly as she lifted the lid, and six pairs of eyes blinked when she did, and there was a collective catch of breath.

Inside was a pair of hair combs, studded with real pearls and sapphires. They were brilliant even in the indifferent lamplight of the dressing room.

Pearls and sapphires. They were the colors, of course, of Molly's fair skin and eyes. She would look like a queen with them tucked into her chestnut hair. The combs were another strategic little gift.

Molly slowly lifted them, held them up to her hair wonderingly, and stared at herself in the mirror. It was clear that her confidence of a moment ago was shaken; her bravado gone. Sylvie rather knew how she felt. For Etienne's gifts had gradually increased in expense and glory, until at last she was lifting out of boxes intricate jewels designed just for her, furred pelisses, things that so spoke of his wealth and power they managed to make her feel somehow both immensely important and much smaller all at once.

Sylvie's hand went up absently then, circling the wrist of her other hand. She rubbed at it gently. A peculiar reflexive gesture, as though she wanted to ascertain they weren't bound. She turned away from Molly's reflection swiftly.

"Yer new bloke sent these, Molly?" Lizzie asked. "When can we see 'im?"

"'E's only been but twice. But 'e took a box when 'e did," Molly said, trying to sound important, but still sounding half-awed. Even a little subdued. The theater boxes, as they all knew, were terrifyingly expensive to take, and only very wealthy men could afford the discretion they provided. And no one was ever certain precisely when the boxes were taken, for the curtains were drawn about each one during each show. "'E sends 'is man to meet me after the show, an' takes me to 'im. An' 'e's not '*alf*' 'andsome, I tell ye. 'andsome as Mr. Shaughnessy."

The faces of the girls instantly became skeptical, as if this was an impossibility.

"'E *could* be a bloody duke," Molly insisted. "And 'e's only kissed me but once. 'Ere." She pointed to her fair cheek. "'E jus' asks about everyone 'ere, and asks about my day, and listens to me talk and talk. Says 'e wants t' court me proper fer a time."

The room fell silent, as every girl in it wondered what it would be like for someone to court her proper.

෴ ෴ ෴

"*. . . send me, send me to my reward, hmm, hmm, hmmm . . .*"

In his office, Tom found the message The General had mentioned centered on the plans for the theater on his desk. He recognized both the seal and the handwriting, and frowned very slightly, a little puzzled but not terribly concerned, as he slid a finger beneath the seal to break it.

The words stopped his singing.

He stared at them, scowled at them a moment, absorbing the small unwelcome shock, breathing through it until it ebbed. He was faintly amused to realize that it ebbed more slowly than it might have a few mere weeks ago; risk was as native to him as breathing, typically, and he recovered from disappointments quickly enough.

It was an admission to himself that more was at stake now.

Specifically, the future of a small boy in Kent.

⚜   ⚜   ⚜

"The major backed out of the Gentlemen's Emporium, Gen."

Outside the walls of the Satyr room, the sounds of men rumbled more thickly than usual, which Tom found comforting. One of the boxes would be occupied this evening, too; a discreet note had been sent to Tom, and he'd arranged for Poe to escort the man in question into the White Lily theater.

"Mmm." The General grunted his own surprise. "Bit late to find another investor now, isn't it? Didn't you commit to the building?"

"He sent his apologies. But no explanation. And he hasn't been to the White Lily of late, has he? And he's been nearly every night for the past year."

"He *knew* he was about to back out, then."

Tom nodded grimly. So the major was avoiding him. Tremendously odd, and he couldn't conceive of a single reason why this should be the case, but it remained manageable as long as the other investors remained. And if Venus proved to be the success he anticipated it would be when they debuted it in a week's time . . .

Well, it would have to be a *very grand* success now to compensate for the loss of the major's backing.

Tom smiled. He was confident it would be a grand success.

"I peeked in at the workshop again tonight, Gen. The oyster shell for Venus will be smashing. You've outdone yourself."

"And in the footlights, Tom, it will be even more incredible," The General said confidently. "I've found a splendid paint—there's this bloke who has found a way to make it glow just so—a special ingredient, you see. And the fish, we'll have them swimming from the rafters . . ."

But Tom heard the recitation of The General's vision in terms of a list of expenses. He ticked off in his head the cost of the shell, and the fish, and the splendid paint, not to mention the costumes for the girls, and knew he would need an influx of fresh capital soon, even more than the healthy amount that flowed in nightly from the shows.

The fire leaped up, devouring a log—another expense, there, wood—throwing almost unnecessary heat into the room. But the fixtures and the murals always looked better in the firelight, and Tom and The General tended to keep it lit for that reason. Showmen, the two of them. He wouldn't begin economizing in that regard just yet. He thought he'd change the subject.

"I meant to mention this before, Gen. Veils. Do you think you could do something with veils?"

"Mmmm . . ." The General said appreciatively, tilting his head back. "Wonderful idea, Shaughnessy. In fact—well, picture this. The girls will be dressed as a harem, and—"

"I have a son," Tom blurted.

The General fell abruptly silent.

Tom didn't look at him. He felt very nearly embarrassed, as though he'd broken wind. He instead took a sip of his brandy, as if the admission had taken something out of him, and he needed to replenish.

A most pronounced gap in the conversation ensued. The General cleared his throat.

"This son. He's in Kent, I take it."

"Yes. Kent."

The exchange of confidences was not what their friendship was based upon; a benign and total acceptance of each other's strengths and flaws and a manly appreciation of all things female comprised the most of it, and an underlying affection based on nothing more than that they suited each other comprised the rest of it. This was new and delicate territory for both of them.

"And he's why you need . . . money? More than usual? It's not just for the Gentleman's Emporium?" was The General's next careful question.

"Yes. In part. Also, because I prefer to be rich." Tom was sounding a little testy now. The revelation had left him feeling a bit raw.

"A preference I share." The General's mouth quirked, an awkward attempt at humor.

Which led to an awkward silence.

"How did you get a son, Tom?" The General asked suddenly.

"The usual way, Gen," Tom said irritably.

The General laughed. "Sorry. It's just . . . well, who's the mother? Do you plan to . . ." The General paused, deciding this next thing needed to be said very, very gingerly. "Do you plan to marry her?"

"I know who she is. I just don't know *where* she is. She left him with her parents." Answering yet not answering The General's question.

Another silence fell.

Tom cleared his throat. "He's almost two years old now. And I find . . ."

He inhaled, and stood up, restlessly paced over to the hearth and stared up at the mural on the way. Satyrs having their way with nymphs, who showed every indication of enjoying themselves as well.

"I find that I want him to go to *Eton*," he said, half-wonderingly, incredulously. He gave a short laugh. "I want him to go to Oxford. For God's sake, I want him to sit in bloody Parliament. I was in that room with the investors, those men the other day, some of them smug, all of them wealthy and comfortable and ordinary. And now I think . . . I want my son to grow up to have a chance to be one of those smug men, I honestly do. I can make it possible if I have enough money. But . . . if the world knows I'm his father, his road will be difficult."

The General inhaled deeply, exhaled, taking in these words.

And not denying the truth of them.

"You're a good man, Tom," he finally said. It was inadequate, but it was about all that could be said.

Tom looked at The General wryly. "Hardly, Gen."

"I mean it. You're the best *I've* ever known, anyhow."

"Now that I can believe."

The General snorted softly, a laugh of sorts. And then he took a long draught of his tea, his own form of replenishment, and shifted his legs up onto a plump ottoman. Tea was the strongest brew he took since the days Tom had found him slumped against the wall outside the Green Apple Theater. He in fact took it so strongly that Tom could smell it from where he stood, even through cigar smoke and the wood being consumed by the fire.

"I've noticed there have been fewer duels lately, Tom. Smiling less?" Slyly said.

Tom gave him a sharp look. "Busy," he said curtly.

"Or just smiling *more* . . . at one particular woman?" As though Tom had said nothing at all.

At this Tom threw a sharp warning glance at The General. The little man was a bit too observant.

"You do know it's unwise, Tom," The General said. "For too many reasons to enumerate. The other dancers, for instance, would perhaps expire from jealousy or heartbreak. You could confidently anticipate a mutiny."

"I know it's unwise." Tom smiled crookedly. "My whole life has been an exercise in the unwise."

"But perhaps . . . well, you might make things easier for yourself if you . . ."

Tom looked at him expectantly.

"Oh, bloody hell. Never mind." The General sighed.

Tom absently worked his stiff fingers, bending them. Too much writing lately had made the old wound complain, even occasionally waking him up in the middle of the night, but there were plans and inquiries and ideas and permissions to be obtained before the dream of the Gentleman's Emporium could take tangible shape. Securing the backing of his investors was only a very small part of it all.

Odd how soft and amorphous-sounding the word "dream" was. So many practical things, bits and pieces, tangible things, nails, wood and pound notes and people, went into the making of dreams.

He rather liked all of it, the dreams, and the bits and pieces. He liked making it all look effortless. He liked giving jobs to people.

"He's too young to know who I am, Gen. The boy. And sometimes . . . well, I've begun to think I should just settle some money on him and quietly step aside."

The General rolled his eyes. "Ah, yes. That sounds like you. Someone who would 'quietly step aside.'" The General pointed at Tom's hand. "Tell me again how you got the scar? This theater?"

Tom stopped working his fingers, glanced down at them. "This is different," he said shortly.

The General apparently didn't believe he was qualified to argue this particular point. He was quiet, and after a moment he simply said, "So . . . harems, eh?" and stood, reaching for his coat.

"Have you heard of the story of Scheherazade, Gen?" Tom reached for his own coat.

And the two of them, immensely relieved to be talking of business again, prepared to plunge into the theater to greet their guests.

∂ℓ   ∂ℓ   ∂ℓ

After the evening's performance, back in the dark of the theater, Sylvie saw the girls take off out the door; saw the fine carriage taking Molly away, and turned once more to go up to her little room.

But she saw a light shining in Tom's office. Once again she couldn't resist the urge to peer in.

Tom lifted his head a little, frowned, then leaped to his feet, hand on what she knew to be his knife, and peered out.

She jumped back, hand over her mouth.

He went very still when he saw her. And said nothing for a moment, only dropped his hand from his knife. "You were peeking, Miss Chapeau."

"I wasn't," she said quickly. She was beginning to be tremendously sorry she'd given such a ridiculous name. She suspected he enjoyed using it for that very reason, and would have otherwise called her Sylvie the way everyone else did.

"You *were*," he disagreed firmly. "You did"—Tom broadly mimed furtively peering around a corner, then ducked back and put a coy hand over his mouth, eyes wide—"this. I saw you."

She tried, she did. But it proved impossible not to laugh.

"And did you see anything you liked while you were peeking?" he asked with all evidence of politeness.

Really, if a contest for flirting were ever held, Tom Shaughnessy had a duty to represent England.

"I saw a light, and wondered who it might be," she told him coolly.

"This is my library. It's where I work. You perhaps expected to see someone else in my place?"

He waited, and apparently decided just this once perhaps to not corner her into a response that would amuse him further. He sat back down at his desk and became brisk instead. "I've noticed that you and The General seemed to have reached a sort of détente. He doesn't like you, but he doesn't really like anyone, except perhaps me. And Daisy."

"One would think he likes Daisy least of all."

"One would think." His smile was enigmatic and swiftly gone.

There was a silence while they regarded each other. And then Tom made a self-conscious little gesture, smoothing a hand over his hair, pushing it away from his face. She found it oddly touching. Though he obviously reveled and took advantage of his splendid looks, it was clear he wasn't a slave to them. This little bit of vanity was clearly for her benefit, and it pleased her.

"Well? Will you sit down then?" He said it impatiently, in a rush, as though he'd actually issued an invitation and she'd been standing there mulling it in silence.

No, she thought. *Because that would be foolish, foolish, foolish.*

"All right," she said evenly, softly.

She looked back at him for a moment. His fingers were stained with ink, his shirtsleeves rolled up to expose strong and corded forearms. Long fingers, tapered, hands blue-veined and strong and tanned, that scar across one, white, drawn tightly at the edges. His shirt was open at the throat a few buttons, cravat dispensed with entirely, and she struggled to keep her eyes from peering at the opening to see whether his chest might be smooth, or whether, as on Etienne, hair curled there. Regardless, his chest was certainly broad and in the lamplight, a lovely shade of gold, a sort of tea with a hint of milk. Whether it was the quiet of the evening, the dark of the theater, the lack of other things to occupy her senses, everything about him, all the little details suddenly stood out in stark relief. The scar on his hand, his lashes, the faintest, faintest of lines beneath his eyes.

He noticed her regard, and she looked up sharply to meet his eyes.

"Who are you *really,* Miss Chapeau?" He said it winningly, coaxingly, with a grin. As if the sheer outpouring of charm would flood the answer right from her.

And this made her laugh. "I am merely a visitor to England, Mr. Shaughnessy, who was unfortunate enough to lose all of her money."

"When you first arrived, the General suggested you might be a . . . ballet dancer." He said the words the way he might have said "a native of Borneo."

She tensed a little with wariness, knowing The General had promised not to reveal her identity. Gave a pretty little laugh. "I wonder why he would think such a thing?"

Tom leaned back in his chair and regarded her for a disconcertingly long moment, hands linked behind and above his head, which only served to emphasize how very broad his chest was. She managed to look back at him evenly, eventually choosing to focus on his left eye, lest she go cross-eyed. She had the distinct sensation he was doing the very same thing to her that she was to him a moment earlier: inventorying her features.

And in the end, he looked more puzzled and a little uncomfortable more than anything else, which wasn't terribly flattering.

"Do you know how I met The General?" he said, unexpectedly.

"I cannot begin to guess."

"There's a theater in the East End—the Green Apple. Right rough little place. Perhaps you know of it?"

She gave a tight little smile. He grinned in response.

"No? Well, I got my start in theater there, you see, at the Green Apple. I'd worked at a pub by the docks, and met a fellow who ran a theater, and . . . well, anyhow I decided to create a show, pretty girls dancing. Dressed as flowers. Daisy petals round their heads." Tom circled the air around his face with a finger, illustrating. "Very clever, if I do say so myself. No one else had done anything quite like it, at least in the East End. And frankly, I very much enjoy pretty girls dancing.

"And, well, the first night of it, men came to the show, but not enough of them—the theater wasn't full. And the next time it was the same. The Green Apple's owner— well, he was right miffed, since he'd backed the show and was losing money. And I was getting right *nervous,* since the owner was a mad cove who would happily slit my gullet for losing his money."

He said this matter-of-factly, and Sylvie tried not to flinch. Just when Tom Shaughnessy had begun to seem human, he demonstrated yet again that he hailed from an almost entirely different universe from hers. A universe where one did business with gullet-slitters.

"Well, I stepped outside the theater when the show was over, and I was leaning against the wall, wondering whether to smoke a cigar, my very last one, and wondering what the devil I was going to do, you see, as I hadn't any money left, either.

"And then I heard this voice from somewhere down

around my ankles. A drunk, *slurry* voice. And it said—well, I *thought* it said; '*Organza*.'

"Of all things! So I looked down toward the voice and saw a . . . little man, slumped there against the wall. He was only about as big as a child, thin, but with a full beard. Filthy bugger. And he smelled like a gin still—like he'd been soaked in the brew and tossed there against the wall. One spark from a tinderbox would have sent him up in flames.

"So I said to this filthy bugger, 'I *beg* your pardon?' Because I'm polite, you see."

"Of course," Sylvie said, mouth twitching.

"And so the little blighter says, from down around my ankles"—and here Tom adopted slurry, surly tones. "I said *organza*, you bloody idiot! Hangs better, and you can nearly see through it in the . . . in the"—Tom hiccuped for effect—"*lamplight.* You've got all those girls in *muslin,* you damn fool. You *deserve* to fail.' "

Imitation concluded, Tom looked at Sylvie. "And then, after he'd said these *most* inflammatory things, this nasty little bastard slumped back against the wall. And I was certain he'd blacked right out, and I was about to go on my way.

"And then while I was staring at him, damned if he didn't stir and try to struggle to his feet. Rolling a bit, thrashing. It was taking him a good long while, so I found myself helping him up by the elbow."

Sylvie laughed, and yet something in her was surprisingly, oddly moved. She could imagine the contempt of another man for a small drunken man; she imagined most men would not have listened, would have walked away out of disgust. She wondered whether it was innate curiosity or a streak of mischief that caused Tom to do it. She imagined it was the sort of thing that would get him into trouble as often as it would prove lucky.

And strangely she found herself thinking: Etienne would never be subjected to such a situation in his life. Etienne would never have to make such a choice.

"So I help him to his feet, and the thanks I get is this. 'And if they're *flowers,* you bloody idiot,' he says to me when he's on his feet, swaying like a damn flower himself. 'They need to dance like flowers. *Erotic* flowers.'" He slurred the word extravagantly. "And I swear to you, Sylvie, right there, before my eyes . . . this little man begins to dance like—like—an erotic flower. Staggering about, waving his arms in the air." Tom waved his arms about in wide loops.

Sylvie burst into laughter; she couldn't help it.

Tom looked at her, smiling, savoring the sound, it seemed. "But even then . . ." He sat back in his chair. "Even then I could see what he was driving at." He said it wonderingly, as though even now he marveled at it.

"So I took this little man by the arm, which he didn't seem to like, as he kicked me in the ankles a few times, but his aim was poor, you see, because he was full of gin, and he missed more often than he struck home. And then I picked him up—Good God, but I cannot begin to tell you how the man stank—and he wriggled quite a bit. But I was able to hold him out from my body, seeing as how he's small and was very thin at the time, not at all the sturdy fellow you see now, and so he didn't manage to kick me in the baubles, though I assure you, he *did* try. And I got him back to my rooms, which were very near the Green Apple, and locked him into one, and let him dry out. Which wasn't pretty at all," Tom said grimly. "He kicked. He ranted. Said a lot of foul things about someone or something named 'Beetle' or 'Beedle' or some such."

"Did you say . . . Beedle?" This was intriguing. Sylvie knew of a Mr. Beedle, and if the Mr. Beedles were one and the same, this went a long way toward answering a few questions about The General.

"Beedle," Tom confirmed. "Never heard such swearing, not even during the war. But when The General was cleaned up and sober, he proved to be a right decent chap. Knew quite a bit about *organza,* in fact, and a lot more. He knew specific things—how to design costumes, beautiful ones. How to build sets. How to make wonderfully entertaining dances. As it so happened, our talents and tastes rather complemented each other. The Green Apple show became a great success with a quick change of costume and a few changes here and there to the dance. We had our erotic flowers. I gave him some of the money from the show. And he never took another drink."

She was quiet for a moment. "Kind of you to do that for him," Sylvie said softly.

"Perhaps," he mused. "I think it was more luck and curiosity than kindness. But then, as I've said, I've always been lucky in my friends."

"Friends like Biggsy the highwayman?" she couldn't help but say acerbically.

"I warrant most of the other passengers on the coach would consider it rather lucky that I knew him," he said with equanimity. "And Mick managed to drive *you* to the White Lily theater, didn't he? Though I haven't yet decided whether I consider that lucky."

He smiled at her; she narrowed her eyes.

"Which brings me to my point, Miss Chapeau. I've known The General for a good many years, and during that time I've learned to rely upon his decidedly singular body of knowledge. So if he believes that you're a ballet dancer . . ." He paused again. "I'm inclined think his opinion has merit."

"Based simply upon his opinion?"

"That, and because, Miss Chapeau, you're *clearly* not a lady."

She was struck silent.

"I beg your pardon?" She nearly choked out the words.

He continued, seemingly oblivious to her outrage. "I've known many women . . ." He paused, tilted his head back as though they were parading across the ceiling, and a faint smile turned up his lips. ". . . *many* women," he confirmed, wryly and emphatically. "Women from all walks of life. Some with titles, many without. And you are neither a lady nor in service. You are accustomed to being looked at and to getting your way, and you haven't the air of a married woman, because you haven't the air of someone accustomed to being . . . well, looked after."

As this was startlingly true, Sylvie was rendered speechless.

"You've a different sort of confidence. Something explains this, and I'm not certain what it is. So I've told you a bit about me . . . why don't you tell me why you're in London."

"I have come to London to visit . . . a relative," she offered finally, tentatively. He deserved that much, she supposed. "I found my relative unexpectedly not at home."

"Ah. So the . . . Chapeau . . . family was called away suddenly on urgent affairs? Perhaps they've gone to visit your cousins, the Pelisse family of Shropshire?" He asked it innocently.

She was tempted to laugh. Tom Shaughnessy was cleverer than she wanted him to be. She considered whether to confide in him: *My sister is married to a viscount, and apparently every opportunist in the land is claiming to be her sister, and, by the way, there's a large, grand reward for the apprehension of these opportunists. You might have heard, as the rest of London seems to have. And didn't you mention you needed a good deal of capital for your new theater?*

"Their house was dark, there were no servants about, no one to allow you in?" he pressed. "No one expected you?"

"No," she said shortly. "No servants."

"And you will leave the White Lily when your relative returns?"

She hesitated. "Yes."

He was quiet for a moment. "You don't trust me. I was hoping you would."

"No," she said shortly, with a little smile.

And to his credit, after a moment, he smiled too. "Perhaps you shouldn't."

The flirtation was back in his words, but faintly, as though he was forcing it there to make her feel more comfortable. An odd little silence passed by. He cleared his throat.

"If you are in any danger, Miss Chapeau, you can tell me. I shan't let you come to harm."

He said it almost gently. But with absolute quiet conviction. And she understood now that this sentence, this offer, had been the entire point of his interrogation.

"Thank you," she said finally. Feeling nearly shy.

Tom was watching her, his light eyes serious. "Your lover is a fool," he said swiftly.

"He is *not* a—"

"Yes?"

Sylvie squeezed her eyes closed, infuriated. And then something fought up in her: a reluctant amusement at and admiration for his ability to find precisely the right places in her pride and temper to prod in order to get her to confess things. She suspected it was his particular talent. She preferred not to think of it as her particular weakness.

She opened her eyes, found him watching her, but strangely, not smiling. "Your temper, Miss Chapeau, may one day be the death of you. But it makes you truthful, I believe. And your lover . . ."

He waited, to give her one more opportunity to deny the existence of a love. She wouldn't give him the pleasure of it.

"And your lover can't be a very good one."

She should have been outraged.

Instead: *Why?* She wanted to ask. *Is there something about me that betrays this? Are there different kinds of lovers? What makes a good lover? Do they scramble your wits and make you laugh one moment and furious the next and make you want to feast with your eyes upon the details of their faces?*

Or do they take you, then fall asleep leaving you unsatisfied more often than not, and tell you they love you as often as they remark about the weather and promise everything you've always wanted? Safety and peace and wealth and comfort?

She decided to call his bluff. "What on earth makes

you think so, Mr. Shaughnessy?" Her voice was light, nearly inviting.

The candle guttered in its glass globe. It changed the shadows in the room ever so slightly, made Sylvie aware that she had been sitting alone with him for perhaps too long.

"Because you are here with me right now and not with him."

The logic of this seemed unassailable when delivered in a voice low and soft, nearly husky. He sounded gently patient. As though he'd been waiting for her to arrive at the answer on her own.

And then she tore her eyes away from his and took a deep breath, and the spell he'd managed to weave with his soft voice drifted away.

"I told you why I am in London, Mr. Shaughnessy. It has naught to do with him. Or with you."

Another silence, as Tom seemed to be contemplating his next question.

"You admit you are an ambitious woman, Miss Chapeau."

"Yes," she said tersely.

"And your lover—"

"Will give me what I need." She completed firmly for him.

Tom dropped his chin once, almost a nod, as if taking this in. He took up his quill, twirled it absently between his fingers. And then he looked up, and his voice was dangerously gentle.

"But what do you *want*, Miss Chapeau?"

Such a simple question. And yet, for a moment, it shocked her motionless.

Jesus was buried and rose from the Grave: Justifying our faith that we too shall rise like him.

Romans 4:25 .... Job 19:25, 26

Man can be saved to Eternal Life: By repenting of our sin. And than pray to him in Faith Believing. Trust him, God's Son Jesus Christ as our sin bearer savior.

John 3:16 .... Joel 2:32

Salvation is a Free Gift: And not by works of righteousness.

Ephesians 2:8, 9 .... Isaiah 55:1

That if thou shalt confess with thy mouth the Lord Jesus, and shalt believe in thine heart that God hath raised him from the dead thou shalt be Saved.

For with the heart man believeth unto righteousness; and with the mouth confession is made unto Salvation

Romans 10:9, 10

For whosoever shall call upon the name of the Lord shall be Saved.

Romans 10:13

BIBLE DOCTRINE of SALVATION

God is our Creator: Man is his "crowning creation". It is in him we live, move and have or being.
Acts 17:28 .... Psalm 100:3

God is Love: He loves man with an everlasting love.
I John 4:16 .... Jeremiah 31:3

Man's reasonable response: Is to Love, Honor and Obey God.
Luke 4:8 .... Deuteronomy 10:20

Man deliberately disobeys God: All men have sinned.
Romans 3:23 .... Ecclesiastes 7:20

God is Holy and Just: God must punish sin. Sin's consequence must be paid. And that is Death.
Romans 6:23 .... Ezekiel 18:4

Since God is Love: He has an infinite love for man, who is his "crowning creation". So he sent his only begotten Son, Jesus Christ, to pay man's sin penalty.
Romans 5:8 .... Isaiah 53:10, 11

Jesus died on the Cross: For man he experienced death. His divine blood was shed, making atonement and redemption available to man.
I Peter 1:18, 19 .... Leviticus 17:11

Finally, she laughed shortly. "There's no place in my life for 'want' in and of itself, Mr. Shaughnessy. And I have . . . earned . . . *everything* I need."

"And *everyone* you need?" he said ironically.

She stood quickly. "I should retire and leave you to your . . . your work."

"Very well, Miss Chapeau. But wait—" He frowned suddenly. "There's something . . ."

She paused, hovered, uncertain, sat again.

"You've . . . a mark of some sort on your cheek." He narrowed his eyes, as if trying to ascertain just what it might be. ". . . allow me to . . ."

He leaned over the desk toward her, suddenly. She held her breath, willing herself not to turn her head as those silver eyes came closer, knowing this was a dare. And yet her eyelashes fluttered, her eyes began to close, then did close. Her speeding heart made her breath come short, and each breath took in the scent of warm man, and each breath scrambled her senses just a little more. She waited.

"I was mistaken," his voice came to her, softly, after what seemed an eternity. So close it seemed to be coming from somewhere inside her own body. The breath of his words brushed her cheek. "Perhaps . . . it was just a shadow."

Her eyes opened again in time to watch his long body lean slowly back in his chair.

She had expected him to be wearing a faintly victorious smile.

Instead, he looked just as unsettled as she felt; his face had gone strangely taut. His eyes were darker now. Slate.

Sylvie was conscious that her shoulders were moving more rapidly with her breathing. The pierce of anticipation ebbed, leaving behind a peculiarly acute disappointment. As though a gift proffered had been yanked away.

"I believe you've crushed your quill, Mr. Shaughnessy."

Tom glanced down at the mangle of feathers in his hand. And for a moment he looked genuinely puzzled.

And then he deposited his broken quill almost tenderly on his desk.

"Good night, Sylvie," he said softly. "And it might be wise to keep in mind that I'm not a gentleman. I'm not obliged to play fair."

Sylvie stood and whipped about so quickly that her skirts nearly tripped her. She took a swift step toward the door.

"And Sylvie—"

She paused but didn't turn around.

"Sometimes . . . sometimes they're one and the same."

She knew he meant want and need.

And oddly, it sounded as though it was a revelation to him, too.

CHAPTER ELEVEN

FOR TOM, days had always passed quickly, but with the addition of visits to Kent to his week as well as preparations for the Venus show—they now had a song, there was a dance for the girls to rehearse, and the oyster was nearly complete and required his opinion—the rest of the week was a bit of a blur.

He saw Sylvie Chapeau every day, stoically smiling and patting fannies, learning to be a water nymph. He kept a safe distance, at the foot of the aisle, considering what it meant to *him* to want and need.

Toward the end of the week as Tom was ensconced in his office, poring over expenditures for The Gentleman's Emporium and planning new ones, another message arrived.

He eyed it warily, but knew he had no choice but to open it: He broke the seal.

Lord Cambry offered his apologies, but regretted he could no longer invest in The Gentleman's Emporium.

The words struck like an adder bite.

He'd scarcely had time to register them when he looked up and saw a woman dressed not as a fairy or a pirate or a water nymph, but in a walking dress, a rather nice one, and it took him a moment to recognize Molly. It wasn't the sort of dress one could afford to have made on her salary unless one saved for a good, long time. He wondered, briefly, if the bordering-on-demure, well-cut gown meant that yet another girl had acquired a wealthy protector or a willing husband and had decided to retire from the White Lily.

The timing would be inconvenient regardless, given the role they planned for Molly in the Venus show. But Tom philosophically began considering alternatives— none of them Daisy Jones—even before he spoke.

"You've arrived early today, Molly, haven't you?" he managed cheerily enough.

"Josephine needed 'elp wi' the sewing, an' so I offered to come in."

Molly had never struck Tom as the type to volunteer for extra work. He frowned a little, bemused. "She needs additional help? Isn't Sylvie helping her with the sewing? All the costumes have been sewn—it's only mending, is it not?"

"Well, that's just it, Mr. Shaughnessy. Sylvie ought to 'elp, but now she goes off to meet 'er lover midday of late, so Josephine asked fer me help."

Time stopped. Tom's breathing stopped as well.

"Sylvie goes off to meet her lover?" he managed to re- peat levelly.

Molly fingered the corner of his desk. "Every day, middle o' th' day, Josephine says. Past few days." Molly was the very picture of innocence. "All of a sudden, like. She leaves early, and comes back mussed and red in the face, like, and she looks . . . 'appy. *Real* 'appy."

"Thank you, Molly." Tom breathed in, breathed out, to

get his lungs, his heart moving again. He didn't want to hear any more. "This is interesting."

She looks 'appy.

"Yer own needs bein' met, Mr. Shaughnessy?" Molly asked frankly.

"Mr. Shaughnessy?" she repeated, when he didn't answer her.

He did manage to get his mouth to turn up, but the motion was painful, seemed as unnatural as bending in half backward. "Your concern is touching, Molly, but I haven't any complaints in that regard."

"My concern *is* . . . touching, Mr. Shaughnessy," she said quite seriously, with a duck of her head. She trailed a hand provocatively across her collarbone, then, very casually, down across one full breast.

He was a man, after all; he watched the hand's entire journey. The trouble was, it all looked rather like choreography to him now.

"Thank you for considering my needs, Molly, and I *am* flattered. But I believe you know my policy." He said the words firmly, with a small smile to soften them.

Leave, he thought. He wanted her to leave so he could be alone with the alien sensation pressing inside his chest. If he didn't know better, he would have called it an ache.

He kept his voice level. "You said you believe Sylvie creeps off to see her lover rather than doing the work she was hired to do? And this is why you've decided to pay me a visit?"

"Oh, yes," Molly said somberly. "Right about this time o' day."

ॐ ॐ ॐ

The top half of the White Lily was divided into two spaces: one, the attic room in which Tom felt most comfortable, because smaller spaces made him feel more secure somehow. And the other, a room that hadn't been used for decades for anything other than storage.

When he arrived, he discovered the determined sunlight filtering through the dust-caked windows, creating a sort of twilight in the room; the floor, he noticed, had been swept, barrels and crates pushed aside to create a clearing. A stage.

Tom hovered behind in the dark hallway as she left her room, closed the door behind her, and furtively, hurriedly took the stairs up a flight toward the attic room, her feet touching the stairs lightly as a cat. Inexplicably, as the day was warm and the heat had risen to fill the upper rooms with a sultry density, she had covered herself in a cloak. A disguise?

Or did she spread the cloak over the floor so she could lie upon it with her lover?

His hands squeezed closed into involuntary fists, echoing what his heart had done at the thought.

Still, he followed her, taking the stairs as lightly as he could, and keeping his head down. What did he intend to do? Leap out and cry *"A-ha!"*

He should leave.

He couldn't leave.

And then, at last, the foreign tightness in his chest eased a little when all he saw was Sylvie.

She was standing in the middle of the room, head down, shoulders back, arms curved out from her body as though she cradled a great invisible heart between them, the fingertips of each hand just shy of meeting below her belly. Her feet were pointed out, her hair pulled back, combed smooth and pinned so tightly the sun glanced off it as though the surface was mirrored—sable with a sheen of fire.

The cloak had been folded neatly and set aside; he saw it. And she wore a dress that, scandalously, remarkably, exquisitely, exposed a length of elegant ankle and calf. The reason for the disguise, he supposed. Fragile, the skirt of it seemed to hover like mist above her calves, looking ready to flutter up should she move or breathe.

Her throat was long and white, so fair he could see the faint blue trace of a vein in it. It should have made her seem vulnerable; instead, everything about how she held her body at the moment spoke of power and intent.

And for a moment, it seemed, he couldn't know for certain whether the light radiated from her or came through the window, or if it was merely an agreed-upon exchange between Sylvie and the sun.

And then he noticed the smile. Faint, but so privately, confidently joyous Tom could nearly *feel* it. Nearly. It was both bitter and sweet, taut and rich, like the first bite of a plum, because he was certain he'd never worn that kind of smile, felt that kind of joy.

It was very like the smile one would give a longtime lover, he imagined.

The smile became softly inviting; she stretched her arms out toward some invisible partner, and balanced—floated—it seemed, on one leg.

Then she swiftly gathered her limbs together and pirouetted, rising all the way up on her toes, and like a dandelion caught in a breeze, covered the distance of that rough floor with leaping steps and turns, before stopping to arch backward, one knee drawn up, her body lithe as a ribbon. And he saw now that her dress was less a costume than very nearly a pair of wings, for it merely enhanced the sense that he was watching a creature of flight.

Mesmerized, Tom watched her, pressed back against the stairwell, breathing all but suspended, the better to hear, to feel her dance. He'd seen paintings of ballerinas before, but the dance itself never interested him; he'd considered it a conceit for those at court. And, of course, there wasn't any money in it.

But now, something like awe and panic warred inside him, and amused him distantly. Truly, he felt as though he'd stumbled, sober, across an actual fairy, the sort his Irish mother had so fervently believed in and feared, not the sort that he and The General swarmed the stage with to ribald acclaim. Sylvie no longer seemed to belong to the same species as he did; she didn't seem crafted of flesh and bone. Rather, suddenly she was made of fire or water, something that burned or flowed.

And Good God—just look at that. She could bend nearly in *half.*

Backward.

The prurient possibilities of this did not escape him.

He could almost hear the music Sylvie moved to in his head, could feel the story of it as she danced. He sensed, even through the pleasure on her face, that she was meticulously counting the steps off in her head, each placement of her foot precise and calculated as it thumped lightly on the floor in satin slippers, or left the floor to sail through the air briefly, though to the viewer it would all seem entirely artless. She hadn't mirrors to follow her movements; he wondered if she missed them. She must know from the way her body felt to her that the movements were correct, the way Josephine could play a song from feel.

And as he watched Sylvie's arms floating upward, rippling, her delicate neck tilted back, he knew this was beautiful; he in fact knew that "beautiful" was an inadequate word for it. This was artistry, and in a way he resented it. For in watching it he felt every bit of his own roughness, the roughness he had ruthlessly wrestled into submission.

And at the same time, he knew learning to dance like this would have required pain and sacrifice and endless practice, a superhuman determination. The determination of someone who was resolved to be something, anything other than ordinary.

A determination, in fact, rather similar to his own.

The pieces fell into place: the source of this woman's confidence, and her determination, perhaps, to move out of the shadows of the *demi-monde*. Perhaps she, like he, was beginning to understand the limitations of the shadowy place within society they occupied. And perhaps this was the reason she had taken a lover, no doubt a wealthy one.

He will give me what I need, she'd said.

Somehow, Tom had known from the moment she'd landed in his lap in the mail coach that this woman was far, far from ordinary. And now he realized why watching her wield cutlasses and pat derrieres . . . was rather like watching a unicorn pulling a plow.

Then again, he rather liked seeing Sylvie in her fairy wings. He rather liked seeing her dressed as a pirate and patting derrieres. Somehow, they all seemed simply aspects of her: the delicate, the ethereal, the magical. The dangerous, the wicked, the fearless.

Although he'd begun to suspect he'd rather like seeing her dressed in anything at all.

Tom watched, and knew the longer he watched, the greater the risk she would see him. And now he almost wished he hadn't followed her, for he knew the image of her dancing, of that smile, would haunt him. He felt nearly as conflicted as if he'd actually caught her with a lover.

And in a way, he knew, he had.

She looks . . . 'appy.

He backed slowly, carefully, down the stairs, wondering why he should feel guilty, why he should feel as though he'd been intruding, when everything in this theater belonged to him, including the room she'd cleared to become her own private stage. His own determination and passion had made it so.

He'd forgotten the final step that had always creaked just a little. And it made no exception for him this time.

ৡ৴   ৡ৴   ৡ৴

Sylvie stopped dancing, turned, swiftly alert, when the stair creaked.

And she froze, her throat stopped, when she saw just a flash of bright hair and an unmistakable pair of shoulders vanishing from sight.

ৡ৴   ৡ৴   ৡ৴

Sylvie arrived a bit late to rehearsal, shedding her ballet slippers and dress in her room in a frantic hurry, dressing in an empty dressing room, scrambling just in time to join the other girls onstage, her cutlass thumping against her hip as she ran.

The General had wanted to rehearse the pirates today, as he wasn't satisfied with them just yet. Everyone was already in place aboard the great pirate ship, and with a warning disciplinary frown at Sylvie for her tardiness, The General waved a hand at Josephine. The music began.

This was when Sylvie noticed Tom Shaughnessy standing at the foot of the aisle. Stern-faced, distracted. Determined, it seemed, to pass judgment. Sylvie suspected she knew why, and her heart lurched in her chest, making her feel, perhaps appropriately, just a little seasick.

The girls all clambered aboard the little ship and prepared to walk down the gangplank, brandishing their cutlasses. The General had wisely separated Sylvie and Molly, and though he lamented the slightly uneven row of girls—as Sylvie was just an inch or so shorter than Molly—he was more committed to keeping relative peace. Daisy had already squeezed down into the hatch—today, thanks to skillful sawing, she only needed a little surreptitious assistance from two of the girls, who tamped down on her ample shoulders with the balls of their feet until Daisy's great pirate hat finally disappeared from view—and Josephine began playing the bawdy sea chantey.

Two bars into the song, Daisy's pirate hat and enormous bosom popped out of the hatch, and, using her hands and struggling just a little, she hoisted the rest of herself out onto the deck more or less gracefully and launched into the tune, which was only enhanced by the fact that she was breathing a little heavily from her exertions.

*Now, thrust your sword, laddie, now thrust your
sword!*
Send me, send me to my reward!

Meanwhile, Sylvie, with the rest of the piratesses, dutifully pointed and thrust and rubbed her cutlass.

Given the gaiety of the onstage entertainment, Tom
Shaughnessy's stern face glaring up from the foot of the
aisle was tremendously jarring. Sylvie found herself unable to turn her lips up into the requisite smile. Grimly,
she felt as though she were dancing before her execu-
tioner.

The General had taken one of the front-row seats to ob-
serve; his feet were draped over the seat in front of him.

But even he jumped when Tom gave a sudden thump
with his walking stick.

"Josephine," Tom barked.

Startled, Josephine and everyone on stage stumbled to
a halt.

All eyes were on him, wide and expectant, waiting for
the suggestion or reprimand.

"*She*—" Tom pointed with the gold top of his walking
stick at Sylvie.

"Sylvie?" The General queried carefully, staring at
Tom as if he'd gone mad.

"Sylvie needs to be smiling."

In contrast to his orders, Sylvie found herself glaring at
Tom.

Who was studiously avoiding her gaze.

"It's really not that difficult, Sylvie." The General
jammed two of his fingers into the corners of his mouth,
pushing it upward. "It looks like *this*, a smile does. Give it

a try. I assure you, the gentlemen who attend our entertainments don't want to see a . . . a . . . glowering stick."

Giggles tinkled, as surely as if Josephine had run a brisk hand over the pianoforte's upper registers.

"Nor do they want to see a pack of females entirely bereft of grace."

This came from Tom, and so sharply it surprised everyone, including The General, if the abrupt elevation of his eyebrows was any indication. The girls onstage froze in astonishment, whirled as one to stare at him, all lower lips dropped wonderingly.

And Tom wasn't finished. "Some of you have decided you needn't try anymore." He landed a distinctly uncharitable gaze on Molly.

It occurred to Sylvie, with a peculiar warming of her cheeks, that the man had, in the span of a minute, singled her out for a picayune criticism, then promptly and vehemently come to her defense at the expense of someone else.

And he was still studiously refusing to look at her.

Tom Shaughnessy was *rattled*.

"Wot's '*beref*'?" Rose whispered to the girl next to her.

"'Avin' none," Lizzie clarified on a hiss.

"As in, 'Mr. Shaughnessy is nivver beref' of someone to warm 'is bed,'" Jenny elaborated, to show off her vocabulary skills.

More giggles.

Not from Molly, however. Molly was absolutely rigid— and magenta—with outrage at Tom's implied reprimand.

The General silenced all the girls with a potent saturnine glare.

"You are pirates, ladies, dangerous and *desirable* pirates.

And capable of dancing without colliding with each other or otherwise disgracing me." Tom's voice entirely lacked the glib lilt it normally had. He sounded decidedly peevish. "I've seen you do it. Please do it again."

He turned toward Josephine, who was watching him with mouth dropped. "Josephine?"

Josephine gave a start and all but fell on the pianoforte, fingers flying with more than her usual vigor, as if the rare reprimand from Tom Shaughnessy had been all for her.

The girls obediently glided down the gangplank brandishing their cutlasses, snarling charmingly, hips swaying.

Tom lingered for a moment, watching; he lowered his walking stick to the ground, twisted it idly about. Looking at, but not seeing, the stage. He gave one absent, half-hearted sort of thump, then stopped, as if his mind was too full to allow him to both thump and think at the same time. He lingered a moment longer.

And then he turned abruptly and strode toward his office.

Through the pianoforte music they all heard the sound of a door being shut a bit harder than necessary.

ஸ்   ஸ்   ஸ்

Sylvie could scarcely get through the rest of rehearsal without thoughts of what Tom Shaughnessy might do. Would he . . . "turn 'er off"? Would he "sack her" and leave her to her own devices in London? Would she have the nerve to blame The General?

And so when The General gave them leave to go, she lagged behind, watching the other girls vanish into the dressing room. She saw Molly cast a glance over her shoulder, toss her head again, murmur something to Lizzie.

And then, her heart thumping as surely as if Tom Shaughnessy were marking time with his walking stick, Sylvie made her decision.

She turned and marched stoically toward Tom's office.

He was shaking off his coat when she appeared in the doorway. He froze midmotion, one arm in a sleeve, one arm out, when he saw her. His cravat had already been tossed over the globe in the corner, as though he'd entered the office and violently rid himself of a noose at once.

It occurred to her then, very suddenly: *He wears a costume, too.* The man she saw leaning over his desk at night, shirtsleeves rolled up, two buttons open to free his movements—the stripped-to-essentials Tom was the real Tom Shaughnessy.

They stared at each other, frozen in an indecipherable moment, trying in vain to ascertain what the other was thinking.

"I saw you."

They both said it at once, in a rush. Both faintly accusatory. Faintly apologetic.

Tom's face was difficult to read. He turned from her and finished getting out of his coat, draped it over his chair carefully. Absently unbuttoned the cuffs of his shirt, then rolled them up, and she watched every motion, and watching him reveal his arms seemed somehow as intimate as watching him undress completely. It wasn't at all what a gentleman would have done in front of her during the day. She could not for a moment imagine Etienne rolling up his sleeves in front of her, though she had of course seen every inch of Etienne uncovered.

Tom looked down. He fumbled with the papers on his desk, then appeared to realize he was fumbling and stopped. He let his eyes wander over to the window, over to the bookshelves, back to the desk.

In other words, to anywhere she wasn't.

"Well, then. Did you come to see me for a reason, Sylvie?" Stiffly said, and formally. It sounded like a foreign language coming from him.

She watched him, unfamiliar with whatever this mood happened to be. She sensed he was unfamiliar with it, too.

"Are you . . . angry?" It was at least a place to begin asking questions.

He looked toward the bookshelf and appeared to consider this. As though he was having difficulty deciding precisely *what* he was.

"No," he finally said. To the bookshelves, not to her.

An awkward silence.

"All right," she said softly. "I'll go."

"There's no money in it," he said quickly. Abruptly. Almost as though trying to convince himself of something.

She remained where she was.

Which was when he did finally look at her. He nearly blinked when their eyes met, as though receiving a tiny shock. His expression was oddly . . . defiant. Uncertain. As though, for heaven's sake, he was being required to defend himself and didn't know quite how to go about it.

In short, Tom Shaughnessy was for some reason decidedly *uncomfortable.*

Not angry. Not glib. Not amused.

Not even flirting.

Sylvie stared at him, fascinated. She'd watched him gracefully and adeptly field highwaymen and earls and frightened women and incensed husbands with scarcely a ripple in his authority and good humor. And now . . .

Me, she thought. *I did this to him.* With her dancing, her own form of brilliance, she'd shifted his balance. She'd made Tom Shaughnessy feel . . .

Vulnerable. Ah, yes, that was it.

It pleased her inordinately. Particularly since this was a man who had made the ground beneath her feet feel nearly as wobbly as the deck of that ship that brought her across the Channel. From the very moment she'd clapped eyes upon him.

She suspected her eyes began to glow a bit, because that's when his eyes went dark and something like firm resolve crossed his face. He took two decisive steps toward her.

Which made her suck in a nearly audible breath and take an almost imperceptible step back.

Which made his mouth twitch just a little.

It took every bit of her courage to hold her ground as he slowly closed the distance that remained between them, until he stood so close that the heat of his body and the singular scent of him wound her in a cocoon. She should have known a man this wicked would smell like paradise: tobacco and soap and some hint of spice. Sweat, just a little. Clean linen.

And the unmistakable, most singular, subtle scent of all—desire. She knew the scent. For she was not, as he had guessed right from the start, an innocent.

It was the first time, however, that she had gloried in this.

Words. I need words. Words to parry with and to build

a net of safety with. "Do you see something on my cheek, Mr. Shaughnessy?"

The words were, unfortunately, a nearly breathless rush of sound. Her speeding heartbeat was making her blood ring in her ears.

It didn't appear as though he'd even heard the question.

"I believe I mentioned that I'm not obliged to play fair, Sylvie." He said it softly, his voice low and level. It was a warning. An apology.

And a dare.

And it was the last that made her determined to stand her ground.

Even with her speeding heart sending the blood whooshing in her ears and all but freezing her lungs. Even as the intent became very clear in the set of his jaw, in the heat of his eyes. Even as the want in her rose so fiercely that she thought she would simply die if this time he didn't . . . if he didn't . . .

And now he was so close she could see the facets of silver in his eyes, the fine creases at the corners of them, like the rays of stars.

But when his lips touched hers she saw nothing more. Her eyes closed as the kiss detonated in her.

So very nearly painful in its sweetness. As though she'd been cracked gently open, only to discover she was full of nothing but brilliant light.

And then it was over. Her eyes fluttered open to discover why.

She saw that Tom had taken a step back from her. His silver eyes had gone pewter-dark, stunned. For an instant, they were motionless together. Assessing. Reassessing.

For with one near-chaste kiss both had managed to

strip themselves of pretense and combat and flirtation and all the other little things they used to defend themselves against each other. They were suddenly equal. And equally uncertain.

A moment later, one of them became certain, and naturally it was Tom.

He stepped swiftly toward her; his hands came up, held her face lightly. A statement of intent. And like this, for the span of several breaths, he waited. *Not obliged to play fair,* he'd said to her. And even now, she knew he wasn't playing fair: For he was forcing her to choose.

And she could have twisted away from his touch, or taken a step back. It would have been such a simple thing to do, a wise thing, perhaps.

Instead, when his face at last came to hers again, she exhaled softly, in relief or pleasure, she knew not, and angled her head to meet his lowering lips with her own.

Sylvie hadn't known a kiss could begin like this: as scarcely more than a sigh of a touch, as another pair of lips brushed soft as breath across her own. But this was how they learned the shape and texture of each other; this was how, this was why, little by little, her bones became molten, and she murmured his name.

And then Tom nipped very softly at the lush curve of her bottom lip, brushed, lightly, lightly, with his lips, the corners of her mouth. Mesmerized, caught up in the delicacy of it, Sylvie at first allowed him to lead this dance, to caress her with his lips only, until the tension in her pulled tight as a crossbow, and she could no longer bear it. It was she who parted her lips, who touched her tongue to his lips, inviting him in.

He made a sound low in his throat when she did, and

his hands stroked over her cheekbones, trembling, coaxing her head back just a little so he could take the kiss deeper, the pads of his fingertips rough, his touch gentle against the skin of her jaw. Dizzying, the taste of him, the textures of him, the heat and velvet of his tongue and lips. She fumbled for fistfuls of his shirt for balance, pulled herself closer; beneath her hands his hard chest rose and fell swiftly, and she felt against her thighs the hard, hard swell of his erection. She shifted herself to fit herself tightly against him, heard the sharp intake of his breath when she did. Excitement spiraled drunkenly in her, demanding appeasement. She was of a mind to satisfy it; she thought, in that moment, she would have done anything at all to satisfy it.

It was then the kiss grew fierce, each of them battling to give and take more. Tom's palm drifted down from her cheek, spread wide; brushed against her breast, lightly, lightly across her already achingly taut nipple. His touch split through her like lightning. She arced from it, her breath caught, jagged in her throat.

And as though they had both just received confirmation of potential grave danger, they went still. His hand risked nothing more; he dropped it to his side. And the kiss ended. Not abruptly, but as though it had come to its choreographed conclusion.

Leaving behind the harsh rush of breathing, the musk of desire fanned, interrupted. Confusion.

In silence they regarded each other across this new and treacherous terrain they had created. And they didn't speak, but Sylvie wasn't conscious of the stretch of time; it could have been an eternity; it could have been mere minutes. The kiss had upended the universe, and she seemed no longer ruled by time at all.

"You have another rehearsal, Sylvie," Tom's voice was a little hoarse. He cleared his throat, and added, "If your legs will hold you up."

Said as if mundane words could restore things to the way they had been.

She could still only gaze dumbly back at him. Rendered entirely new by one kiss, she had no language yet with which to speak.

When she said nothing, his faint smile faded completely, and he ducked his head, looked at the floor. His shoulders were still moving, his breathing still unsettled, as surely as if they had indeed danced a whole ballet together. She watched him, bereft of speech, both gratified and a little frightened that he was so clearly shaken, too, this man who had no doubt partaken of a veritable pageant of lovers from all walks of life from the time he'd been able to . . . thrust his sword.

It merely proved there was something between them that would demand resolution, regardless of what was wise or safe.

And then Tom looked up, as though he'd found a decision on the floor.

"My room is at the top of the theater, Sylvie, as you know. You'll find me there . . . most nights."

And he turned and left her, closing the door quietly behind him, as if to leave her alone with those words.

Most nights. The words sank home.

And when they did, she almost laughed. She almost cried.

If she'd had something to throw, she might have thrown it at the door.

And this was Tom Shaughnessy, forever causing her to feel everything she possibly could feel all at once, and in so doing making her feel more alive, somehow, than she'd ever felt before. It infuriated her, because she didn't want to feel . . . *alive.*

She needed, in the end, to feel safe.

And nothing, *nothing* about this man was safe.

Most nights.

She almost cursed him for leaving the choice in her hands. A fine time for Tom Shaughnessy to pretend he was a gentleman.

CHAPTER TWELVE

SYLVIE DIDN'T SLEEP. She tossed this way and that in her narrow bed, marveling, resenting the fact that her body seemed to be mutinying against the discipline she'd imposed upon it for years. It wanted something that made no sense and had no order or purpose.

He would shoot the heart right out of a target, he knew how to use a knife for something more sinister than slicing cheese, he might very well be keeping a mistress named Kitty in Kent. *What does it matter?* Her body wheedled. *What does any of that matter? Take him. Take him. Take him.* Her body wanted Tom Shaughnessy's hands and lips upon her skin, wanted his body covering hers. It was as simple as that.

And so she but sleepwalked through the rehearsals the following morning, smiling, bending, patting bums without feeling them, eliciting The General's approval for once. "Thank you for not pulling a face when you pat Molly, Sylvie!"

She'd joined Josephine for an hour or so to repair fairy dresses and gossamer clothes for nymphs and pantaloons for pirates, driving needles into them to stitch their wounds closed, and absently wished the solution to her own troubles was quite so simple. A wound had not been opened in her by the kiss. It was more like a portal. She didn't know where it led, she hadn't known it was there, and she couldn't close it again. Her choices were to walk away from it, knowing always it stood behind her, missed.

Or to walk through it.

Or to lose herself in dance, where everything was choreographed and planned and made perfect sense, where discipline was required to make beauty, and not consider it for an afternoon.

She excused herself from Josephine early, offering no explanation, and left for her attic room to dance away her thoughts, if she could.

And now Sylvie stretched and balanced, arms floating out straight like wings aloft on a current of wind, one leg outstretched. A perfect—no: nearly perfect—arabesque. She could almost hear Monsieur Favre's voice in her head. *Mon dieu, you are dancing, not pulling a plow, Sylvie.*

She arched her back a fraction of an inch, extended her arms forward aaaand . . . *there*. That was perfect. She could feel it.

"What do you call *that*?"

Sylvie congratulated herself on not toppling over. She nearly flinched, but when she heard the voice, she was proud she managed to do nothing more than blink.

"Ballet," she said simply, to Molly. As though she'd been expecting to see her all along.

Sylvie drew her arms down, dropped her leg, curved her arms above her head and dipped into a *plié* to stretch her muscles. Her body knew the position from feel, could create the movements of a dance the way a musician's fingers could find a song by memory. Still, she wished for a mirror and a barre. She almost wished for Monsieur Favre.

Mostly she wished—though this was probably the most futile wish of all—that God would roll back time to the point just before Molly had discovered that Sylvie danced at the top of the theater, and then perhaps knock her unconscious.

She imagined Molly had followed her here, just the same as Tom had. Soon the bloody attic would boast as much traffic as the bottom of the theater.

"'Oo would want to watch ye . . . squat?" Surprisingly, Molly didn't sound entirely scornful.

"Princes," Sylvie said idly. "Kings." She moved her feet and arms into fourth position. *Relevé.* Still, her heart was beating a little harder than usual with the effort to sound nonchalant.

Molly snorted.

It was the snort that made Sylvie do it. She stood *en demi-pointe* and thrust her arms up over her head, then spun in a dazzlingly effortless series of *ronde de jambe* turns across the room, the room blurring in circles before her eyes. She concluded *en attitude croissé,* then arched her back and sank into a kneel; her body, she knew, looked as soft as folding velvet.

She rose once more, her face expressionless, and assumed third position.

A moment later she flicked a glance at Molly.

She saw in Molly's face longing, and an impotent sort of fury. A helpless admiration that no barbs or amount of pride could ever hope to disguise.

Sylvie knew a deep shame. It had been unworthy of her, unfair, her cocky demonstration of something that had taken her years of sacrifice and work to render effort-less. Her own pride had made her momentarily cruel.

Molly was flushed. She swallowed and looked toward the window, studying it. "Wants cleaning," she muttered.

"Mmmm," Sylvie responded. She returned to her exercises. She lifted one arm over her head in a gentle arc, raised the other lightly across her waist. From fourth position she would—

"Why . . . why do ye do it? So men will admire ye?"

Sylvie paused and looked at Molly, who was struggling for understanding through her own pride. The question was asked in all seriousness.

"Because . . . No. So that *I* will admire me." It was an answer, but only in part.

Molly was quiet again.

"And is ballet why ye've got no—" Molly gestured with her finger to her breasts, one at a time "—t' speak of?"

It was an entirely serious question. Sylvie didn't know whether to laugh or sigh.

"It might be," she allowed at last. "Did you follow me here, Molly?"

Molly said nothing for a moment. "I thought . . ." She turned, didn't complete the sentence. She instead wandered across the room, found something fascinating about an old barrel, studied it with her back to Sylvie.

"Why do you dislike me?" Sylvie thought it might disarm her to be direct.

Molly turned to her, and Sylvie was slightly amused that she didn't deny it, and Molly had a half-admiring tilt to her mouth. She actually seemed to be giving the question some thought. As though she wanted to give precisely the correct answer.

"'E looks at ye. *Really* looks." Molly looked away from Sylvie as she said this. "'E doesna see the rest of us. Never 'as," she added, half-bitterly, half-amused.

"Who?" Sylvie asked. Though she suspected she knew, and something inside her gave another grand leap.

"Who?" Molly scoffed. She might as well have added, "you fool," for that was precisely her tone.

She didn't complete the sentence. Sylvie didn't ask her to.

Molly studied Sylvie. There was a resigned twist to her mouth, and wry pain, suppressed, in her voice. "'E's the best man I've ever known."

Sylvie was struck silent. It would never have occurred to her to describe Tom Shaughnessy in quite that way.

"What of your lover?" Sylvie asked gently. "The one who is as handsome as a duke?"

Molly paused, and then her mouth twisted again. "'E's a man." A lift of the shoulder. And the faintest hint of scorn, for herself, or for her lover, Sylvie wasn't certain. 'Even *'e* asked about ye. Said ye looked . . . wrong." She looked half-pleased, half-troubled by this assessment. "'E wondered why ye were 'ere at the White Lily at all. I told 'im ye'd a lover right 'ere at the White Lily, that was why," Molly said half-casually, half-spitefully. And tossed a glance over her shoulder again.

Uncomfortable, suddenly, with the drift of the conversation, unwilling to engage in any sort of confirmation or combat, Sylvie touched her hand to a barrel for balance and dipped into a *plié*. She allowed Molly to watch her. She imagined she did look wrong onstage, despite her best efforts to sway and bend and pat derrieres. Odd, but she was a little stung by the criticism.

"Is it difficult to learn?" Molly said. She said it casually. "This way of dancing?"

Brutally difficult. It takes everything from you, it requires all you have, it will make your feet ugly and your body thin and powerful and you will never know a moment when a part of you does not physically ache. Only a very few are truly wonderful, and I am the best, the very best, and I worked *to be the best.*

Molly sought the answer in Sylvie's face.

And Sylvie thought she saw the faintest traces of a bruise remaining below her eye on that fair, smooth skin, the mark left by Belstow's hand. It was the price Molly had paid for living so men would admire her.

And then Sylvie understood then that her answer to Molly had been almost unfairly untruthful.

For she had committed her whole self to the dance in order to have a life other than ordinary. In order, in many ways, to attract a man like Etienne, who would give her a future so different from the one Claude now lived out, with its careful, spartan economies, tawdry memories, resigned to the loneliness and bitterness of living out her days in the twilight of society in a tiny apartment with an intelligent, foul-mouthed parrot.

In short: Sylvie had done it so men *would* admire her. She had grown to love the dance, but the reasons she had committed herself to it were twofold and inextricable from each other.

Still: She knew to own such a skill was to own magic and power.

She gazed at Molly and couldn't believe what she was about to say.

"Would you like me to show you how?"

CHAPTER THIRTEEN

A MIDST HIS PLANS for the Gentleman's Emporium was correspondence from the man who was to provide mirrors for the dressing rooms, and that afternoon, while Sylvie danced in the attic Tom fished it out, smiling to himself. He had a marvelous idea. It involved mirrors.

And then he saw another missive centered on the plan in the middle of his desk. A different seal, a different handwriting.

But Tom knew what it would say even before he opened it, and the smile disappeared.

Ↄ   *Ↄ*   *Ↄ*

"Viscount Howath backed out," Tom told The General before the evening's show. "He sent a message today."

It was odd, this one-by-one backing out by his investors. Like death by little\cuts, and highly uncharacteristic of this group of men, who had been friends and patrons for some time now. And *none* had been to the theater lately. He hadn't seen them about town.

Which could only mean they were avoiding him.

It was the sort of thing he found maddening. He could persuade, he could cajole, he could convince with facts and charm. He would happily—perhaps not happily, but at least logically—accept a reason for backing out at a very inconvenient moment. He could deal with *anything* directly.

But he loathed the quiet and evasion. He considered it cowardly, and there was nothing he could do to combat it. It was inexplicable, and it was difficult not to attempt to ascribe it to a single cause.

And yet he couldn't think of one.

He was distantly amused. Not since he was a small boy had everything in his world seemed so precarious. And odd how that even as one dream took shape, began to crumble in his hands, caused him to scramble to salvage it, something else presented itself, and it was this, too, that made his world seem more precarious than usual.

He'd thought to solve this yesterday, with a kiss. He'd kissed women before, naturally, and enjoyed it; kisses were typically preliminaries to very pleasant foregone conclusions. He'd imagined, before he kissed Sylvie Chapeau, that kissing her might at last restore balance to his world. Desire, once indulged, inevitably faded, and curiosity, once indulged, ceased to plague. She had been both—curiosity and desire—since she'd landed on his lap and poked him with a knitting needle.

He hadn't known that from the moment he'd idly touched her that touching would simply never be enough. And he hadn't known a single kiss could become howling, impatient hunger that robbed him of sleep and also made him want to lay the moon at her very feet.

Well, if he couldn't bring down the moon for her, he would begin with . . . mirrors. He smiled a little. She would see them soon enough.

"Have you ever been in love, Gen?"

The General's head snapped toward him. An irritated dent appeared between his eyes.

"Good God, Tom, how much of that brandy have you consumed? Are we going to do this every evening now, like a pair of girls? Exchanging our 'hopes and dreams'?" he mocked in a girlish voice. "I want none of it."

Tom laughed silently. "I want to know, Gen."

"Are you wondering whether *you're* in love, Tom, is that it?" The General said slyly. "Why don't you just say it?"

Tom stared at him evenly. "*I* found you filthy, drunk, lying on the street—"

The General shot him a black look. "Good God, but you play dirty, Shaughnessy."

Tom shrugged cheerfully.

The General sighed. "All right. Yes. I've been in love."

"And?"

"It makes you feel ridiculous, helpless, awkward, glorious, and immortal." The General sounded downright surly, and as though he was ticking off a list. "Happy now?"

"And?" Tom urged.

A long pause.

"She thought I was too short." He said it lightly.

Tom felt the words as surely as if a tiny knife had twisted right into his own heart.

"You're the biggest man *I've* ever known, Gen." He made sure he said the words lightly, too.

"And that doesn't surprise *me* in the least."

Tom laughed. Smoothly, he said, "So shall we do a harem bit in a week or so? I think Daisy might make a splendid centerpiece for the harem bit."

"Daisy might make a splendid Christmas ham," The General muttered darkly.

"Oh, you might be right. Pink, and plump, and warm, and succulent . . ." Tom mused, drawing each word out, mischievously, deliberately.

Tom noticed that The General's ears went decidedly pinker with each word.

ঞ   ঞ   ঞ

A day away from an incendiary kiss and a good night's sleep after last evening's show made Sylvie feel much stronger. It in fact seemed downright possible not to think about Tom Shaughnessy for entire minutes at a time.

Until she arrived that afternoon in the attic.

She stopped at the top of the stairs, nearly blinded by the dazzle. It took her a moment to realize why.

Mirrors. A series of mirrors had been propped along one wall, each tall and rectangular.

And the sun came through brilliant now, nearly blinding, striking light from them.

The windows of the little-used room had been scrubbed clean, both inside and out. One of them had even been pried open, and a breeze had pushed its way in. As this was London's East End, a number of unidentifiable and objectionable smells came in with it. But a breeze would be lovely on the back of her neck as she danced.

Sylvie put her hand to her cheek; her heart gave a sudden *grand jeté* of sweet, strange joy. She was breathless with the surprise of it and didn't know why. She'd been given gifts before. Etienne showered her with gifts. Most of them jeweled or scented or lushly crafted of silk or fur or velvet.

But when she looked, she saw her awe reflected in Tom's gift to her, those mirrors.

Six of them, spanning one side of the room. It was perhaps the first gift she'd ever received that was specific to her, that some other woman would not have been just as happy to have.

And she studied her face, for it was an expression she'd never before seen on it, and it was like seeing a vivid, joyous stranger who might just be related to her. And it made her wonder about Susannah. Whether living a different life would have given her sister different eyes, whether they would be bright with curiosity and joy, or dull with complacency. Whether they would be more or less knowing than Sylvie's, more or less kind.

More or less awed by a simple, perfect gift from a beautiful, dangerous man.

There's no money in it. Tom Shaughnessy, gaudy on the surface, shrewd penny-squeezer who slept in an attic beneath, had decided to indulge her gift, anyhow.

There was a creak on the stairs, and her heart lurched. She whirled.

Somehow, she didn't want to see him just yet. And somehow it seemed unlikely he would seek her here to witness a response. She wanted to be alone with the fullness of her thoughts, to decide what it was she wanted.

Wanted. Simply to take something because she wanted it seemed a foreign concept, and her mind fumbled at it like a child attempting to pick up a toy too big for its hands.

Sylvie turned toward the stairs and saw nobody. But still the footsteps creaked up. Slowly, steadily up.

Which is when she realized it must be The General if she couldn't yet see the top of his head.

And it was.

"Well," he said, when he saw the mirrors.

The word was full and eloquent. The General was no fool, naturally. She would not have been able to obtain those mirrors and haul them into the White Lily on her own.

She gazed at him, eyebrows lifted, waiting for the next words.

"You've transformed the room quite a bit since I saw it last," he said finally. "You . . . hadn't mirrors." Again, meaningfully.

"No," she said carefully. Waiting for the next, more specific question. The one she didn't want to answer. "I hadn't mirrors."

The General's eyes, she decided, were decidedly too shrewd, too knowing. She suddenly realized she knew how to deflect that gaze.

"Do you happen to know a Mr. Beedle, General?"

Ah, and the result of that question was deeply gratifying. Those sharp eyes flew wide. Hectic color flooded his cheeks. He blinked rapidly several times.

Then all of it disappeared—the blinking, the color, the wide eyes—as he gathered his composure.

"Why?" he demanded curtly. And then: "Do you ask?" he completed, as if this would make the question more polite.

She drifted across the room, viewing herself in yet another of those mirrors. She felt as though she wanted to see herself in each one.

"Because I once knew of a Mr. Beedle, an English choreographer, very talented. He visited the Paris Opera, and we danced for him. He married one of his ballerinas, I believe. Maria Bellacusi. She was quite gifted, too. I lately heard he worked in the English court. But ballet is not so popular here in England."

"No." The General narrowed his eyes. "Not so popular."

"Just at court. For the king."

"Yes. Just at court. For the king."

Sylvie smiled at him and tilted her head. "You love ballet, perhaps. But not . . . ballerinas."

The General let out a startled bark of laughter.

And then he paced a bit across the room, almost as if taking the measure of it, the bright sun counting off the shiny buttons on his coat. He turned to look at her.

"It was more, Miss Lamoreux . . . that a ballerina did not love me."

Honored and startled by the confidence, Sylvie was quiet for just a moment, but made certain to speak before he felt awkward.

"Did you come to pay me a social call, General, or to

tell me I am needed somewhere else in the theater?" she said to him.

He clasped his hands behind his back. "I came, Miss Lamoreux, because I have an idea."

He said this with all appearance of dignity, but she could see the anxiety in the clasping of those hands. And what very much looked like . . . hope . . . taut in his face.

"An idea?"

"For a . . ." he cleared his throat. "For a ballet."

ঞ   ঞ   ঞ

"I meant only to protect her."

Claude Lamoreux and Guillaume the parrot had been reunited. From a perch on her shoulder, Guillaume every now and then gave loving nibbles to Claude's ear. Claude sat, pale and distraught, dabbing at the corners of her eyes, across from the Viscount and Lady Grantham. Her hair was dark, with threads of silver running through it at the temples. Eyes very large, very dark, puffs of fatigue bulging beneath. Grooves were worn into her face on either side of her nose. Time was drawing her face downward; she would, in a few years, Susannah could see, have laps of skin on either side of her mouth. It looked as though life had not been easy, on the whole, for Claude Lamoreux, who had never truly been pretty and who had never married.

"I feared what would become of Sylvie if she knew the truth of her life. If Etienne, her lover, knew the truth of her life."

Susannah knew she should be more worldly, but really,

the use of the word "lover," as though it were "settee" or "teapot," would take a bit of getting accustomed to.

"He wants to marry her, you know, and she will have a good life, a much better life than ever I had or could ever give her. He is a prince. Of the House of Bourbon."

Claude could not entirely disguise a very small bit of smugness in this. A prince certainly outranked a viscount.

"So I burned the letters you sent, Lady Grantham. I am sorry, Lady Grantham. I was afraid, both for Sylvie and for myself."

Susannah had been torn between wanting to depart for England immediately in search of her sister and wanting to wait for Claude, but the shipping schedule ultimately made their decision for them. It would be days before a ship could take them home. And so they sat now in the room in which Sylvie, her sister, had lived for almost her entire life. Small as a closed fist, the apartment seemed, careful years of economy epitomized in the plain worn furniture and carpets, with one bright window letting light into the parlor, landing a beam on Guillaume's perch. He clearly had the run of the place, as Susannah could see feathers and fluff scattered about. No doubt they were the bane of Madame Gabon's existence.

Susannah reached out and covered Claude's hand with her own. "Thank you for caring for her all these years. I know what a risk it was."

"I danced a bit at the Green Apple long ago, you see, which is where I met Anna, and Daisy Jones. I learned through Daisy of your . . . plight . . . and when I returned home to France I . . . I brought Sylvie with me to raise as my own. And as no one ever heard from Anna again . . . I never told Sylvie about her, as there never seemed a need to trouble her with it. I never knew what became of the other little girls—of you, Lady Grantham, or Sabrina. And it was wisest not to write of it to anyone, for the danger was . . . the danger was . . ."

Guillaume murmured an English obscenity tenderly and gave Claude another nibble.

Claude looked up apologetically. "He belonged to a sailor once, long ago," she said. "He has a remarkable vocabulary."

Remarkable did not begin to describe Guillaume's vocabulary.

Susannah gave her a weak smile. Kit held her hand in his, and squeezed it. He, she suspected, was trying not to laugh.

"I'm sorry, Susannah." Claude's voice thickened again, and she dabbed at her eyes.

"Oh, Claude, I am not angry," Susannah told her, "for I likely would have burned the letters, too, for someone I love. You told us that Sylvie's letter said that she went to England. Do you know where she might have gone when she arrived?"

"I do not know. I am sorry. Daisy Jones is my only English friend, you see. But I do not believe that Sylvie knew of her."

Claude sniffed. "I am worried. As you can see, our life is not grand, and it was not easy when she was very young. But Sylvie . . . she is now the finest ballerina in Paris. Everyone knows she has gone. Monsieur Favre . . . Madame Gabon tells me is very angry."

"Sylvie is a ballerina?" Kit repeated, fascinated.

And Susannah was instantly a wee bit jealous, because it *did* seem like a fascinating thing to be.

And then she was a wee bit proud, because it was fascinating to be related to a ballerina.

Who had a *lover.*

Claude took a deep breath, steadying herself. "If you find her . . . when you return . . . will you tell her I am sorry? I never meant to hurt her. She is very disciplined, my Sylvie. It is so unlike her just to run. But, oh, she has a temper, and I fear this time impulse sent her across the sea, and possibly she will not be safe on her own."

Susannah saw Kit glance sideways at her.

So Sylvie was not the only one in the Holt family to possess a temper. Somehow, Susannah was pleased to hear it, and felt closer to her sister already.

      ᴥᴑ   *ᴥᴑ*   *ᴥᴑ*

Because Tom and The General loved drama, that afternoon they positioned the girls as well as Daisy in the audience, a view they seldom enjoyed. Almost like little girls being brought on an outing, they were quiet and wide-eyed, perhaps tense with anticipation, well behaved. No giggles or murmurs.

For they knew why Tom and The General had gathered them here.

Sylvie slid a sidelong glance at Molly, only to find it intercepted by Molly's sidelong glance. After their conversation in the attic yesterday, Sylvie knew Molly was certain that Sylvie would be appointed Venus.

A portentous thumping noise, sliding, a few crashes and some swearing were heard from behind the red velvet curtains.

"The day you've been waiting for has arrived, ladies," Tom announced grandly.

And then the curtains shimmied up.

"Cor!" Rose breathed, perhaps predictably.

An enormous oyster sat on the stage, glowing softly. In the dim light of the theater, they could barely see a series of long, dark ropes attached to it, painted to disappear into the darkness when the lights were lowered. A crew of rough little boys stood at the ready to tug on them, to open the great creature's maw.

"It will look lovelier at night," The General assured them. "We shall surround it by waving seaweed and floating fish . . ." With his hands in the air, he sketched the picture of them, and the girls' eyes followed his hands, envisioning it.

"Venus," Tom told them, from where he stood onstage, "will have the honor of waiting inside the oyster and being revealed, slowly, to a breathlessly waiting audience. She will truly be the pearl in the oyster, and she'll rise, gracefully, and sing a song recently composed by our beloved Josephine."

Josephine nodded graciously.

Sylvie immediately thought: *Pearl, girl* . . .

What had this place *done* to her?

"And since I know all of *you* are breathlessly waiting to be told who she will be . . ." Tom continued.

They *were* breathless.

Sylvie was breathless, in particular, hoping, praying, it would *not* be her. And in truth, she hadn't the faintest idea what to expect from Tom Shaughnessy, whether he would consider such a thing a gift . . . or whether it would amuse him to put her in the shell when he would know she so clearly didn't want to be there. She supposed she could protest, but he still provided the roof over her head for the time being.

No: He was a practical man, and she would make a dreadful Venus.

He allowed the silence to gain in momentum, drawing it out the way an orchestra conductor draws out the violins, perhaps.

"Molly," Tom Shaughnessy said quietly. "Would you please step forward?"

The exhale of breath from the girls in the audience nearly lifted up the curtains.

"*Ohhhh* . . . Molly . . ." Congratulatory murmurs rose up. Mostly unsurprised murmurs, as Molly's supremacy was all but unquestioned. Mostly, to their credit, pleased murmurs.

Molly, as though it were her very own coronation, rose, and all but floated toward the stage.

And when she turned around again, her smug smile could have lit the entire theater at night.

"Let's applaud Molly, shall we, ladies?" Tom said with appropriate gravity.

Gracious applause fluttered from the seats, and Molly basked as The General and Tom flanked her.

And Daisy Jones lifted herself up from her seat and quietly, with dignity, made her way toward the back of the theater, toward her velvety pink room, like a storm retreating in the face of the advancing sun.

Sylvie watched her go. The woman had never spoken to her directly; Sylvie had never seen her speak to any of the girls directly. Daisy kept a precise boundary between herself and those she perhaps considered beneath her.

She looked up, saw Tom smiling down at the girls. But The General was watching the majesty of Daisy's retreat, his expression difficult to fathom.

ग़ॎ   ग़ॎ   ग़ॎ

The next hour or so was devoted to Molly's learning how to fold herself into the oyster shell and rise from inside it as it slowly, slowly opened. Every girl wanted a turn at it, which took a bit of time, and The General, flush with his success, indulged them just this once while Tom solemnly discussed with the boys the timing of the pulleys, the angle and speed at which to tug the ropes to most gracefully reveal Venus. He demonstrated this himself.

Sylvie peered closer at the huge oyster, ran her fingers over the satin of the inside, admiring the sheer whimsical brilliance of the craftsmanship, and the very idea that had spawned it. It was lined in rippling, pillowy pale pink satin, as befitted the throne of an undersea queen. It would gleam in the footlights softly, reflecting Molly's fair skin. It was, indeed, the ideal setting for a pearl.

The seed for it, the mind that had seen the potential for the beauty and whimsy and sensuality of it, had been Tom Shaughnessy's.

Sylvie thought of Tom as a boy in the rookeries, stealing to eat. Hiding from those who might drag him off to the authorities, as though he was merely something to be disposed of, like a feral cat. Learning to fight and to survive with the tools at his disposal.

Lucky in my friends, he'd said.

And as she caressed the inside of that absurdly beautiful, magnificently silly oyster, she knew it might as well have been Tom himself she was touching.

She glanced up, knowing somehow his eyes would find her.

He was still discussing the mechanics of the pulleys with the boys, and he noticed, perhaps, the shift in her posture, and it was but a glance, a swift hold of her gaze. His eyes darkened even then. And then he returned to the business at hand.

Most nights.

CHAPTER FOURTEEN

THE NEXT DAY, Molly arrived in the attic shortly after Sylvie did. But she wasn't alone. She'd brought the rest of the girls with her.

And all of them stopped and stared, wide-eyed and silent, at Sylvie, who stood with her hair pulled tightly back, the lovely exotic dress she wore to practice her dancing floating about her calves.

Molly finally spoke. "I told them about the ballet, and the princes and kings." Her chin was up.

"And you would all like to learn to dance this way?" Sylvie asked them.

She had never before taught a roomful of girls, though she had advised younger students about form, and every now and then wiped away Monsieur-Favre-instigated tears.

"Can ye show us?"

Sylvie looked at those lovely girls, with their round bodies accustomed to very little work at all apart from, perhaps, the sort that took place on a mattress or the sort that took place on the White Lily's stage. And wondered how they would cope with the pain and discipline, the nuance and complexity—

But she needn't tell them it was difficult, or painful, or that few really excelled at it. She would show them, and they could decide for themselves whether or not they found it so.

"Yes. I will teach you."

They looked back at her, and shy smiles were exchanged.

But Molly's expression shifted as something occurred to her. "The mirrors . . . ye'd no mirrors before." She looked almost accusingly at Sylvie.

But before Sylvie would respond she heard more creaking on the stairs.

They all froze, and Sylvie saw for an instant a stricken expression flicker over Molly's face. *She thinks it is Tom coming to meet me,* Sylvie thought.

But Sylvie recognized the step of The General, for she had invited him to meet them here.

"They would like to learn the ballet," Sylvie told him very calmly.

The General stared at the six girls, six very beautiful and very different women reflected in the mirrors of this cramped little room, the context so different from the White Lily's stage.

And at first, the faintest hint of incredulity shadowed his brow. Or perhaps it was bemusement.

And then . . . a glimmer of inspiration dawned in his shiny dark eyes. It was a familiar gleam. A nearly *fanatic* gleam.

She'd seen it in Monsieur Favre's eyes before.

"Will you work hard and do what I say and not complain? I will only ask once, and if you complain even once, I shall refuse to work with you."

This he directed to everyone except Sylvie.

Five heads ducked up and down. No harm in agreeing, no doubt they imagined. They had no true idea what was in store for them.

"Well, then. Shall we begin?"

ॐ   ॐ   ॐ

It was to be a night of pirates, fairies, damsels and a mermaid on a swing, and the girls, after their first simple lessons in the ballet earlier in the day, settled down at their tables to the task of becoming fairies first of all. All was, as usual, noisy chatter, and the air was nearly clouded with powder, complaints, and exclamations over gifts that had been delivered by the ever-present crew of little boys.

Sylvie arrived in the dressing room to find her little table to prepare herself for the performance, and slowed when she saw what was atop it—a little box.

"Oh, look! Ye've an admirer, Sylvie!" Rose said encouragingly. The unspoken words were: *at last.*

Compared to the gaudy things that arrived on their little dressing tables each night, the clusters of blooms and baubles, the gift on Sylvie's table seemed exceedingly modest. She stared at it, wondering, half-bemused, how on earth she would respond to an admirer from the White Lily's audience.

Just then, Molly lifted a silk shawl out of its wrappings, the latest of her gifts from her anonymous admirer, the one who watched the shows from the private box intended to court her "proper." It was a thing of limp, luminous beauty, and a collective sigh went up when it was revealed. The girls flocked to it. They all wanted to touch it and wrap it about their own shoulders, and Sylvie and her tiny gift were instantly forgotten.

She approached the box almost cautiously, as though it might turn into a great moth and fly at her, and took it up gingerly in her hand. It was of wood, and it fit neatly into her palm, with a heft that belied its petite size.

And then she saw, painted, very delicately across the top: a ballerina, her dress floating like a cloud about her, her arms stretched overhead, her face rapt.

Sylvie felt the first rushes of heat in her cheeks, the sort of heat that always stole her breath, made her heart feel like a tiny sun in her chest.

Attached to the box by a thin gold cord was a petite gold key.

With trembling hands, Sylvie fumbled the lid of the box to reveal the shining drum at that would turn to spill the music out. For it was indeed a *boîte à musique*.

A music box.

She fitted the key into the slot, not unaware that the very act of inserting a key into a slot to create music had a certain poetry and prurience to it. A certain symbolism, given who had left this box for her, and somehow she doubted it had been lost upon him.

What do you want, Sylvie?

And so she turned the key. And a little tune began softly, scarcely audible in the roomful of laughter and chatter. Playing just for her.

჻   ჻   ჻

Later, after they'd been pirates and fairies and were waiting to be damsels behind the curtain, watching Daisy in the swing and taking wagers on whether it would hold, Sylvie felt Tom stand behind her briefly. Over the top of their heads he watched Daisy in the swing. He didn't look at Sylvie at all, or speak to her or Molly or Rose, nor did Sylvie turn to meet his eyes. He was distracted and alert, overseeing his show from every angle, just as he did each night.

But when he turned to leave, his hand brushed against her back, a light, seemingly accidental drag of fingers. Scarcely even a touch.

And then he was gone, off to see to the Earl of Rawden, the famous poet earl, who had just arrived with the gust of authority he always brought with him and was swiveling his head about looking for Tom, and off to pay the king's man, Crumstead, who had arrived for the show and for his bribe.

Scarcely even a touch. It might even have been construed as accidental. Certainly the other girls had noticed nothing, for they were still peering out at the audience from where they stood next to her, whispering comments she'd ceased listening to.

But this was Tom Shaughnessy after all, who did have a certain talent for timing and drama. The touch had been deliberate, she knew. A message, a fleeting moment enclosing the two of them in a silent understanding:

I want you.

In that instant, joy and fierce desire battled with anger, and with the fear of all that she felt. And there was resentment that she should feel it at all, when all her life she'd channeled her passions so effectively, when everything in her life had been as choreographed as the dance, and she knew the next step she should take, and the next.

But with mirrors and a music box and secret proprietary touches, Tom Shaughnessy was wooing her with an intuition and a subtlety at odds with everything he appeared to be, and in so doing had somehow managed to sink through the walls of her reason as water sank into hard earth, undaunted by the challenge.

Made for the challenge, in fact.

And then she wryly corrected a word in her mind. He wasn't wooing her. He was seducing her. The ends were altogether different.

'E doesna touch the dancers. She heard Rose's words again. The theater was everything to Tom, and he wasn't a foolish man. He used his own appeal skillfully with his employees while maintaining a sensible distance, aware of the delicacy required to keep everyone happy, everything running smoothly. And because Sylvie knew how important the theater and everyone in it were to him, she knew the sheer subtlety of his campaign meant he had not undertaken it lightly.

The implications of this made her breathless.

She had felt often that Etienne's wooing had been more or less ceremonial, that the outcome had never been in question for him.

But here . . . here she had a choice.

And though she had at first resented Tom for leaving the choice in her hands . . . she now saw it as the most splendid of his gifts.

ঞ্চ   ঞ্চ   ঞ্চ

Later, Sylvie, once again in muslin, rouge rubbed from her cheeks, hair twisted once again into a sedate knot, watched the girls leave for the evening, and waved her good-byes. She lifted a hand to Poe at the door. He lifted a hook in return.

And when everyone was gone, she turned away, availed herself of a lit candle, and took the stairs up to her room. But before she did, she glanced for a light in the depths of the theater; the door to his office was closed, and no light shone from beneath the door.

The evening had been long and raucous. Invitations had been issued to Tom; she'd heard them as he'd greeted the guests near the door and as they'd said their farewells. The Velvet Glove had been suggested to him more than once.

Most nights.

She went up to her room. She unpinned her hair, and brushed it smooth. She stepped out of her dress, untied her stockings, rolled them down, and lifted her nightrail in her hands, preparing to drop it over her head.

But then she paused and saw her reflection in the mirror. And she thought about life as choreography, and about mirrors, and a music box. At the top of the White Lily there was a proud, beautiful man who wanted her. But with these small gifts, he'd shown her that he *knew* her, too. The gifts told her so much more about him than he realized.

She set the nightrail aside, laying it carefully on the bed. She dropped the dress over her head again, took her cloak from the hook on the wall, and wrapped herself in it. And then she took up the candle again.

ఎ   ఎ   ఎ

It wasn't until he heard the creak of a light step on the stairs to his room that he admitted to himself that he'd been waiting to hear it for days now. That he'd lain awake for nights desperate for it, every one of his senses honed to razor alertness, hoping for it. Denied invitations, conducted a campaign of quiet seduction so unlike him it unnerved and distantly even amused him. Never had he wanted anything more, it seemed. Never had he been so uncertain about getting it.

Tom sat up in his bed, struck the flint to light the lamp next to his bed, and the tiny room glowed in the warm light. His hands shook, for God's sake, even as he did it. His heart had set up a drumming in his chest.

He saw the light of her candle quiver against the wall first, then the shadow of her, and finally the woman herself. Her cloak was wrapped around her; beneath the hem, he saw light muslin.

Her hair was down, a sheet of silky darkness burnished by the dueling lights of her candle and his lamp. He could scarcely breathe. When she saw his lit lamp, she lifted her own candle with hands that trembled, and puffed it out.

He couldn't speak.

In silence, he watched her drop the cloak. Saw, in the shadows, the outline of her lithe body through her dress, her long legs, slim waist. And in silence he watched as matter-of-factly she reached for her dress, and pulled it—Oh God—right over her head.

The sight of her body completely bare to him all at once was an exquisite physical shock. He stopped breathing.

She began to fold the dress. He remembered to breathe again in order to speak.

"For the love of God, Sylvie, leave the dress." His voice was low, hoarse.

She dropped it and laughed then, a soft, shaky little laugh. Lifted her hand to push back the long mass of hair, and he watched, mesmerized, the lift of her small, perfect breast when her arm rose, then the waterfall sheen of the hair spilling behind her.

A woman who had been nude in front of a man before—not coy, not ashamed, and yet not wanton, either. A woman who understood the purpose of bodies. A woman who knew, no doubt, how to use her body for work, and for art . . . and for pleasure.

And at this last thought, a peculiar current of jealousy arced through Tom's excitement. Someone else, at this moment, somewhere, was perhaps missing her. Had touched her. Someone else no doubt felt he had the right to her, and Tom knew he should entertain guilt or regret.

But she was *here* now.

Lover or no lover waiting for her somewhere else, she had crossed the theater tonight, candle in hand, climbed each creaking stair to be with him.

ॐ   ॐ   ॐ

She sat down on the edge of the bed near him, curled her legs up beneath her.

"Sylvie." A whisper. Nearly rueful.

Tom shifted slightly, and his light blanket slipped away from his chest, folding to his waist. He pushed it impatiently aside, and there before her, inches away from her touch, she saw the broad line of his smooth shoulders, the hard muscles cut into his chest, the slim waist. And curving up against his flat belly, the evidence of how badly he wanted her. Her senses flooded; she could scarcely believe she was here.

His hand extended, hovered an instant so close to her, deciding. Then, delicately, he rested the backs of his fingers against her ribs, as though testing the temperature of water, wondering if it perhaps would scald him.

And the entire surface of her skin began to glow like something gently set aflame.

She turned her head from the expression in his eyes. Somehow it was too much to take in all at once.

Tom's hand moved then; she could hear his breath catch as he slid it up slowly, slowly, over her ribs, leaving a trail of sensation behind. He tipped his fingers up to cup her breast; the rough pad of his thumb dragged over her nipple. Shocking, the serrated pleasure suddenly everywhere in her. She closed her eyes. It stilled the breath in her lungs; she heard the ragged catch in her own breath.

"Small," she whispered roughly, self-consciously.

"Soft," he said at once, like a correction, his voice low and rough. As erotic as his touch.

His hand slowly dropped away; he seemed to sense her tension.

And together for a time they sat in silence so thick and heated it was like another entire body between them.

"Show me then, love, how you'd like it to be," he said softly.

Sylvie opened her eyes and inhaled deeply, and took in

with her breath the musk of his desire, the warmth of his skin, and it was potent, harsh and sweet; it was wine, it was opium. It dissolved what remained of her ability to think, but this seemed almost a relief; she had come here for one reason only, after all, and thinking had nothing at all to do with it.

Sylvie leaned forward and looped her arms loosely around his neck. Rested them against the warmth of his bare skin. Her mouth nearly touched his; her nipples just brushed the skin of his chest, sending a swift scorch of pleasure through her. His breathing was shallow and swift, and she could feel it against her mouth, and yet still he merely watched her, thoughtfully. His eyes never moving from hers, his hands waiting, curling into the blanket at his sides.

And then she leaned back, her weight pulling him slowly down with her. He came down over her; heat and smooth muscle covering her; she wrapped her legs around the furrowed contours of his thighs, cradling him, capturing him with her body, slid her ugly dancer's feet down his hard calves in a caress. Shifted so that the hard length of his arousal fit perfectly against her. Saw his eyes darken when he sensed she was ready for him even now.

They breathed in and out, swiftly, their bodies so close their ribs moved together in time; it seemed they drew in, exhaled the same breath. His mouth was a tense line.

Tom searched her eyes for doubt or surrender or intent, perhaps; she truly didn't know what he would find there. *Want,* was all her mind and body said. *Want.*

"No mercy, then," he whispered.

His mouth fell hard upon hers; she felt his low groan vibrate through her as they tasted each other again at last.

There were few preliminaries; she needed none, for it seemed necessary to take him in all at once, like an antidote. She arched her hips up against him to take him inside her, and she took him as equally as he took her, nearly crying out her pleasure when they were joined.

He propped himself up over her and gazed down. And continued to gaze.

"Tom—*s'il tu plait*—fast—*vite*—"

He stared down at her, his eyes still so dark, his mouth curved up. She could feel the sweat starting over her own skin. And still he didn't move.

Her voice became a rasp of urgency. "Tom—you must— I want—"

"No."

Sylvie felt the breath of his word against her lips. She opened her eyes; his face almost touching hers. He'd managed to make his refusal sound nonchalant, but the perspiration gathering, gleaming on his chest, the muscles trembling beneath her fingers, made a liar of him.

"I need—"

"Beg me, Sylvie."

"*Please*, I beg of you—"

"Hush, love. You should never, never beg."

She half laughed, half groaned. *"Tu est un bête."*

"A beast, am I?" She heard soft laughter in his voice. He drew his hips back from her, slowly, so slowly, allowing both of them to feel every inch of each other, the sensation exquisite, too much, too much. "Is it this . . ." He swiftly thrust, once, twice. Stopped. Hovered over her, again, his arms propping his body above her. "Is it this you want, Sylvie?"

She tried to swear; English or French, it would not have mattered, but God help her, she could only moan her assent. *Bloody man.*

He dipped his head then, brought his mouth to her ear and confided in a whisper: "It's what I want, too."

She nearly laughed; it became a shameless moan instead, when he moved inside her at last.

Eyes locked with his, she clung, conscious of the blanket scraping against her back as she arched up to meet his thrusts, of the squeak as they taxed the springs of the narrow bed, the chafe of his whiskers exquisite against the skin of her throat as he ducked his head to kiss her arched neck. Of her hands sliding over his sweat-slick back and the low roar of swift, mingled breathing, and their mouths finding and losing each other again in the ferocity of their coupling. And then her nails biting into his shoulder blades for purchase and the primal sound of bare skin meeting bare skin swiftly and hard as urgency drove them toward release.

Too soon it had Sylvie in its teeth; and then all at once it engulfed her, shocking, total, a pleasure indescribable.

"Tom—"

She would have screamed it, but he covered her lips with his, took his own name into his mouth as she came apart beneath him, the pleasure savage, seismic. Her body bowed up from the force of it, and still he moved in her, and moved, until his eyes closed and his body stilled as the consuming pleasure of his own release took him.

Tom lowered himself slowly, careful not to crush her; his breath was hot, rough, in the crook of her neck.

A peace like nothing she'd ever felt cupped Sylvie inside

it. She listened to his breathing, floated on the sound of it, as though it was soft music. After a moment, she wrapped a spiral of his hair around one finger, pulled it straight, released it to watch it snap back into its loose wave.

She felt him smile against her throat.

Languidly, he lifted his head, as though the effort cost every bit of his strength, and gazed down at her, studying her as if seeing her for the first time. For so long and so quietly she began to feel uneasy.

"Your mouth . . ." he began.

But then he shook his head once and kissed her instead. And this kiss was all softness. All tenderness that silenced her, made her shy.

He stopped, and they lay in peaceful silence for a moment.

And then he propped himself up on his elbow. "And now may I show you how I'd like it to be?" Eyes serious, the question solemn.

Feeling breathless, she hesitated. Then nodded. And waited.

His head lowered; his lips brushed hers again, very softly.

And though they were places he had been planning to kiss her from the moment he'd seen her, a way of stating his intent to discover every corner of her, he kissed her. Her earlobe. Her temple. The base of her throat. Her collarbone. As if every place on her was precious, worthy of exploration. She discovered the places along with him, felt them all but sing beneath the touch of his lips.

"When I saw you dancing, Sylvie, it was like watching a . . . flame. And yet, here is your body, as solid, as strong as . . . as strong as an ox . . ." He dragged his fingers, softly up the curve of one slim thigh, moved his face there to kiss a tiny mole on the silky skin between them.

"An *o-ox?*" The last word began as indignant and ended as a gasp when his tongue dipped into her navel.

"An ox," he repeated firmly. "I am not a poet. So strong . . . so fine . . ." He flattened a hand over her taut belly, traced outward to the sharp corners of her hip, then kissed the smooth curve of it and turned his cheek so she could feel his whiskers against her tender skin. Goose-flesh swept over her.

"I'd never seen anything so . . . so beautiful, Sylvie." His voice grew thicker.

He dragged his lips lower, and lower, into the silky dark triangle between her legs.

She gasped when his tongue reached its destination. Dipping into the wet heat of her, a deliberate, skillful caress.

"Is it good?" his voice low and taut.

"Dieu." She breathed it.

"It will get even better." His voice low and dark with promise.

With tongue and lips and breath, he proved it.

And it was difficult, for this was a different kind of surrender, this allowing him to give to her. This opening up of herself to this searching, skillful lover, who made love to her as though he wanted to know every bit of her. And even as her body wanted to submit, surrender, lose itself to him entirely, a part of her resisted, was very nearly afraid, and she could not have said why.

And he knew.

"It's all right, love," he murmured. "I have you. I have you. It's all right to let go."

And inexorably, little by little, fear gave way beneath his fingertips, his tongue, his breath, his lips, and the word dissolved until it was comprised only of his touch and her body's response to it. She moved with him, at first learning how to take, then learning how to demand, with sighs.

"So beautiful," he murmured. And he gave more, until she thought she could no longer bear it.

Lost.

It wracked her when it came, her release, a great wave that rippled from somewhere inside her, and it seemed to go on and on, tossing her with it.

"I want to be inside you again, Sylvie." Tom's voice came to her distantly, a hoarse demand.

"Yes." It was the only word she knew at the moment.

He lifted her hips and guided himself into her, slowly, slowly, and she took fresh pleasure, fresh awe, in watching him lose himself in her. He moved rhythmically until she saw the cords of his neck draw tight and his eyes close. And with a ragged gasp, he spilled into her, his body jerking.

He withdrew, sank down next to her, and held her loosely against him. And for a long time they lay like that, two sated bodies, damp with sweat. His hands moved in her hair, stroking out the tangles, as though he had all the time in the world to do just that.

Her hair was long and fine, a skein of silk. It tangled so easily.

"He didn't ask before he took you, did he, Sylvie? This . . . lover . . . of yours."

Her breath nearly stopped.

It was the tone of his voice. She didn't like it . . . and

she did. A tight, low band of sound. Gentleness shot through with veins of fury.

She couldn't answer him, any more than she could seem to stop the tears that astonished her. They spilled slowly, large and cold. Old tears. As though they'd been inside her for a very long time.

She impatiently brushed them away. "I was a grown woman. I did not refuse him."

"Ah. That makes it all right, then." Ironic now, and harder.

She heard his breathing grow rougher, but his hand was still gentle. Tracing the lines of her, the sharp blades of her shoulders, the fine strong muscles of her back created from the magic of the dance, which allowed her to continue to make such magic. The small even bumps of her spine. Gently, gently. Stripping her down to nothing with this relentless, searching, tenderness.

"How did it happen?"

"Does it matter?"

His silence told her he realized that it did not. "But it did. Happen, that is. He just . . . took."

Sylvie closed her eyes and tried to focus on the path of his hand over her.

She remembered Etienne's charm, his words; she'd been flattered and overwhelmed and an accomplished coquette, and so she had found his pursuit exhilarating, a game, even as she recognized the dangers inherent in it. She remembered the day: He'd stolen a kiss, as he had a half dozen times before. And then she'd been in his arms, up against the wall, his mouth hot against hers, and she had returned his kisses with ardor and skill, because it was thrilling, and part of the game.

And then his hands were beneath her skirt, and it had felt . . . interesting, and new. She sensed rather than saw him open his trousers. Too afraid to deny him, half-enamored of her own worldliness, too proud, in a way, to protest what she knew was about to happen and what did happen.

She'd realized when it was over that she hadn't been worldly at all.

He had smoothed down her skirt and promised her the next time would be better. That he'd been overcome and perhaps hasty. He'd been all apologies and charm and flowers and gifts. And . . . it *had* gotten better. She had learned to take pleasure as well as to please.

But no, there had never been any asking. He had never given her a choice.

Had never assumed that she might want one.

And he had been her very first.

"He loves me. He wants to marry me."

Tom's hand stilled on her. Sylvie was glad for the moment for the chance to gather herself. And glad when it resumed moving over her again, because for a moment she'd feared he no longer wanted to touch her.

"Do you love him?" He asked it gruffly.

The truth was she didn't really know. "He is a prince."

She felt Tom's body go utterly still. "Metaphorically speaking, or an *actual* prince?"

"Meta . . ." Not an English word she knew.

"Is he truly a prince?" he clarified for her. "A real prince?"

"He is truly a prince," she confirmed. In such a way that Tom knew that she meant it.

There was a beat of silence. "Christ, Sylvie." He actually sounded darkly amused.

He sat up abruptly and swung his legs off the edge of the bed. Though she doubted he'd be going anywhere, since he was naked and his clothing was on the other side of the room and this *was* his room, after all.

☙ ☙ ☙

"Do you love him?" he had asked her. In truth, she really didn't know. What did she really know of love? Etienne promised her safety and permanence and status and all of the things she had wanted for so long. A long future of comfort. Of certainty.

But oh, it was nothing, nothing like this.

She was tempted to call this love, this savage, tender want for Tom Shaughnessy, but she wasn't entirely sure it was; she was afraid to think that it might be, and what she would then be giving up when she left him. Easier to call it desire, for such a thing could ostensibly be appeased, spent.

She felt shy, suddenly, admiring the broad spread of his back in the lamplight, the smooth golden ridges of muscle on either side of his spine. Utterly unself-conscious in his nudity, his hair poking up in odd peaks and horns created from sweat and passion and her hands rummaging through it, his small white buttocks looking oddly vulnerable, both comical and uncompromisingly masculine somehow as he sat there at the edge of the narrow bed.

He suddenly seemed a stranger, this strong, clever, beautiful man. A complicated man, for all of that.

She supposed it could be love, this surprising ache that spread through her, and seemed to need . . . all that he was . . . to ease it. The dazzle, the temper, the roughness, the tenderness, the pragmatism, the passion. But how could it be love after so short a time?

Perhaps a better question was: How could such a short time seem like forever?

And yet Tom Shaughnessy had nothing at all to do with the life she wanted and needed. She had taken him, and he had taken her. And perhaps that was all this could be.

A moment later she inched toward him, wrapped her arms around his back, pressed her body against him, held him loosely. Little by little, she felt the tension leave him as he relaxed into her. And oddly, nothing had ever made her feel more powerful than the knowledge that she could give comfort as well as pleasure to this man.

"Come to sleep," she murmured.

He turned and looked at her over his shoulder. "Stay with me?"

She nodded. He turned and slid into bed, lifting the blanket for her, and she slid next to him.

He wrapped an arm around her. She waited for him to sleep before she allowed herself to do so.

    *   *   *

Tom was awakened the following morning in what he was certain was the very best way any man on the planet could hope to wake:

A soft hand was sliding down his thigh, and silky hair was dragging behind the hand.

"Sylvie?" he murmured sleepily.

He opened one eye; he didn't see her on the pillow next to him. He fumbled a hand down beneath the blankets and found his hand tangling in her soft hair. "Good morni— *God*. Oh God."

Her tongue had just slid down his shaft, which was immediately more than alert.

She paused. "Good morning to you," she said politely, somewhat muffled from beneath the blanket. And then giggled.

"*Unh*," he gasped in response.

She laughed again, a low rumble against his sensitive flesh, and the sound was painfully arousing.

She took the length of him into her mouth, slowly, gently at first, and he sucked in breath, and stirred, opened his legs wider. And then he slid his fingers from her hair to pull the blanket back, because he wanted to watch.

He surrendered languidly to the skills of her mouth and hands, hot and delicate on the insides of his thighs, clever and insistent over the length of his shaft, and in so doing she took him from lazy, floating bliss to the gasping, knife-edge of release.

He grasped her hair in his hands to stop her.

"Sylvie." He gasped out the word. "I want you."

She looked up, saw his face, and came into his arms, because she knew that's what he meant.

He rolled her over so he could slip inside her. Gently he tipped the two of them so they were lying side by side. So he could kiss her mouth, and watch her eyes as he moved in her, feel her breasts chafe against his chest. Beautiful eyes. Her eyelids heavy with pleasure, slit with it; her dark lashes quivering; he watched the flush rush over her cheeks and throat as they clung and rocked together, slowly this time. His hands brushing over the silk of her lithe back, of her legs, tangling in her hair. Their lips brushed against each other, taking small kisses, murmuring unintelligible things, endearments, sensual requests.

"Je t'aime," he thought he heard her sigh against his lips.

"Say it again," he demanded in a whisper.

She didn't. But she did say his name when she came shuddering in his arms, and she'd made it sound very nearly the same.

CHAPTER FIFTEEN

Sylvie threw her dress on over her head, smoothed her riotous hair out, with Tom's help, and got it twisted into a more decorous knot, and then sat on the edge of his bed and watched him get into his clothes. She studied every move of it—the buttoning of trousers, the tying of the cravat—fascinated, for some reason, as if the very act of dressing was something wondrous and new.

It was only because *he* was doing the dressing, she knew.

And when he caught her watching, he froze and smiled, and then sat down next to her. Her breath hitched. And this, this sharp thing inside her chest, sharp and brilliant, felt quite a bit like joy.

He cradled the back of her head in one hand, and his fingers, briefly, tangled in her hair, touched, lightly, the nape of her neck. He looked down at her for a moment, his silver eyes looking every bit as bemused as she felt. And then, kissed her, and it was warm and lingering and thorough.

And this was how their day began—with no conversation, just a kiss. She preceded him out of the attic room, and he followed her, and with a smile over her shoulder, she went to her rehearsal, and he went to his library, or to wherever he needed to be. She didn't ask.

ॐ   ॐ   ॐ

Did it show, she wondered, as she arrived in the dressing room? The night she'd spent in the arms of Tom Shaughnessy? Not a single girl in this room was a virgin, not by far. Could they tell from the faint traces of blue fatigue beneath her eyes, by her kiss-swollen lips, by her eyes that looked at all of them but somehow saw only last night before them, like a waking dream?

Regardless, everyone chattered just the same, and stripped out of their day dresses to get dressed as water nymphs, and no one seemed to notice that she didn't say a word, unless it was Molly, who always seemed peripherally aware of her, regardless.

"'Ello, everyone."

The voice was soft, but the laughter and chatter in the dressing room stopped as abruptly as if someone had struck a gong. They swiveled as one toward the entrance.

The girl standing there was beautiful even by the White Lily's standards. Fine silvery blond hair coiled up off her face, a few spirals of it touching her cheeks and forehead; a sprinkle of pale freckles across her nose and delicate cheekbones. Brandy gold eyes, doe-sized and luminous. Her clothes were well made, even expensive, suited to her coloring; a walking dress in sarcenet, a bonnet lined in a rich red-brown, matching ribbons tied beneath her chin.

But it wasn't the girl that riveted everyone's attention. It was the small bundle she held in her arms.

Tiny reddish fists popped out of it. And then it made a mewling sound.

The air in the dressing room immediately all but combusted with the collective rabid curiosity.

"Does it 'ave ginger 'air?" one of the girls whispered.

Sylvie felt faint. *Kitty.* This was Kitty, Tom's favorite, ostensibly. The mysterious disappearing girl. Right here in the doorway.

And there was a baby in her arms.

"Kitty!" Rose was the one who rose to kiss the girl on the cheek. "H'it's a *looovely* babe! And ye're in splendid looks. Ye've been missed."

" 'E's a boy," Kitty said proudly, not to the room, but gazing down at the bundle. "Strong an' loud. I'm right lucky 'e's sleepin' now. Must be all of these women. 'E's playin' possum, like. 'E knows we rule the world."

She smiled softly at the baby and made little clucking sounds.

"D'yer name 'im Tom—*Ow!*" Rose was elbowed by the girl next to her.

Kitt looked up dreamily. "I should 'ave done." She looked down again with a soft smile.

An excruciatingly *enigmatic* smile to just about everyone in the room.

Rose peered into the bundle. " 'E's got *no* 'air," she announced meaningfully to the room.

Kitty seemed oblivious to the silent turmoil she'd caused. She was protected by a bubble of new motherhood, and nothing that didn't directly affect her infant could touch her now.

"Then what *d'yer* name 'im?" Rose asked.

Kitty looked up and smiled impishly then. "The General."

And at the collective dropping of jaws, Kitty laughed merrily, which made her little son protest with baby noises. And the laughter lit her face and eyes, and made it clear that she was more than beautiful, she was unique.

Sylvie felt the fear sink through her. *Tom's favorite*.

And Sylvie remembered the toy horse on his shelf: there and then gone.

"I just wanted to see all of ye. I thought ye might 'ave worried over me. But we're doing wonderfully well."

It almost sounded defiant; it felt rather like a final good-bye, and no doubt it was. Kitty had perhaps come to take a look at her old life, perhaps to prove something to everyone in that room, perhaps to prove something to herself.

She turned and left.

"Someone go an' ask 'er."

"She willna tell, that one. Mum's the word, 'er."

"Ask 'er if she lives in Kent. Go, go!"

"*You* go."

And more such whispers rustled.

Sylvie noticed how strangely pale Molly had become. Silent, too.

Sex, Tom Shaughnessy had said. What the White Lily was about, what it celebrated. What she and Tom had celebrated together last night, this morning. It wasn't as if she hadn't known all along, she told herself. It wasn't as though he'd betrayed her in any sense, or promised her a thing. She'd taken her pleasure, and pleasure had been taken from her, and this must be the cost: the plummeting feeling in her stomach, the ice that settled in there, and she couldn't begin to explain why this would be.

She waited an interval, silent. And then moved out of the dressing room, with the thought of perhaps blindly seeking refuge, perhaps in her little room. To breathe through the pain, or walk it off, as though she'd simply twisted an ankle.

And camouflaged by the chatter, she made her way out of the room, still in her day dress.

⚜   ⚜   ⚜

Tom had his gloves and hat and walking stick in hand and was hurriedly moving toward the door from his office.

"Sylvie." He stopped when he saw her. She saw the memory of last night in his eyes and in his smile, and she was suddenly warm everywhere from it, even as uncertainty and her own pride made her cool to him.

"You are off to visit your family, then?"

He looked shocked. "My . . . family?"

"To Kent?" Sylvie said. Perhaps he was shocked that she knew.

"My family." He repeated. Staring at her oddly. And then he made a little sound of wondering incredulity. "Well, I suppose I am. But . . . how do you . . ."

"And so you take them with you now . . . Kitty and the baby?"

"With Kitty and the—" And now he seemed utterly baffled. "What on earth are you running on about? What do you know of Kitty? Does—"

"Kitty was here with the baby," she said flatly.

"Kitty was here?" He sounded mildly surprised. "Is she still here? Is she well? And the baby? I imagine Poe or Stark must have let her into the building."

How could he be so cavalier about this? Unless . . . "They are both well," she said cautiously.

"Good, then." He smiled at her.

She couldn't return the smile. She frowned slightly, looked up at him, and said nothing, utterly tangled in this conversation, not to mention her own thoughts and emotions.

And then she turned to leave.

He closed a quick hand around her arm, stopping her. "Sylvie, what the bloody hell is troubling you?"

She saw the rest of the girls filing out of the dressing room; a few heads turned, then paused, lowering their voices to talk as they saw them.

She wasn't certain Tom saw the other dancers. For he gently, slowly, released her arm. Made the release somehow a caress.

She had no right to say it, to think it, to demand any sort of clarification from him. She had no right or reason to expect he was anything other than what he appeared to be.

"They say . . ." She paused. "The girls say . . ." She cleared her throat. "They say you . . . They say Kitty . . ."

He frowned a little. And then his head went back slightly as understanding dawned, came down in a short nod of comprehension.

"Do 'they' now?" Ironically drawled.

She lifted her eyes up swiftly, tried looking into his eyes, but found it difficult somehow. So she looked down at his boots instead. Shiny. She could see her face in them, and what she saw chafed her pride, for she could see that she was feeling hurt, and that meant he could see it, too.

"Tell me truthfully, Sylvie: Would it trouble you if the things 'they' say are true?" His expression was careful now.

It should not trouble her. It should not even surprise her. She certainly hadn't a right to feel any particular way about it at all.

She did look up then.

He was fussing uncomfortably with his walking stick, twisting and twisting it in one gloved hand. Using it to help him think, perhaps. Watching her, his own face tense.

Still, she said nothing.

And then he breathed in deeply, exhaled deeply, either in resignation or like someone gathering courage.

"I would be pleased if you would accompany me to Kent, Sylvie. Will you come?"

The invitation sounded awkward, nearly formal.

"With Kitty and the—"

"No."

She frowned a little, confused, and feeling stubborn now. "The sewing—"

"Will wait."

"Rehearsal—"

"Sylvie." The impatient word stopped her. "I employ everyone here."

Meaning: If he chose, he could order her to accompany him.

A man like Tom Shaughnessy. She remembered thinking that the night she arrived. What he seemed to be warring with, what she felt him to be.

She sensed something waited in Kent that would finally, definitively tell her what this truly meant.

"I will come with you."

ৡ৸   ৡ৸   ৡ৸

He was witty and entertaining on the ride there. He taught her another bawdy song having to do with pirates, one deemed far too risqué for the White Lily's show. But he didn't touch her, or kiss her, or speak of the previous evening, and a hired closed carriage seemed the *ideal* environment in which to dally. Certainly, Etienne had taken liberties in closed carriages.

"We're visiting the May family of Little Swathing," is all he told her. "And you're my cousin," he said to her, as they reached their destination.

This made her snap her head around.

He was laughing silently. "For the sake of Mrs. May. She already finds me scandalous, so you're my cousin for the afternoon. I doubt she'll be fooled, but it's a lie she can be comfortable pretending to believe, I think."

The Mays' cottage was small and worn and comfortable looking from the outside, wrapped around by a flower-and-vine-tangled picket fence. Mrs. May, a solemn-faced woman, greeted them at the door, and even before introductions had been exchanged, a little boy toddled from behind her and flung his arms up toward Tom.

"Tah!"

Tom bent down and scooped the boy up and plopped him down on his shoulders, which made the little boy giggle and curl his hands into Tom's hair.

"Owwww!" Tom's howl was especially for the child's

benefit, and it worked a treat, as Jamie laughed. Tom reached up and gently loosened ten little fingers from his hair. "Not so tightly, thank you, my good man."

And then Tom turned and met Sylvie's eyes, and her heart nearly stopped. Two faces looked back at her:

Tom and a little twin of Tom. One pair of eyes wide and wondering and innocent; the other pair searching, a little guarded. Decidedly not innocent.

And unapologetic.

"He says that now, Mr. Shaughnessy," Mrs. May said. "I think he's saying 'Tom.' He asks for you."

And when Mrs. May said that, a confluence of emotions raced over Tom's face. Startled pleasure, Sylvie would have said. Or startled pain. It was difficult to know the difference, for the moment was fleeting.

Mrs. May had all but completely succumbed to Tom Shaughnessy's charm, and had over the past few weeks become something approximating warm, which had some to do with the fiscal contributions Tom made to their household, and much to do with Tom himself.

Or so Tom flattered himself into thinking.

"Clever boy," Tom said, lowering his son to the ground. "What else does he say now?"

"Ball!" Jamie hollered, as if in answer, and squirmed to be lowered to the ground. His father obliged him. And then Jamie reached for his ball, and he toddled over to Sylvie and offered it to her.

Sylvie couldn't speak. Little James was a walking, miniature imprint of his father. Not a shy child, either, she could see; he was all joy and curiosity and restless energy. She supposed the Mays were in part responsible for the joy. But she wondered if Tom saw those qualities in Jamie, and whether he recognized them as his own.

She leaned forward to take the ball from him. Jamie dropped it in favor of seizing her nose in one small hand and squeezing it hard.

"Nose!" Jamie bellowed gaily.

"*Unnnh . . .*" Sylvie's eyes began to water with the effort not to scream in pain.

"He says 'nose' now, too," Mrs. May said.

Tom was laughing helplessly, if silently, the bloody man. He knelt and gently removed the pincers of his little boy's fingers from Sylvie's nose.

Sylvie reached up to feel if her nose was still in place. It was on fire.

She had very little experience with children. She knew they made loud noises, emitted noxious smells, and were often effortlessly enchanting. Even as her nose burned, Jamie's face split into that smile that took up nearly his entire face, and she was moved.

"I've often been tempted to do that, myself," Tom said this half to Sylvie, half to Jamie, mostly for his own amusement. "It's a fine nose."

And then he swooped Jamie up and bounced him back up onto his shoulders.

"What word of Maribeth?" Tom asked of Mrs. May, quietly.

"None, I fear."

And they began to talk of Jamie, while Sylvie watched and listened—his words, how tall he was getting, what he was eating and refusing to eat. What else he might need in a few weeks time—clothes, shoes. As matter-of-factly as Tom discussed costumes and bawdy songs.

Sylvie listened, fascinated, and watched as little Jamie delved about in Tom's hair with his hands, and kicked at Tom's chest once or twice with a small foot, while Tom absently jounced him a bit, and absently but firmly removed Jamie's fingers when they probed into his ear. He somehow looked as natural with a small boy at his head as he did when he greeted the guests arriving at the White Lily.

"Mr. Shaughnessy, I'm afraid he's named the horse . . ." Mrs. May lowered her voice to a whisper, and turned a shade of pink. "Bloody Hell." She sounded faintly accusatory.

"I'm terribly, terribly sorry, Mrs. May." Tom was struggling not to laugh. "Perhaps he'll grow out of the horse and forget all about it."

"He's growing so quickly. I thought . . ." Mrs. May paused and cleared her throat. "I thought you might like to take him for a day, Mr. Shaughnessy. You should hate to miss any new words."

It wasn't a dramatic change in expression, really. But Sylvie noticed the shift. Tom's lighthearted pleasure became a mask over something careful.

"Perhaps," he said lightly, and lowered Jamie to the ground. "Perhaps we'll discuss it."

ჟ   ჟ   ჟ

"Why did you not tell me about him on the way here?" Sylvie asked him when the carriage was once again pulling them home.

"I wanted you to see him first. Before you judged me," he said.

For of course he knew she ultimately would be judging him. She understood his point, even as she hadn't enjoyed the suspense.

"Who is his mother?"

He cleared his throat. "Maribeth May was an adventuress of the first order." Tom smiled wryly. "She and I enjoyed each other on several occasions"—he gave the word "enjoy" an accent of irony—"and then she left for . . . oh, I believe it was Shropshire, word had it . . . with another man, one who doubtless had more money or perhaps prospects than she assumed I had. She was ambitious, Maribeth was, and one could scarcely blame her. I was not heartbroken, nor was I terribly surprised, given what I knew of her. I was informed of Jamie's existence by letter."

As he spoke Tom absently, slowly, worked the fingers of his scarred hand with the other fingers. "I imagine she found him an inconvenience, perhaps financially. Or perhaps she found him a . . . a hindrance to her pleasures." The last words seemed difficult for him to say.

They both fell silent for a moment.

"I have no doubts he is my son," he added.

No one who laid eyes on the boy could ever have any doubts, either, Sylvie knew. She simply nodded. "He is beautiful," she said gently.

Tom looked up quickly, some emotion flaring in his eyes. And then he gave her a swift smile, teasing her, knowing she'd just complimented him, too. "You haven't asked about Kitty."

"And Kitty?" Sylvie obliged him.

"Kitty was . . ." Tom smiled faintly. "Quick-witted, more so than the other girls. Lovely. I did like Kitty. But then she came to me and told me she was pregnant. She was afraid I would be angry and let her go, and it was a valid fear: I would have *had* to let her go, regardless. I can't put a pregnant girl onstage, God knows. Her man had no employment at the time, and so I . . . I gave her some money. Enough for them to marry. To find their own rooms in town. I made some inquiries and found a position for her husband."

"But this . . ." He paused. "This was after I learned of Jamie."

Telling her, quite frankly, that his Jamie had perhaps changed the way he viewed the world. That perhaps his generosity toward Kitty had a little something to do with his own guilt.

"Give your hand to me," Sylvie said quietly.

Tom looked up, surprised.

"Give your hand—" But then she stopped and simply took his hand in hers.

She skillfully began working his fingers, kneading between them, stretching them, gently rubbing the joints. She was an expert at this since it was a necessity to do this to her feet after rehearsals, after performances. She knew intimately the little universe of bone and muscle and sinew in her own feet.

"Good?" she asked.

He nodded. But his expression was guarded, a little bemused. As though struggling with or suppressing something, and so he couldn't speak. She thought of the ways in which Tom Shaughnessy had always looked after those around him, including her, in his way. She wondered if anyone had ever truly looked after him. It was almost as though he didn't know how to allow someone to do it.

"He's your only child," she said, half statement, half question.

"The only one I know about."

Ironically said. And no doubt something that could be said for nearly any man, even—perhaps especially—someone like Etienne.

Finally, Tom sighed and closed his eyes slightly, leaned back against the carriage wall, accepting her ministrations.

What a pair we are, she thought half-ruefully. *I rushed across the Channel from the arms of one lover to learn about my past, to learn who I am. Never dreaming I'd land in the arms of another lover.*

And finally, she stopped massaging Tom's hand and simply held it for a moment, drew her fingers lightly over the lines in his palm, daring a caress. He opened his eyes then, and slowly withdrew his hand from hers, lifted it to her face. With his thumb, he traced, very lightly, the line of her jaw. She turned her cheek into his hand; for a moment he cradled it.

And she thought he might kiss her, but she wasn't certain whether she wanted him to kiss her just now. She wanted to sit quietly and absorb this matter-of-factly recited tale of a casual liaison with a woman that had resulted in a beautiful bastard child, and to picture how Tom had looked a moment ago when he held that child.

And to remember the look in his eyes when he hovered over her, moved inside her. When he had kissed her for the very first time. The stunned darkness in his eyes.

And when she did, like a wave it swept through her, the desire, fierce and complete, spinning her head.

She wondered if today's journey was his way of warning her away. *This is who I am.*

Or whether, in showing her Jamie, he had just shown her the inside of his heart and was waiting for her to tell him what she thought of it.

He didn't kiss her. He took his hand away from her cheek, then turned his head toward the window. He remained silent for the rest of the journey.

ე   ე   ე

When the White Lily's brilliantly ostentatious sign was once again in view, the coach stopped.

Tom reached out a hand and helped her down from the hackney, then paid the hackney driver, counting out coins and seeing him off with the lift of a hand.

Sylvie shook out her skirts and looked for Tom.

He wasn't looking at her; his head was pointed toward the center of London, squinting in the sunlight. He had the abstracted air of one looking through a telescope, attempting to bring something very far away into focus.

She noticed he was standing very still, lightly tapping his walking stick absently into the ground.

"Your prince . . . is he very wealthy, Sylvie?"

"Yes," she answered, after a hesitation.

"Can he give you a life of comfort and certainty?"

She watched him, attempting to gauge his mood. She frowned a little. Reluctantly—as though she didn't want him to arrive at whatever conclusion he seemed to be seeking, she answered: "Yes." Her heart had begun knocking strangely.

"And he loves you."

It was a statement; he already knew the answer to the question, for she had told him the night before. He seemed to be adding all of this up in an equation of sorts in his mind.

Suddenly, Tom looked at his hat, as though he'd just remembered he was holding it, and then placed it on his head. Ruefulness in the gesture, as though he knew a real gentleman would not have forgotten to replace it once removed.

"Then you'd be foolish not to marry him."

He looked at her evenly when he said this.

And when she didn't speak, because she couldn't speak in the aftermath of those words, he nodded shortly, as though she'd answered some sort of silent question.

He turned and pushed open the door to the theater, and she watched the White Lily swallow him up.

ⁿ   ⁿ   ⁿ

The note was in The General's handwriting, and was succinct, as befitted the gravity of it. It had been placed under the paperweight that Tom had finally, wisely, acquired, given The General's penchant for gusty sighs.

Pinkerton-Knowles backed out. That's the last of them.

Tom didn't swear. Or toss the note down. Tom simply held it, felt some cold sensation wash over the back of him. The wave of disappointment, followed by the wave of inspiration, which would normally have followed such a total defeat—it wasn't as though he'd never known defeat—had given way instead to a peculiar quiet fury.

Something was amiss, and he couldn't begin to guess what that might be. When the enthusiasm had been so uniform and total, when the idea was so good, when all of it had been taking shape so splendidly. When his days were spent marshaling builders and making plans.

When he had already committed all of his own spare capital to it. And now, in the absence of a strong dose of capital from some other source very soon . . . he would be swiftly ruined.

◈ ◈ ◈

It started as just a tiny spark, a spark that resulted, she supposed from striking his words over and over again in the tinderbox of her temper.

Then you'd be foolish not to marry him. Then you'd be foolish not to marry him. Then you'd be foolish not to marry him.

They played in her head beneath the words of the silent music she danced to as she taught the girls the steps to the ballet that afternoon. She heard them in her mind as she praised their form, laughed with them. She heard them in her mind as she argued with The General over what the next step in their dance should be.

And then the spark grew when she applied the little puff of her pride to it. She supposed she wanted to be the one to tell Tom, "Oh no, this could never be. I am promised to another. Thank you for the moments of pleasure." Sylvie Lamoreux, the much-desired queen of the Paris ballet, had taken a lover, a ruffian of a lover, as a lark, and now it was over. She had sampled something she wanted, and now it was over.

But Tom Shaughnessy, the name purred most often on female lips throughout London, or so it was said, had tired of her after one evening of sensual pleasure. She told herself this to see if perhaps it felt true, to see if this was why she was so furious, so that then she could spend her uncomfortable anger on it and have it be done.

But no. This didn't feel true, either. So she probed about in her mind for whatever it was that seemed to be feeding her temper, flushing her skin until it felt burned.

And then realized she should be probing about in her heart instead.

And that was where she found the answer.

And that was when she became well and truly furious.

ঞ   *ঞ*   *ঞ*

She flung open the door to his office, heedless of who might see her enter, slammed it again, glanced about, seized his paperweight, and heaved it at him.

It would have struck him square in the chest, but Tom caught it just in time, looking startled and very briefly impressed, either with his own reflexes or with her aim.

"What the bloody he—"

"Tu est un lâche!" Sylvie reached for a book and hurled that.

But Tom was a quick study. He nimbly dodged it, backed away from her around the desk.

"What am I?" He was genuinely befuddled, backing away from her. "What the devil are you—"

She stalked him around the desk. And finally, in the flames of her temper, she found the English word and spat it:

"Coward."

She saw it happen, the instant and terrifying transformation: his eyes go the color of slate, his mouth become a tight, white line. She'd made him furious.

"Explain yourself."

Any sensible person would have been frightened and backed away. She'd witnessed his temper, and knew it was easily the equal of her own. But she was too angry to be sensible.

"'Then you'd be foolish not to marry him,'" she mimicked nastily. "Coward! You are just afraid because . . . because . . .

"'Because'?" he snapped.

"Because you are in the love with me."

Tom blinked as if the words had struck him between the eyes.

Silence fell, guillotine-swift.

Then Sylvie became aware of the sound of quick breathing, her fury mingled with his.

His eyes never left her face. His hands remained tensed at his sides, at the ready to defend himself if she intended to throw anything else.

And this struck her as somewhat comical, even as Sylvie was aware that neither of them had blinked for an unnatural amount of time.

And then—and then—the bloody man's mouth slowly tilted up at the corners. And as usual, anything approximating a smile transformed his face.

"'In the love with' you?" he repeated softly.

She squeezed her eyes closed. *Damn.* Her cursed temper had made smithereens of her English. She took a deep breath, soothing her mind, recovering her dignity.

"*In* love," she corrected quietly. "*In* love with me."

She watched the rest of his anger leave him. And somehow, the silence had gone from fraught . . . to velvet.

"Well, *I* think," Tom countered finally, softly, "that you are 'in the love' with *me,* Sylvie."

Neither of them confirmed or denied a thing.

Simply watched. Simply breathed.

But finally, this silent stubbornness of his was enough to stir the cinders of her temper again.

"And because you are afraid"—Sylvie waved her hand abruptly, in helpless frustration—"this is why you push me away."

He stared at her wonderingly. The beginnings of a frown creased his forehead.

And then he drew in a breath so deep it was as though he was trying to suck patience from the very air. He sat down hard in his chair at the desk.

"Listen to me. You saw that child today, Sylvie."

She nodded, though she knew he didn't require it.

His words were careful, and they almost had the sound of a recital. She imagined he'd rehearsed them in his head during their silent ride back to London.

"I never knew my own father. My mother and I were always desperately poor, and she died when I was very young. Much of what I did to survive—*most* of it—I would never boast about, or even wish to describe to you. I did what I needed to, and to this day I count myself bloody lucky that I'm not in Newgate, or didn't end up swinging from a gallows. I suppose," he said almost wryly, "if I were to reflect, I could arrive at a *few* regrets. But they wouldn't include Jamie, and they wouldn't include . . ." He looked up at her, seemed to lose his words for a moment. "They wouldn't include you," he concluded quietly.

"But I also know now it would be bloody . . . *unconscionable* to subject someone to the uncertainty of my life, of my reputation, when something so much better can be had for them."

She wasn't certain about the word "unconscionable," but she was virtually positive it meant "wrong."

"And Sylvie, this doesn't make me a—what was your word?"

"Lâche?" she supplied.

"Yes. It doesn't make me a *lâche*. If you truly understood how . . . if you knew you would . . ." He dragged impatient hands over his hair. "You would know that it makes me . . . it probably makes me a . . ." He paused, as a revelation flickered over his face. "A damned *hero*."

He ground out the last words, oddly, darkly amused, bemused. Clearly it was the last thing he'd ever, ever expected to be.

She considered them.

"It makes you bloody stupid," she said flatly.

His head jerked toward her.

And then in one smooth startling motion he stood up, crossed the room, and grasped her chin in his hand.

She gasped when he tipped her face sharply up to him, tried to jerk her chin away. He held it firmly.

"Tell me, Sylvie, and answer me honestly for once: are you angry with *me* . . . or with yourself?"

"I—"

But then his mouth was on hers, hard.

It was a kiss that infuriated, confirmed, stirred, and then somehow . . . despite everything . . . became all she'd always needed, suspected she would ever need, which infuriated her all over again.

And it felt entirely final.

And then he stopped, released her chin. He closed his eyes briefly.

They were both breathing roughly. When he opened his eyes again, she saw the iron resolve in them.

"So stop blaming *me,* Miss *Chapeau.* It's simply how things must be. If you gave it a moment's thought instead of indulging your temper, you would realize that I'm right. And it's just your own bloody misfortune to love two men."

"I don't—"

"Yes?" he said swiftly. His face tense. Waiting.

But when she said nothing, he nodded once, curtly.

"Tell me now who's 'bloody stupid,' Sylvie. Tell me now who's a coward."

She looked at him. And for a moment she forgot his words, and simply looked, fell into the beauty of his hard, elegant face, the character and wear of it. Looking for a reason to hate him.

Finding only that it resembled her own heart. And this brought with it a quiet sort of terror.

"Don't feel you need to stay," he said softly. Ironically.

She turned abruptly.

And to spite him, because she knew he was looking for passion . . . she closed the door quietly behind her.

CHAPTER SIXTEEN

I T WAS SO DARK in her little nun's cell of a room; her eyes remained open, and still it was as though she was looking at the inside of her eyelids. She'd found it comforting before, and snug. Tonight, somehow, it seemed to mock her mood. Shame was not nearly as comfortable a bed partner as a warm, passionate man.

A quick temper was her curse; she relived throwing things earlier today, the shouting, and put her hands up to her cheeks. *Mon dieu.* She wondered if her sister had a temper. It would be lovely to have someone with whom to commiserate about a family trait.

I think you are in the love with me, Sylvie.

Are you angry with me, or with yourself?

She knew how to be with Etienne, knew what to expect. Knew how the days of her life would play out. And she knew a moment of regret for ever leaving him, for now she was all too aware of the places in her he would never be able to stir.

And more aware than ever of the things he could offer her that someone like Tom Shaughnessy could not.

Indeed, *had* not.

This was the trouble, she realized, with surrendering to want.

And as she'd left his library today, she'd glanced down and seen the note that had been tucked beneath the paperweight she'd hurled:

Pinkerton-Knowles backed out. That is the last of them.

She knew what this meant: Tom had lost all of his investors, and thus all of his capital, too. His future was now nearly as uncertain as it had been when he was a child, stealing cheese. She felt it on his behalf, the winds of the abyss whistling at her ankles. She had fought too long, her entire life, to dance away from that abyss.

Sylvie stood and lit a candle, pushed open her trunk, unfolded the miniature of her mother from where she kept it wrapped, hidden, in a soft cotton shift. And stared down at it, holding the candle away from it so the wax would not drip down.

I will tell him who I am, she thought.

It was something she wanted to give to him, a gift in parting—an apology, and her trust. To tell him he was right about everything after all—this was all it could be, and that she understood that this interlude was indeed over, and she would no doubt be gone soon.

To thank him. The gratitude didn't seem specific. Perhaps she simply meant to thank him for being.

Her heart knocking, she traveled the dark hallway and found the stairs leading to his portion of the attic.

The room was dark. She hovered near the last step, listened for breathing, and heard none.

"Tom?" She whispered. She took the last step, lifted her candle.

The bed was tightly, neatly made. He hadn't slept in it.

You can find me in it . . . most nights.

The pain was savage and instant and utterly shocking, and for a moment, it hurt to breathe, as though her lungs were suddenly made of rough-edged glass. She simply stood there on the step and stared at Tom's made bed, in a room that smelled and felt so strongly of him it seemed impossible he wasn't in it.

And this was when she admitted to herself that she hadn't come to apologize for her temper. That she hadn't come to tell him who she truly was. Or to tell him he was right about everything.

Though she *might* have done those things after they had made love again and again.

A clock somewhere bonged 3:00 A.M.

So she left, no less ashamed than when she had set out to find him.

CHAPTER SEVENTEEN

DOWN THE HALL girls were dressing for the show in nymphlike togas, shimmering organza to match the shimmer of the grand oyster, smoothing rouge onto their cheeks, while Tom and The General discussed the final details of Venus. For tonight was the night: In the absence of all of his investors, the success of Venus was the pivot upon which Tom's future turned.

"We need to make a damned fortune on this show, or we're sunk." Tom managed to say the words easily. This, in itself, did not come easily.

"We'll make the damned fortune." The General was quietly confident.

Tom shifted restlessly in his chair, patted his hand on the arm of it for a moment. "Gen . . . I had an inspiration."

"Mmm?" The General looked up alertly.

"Well . . . what if I made the Gentleman's Emporium a . . . Family Emporium."

"A *what?*" The General sounded alarmed.

"Family Emporium."

"Family," The General repeated slowly, lingering over the word as if he'd never heard the word before in his life. "Emporium."

"That *is* what I said, Gen," Tom said irritably. "I thought, perhaps, there could be a floor for mothers to take tea together, and then a floor for fathers to drink with other fathers, we'll have cards and games, a place to get ices and cakes, a floor for entertainment that men can bring their wives to, a place for children to play together on little pirate ships, and in castles, and . . ."

He trailed off at the look on The General's face. As if he wanted to test Tom's forehead for fever.

"Things of that sort," Tom finished uncomfortably.

The General seemed to be searching for diplomatic words, which was highly unlike him.

"You have an area of expertise, Tommy . . ." he began slowly.

"Area*s*," Tom corrected testily.

"Very well, then," The General humored him. "Areas. Which is why you're rich now."

"Was rich," Tom corrected. "Now every spare penny I had is in that building across town, and as I said, if we don't make a fortune tonight . . ."

The General waved that away impatiently. "*This* . . . is what you know. Venus . . ." The General said over the word lovingly—neither one of them could say the word with any other sort of intonation—"is what you know. They resulted from your instincts, and following your instincts has made you a success."

"It doesn't mean I can't develop other areas of expertise," Tom said irritably.

"No," The General agreed. Sounding as though he was humoring him.

"And it's not a bad idea, though, is it?" Tom insisted. "A Family Emporium?"

The General shrugged. Which was something of a concession.

Tom fell into a near-brooding silence. Which was highly unlike *him*. "She called me a coward and threw things at me." It was becoming a habit, it seemed, this exchange of confidences.

The General was quiet for a moment.

"The French," he finally said, shaking his head in commiseration.

It amused Tom distantly that The General knew precisely who he was talking about, but perhaps he shouldn't have been surprised.

Then The General's head snapped toward Tom. "Wait. She called *you* a coward?"

"A *lâche*, more specifically."

"And she's still alive?"

Tom grunted a laugh.

"Should I ask *why* she called you a coward? And does this mean . . . do you mean to say . . . are you confessing that you did . . . *finally* . . . touch a dancer, Tom?" The General's lips were pressed together, as if he was struggling not to laugh.

"I touched a dancer, Gen." Tom sounded surly. "And she *is* a real dancer, as you said."

"Mmm." The General's way of agreeing. His gaze drifted then, as if he didn't want to look Tom in the eye. He sipped at his tea.

"The dance," Tom began. "She . . . It's . . ." He struggled for a word.

"Beautiful?" the General said.

"Yes." Tom said, sounding defeated.

"So you saw it?"

"Yes." He paused. "But there's no money in it," he added hurriedly.

"Mmm," The General said. His gaze drifted again.

"Have you noticed that all the girls seem to be getting just a little thinner, Gen?" Tom peered hard at The General. "Almost as if they've been getting more exercise."

"Hadn't, really," The General said, still looking elsewhere. "So . . . she threw things and called you a coward because . . ."

"A wealthy French nobleman apparently wants to marry her. I told her she should marry him. That she'd be foolish not to."

He looked at The General, whose face, at the moment, was completely unreadable.

The General continued to stare at him. And then he frowned a little, looking oddly puzzled. His eyes scoured the murals searchingly, as if looking for the answer to whatever question was silently plaguing him. "Tom?"

"What is it?" Tom said curtly.

"Who's that noble cove you told me about from the Greek myths, when we were having the murals painted? The one who lives with a wound, or some such, and suffered every day, and grew wiser for it?"

"Chiron?" Tom supplied, confused.

"Right. Chiron. Here's the rub: *You,* Tom Shaughnessy, are *not* a noble cove. Not even close. It's just not your nature, that martyr bit. That"—he pointed to Tom's hand, and Tom stopped rubbing—"and this"—he made an eloquent circle with his hand to encompass the theater—"is *your* nature. You *fight.* You fight dirty, if you have to, for what you want. You like a little drama. All of which are benefits of *not* being a gentleman. You don't"—he drawled the words mockingly—"'quietly back away.'"

Tom considered this. "This is different, Gen," he said ungraciously.

The General stared at him, those intense dark eyes bright beneath those thick brows, which then dived nearly to a point at the top of his nose.

Tom matched him glower for glower.

"Well I'll be damned," The General finally said, wonderingly. He gave a short incredulous laugh. Then he reached for his watch from his coat, peeked at the time. He stood and stubbed out his cigar.

"What?" Tom snapped.

The General slipped into his coat, headed for the door, and said the words over his shoulder.

"She was right."

      ஜ   *ஜ*   *ஜ*

Seats creaked and coats rustled, a few throats rumbled to clear, then silence dropped, heavy as the velvet curtain that obscured the evening's promised delights. And as raucousness, not silence, typically reigned at the White Lily, right up to and during the show, this silence underscored the momentousness of the occasion, built upon itself until the anticipation in the audience was so palpable it could almost be beaten like a drum.

Tom looked out from the back of the theater: row upon row of heads were upturned, pointed raptly at the stage. Behind that curtain, in the wings, a crew of boys were poised to fan the fish and pull open the oyster; the girls dressed as

water nymphs were poised to drift out when Molly began
her song.

Tom's gut tightened in a way it hadn't since the owner
of the Green Apple Theater had threatened to slit his gullet for losing money on a show. So much rested on this
single evening.

Josephine's head, pale in the darkness, was turned over
her shoulder, watching for his signal; at last, he lifted a
finger, and she nodded and dragged her fingers across
the pianoforte in a long glissando. The velvet curtain
lurched up.

Tom heard the collective gasp with satisfaction, and
exhaled his relief.

An enormous oyster shell rose up from the stage, ruffled at the lip and ridged across its roof, glowing in the
footlights with an otherworldly luminescence. Wooden
seaweed, painted a deep black-green and carved into appropriately, aquatically curved shapes, rippled by virtue
of boys backstage drawing it slowly back and forth with
pulleys. Enormous, gaily painted exotic fish hung from
the rafters of the theater like Piscean kites, and were made
to swim by boys perched there in the rafters, hidden away,
wafting them with bellows.

The General was virtually vibrating with pride next to
Tom. It was a triumph, a thing of wonder and beauty.
Lacking only diaphanously clad maidens singing bawdy
songs, which it would have in mere moments.

Josephine, as befit the gravity of the moment, was
playing a variation of a delicate sonata. In three bars, the
shell would glide open on pulleys to reveal . . . at long
last . . . *Venus.*

Josephine played one bar . . .

... then two bars ...

... then three bars ...

But nothing happened.

She continued to play. Bar after bar of the sonata rolled through the theater, but nothing whatsoever moved on the stage. And soon the rustle in the audience became one of restlessness rather than anticipation.

"What the bloody hell is wrong?" Tom hissed to The General, who had gone rigid and alert.

Suddenly one plump white arm suddenly popped out from between the oyster's ruffled lips.

The crowd gasped.

The arm waved about for a bit, frantically, as if feeling for direction, looking for assistance. Disappeared into the shell again.

Sweet Merciful Mary.

"Bloody hell—that isn't *Molly.* That's—that's *Daisy!*" Tom growled. "I'll *kill* her."

The crowd began to murmur wonderingly. Murmurs were *definitely* bad for business.

Josephine rolled panicked eyes toward Tom, but her fingers continued dutifully moving. The dreamy strains of the sonata continued to wash through the theater like the sea washing over the shore.

A leg burst out from between the oyster lips. The crowd gasped and visibly jumped in their seats.

It was really only part of a leg. A foot and a plump calf, covered in a pink silk stocking.

The leg kicked about a little.

"Did the thing ... eat her?" someone in the audience speculated loudly, sounding half-confused, half-hopeful.

In the dark Tom could see The General's face glowing

with frantic perspiration. He darted a few steps up the aisle, then darted back when the shell began to creak open.

To reveal that it was, indeed, Daisy. On her knees, pushing up the ceiling of the shell with both hands, like Atlas, for God's sake. One leg draped over the side.

"Oh, God!" The General squeaked, frantic, his hands gripping his head. "It must be the boys. Those bloody damned boys! The pulleys! What the bloody—"

Daisy beamed at the crowd, though her eyes were a little wild and her cheeks were flushed with the effort of holding the shell open.

But slowly, inexorably, despite her best efforts, it began to creak closed, buckling her little by little. And then the crowd, and Tom and The General, got a final swift and potent glimpse of Daisy's panicked face before the shell clapped shut again and Daisy disappeared.

Laughter exploded.

All the while the liquid notes of the sonata poured caressingly through the theater, as Josephine dutifully played on.

"DO. SOMETHING." Tom commanded in a growl to The General.

The General bolted toward the back of the stage.

For a moment, all was quiet. The oyster remained still, glowing its soothing, glorious nacre colors, while the sonata delicately scented the air, and the audience waited, primed now: Tom could sense it.

And then the shell inched open. *Creeeeeeak.*

The audience inhaled in anticipation.

Abruptly the shell clapped shut again. *Clack.*

A collective exhale.

The shell inched open again. *Creeeeeeak.*

Another inhale of anticipation.

Then clapped shut again. *Clack.*

It looked like—dear God—

"I think it's *chewing* her! It looks like it's chewing her!" Someone in the crowd marveled.

Like that.

The laughter became utterly helpless then. There really was no hope for it. Great roars of it ripped up the rows, a conflagration of mirth. Men began thrashing in their chairs, and the percussion of knees and backs slapped joined it.

"Bloody brilliant!" someone bellowed. "Shaughnessy, you're a bloody *genius!*"

The oyster *creeeeeeaked* open again. Steadily this time: an inch, then six inches, then a foot, and then three feet.

The audience settled somewhat, leaned forward, eagerly waiting.

Until it finally opened enough to reveal Daisy. Disheveled, wild-eyed, a grin pasted on her mouth. Tentatively she began to raise her arms into the air in a pose; at the same time, she cautiously peered back over her shoulder at the shell.

It clapped shut abruptly and she vanished.

The audience roared.

Josephine, clearly at a loss for what else she might do, dutifully continued to play the sonata. From where he stood, Tom could see the perspiration gleaming on her face, too.

The delicate music was all but drowned out beneath the stamp of feet and roars of men.

The shell creaked open again. Slowly, slowly, slowly.

Daisy, her optimism clearly spent, was curled up in the center of it, her arms wrapped protectively over her head.

But when the shell remained open, she lifted her head up, peeped cautiously over her shoulder at it. Wildly mussed strands of her ruddy hair were puffing out around her ruddy face.

"It wants you for dinner, Daize!" an audience member bellowed. "Run! Run while you can!"

"You can be the pearl in my oyster any day, Daisy Jones!"

The shell remained open. Cautiously, tentatively, Daisy rose to her knees, facing the audience. She peered suspiciously over her shoulder at her nemesis, the oyster.

"Harpoon the beast!" someone suggested in a bellow. "Kill it before it eats you, Daize!"

More gusts of wild laughter.

One of Daisy's enormous breasts had nearly freed itself from her gracefully wrapped toga in the tussle, and now, as she began to rise, it glowed in the footlights, a luminous, miniature twin of the oyster from which she'd emerged.

"Oh . . . my . . . *God!*" Someone howled in helpless mirth.

Daisy took a visibly deep breath, her bosom cresting and falling like a tidal wave, and gave her toga a twist to recapture the breast.

And finally, when it became clear the top of the shell would remain aloft, Daisy flung her arms triumphantly into the air and crooked a knee.

The lascivious, buxom, grinning antithesis of Botticelli's Venus.

"Bravo! Bravo!"

The applause was thunderous; hands had never beat together so violently before, and the theater resounded with stamps and cheers. Suddenly the air was filled with glittering things: coins raining toward the stage. Then a hail of flowers. Then cravats and shoes and watch fobs.

All was spectacularly successful mayhem.

From where Tom stood in the back of the theater, he could see the wild look slowly fade from Daisy's eyes, and little by little her desperate smile made the subtle transformation from panic . . . to uncertainty . . .

To triumph.

Ah, well. Daisy was a diva. It was perhaps the way of divas to prevail.

The General had returned, looking considerably more sweaty and disheveled. "The damn boys with the pulleys had disappeared."

"Sack them if you ever see them again," Tom said flatly. "Why was the oyster chewing her?"

"I tried—several times—but when *I* pulled on the pulley, I only dangled. Couldn't get it to open far enough." He said this matter-of-factly, accustomed to the myriad trivial inconveniences of his size. "Several of the girls helped me get it open."

They both took a moment to watch Daisy basking in the waves of applause.

"That bloody woman is going to do that exactly the same way every night this week," Tom said with grim satisfaction.

ঞ   ঞ   ঞ

The congratulatory crowds had finally cleared away from Daisy's dressing room, leaving her alone amidst a veritable forest of flowers. She considered whether to call a carriage to take her home. Alone. Perhaps she should stop in to see Tom before she did.

It wasn't a conversation she looked forward to having.

A tap sounded on her dressing room door, surprising her. She quickly blotted her eyes and huffed out the nearest lamp. In the shadows, she hoped it would be difficult to see how red they had become.

"Come in," she sang out, hoping her voice didn't sound as thick to the person on the other side of the door as it did to her.

The door opened. The General stood in the doorway.

He said nothing at all. Merely regarded her with those intense dark eyes. She returned his stare.

"Well?" she all but snapped, finally.

"You've been crying," he accused.

She turned away from him and began fussing with the petals of one of the flower arrangements. Hothouse flowers, which is what one earned when one was feted by dukes and earls. They'd been brought to her for years, a consequence of her notoriety. She wondered how much longer she could expect them.

The General, of course, was empty-handed. "You were an enormous success this evening," he began.

"Ha," Daisy said this to the mirror. "'Enormous' is the word."

He said nothing.

She tried not to, but she did anyway: she sniffed. *Bloody hell.* And so now he knew for certain that she *had* been crying.

"I suppose I should apologize to Tom," she said tentatively.

"Oh, I think Tom has forgiven you," The General said with faint irony.

No one said anything for a time.

"I paid 'er a guinea. Molly," Daisy confessed.

"I should have thought Molly could be bought much cheaper."

Daisy almost smiled at that. "I just thought it would be so . . . pretty," she said wistfully. "I wanted it to be me. All the girls were so damned . . . they gloated about it."

As this was true, and partially Daisy's fault for being such a diva, The General remained silent.

"I'm sorry I ruined yer beautiful show." She meant it.

He gave a one-shouldered shrug. "They loved it, the crowd did. They loved you."

"But not fer the reasons I wanted them to love it."

He conceded this with silence. "Perhaps it's for the best."

Daisy knew this meant that perhaps her future featured comic roles and not roles for a youthful siren, and that she might as well become accustomed to it now.

"I'm not pretty anymore, am I, Gen?"

"Oh, Daisy. You were never pretty."

She whipped her head toward him, her eyes enormous with horrified astonishment.

He rapidly closed the distance between them then. And to her amazement, reached out, and with his thumb gently dabbed a tear on her cheek.

"Don't ever use words like 'pretty' to describe yourself, Daisy Jones," he said, softly, but firmly and unapologetically, too. "Pretty is far, far too tepid a word for what you are. And no one will *ever* forget you, you know."

And suddenly Daisy Jones, who had sported with dukes and earls atop her cherished nearby pink velvet settee, who'd been feted and showered with gifts by the richest men in London, felt as shy as a girl before the message she saw written in The General's dark eyes.

Gently, without hesitation, he lifted her chin up to touch his lips to hers. And then he proceeded to kiss her in a way that stripped away all her years and experience, all notions or cynicism about romance, and left only the two of them alone.

"You know I love you, don't you?" he said softly when he was done.

"I do know." She sounded as breathless as a girl.

"And?"

"And I love ye, too, ye wee bugger."

"That works out nicely for the both of us then, doesn't it?" he said gruffly. "And speaking of that guinea, Daize . . . I know of a better investment than Molly. And it has to do with Tom."

ॐ   ॐ   ॐ

Tom kept to his word. Every night that week, Daisy climbed in the beautiful oyster shell, struggled to free herself from it, was chewed, nearly lost a breast out of her toga, and in the end was cheered wildly. She was also supposed to sing a bawdy song, but occasionally the cheering made it all but impossible.

The theater was filled to the rafters day after day, so they added shows, keeping Daisy exceptionally busy. And Tom began to breathe a little more easily. He had no investors, he was in debt up to his eyes, but his coffers were refilling just a little, and another few weeks of this kind of roaring success would buy him enough time to rally more investors before the costs of building the Gentleman's Emporium dragged him under, and with it the White Lily and everyone who depended upon it . . . and him.

But Daisy's Venus so warmed up the crowds that nearly anything they would have put onstage after it would have elicited howls of approval. Fairies, pirates, damsels—it would not have mattered if he had dressed all the girls as horses and trotted them out.

An equestrian theme!

It just demonstrated that inspiration was always just one thought away.

But then he thought of a wooden horse named Bloody Hell that could be pulled on a string. And suddenly he pictured how much small boys would enjoy playing with other small boys on hobbyhorses. How much they might enjoy a *show* featuring hobbyhorses.

Or maybe puppets . . .

She was right, The General had said.

You fight, he'd said. *Dirty, if you have to.*

There simply had to be a way to have everything he wanted, for he always had.

And so his thoughts warred with accepting that he might not be able to have the things he wanted and grappling and rejecting ways to get them.

ॐ   ॐ   ॐ

For a few nights, he waited until his eyes were raw from lack of sleep for the creak of footsteps on the stairs.

But he saw her only onstage: a fairy, a pirate, a damsel, game but reluctant, fiery and proud.

Other nights he left looking for other female company,

other arms, other hands, that could do things to and with him to remind him how easily passion could make one forget, and how much pleasure could be had from one's own body without complications. Without involving anything other than the body.

But he'd always lost the will halfway to the Velvet Glove, where they had no doubt become lonely for his company, and instead spent an evening staring at the building he intended to transform into the Gentleman's Emporium, sipping at a flask of whiskey and making plans. And thinking, mordantly amused, about the flawed things he suspected he loved. A dwarf choreographer and an aging diva and a little boy with a wooden horse named Bloody Hell and a beautiful, bad-tempered, achingly tender ballerina who made love as though she were both dancing and fighting for her life.

It wasn't as though he didn't know where she slept. As if he couldn't have made a meal of his own pride and gone to see her.

But it was for the best, he told himself. She would be leaving, and life as he knew it would resume without her.

ॐ   ॐ   ॐ

Augustus Beedle hadn't aged well, but The General found to his surprise he didn't look upon this with any particular satisfaction. His hair, once a leonine sweep, now began much farther back on his head, leaving an expanse of lined forehead; five lines, he counted, evenly spaced, like a staff of music awaiting the notes of a composition. His waistcoat bulged just a little. *How about that.* The General thought. The famously lean Beedle now sported a wee paunch.

Given the missing hair and the forehead lines, The General suspected that being married to a temperamental ballerina was perhaps more challenging than Augustus Beedle had expected.

And at this thought, The General *did* experience a twinge of satisfaction.

They exchanged bows. Once upright again, they took a quiet moment to eye each other, assessing. The General saw Beedle whisk a look over his clothes, trace their genus to Weston, and do the math of their cost in his head, for his face ultimately reflected a begrudging approval.

What he lacked in height, The General had always made up for in flair. Beedle had never been able to compete in that regard, at least.

"You've been missed," he said finally. "Your gift for sets has been unsurpassed, and your eye for choreography—"

"It's been a very long time, Beedle," The General said wryly. In other words, doubting the sincerity of all of this.

Beedle smiled wryly, acknowledging the little jab. "Your talent was exceptional, and I did enjoy working with you. Should you need a—"

"I'm happy where I am." The General thought of Daisy for a moment: warm, round, loud, honest, kind, proud Daisy. "Very happy."

Beedle cleared his throat. "I should like to say that I'm grateful for this opportunity to apologize for our misunderstanding."

"Maria was not a 'misunderstanding,' Beedle."

The General had forgiven Beedle, for despite the friendship between the two men, it wasn't precisely Beedle's fault that Maria had chosen not to love a short man and that The General had chosen to drown his broken heart in all manner of liquor in every major city on the Continent. But The General's strategy required keeping the other man off-balance and feeling guilty and uncomfortable for the time being.

In other words, he needed him in the proper condition to do a favor. For this was his sole mission today. It was a mission, coincidentally, that Tom Shaughnessy knew nothing about. And the mission was entirely for Tom's sake.

"She is well?" he asked solicitously. Keeping his voice ever-so-slightly strained. Brave-sounding. "Maria?"

Beedle smiled tiredly. "Yes."

"Very good." Again, just a hint, a crucial hint, of noble strain in his voice.

The General allowed the silence to stretch until it was officially awkward. And then:

"You're familiar with the White Lily, Augustus?"

A small, appreciative smile. "Yes. Tom Shaughnessy's theater. Beautiful girls."

"I thought you might be interested to know, Augustus, that I've formed my own *corps de ballet*, very talented dancers, all. And they were all employed by the White Lily."

Augustus Beedle's eyes went gratifyingly wide. "Where can I see them?"

"Well, that's just it, Augustus. They will be featured as part of a new, grand entertainment center. A . . . Family Emporium."

"Shaughnessy's idea?"

"Yes."

"Then no doubt it will be wildly successful."

"No doubt," The General said. "And I'd like to beg a favor of you, Augustus."

"Anything," Beedle promised.

"We could also use a blessing from an exalted source. Specifically, a very well-known patron of the ballet."

It took Beedle but a moment.

And then he smiled. "That, my friend, should not be difficult."

⁂   ⁂   ⁂

Sylvie was sitting quietly with Josephine in the sunny room, next to where all the hammering and swearing normally took place, stitching a rent in a fairy wing, when the housekeeper, Mrs. Pool, interrupted them.

"Ladies, a Viscount Grantham and a Lady Grantham are downstairs."

Sylvie stood so abruptly that her fairy wing tumbled from her lap and lay upside down on the floor, like a big butterfly shot from the sky.

"They are looking for a girl named Sylvie Lamoo... Lamosomething. A right fancy name. They thought she might have come to the White Lily." Mrs. Pool gave a merry laugh at the absurdity of the very idea. "Mr. Shaughnessy sent me up to find you. Shall I send them away?"

"I—" It was an airless squeak. Sylvie gaped for a moment at the housekeeper. Then she turned and gaped at Josephine.

Then she smoothed her hands nervously over her hair, and nervously down her skirt, then gave up on the grooming and simply bolted down the stairs.

⁂   ⁂   ⁂

Near the door of the theater, near the stage, three people stood. Two men, one very tall and fair-haired, an air of easy importance and casual danger, rather the sort of air Tom Shaughnessy wore like a coat. This must be Viscount Grantham.

The other man was Tom. His face was quiet, oddly pensive. He didn't smile when he saw her. Simply watched her, standing very still. She felt his eyes on her, physical as hands drawing her to him.

But it was the third person, the small person, the woman, who riveted Sylvie.

She slowed, then stopped a few paces away from her, and stared, folded her hands into her skirt in front of her.

She's pretty. She doesn't look quite like me. Dear God, she looks like Mama. Look at her beautiful dress. She is my family. My family. My sister.

The thoughts collided in Sylvie's head, competing for expression and attention, ultimately making speech impossible. Mouth parted slightly, she gaped at Susannah Whitelaw, née Holt. Lady Grantham. Her hand went up to her mouth in sheer wonder. Tears stung her eyes.

Luckily, Susannah was doing all of the very same things at very nearly the same time, so she needn't have feared she would be considered rude.

It was Sylvie who finally managed the curtsy. And her sister, Susannah, Lady Grantham, gave a short giddy laugh and curtsied, too.

They approached each other slowly, tentatively, as if they each feared the other would evaporate. They each reached out their hands; their fingers met and clung. *My flesh and blood,* Sylvie thought wonderingly, holding her sister's cool palms.

"You look just like her," Sylvie finally said breathlessly.

"*You* don't," Susannah said just as breathlessly, just as wonderingly.

"I must look like *him*," Sylvie told her.

They laughed together, giddily, though nothing was funny. Joy. The sound of joy and disbelief.

Then silence, slightly awkward, slightly awed.

Tom broke it. "Why don't you take your sister to your room upstairs, Miss Lamoreux?"

And Sylvie did start at the sound of her name, her real name, from Tom's lips.

"Thank you," she said softly, trying to give the words every meaning possible. She held his eyes for a moment.

And she took Susannah by the arm and led her upstairs.

JP   JP   JP

Susannah and Sylvie sat together, a pair of shy strangers who were not strangers. In their hands they held their miniatures of their mother. It was a family reunion, of sorts.

"Your maid—" Susannah began.

"Madame Gabon?"

"Yes. She said you were a dancer, Sylvie. She said you were famous."

"I am a ballerina," Sylvie confirmed. "And I *am* famous," she said with an utter lack of conceit. "In Paris, at least. And I am known in other countries."

"Oh, my," her sister, wife of a viscount, breathed. "It seems everyone in the family is a dancer, except me. Unless you include the waltz."

"We must *always* include the waltz," Sylvie said somberly.

Her sister laughed, and this was grand, as Sylvie suspected Susannah loved to laugh and would do it easily.

"Sabrina is our other sister?"

"Yes. We must find her, too."

"I wonder if she's a dancer, too."

"Miss Daisy Jones said she thought she might have been raised by a curate."

"Miss Daisy Jones?" Sylvie looked at her sister blankly. "Why would Miss Jones know about Sabrina?"

"Daisy knew our mother! Didn't you know?" Susannah was astonished.

This was stunning news. "Miss Jones does not speak to the other dancers here at the White Lily."

And here was something that Sylvie half understood, and wasn't certain that Susannah would: why Daisy would keep her distance from the other dancers. Having no doubt come such a great distance in life, Daisy wanted to keep a safe distance between herself and her past. For a distance reminded her of how far she had come, and kept her safe from the gravity such a past might exert.

"I shall speak to Daisy, soon," was all she said.

A lull, for they were still discovering the rhythm of being sisters.

"Your housekeeper said you were beautiful," Susannah said gently. "When you danced."

"I am," Sylvie said firmly.

Susannah laughed delightedly. "Now I *know* we're related."

They exchanged proud, smug, amused glances, perhaps their first of sisterly solidarity.

And Sylvie squeezed Susannah's hand, and hers was

squeezed in return. Lovely to take for granted this exchange of warmth.

But she had a pressing question.

"Do you . . . do you have a temper?" Sylvie wanted to know.

"I *slapped* a man once in a fit of temper," Susannah confessed shamefacedly. "I threatened a man with a vase when he tried to take my dresses."

Sylvie felt immensely relieved. "So it is not only me. *Mon dieu,* it plagues me, I fear."

"Daisy says Mama had—has—a temper."

When Susannah stumbled over the verb tense, they both fell quiet for a moment.

"Do you think she's alive?" Susannah finally dared to ask.

"I think, even when I was very small and alone with Claude . . . somehow I didn't believe she was dead when Claude told me so. Mr. Bale said there had been a . . . trial?" she ventured.

And so Susannah told Sylvie, who drank it in thirstily, the extraordinary tale of their mother and father: Anna Holt, who had been blamed for their father's murder and forced to flee, leaving her daughters behind, and of Richard Lockwood, their handsome—naturally—and much-beloved politician father. Of Thaddeus Morley, another politician who now moldered in the Tower, waiting to learn whether he would swing for the crime of the murder of Richard Lockwood.

"Do you think we will find her?" Sylvie dared the question.

"We will try," Susannah said firmly, and Sylvie nodded,

approving of Susannah's resolve. Not a pair of milquetoasts, not the Holt sisters.

"And what of your husband, Susannah?"

A lovely, soft pink slowly flooded Susannah's cheeks, and she went quiet.

Sylvie laughed. "Ah, so you are in *love* with your husband!"

"He's . . ." She stopped and shook her head, as if she could never complete that sentence to her own satisfaction. She cleared her throat.

"And you . . . you have a lo-lover." Susannah stumbled over the word, trying to look nonchalant about it, which amused Sylvie. "Etienne. Your housekeeper said his name is Etienne."

"Madame Gabon told you about *Etienne?*" Sylvie would need to have a word with the garrulous housekeeper. "She is too talkative."

"Madame Gabon said he came to find you, and she told him you had gone to England. He wasn't happy to find you gone." There was a pause. "Are you in *love* with *him?*" Susannah asked shyly.

Sylvie laughed to deflect the question. "He is very handsome."

Susannah was no fool. She tilted her head and studied Sylvie curiously, which was disconcerting. And Sylvie began to comprehend that sisters might very well come with some disconcerting features, too. It was lovely to be cared for, and lovely to be scrutinized, even as it wasn't entirely comfortable.

"When did you know you were in love with Kit?" Sylvie braved the question. She'd never before had a woman to ask such a question of.

Susannah's head went back a bit in thought. "I don't think there was a *when* I knew, necessarily. It almost felt . . . as if it always was. He seemed all wrong, at first. He was not what I expected, I suppose. But . . ." She gave a little self-conscious laugh. "He was everything I needed. He was like . . . air." She blushed again. "I cannot explain. I'm sorry."

Sylvie was silent, and simply admired her sister for a moment. She was very pretty. She was absurdly pleased to have a pretty sister, who seemed clever, too.

"Mr. Shaughnessy is very handsome," Susannah said idly.

"Do you think so?' Sylvie turned away, traced a little square pattern with her finger on the counterpane.

"Oh, yes. I remember when I met him. He took away my breath. Even as Kit stood next to me."

Sylvie looked up swiftly at her sister. Then looked away just as swiftly.

"And it's not just how Mr. Shaughnessy looks. It's . . ." She paused. "Something about him reminds me of Kit."

And by the silence that followed, she knew her sister was studying her. Sylvie was both pleased and irritated, and imagined this was the way of sisters, too, the feeling pleased and irritated all at once.

"Will you come to stay with us, or will you want to stay here at the White Lily?" Susannah sounded shy about it.

Sylvie finally looked up and ceased worrying the counterpane.

How tempting it was to stay, when there was a little attic room at the top of the stairs with a man who might or might not be sleeping in it at night. She considered its dangerous lure, and how the very thought of its being empty at night ached as if a hole had been driven through her.

Most nights.

No; it would be absurd to stay. Pointless, dangerous, foolish.

"May I stay with you?" she asked Susannah, just as shyly. In fact, she was rather looking forward to greeting Mr. Bale the butler again. Perhaps sticking her tongue out at his back.

"Oh, yes, please!"

They reached for each other and enjoyed their first of no doubt many, many hugs as sisters.

        ॐ   ॐ   ॐ

And so with a hug sealing their bargain, Susannah tripped gaily down the stairs to tell Kit the news about their new guest, leaving Sylvie to pack for her departure from the White Lily.

She lifted the lid of her trunk and saw her mourning dress folded there, lurking like a stowaway. *Her disguise.* Tom Shaughnessy had seen through it straightaway, but then again, he *was* rather an expert at costumes.

She stood and reached for her cloak, hanging from the peg in the wall. For a moment, she lifted it, allowed the weight of it to drape from her hands, and indulged in the memory of how she'd wrapped it around herself when she'd made that journey from this little room to Tom's.

She would never forget the look in his eyes when she had dropped the cloak. As though she, Sylvie, was a gift he'd never, ever dared hope to receive.

"You could have told me. Sylvie Lamoreux. Or is it Sylvie Holt?"

The voice made her jump. Sylvie whirled to find Tom in the doorway, his broad shoulders filling it completely. Her heart skipped, lightly, painfully, a stone cast across water.

It was odd, incongruous, to see him here in this prim little room, this vivid man she associated with every wicked pleasure.

His words hadn't been an accusation, precisely. They had almost been conversational. Almost teasing. His smile was slight, and oddly, his posture almost diffident.

"I wanted to tell you," she faltered. "I did go to—"

She stopped. She wouldn't tell him that she had gone to his room that evening . . . only to find it empty.

And how it had felt to wonder whether he had gone from her arms to another's.

Her chin went up instead; she sought refuge in her pride. "Would you have seen me differently?" she asked him instead. "If I had told you at first?"

"That you were a famous ballerina in Paris and related to a viscount?" Faint irony in his words.

"I feared you might believe I was yet another impostor, someone posing as Lady Grantham's sister. I didn't want you to believe that of me."

"And you thought I might turn you in for a reward." He said it wryly.

She flushed.

"You'd make a terrible impostor, Sylvie. Everything you are is always in your eyes. I would never have thought it of you."

He said it quietly, almost vehemently.

And the words both thrilled her strangely and made her powerfully sad, too. Confused, she looked down and finished folding her cloak, to give her hands something to do.

"Your sister is delighted that you'll be staying with her."

Sylvie felt her cheeks grow warm with pleasure at that; she smiled softly. "I'm delighted to have a sister."

Tom watched her for a moment, as if simply enjoying her pleasure. "I'm glad," he said gently, finally.

She knelt quickly and placed the cloak in the trunk, to avoid looking into that gentleness, to avoid considering how it made her feel.

"Were you running from him when you came to England?" he asked suddenly.

Her head went up in surprise. "Etienne?"

He smiled a little at that. "Yes."

He'd done it again: surprising her into somehow revealing more than she intended, this time the name of her lover. Tom *did* have a point: She'd probably make a terrible impostor.

"I suppose I . . . I did not want to hurt him, and I didn't want him to persuade me not to come to England, so I did not tell him I was leaving."

It was only part of the truth. She still wasn't certain what the entire truth was; it still hovered somewhere, out of reach of her thoughts. Or perhaps she'd skillfully tucked it away in her mind because she was afraid to reach for it. She'd known only one truth for so long.

"Ah," was all Tom said. His face went closed, and he looked away from her then, but the room offered very little for a wandering eye accustomed to gaudy things, and so his gaze inevitably returned to her.

"And you will go back to him?" he asked it almost lightly. "After you spend time with your sister?"

She looked at him. "Yes." *If he will take me.* She supposed this was the truth, anyhow.

Tom inhaled and nodded. And then he straightened, reached into his pocket for his watch. A busy man as usual, Tom Shaughnessy.

"The show tonight. I came up to see if you would be leaving it, or if you would consent to stay for the remainder of the week." Brisk now.

She smiled faintly. "For you, I will be a fairy, a pirate, and a damsel for the rest of the week."

He didn't smile. "That's how I see you, you know. As all of those things."

Startled, she gave a short laugh.

And surprising her even more, he reached out and with his finger slowly traced the line of her jaw, deliberate as a cartographer.

Her eyes closed of their own accord, as if to allow her skin to remember the feel of his touch upon it this one last time.

"Good-bye. I wish you the very best, Sylvie Lamoreux."

And then he turned and was gone.

CHAPTER EIGHTEEN

O N FRIDAY EVENING, the end of the week of Venus, just as the doors had been flung open and a few audience members had begun to filter into the White Lily to be greeted warmly by Tom and The General, the king's man, Crumstead appeared at the entrance. He looked distinctly ill at ease.

Three men Tom had never before seen hovered behind him, looking just as ill at ease. And faintly resolved.

"Crummy!" Tom greeted him. "Back so soon? Didn't we just pay you?"

"We're shutting you down, Shaughnessy." Crumstead said the words in a slurry rush, as though they were so distasteful he wanted them to leave his mouth as quickly as possible.

Tom froze. He shot a questioning frown at The General, who normally made sure Crumstead got his bribe. The General shrugged in confusion.

Tom returned his attention to Crumstead. "You're jesting, are you not?"

"I'm dreadfully sorry, Shaughnessy, but it's the order of the law. We need to shut down the White Lily." He squared his shoulders, as if he needed all of his strength to deliver the news.

Tom gave a short humorless laugh. "Come now, Crummy. If you want more money, you've only to ask. We're friends."

Crumstead mumbled something.

"I didn't hear you, Crumstead," Tom snapped.

He cleared his throat. "Indecency. We're shutting you down for indecency."

Crumstead did have the decency to look ashamed about it. For the White Lily was not the worst of London's theaters by far. Simply the most popular, the most successful, and certainly the most inventive.

Tom glared at Crumstead. And Crumstead said nothing more, as he knew anything else he might say would be absurd. He glanced nervously down at Tom's hand, folding into a fist, then up into Tom's face. Tom could feel the heat of anger begin to flush his skin.

"Tom, if you don't close the doors and stop the shows, we'll . . ." He cleared his throat. "Have to a-arrest you."

"*Arrest* me?" Tom barked. Crumstead took a step back.

"You won't shoot me, will you, Shaughnessy?" Crumstead was not the world's most courageous fellow.

"Oh, for God's sake . . . Crumstead . . . what is this about? Tell me, and we shall take care of it as we always have. This is ridiculous, and you know it."

Crumstead looked miserable. "I wish I could tell you, Tommy, I honestly do. I don't know. I only know that those were my orders. Please. I need to close you down. God knows I don't want to drag you in."

The faces of the men standing behind Crumstead

echoed this—nervous determination to do what they had been ordered to do.

And Tom suddenly realized this lot had been sent to take him in if he resisted.

The look Tom turned upon Crumstead made the man blanch, but Tom wasn't actually seeing Crumstead. He was held motionless by a white fury and an extraordinary realization. He now understood that someone had encouraged—no doubt, *threatened,* rather—his investors to withdraw, and when that didn't appear to ruin him . . . had deliberately arranged to have the White Lily closed. He could only imagine the little web of connections required for something like this to take place—only someone with great wealth and power, the kind of power with infinite reach would be able to discover precisely how to ruin Tom Shaughnessy in particular. It had been a breathtakingly personal campaign.

But who on earth would have taken the trouble? Tom couldn't think of a soul he would call an enemy.

"Closed for how long?" Tom snapped.

"I imagine that will be up to the courts."

Nothing escaped the torpor of the courts of England before years had passed.

The dancers, aware of the tumult below, had moved from the wings and gathered on the lip of the stage, and now stood before the curtains in a row to watch.

Tom looked up, saw the row of white faces. Saw Sylvie hovering behind Molly. Saw her vivid eyes even from where he stood.

He imagined he would never be able to stand within a few feet of her without that pierce of awareness.

Crumstead sighed. "Tom, can I trust you to shut the doors, or will we have to take you with us?"

Tom's mind worked rapidly, sorting through possibilities, abandoning them, taking them up again.

"Tom, I really don't want to—"

"I'll shut the doors," he said tersely.

"I'm sorry, Shaughnessy. You don't know *how* sorry. Give my regards to Molly?" he added sadly. Because he knew the English courts as well as anyone, and understood it could quite simply be an eternity before he ever saw Molly again.

Crumstead and the men he'd brought with him finally slunk away.

And when he did, behind them stood a man Tom had never before seen. Tall, as tall as Tom, nearly, his face obscured in shadows until he took two steps into the White Lily, and stopped, a few feet away from where Tom stood.

He regarded Tom, quiet triumph and a faint contempt passing over his features.

The man's breeding surrounded him almost like a nimbus; the kind saints wore in medieval paintings. So pronounced it nearly hummed. He was darkly handsome and sleekly clothed, so sleekly that it almost seemed as though nothing, no dust, no harm, could ever possibly cling to him. He was the sort of man, Tom realized, who would never hope to be unobtrusive, and probably never wanted to be.

Rather like himself.

And suddenly Tom realized who this must be.

But he was older than Tom had imagined him. There was a weariness about his eyes, a hardness in his face that comes from living perhaps too much. Or perhaps from seeing or hearing of relatives go to the guillotine.

Because he *was* a French nobleman, after all.

The answer came definitively from Sylvie, as a shocked intake of breath: *"Etienne."*

But there was an echo of the name, too, another feminine voice. Stunned, Tom turned to its source:

Molly.

Molly's eyes met his, widened; she gave her head a little shake, and her hands went up to her face. She turned her head away.

Etienne's gaze landed only briefly on Molly. Tom understood that she was merely the implement he'd used to learn what he'd needed to learn, after all; he'd no doubt wooed her with trinkets and lovely walking dresses, intimidated and awed her with his manners, and then had skillfully extracted information from her, information about Tom and Sylvie and the White Lily. And she was no longer useful.

Etienne's eyes swept impatiently over the girls until he found Sylvie: took in her costume, the wand and the dress and the wings.

And then Etienne's expression . . .

With a shock, Tom realized: *This man loves her.*

If he was a prince, no doubt he could have anything and anyone he wanted. But even being a prince couldn't protect this man from the humbling vicissitudes of love. From all of those things on The General's list.

And he imagined that Etienne resented being humbled at the hands of a dancer, even if she was a glorious dancer, the magnificent Sylvie Lamoreux. And no doubt Etienne couldn't believe that *anyone,* let alone the mongrel part-Irish, part-Gypsy, part–God knows who else—though ultimately all English—owner of a bawdy theater might have presumed to *touch* what he considered rightfully his.

And so he had set out to ruin Tom. To teach the dancer a lesson? Or to teach the English mongrel a lesson?

Whatever had flickered over Etienne's face when he saw Sylvie finally settled into a sort of petulant anger. It was this expression that lingered.

Sylvie stared back at him, as if she simply couldn't look away. "How did you . . ."

"You could have told me you were leaving, Sylvie," he said. Nearly flawless English. Scarcely even a hint of his nationality. "And it was a simple thing to follow you, my love." He said it almost condescendingly. "Across Paris, and then to this . . . place."

Tom knew an impulse to seize the man by the cravat and give him a good choking.

The crowd was thickening at the door, wondering why a single man seemed to be blocking the doorway of their beloved theater. Tom saw Bateson's face. And behind Bateson . . . Belstow. The man who had dangled from Tom's fist just a few short weeks ago. Another man who thought it was his right to do as he pleased to women. He suspected Belstow had done his part to assist Etienne in the destruction of Tom.

"You would have stopped me, Etienne, from coming to London," Sylvie said. "And I wanted to know the truth of me and my family. That is all."

Etienne regarded her for a moment, his features unreadable, not denying the truth of this.

"I forgive you," he finally said. "We shall discuss it when we return."

Tom saw Sylvie's hand tighten around her wand and wondered if she intended to hurl it.

This was the man who had . . . taken Sylvie. As if it had simply been his right. As if she wasn't something precious and rare and beautiful, worth winning, worth fighting for. Something to be worthy *of.*

And now he was here to take her back, again, as if it was his right.

You fight. Dirty, if you have to.

Suddenly everything was elegantly simple.

"Name your seconds, Etienne."

A gasp went up. The showman in Tom was distantly gratified, even as he could hardly believe he'd uttered the words he'd heard so many times before. In truth, it wasn't even his right to utter them, as he wasn't, in fact, a gentleman.

But he saw now the uses of honor. He had also, quickly, as he was Tom Shaughnessy after all, derived a plan to fight dirty in the *guise* of honor.

Etienne's mouth curved faintly, condescendingly. His brows might have lifted a fraction, but other than that his expression was bland. As though nothing here could possibly touch him. "You are challenging me to a duel, Shaughnessy? I can't imagine why you feel you'd have the right."

"Since your English has thus far been splendid, I'm rather surprised you need clarification now. But yes, I am challenging you to a duel."

"Tom, for God's sake . . ." The General murmured. "You'll kill him. I mean you really will kill him. He *will* kill you," The General said, as if in concern, to Etienne.

Etienne's head swung toward the sound of The General's voice, then lowered his head to find the man who'd actually said the words. He frowned a little, puzzled by him, too, then returned his eyes to Tom.

A throat cleared. "He's really a marvelous shot, Etienne," Belstow allowed.

London, granted, would be much less interesting if Tom Shaughnessy were to be shot dead. Not even Belstow seemed eager to see it done.

"You've no true right to call me out, Mr. Shaughnessy," Etienne said calmly. "Duels are for . . ." He delicately trailed off, as if it would be ungentlemanly to point out that Tom was patently not a gentleman. "And what on earth would my transgression be, if you please?"

Tom looked at him. The room, and everyone in it, had gone eerily silent.

"You're afraid of me, aren't you, your Highass?"

Not his best attempt at humor, but then again, he'd just called someone out for the first time, and he was wildly, coldly, furious. Tom forgave himself.

Etienne stiffened then. His elegant jaw set. "Oh, come, Shaughnessy. You'll *hang* for killing me."

"But you'll be just as dead as I am, only sooner, as I assure you I'm a *flawless* shot."

"Shoots the heart out of the target every time." Bateson, who was hovering on the periphery of the small crowd, volunteered, voice quavering just a little.

Coldly now, Etienne said, "If men choose not to invest in your endeavors, if the authorities choose to take away your right to this travesty of a theater—"

". . . bit more than a suggestion, from what I hear," someone muttered.

". . . said he'd tell Pinkerton-Knowles's wife he liked to go to the theater to watch pretty girls," another muttered.

"—then that's their choice," Etienne concluded.

"*You* did this, Etienne?" Sylvie's voice was faint with bewilderment. "*You* closed the White Lily?"

Etienne turned his head toward her, opened his mouth slightly, as if to reply, then apparently decided a reply was unnecessary. He turned back to Tom.

Tom saw Sylvie's eyes become green flints.

"Name your seconds," Tom repeated calmly.

The two men locked eyes for a moment, and Tom saw a flicker of panic flash there in the depths of Etienne's dark ones, even as his features remained immobile.

"Etienne—" Molly said.

Etienne flicked her a look of such contempt that her face went white. "I'm sorry," she choked out, meeting Tom's eyes. "Mr. Shaughnessy . . . I . . ."

"Stop," Sylvie said, her voice low, thrumming with panic and fury. "Both of you."

"I shall stop," Tom said evenly, "If Etienne agrees to apologize for what he has done."

Etienne's lip curled condescendingly. "This is business, Shaugh—"

"No, Etienne." Tom's voice was as deadly and precise as his aim. "This is *not* business. I meant that you should apologize to Sylvie. This is about Sylvie. And I think you know why."

Etienne was silent. Hatred, flat and dark, dulled his eyes as he regarded Tom. Measuring him, and not arriving at conclusions he liked.

"Please," Sylvie's voice came again. Thin, taut. "Please stop."

Tom turned to her. "Very well, then. Tell me that you don't love me, Sylvie, and there will be no duel."

Sylvie stared at him, eyes glittering in her stark face. All the heads of the dancers were pointed at her, riveted, lovely mouths dropped open.

"Tell me you don't love me, Sylvie," Tom repeated calmly. "Look me in the eye and tell me, in front of these witnesses, that you don't love me, and there will be no duel, and you can return to Paris with Etienne."

And then he saw her square her shoulders, just a little shift of a motion, preparing herself just the way he'd seen her do right before she'd kissed Biggsy the highwayman.

She looked him evenly in the eye.

"I don't love you."

And her voice scarcely even trembled.

Four words. Each given equal weight. As somber, and as permanent sounding, as a sentence handed down by a judge.

Tom held her eyes evenly with his. Daring her to look away.

"Now tell me you love Etienne. Look me in the eye, in front of all these witnesses, and tell me you love *him*, and there will be no duel."

No color in her cheeks or lips. Her hands, he could see, were shaking, and surreptitiously she pressed them into her dress. Her chin went up.

"I love Etienne."

Tom stared at her. And finally he dropped his head into his chest with a nod.

Then looked up again at the prince. "I'll see you at dawn, Etienne. My seconds shall arrange it with yours."

"But—" The shocked protest came from Sylvie.

"I lied," Tom said, not looking at her.

Etienne made an exasperated sound, turned his noble palm up in apparent confusion. "Come now, Shaughnessy. You've nothing at all to prove. You might as well forgo the drama. She doesn't want you; she just said as much herself. And I'd hate to waste a perfectly good bullet on a mongrel."

Tom nodded along as Etienne spoke, as if this was all very fascinating. "But you've taken away all I have, including Sylvie, who has told everyone here she does not love me, so now I have nothing left to lose, do I, Etienne? Why should I care whether I live or die?" Tom's voice was level. He made it sound like a philosophical conundrum, something worthy of idle discussion over brandies.

"Because I knew there was more pleasure to be had in ruining you than killing you," Etienne said simply. "And you've no right to her. You've never had a right to her."

Tom furrowed his brow a little. "I see. So now that you've ruined *me* . . . Sylvie will love you?" He made it sound as though he was genuinely baffled by the logic. "Because it's clear from all the effort you've gone through to ruin me that you don't believe that she truly does. Or ever will. Despite what she says."

Tom watched with satisfaction as the color drained from Etienne's face, leaving him white with fury.

"You heard her," Etienne said coldly. "She doesn't want you, Shaughnessy."

"I heard her." Tom gave him an enigmatic little smile.

Etienne's breath came quickly now, along with his words, staccato and furious. "Very well. Since you want killing so badly, I will shoot you at dawn."

"Splendid. As I said, my seconds shall arrange it with yours."

Tom turned on his heel and made for the mural room, past Sylvie, past all the other staring faces, through the gasps and murmurs, without looking at any of them.

⁂   ⁂   ⁂

"You're really going through with it?"

The General simply watched, as he had so many times before, as Tom got out his pistols. He hadn't lit a cigar. Just being practical. There wasn't time, of course, to smoke it down satisfactorily, since dawn was a mere hour away.

Tom pried his pistol from its velvet nest. *Inspecting it for perhaps the last time,* he thought mordantly. "Yes."

"Are you going to shoot him?"

"I am," Tom said, hefting the pistol in his hand, "going to do my level best. Should it come to that."

Quiet in this cozy room once more. Kit Whitelaw, Viscount Grantham, was outside speaking with Belstow; he'd volunteered to be Tom's other second. The discussion was a mere formality, for the duel would be as they always were: in the clearing at the edge of St. John's Wood, with pistols, at dawn, just as the light began to dilute the dark.

"And your son?"

"Will know his father wasn't a coward—if anyone remembers me and tells him. I assume that will be you."

The General gave a lift of the shoulder: *Of course.*

Tom looked at him. "You aren't going to remind me that you told me she'd be trouble, are you?"

The General shook his head to and fro. "She might even be worth it," The General said.

Suddenly The General's head jerked toward him. "Wait: 'Should it come to that,' you just said. Does this mean you have a plan?"

"Don't I always, Gen?" Tom grinned.

✍ ✍ ✍

And while Tom was inspecting his pistols, Kit had sent Susannah and Sylvie back to the Grantham town house in his carriage so he could go about the very masculine business of playing the role of second.

In the Grantham parlor, over tea laced with whiskey, Susannah held Sylvie's hand.

Sylvie was dimly aware she was still dressed as a fairy.

"I remember this," Susannah said softly. "I remember another dark night, long ago. And it was you who held my hand."

"You were crying," Sylvie said softly. "I remember, too."

And she remembered she'd scarcely cried since, if ever. She wasn't crying now. She could not. She felt numb clear through. She was made of ice, she breathed ice. Her heart might be beating, but she could scarcely feel it.

"Well, I'm glad I can hold your hand now."

Sylvie said nothing.

"Somehow I knew it would be exciting to have a sister," Susannah added.

Sylvie managed a faint laugh at this. "I think we are doomed to be exciting, given the story of our mother's life."

"Sometimes men have duels and deliberately miss. Kit shot his best friend over a woman when he was just seventeen, and he deliberately missed." Susannah's way of offering comfort.

"Etienne won't miss," Sylvie said dully. "He won't try to miss. His temper . . . And Tom . . ." Her voice broke over the word. "Tom won't try to miss, either."

Susannah was very quiet. And still. Sylvie could feel her almost vibrating with alertness. "Mr. Shaughnessy is very handsome. Ow."

Sylvie had squeezed Susannah's hand a little too tightly. "I am sorry, Susannah."

Another deafening silence.

"You just called him Tom," Susannah added softly.

And a trifle, if Sylvie was being honest, insistently. Which began to penetrate the ice in her mind and heart.

Safety, certainty. These were the things she'd always wanted. Or thought she wanted. The things that Etienne promised, a future that should have seemed enormous and comfortable, a future beyond the *demi-monde*.

Why then, when then, did the idea of it become stifling? Even frightening? *Were you running from him when you came to England?* Tom had asked. And she had known he'd meant Etienne.

She realized then: she'd known he'd meant Etienne, because she *had* been running from Etienne as well as trying to discover her past.

Her breathing began to quicken. Etienne claimed to love her, but Tom's words returned to her now: *So now that you've ruined me . . . Sylvie will love you?*

It wasn't so much that Etienne loved her. Etienne felt *entitled* to her.

And then Sylvie thought about what Susannah had said: That Kit had felt like . . . air. Like everything she had always needed. But he was not at all what she expected.

She thought of Tom Shaughnessy, and how even as he glittered, and even as he reveled in all things bawdy and some things deadly, and even as he took her to what surely must be sinful bliss with his hands and mouth, there was something about him that made her feel . . .

Safe.

It wasn't so much about what he did, or what he owned. It was simply a part of him, that core of strength, of confidence, of—

Oh, this would amuse him:

Of goodness.

He was the best man she had ever known.

"Susannah, call the carriage! Now!" Sylvie yanked her sister to her feet.

"Oh Good *God,* I was afraid you were never going to say that." Susannah stumbled after her.

ஃ   ஃ   ஃ

It was nearly as familiar to Tom as Manton's now, this clearing at the edge of the park. Half a bright moon hung overhead, tangled in shreds of clouds. Dawn was encroaching; the deep purple of the sky was softening, gradually, to mauve.

Two carriages hung on the edge of the park, horses calm in their traces, nipping at the grass, unaffected by the various madnesses of men. They no doubt would scarcely flinch when the shots were fired in a few minutes.

The air was sharp; it was the brink of autumn, after all. An impatient wind gusted, getting in hair, lifting coats, tugging at the carriage reins.

The seconds had loaded the pistols; the surgeon, called from his bed, rubbed at his eyes and stood quietly next to Kit and The General, and Tom and Etienne had counted off.

They now stood the appropriate number of killing paces apart from each other, arms raised, pistols pointed.

When everyone heard the clatter of hooves, a carriage being driven at breakneck speed, pulled by a team of dark horses. The door burst open before it even came to a complete halt.

"Stop!"

A blur of dark flying hair and cloak hurtled out of the coach and planted itself between the two men, undecided, it seemed, as to which way to turn.

"I've heard of this sort of thing happening," The General muttered.

And at first, there was a stunned silence, for the *Code Duello* didn't particularly address women bursting in upon the proceedings.

"Sylvie," Etienne's voice finally cracked in the silence. "Don't be a fool. Step aside. Leave us."

She whirled on Etienne decisively. "Lower the pistol, Etienne, or I will shoot you myself."

And by God, she did have a pistol, which she raised. Who would have given her a pistol? Her *sister*?

Susannah's head was just now peeking out of the coach. The viscount turned and glared at his wife, who made a small "eep" sound and pulled her head back in.

"Susannah," Kit growled.

Ah, apparently so.

"I'm afraid I have to agree with Etienne to some extent, Sylvie," Tom said calmly. "Please don't point that at an armed and angry man."

Sylvie turned to Tom; her eyes caught the early light; she clenched the fist that wasn't holding the gun against her billowing skirts.

"Have they changed the rules for these things?" Kit murmured to The General. "There are usually only *two* armed parties."

"Sylvie—" Etienne's voice was dark with warning.

She turned back to him, and her voice rose so that everyone present could hear it, furious, aching with the need to confess. "I lied! I lied. Damn both of you, but I *lied.*"

"What sort of lie did you tell, Miss Chapeau?" Tom encouraged almost conversationally.

She whirled on him, glaring, breeze whipping her hair out behind her, then across her face, like those shreds of clouds in the sky.

And then she spun back to Etienne. Her voice softened just a little, but the words were firm with resolve.

"I am sorry, Etienne. When *I* said I loved you, I only meant to stop the duel. But since you are *both* idiots, and *must* duel . . ."

Suddenly the fury went out of her. She caught her hair in her fist to keep it from blowing about her face. "I did lie, Etienne. I do not want to be with you. I do not love you. It is . . . it is not you I love."

Tom doubted any man in the clearing truly gloated, for it was clear from Etienne's stance, the frozen posture, that she might just as well have shot him.

It was quiet, except for a horse whickering softly.

"When Molly said . . . when she said she thought she heard you throwing things at him . . ." Etienne lowered his pistol, handed it to Belstow. He gave a short laugh, a sound half pain, half disgust. "I suppose I knew."

His way of attempting to seize a little dignity from the occasion.

Sylvie was silent, gazing defiantly at Etienne. Watching him, daring him to do anything further.

And everyone, for the moment, was utterly still, apart from the rude wind buffeting coats and whipping hair.

And then Etienne nodded, lifted a hand, either in surrender or farewell or dismissal. He walked away, stepped into the coach. Belstow followed a moment later and pulled the door shut behind them.

Everyone watched until the horses lurched and pulled the carriage away.

Tom cleared his throat.

Sylvie turned suddenly. Gazed at him from a distance, very still. And then she knelt so she could gently place the borrowed pistol on the ground. Took two steps toward him. And stopped.

Tom obligingly handed his pistol to Kit.

Then Sylvie broke into a run and flung herself into his arms. He wrapped her tightly, buried his face in her hair, and forgot there was anyone else in the world in the sheer relief of holding her.

"I lied," she murmured again.

"So you said. Pity you lack faith in my aim." His voice was thick. "You thought he would kill me. You wanted to save me."

"I lied because I love *you*," she said indignantly.

"Oh yes, I know that, too. But *you* didn't know."

He held her. Gently touched the rough tip of his finger to the one tear shining on her cheek. Pressed his lips where the tear had once been.

"Well?" she demanded, looking up at him. "And?"

"Oh. Hmm. Well, I suppose if this isn't love, then love doesn't exist."

"Tom." The word was a warning and a command.

"Oh, very well. I love you, too."

He said it quickly. Trying to be glib. But he'd never said the words before, to anyone, in his entire life, and they instantly turned him inside out. He was suddenly glad she was there, warm in his arms, because though he was no coward, he suddenly felt very exposed.

And she knew. Smiled softly up at him.

And the first kiss in the aftermath of "I love you" was different from any other kiss he'd known. He kissed her then, pulled her close into his body, tightly against him, and took her lips with his, knowing he would never grow tired of the soft perfection of that lower lip of hers, of the sweet singular taste of her, hadn't tasted her nearly enough.

He lifted his head.

"Do you see how clever I was?" he congratulated himself. "You thought Etienne would shoot me dead, and there I would be on the ground, the life bleeding out of me. And I knew you would come and stop the proceedings because you couldn't let me go to my death without saying you lo*mmph*—"

She'd clapped a hand over his mouth, very much not wanting to hear the rest of it.

And then, when she realized what he'd been saying, she frowned. And went very still in his arms. And pulled away a little.

"You . . . carried through with a duel so that I would come here and make a scene?"

He refused to release her. Not when he'd just told her he loved her. "Of course. How else would you know that you *really* loved me if I hadn't? How else would you find the courage to take what you really want, Sylvie? And if I hadn't followed through with it, how else would you know that I loved you, too? You might have gone home with Etienne simply to save my life."

She considered this, then narrowed her eyes at him. "That was a risky game."

He smiled faintly. "It certainly was. I've some experience with risk, however."

He noticed her expression and the dangerous little sparks in her eyes, visible even by the waning moonlight, anger stiffening her arms.

"All's fair in love and war, Sylvie."

He *had* fought dirty, of course. But not with Etienne— with Sylvie.

Who was still glaring silently.

"Are you going to begin throwing things, Sylvie? If so, can you begin by throwing your body at me again?"

This won a smile. And so he ran his hands up her bare arms, chilled now, pulled her back into his chest, wrapped his arms around her, and she pressed her cheek against his heart. Held her for a moment.

He noticed, distantly, that Kit and The General had melted away to a polite distance, out of hearing range of declarations of love.

Over near the carriage, Tom saw a distant point of light: the tip of The General's cigar.

"I am sorry," Sylvie said after a moment. "I *was* bloody stupid."

"Quite all right," he said magnanimously.

"Do you need a wife?" she murmured against his chest.

"Are you proposing to me, Miss Sylvie Lamoreux?"

"I believe that I am."

"I'm but a penniless bastard, and you, apparently, are some sort of ballet royalty related to a bloody viscount."

"Not so penniless," she murmured.

"You should have had the decency to allow me to do the proposing," he added.

"Forgive me." She sounded contrite. "How would you have done it? With a bawdy song?"

"Like this, the man of economy that I am: Will you be my wife?"

He knew a brief moment of terror when the words were out of his mouth, and she was silent, still in his arms. It was a dizzying moment, where his world tilted on its axis, and he knew in the next instant, nothing would ever be the same.

"Mmm," she said softly against his throat, nuzzling him shamelessly there. "Yes, I believe I am quite willing to do that."

Ridiculous, awkward, helpless, glorious, immortal.

It called for another kiss, the first one after a proposal of marriage. And this one was different, too. Full of wonder and promise.

"Wait," he said suddenly. "What did you mean by 'not so penniless'?"

She looked up almost guiltily. But her eyes rivaled the rising sun for glow. "The General and I have something to tell you."

∂ℓ∂   ∂ℓ∂   ∂ℓ∂

They decided to divide the party into two carriages for the journey home, and Susannah and Kit were very understanding—more than understanding, if all the raised brows and meaningful smiles and manly pats on the back (for Tom) were any indication—when Sylvie asked whether they minded if she stayed, just for the evening, with her fiancé, Mr. Tom Shaughnessy. It was all in the family, anyhow: The surgeon was no doubt too sleepy to spread the scandalous tale of Tom Shaughnessy and his fiancée, and Kit and Susannah most decidedly didn't care, having done their own share of scandalous things.

And so Kit and Susannah and The General and the sleepy surgeon all boarded one carriage, and the other carriage took Sylvie and Tom.

He pulled her instantly into his arms, across his lap, and he pulled the cloak around the two of them, each warming the other.

"Are you still dressed as a fairy?" he murmured, suddenly.

"Mmm."

And then his mouth was at the base of her throat, hot against her chilled flesh, and his hands were fumbling up her dress. The aftermath of fear and near violence, relief and completion, fueled urgency, and Sylvie helped him, just as desperate for him. Swiftly, awkwardly, the dress was raised sufficiently, trousers unbuttoned. He brought his mouth to hers, covered her breasts with his hands, but still they took each other swiftly and gracelessly, half-laughing in wonder at the sheer raw hurry of it, release coming for both of them in harsh exultant cries minutes later.

Followed by peace.

Tom held her, pulled the cloak more tightly around her. Tucked his head between her shoulder and her chin, in that soft fragrant place. Placed his lips against her beating heart there.

"By the way, Sylvie, I know," he murmured.

She went still. "What do you know?" She tried for innocence.

He laughed softly. "Didn't you notice there were six mirrors? One for each girl. I sensed you might rather take matters into your own hands when it came to the ballet."

A silence. "Clever, aren't you."

"Mmm."

"But there is something you might not know, Tom." And now she was smug.

"Is there?"

"There *is* money in it."

And she told him of their plans.

         ぶ   ぶ   ぶ

London was filled with towers and bridges and other high places, and rumor had it that the day Tom Shaughnessy married Sylvie Lamoreux women flew so thickly from them it was like watching confetti fall from the sky. But then again, exaggeration and spectacle had always followed Tom Shaughnessy wherever he went. Tom, in fact, did his part to encourage the rumor, because it amused him, even as his wife appreciated it somewhat less.

It was, in fact, spectacle enough, some said, to see the formerly infamous Tom Shaughnessy strolling the floors of his outrageously popular Family Emporium, his arm linked with that of his beautiful wife, Sylvie Holt Lamoreux Shaughnessy, a small copper-haired child atop his shoulders.

And the Family Emporium was outrageously popular in large part because Tom Shaughnessy had always been lucky in his friends.

Once Augustus Beedle learned of the Family Emporium from The General, he not only roused the interest of a number of wealthy investors, he persuaded His Majesty, King George IV, to pay a visit to watch a new *corps de ballet* comprised of beautiful girls named Molly, Lizzie, Jenny, Sally, Rose, and Sylvie performing a ballet crafted by The General himself.

Called, naturally: *Venus.*

His Majesty had not required undue persuasion. Few men did where beautiful women were concerned.

"The least I could do for you, Tom," The General told him.

On every floor something delightful took place: Plays for children to watch and wonderful things for them to climb upon, horses and castles and pirate ships; on other floors, places for men and women to enjoy the company of each other separately and together, over tea or cigars or cards.

Watching the ballet was something they did together, primarily because everyone knew the king had done it.

But it *was* clear to everyone that Tom Shaughnessy, having acquired a beautiful wife and a beautiful child— for Jamie had come to live with him—had abandoned his wicked ways for good.

But every night, in a snug little room in a snug little bed, his wife insisted he remind her how very, very wicked he could be.

Don't miss the final book in
Julie Anne Long's
scintillating Holt sisters trilogy!

Please turn the page to preview

The Secret to Seduction

AVAILABLE IN MASS MARKET
SUMMER 2007.

CHAPTER
1

IN THE WINTER OF 1820, Sabrina Fairleigh, daughter of the Vicar of Tinbury, was startled to learn that her future happiness rested entirely in the hands of a libertine.

Or, rather, not just *a* libertine.

The Libertine.

This was how the Earl of Rawden signed his poetry, poetry that scandalized, enthralled, and allegedly caused women of all ages and ranks to cast off their dignity and trail him like hounds on the scent of a hare: *The Libertine.* It was the sobriquet by which he was known throughout all of England, and a million rumors, each one more shocking than the next, orbited the man: He lived openly with his mistress, he'd killed a man in a duel, he spent profligately on gaming and drink and his reprobate friends. His reputation was, in fact, such that word of it had managed to waft, like opium-and-incense-scented smoke, all the way to the tiny, tucked-away town of Tinbury, Derbyshire—where the air, incidentally, had never been scented by anything more controversial than roast lamb, and where life was as sedate, predictable, and pleasing as a minuet. The gentle, low-swelling green hills surrounding the vicarage, not to mention the Vicar of Tinbury himself, seemed to prevent local passions from becoming unduly inflamed. No one in Tinbury seemed in danger of writing sensual poetry.

But neither the gentle hills nor the Vicar had been able to prevent the quietly determined Sabrina Fairleigh from forming a . . . well, *attachment,* was the word she carefully used in her own mind . . . to her father's handsome curate, Mr. Geoffrey Lambert. Her heart used a different sort of word when it thought of Mr. Geoffrey Lambert.

And it was perhaps evidence of the Creator's perverse sense of humor that her father's curate, Mr. Geoffrey Lambert, and The Libertine, Earl of Rawden were cousins. It was a somewhat labyrinthine connection, perhaps, but a connection nevertheless. And it was Mr. Lambert's earnest hope that his wealthy, infamous cousin, the Earl of Rawden, would find it in his heart to finance his dream of being a missionary, and it was the unspoken understanding between Sabrina and the curate that she would accompany him on his mission . . . as his wife.

Much of what took place between Sabrina and the handsome curate was unspoken. Indeed, sometimes

Sabrina thought their communication primarily involved reverent gazing.

So now, on this winter morning after a surprisingly early snowfall, Sabrina was rattling along in a closed carriage while her friend Lady Mary Capstraw dozed, mouth half-open, across from her, and a discreet distance behind, *miles* behind, rolled the carriage containing Mr. Lambert. For the Earl of Rawden had bought a grand home—the grandest home in the Midlands, unoccupied for ages—and in celebration had decided to hold a house party. And through the same fine webbing of connections that linked the two cousins and everyone else of remotely noble birth, invitations for both Mr. Lambert and Sabrina's friend, Lady Mary Capstraw, had been procured, and Sabrina was invited along as Lady Mary's companion.

Many an engagement had been secured at a house party. At this thought, Sabrina's heart gave a tiny hop. The understanding might very well become a proposal within the next fortnight.

Sabrina didn't doubt that Mr. Lambert—Geoffrey, as she now called him, rather boldly, and never in front of her father—with his lean, elegant face and long slender fingers and his wistful, penetrating dark eyes could be related to an earl. He in fact, could have *been* an earl, she decided, though she hadn't the faintest idea what one looked like, as Tinbury featured only a squire or two. But the idea of the Earl of Rawden—*The Libertine,* for heaven's sake—with duels and his mistress and his poetry that caused such a tumult in the hearts of women . . . well, it all sounded so very *impractical*. How dreadfully uncomfortable and inconvenient it must be to be slave to such passions, such untidy emotions. She wondered whether the wear of his life would show on his face, or on his body; surely debauchery would take its toll. She decided, quite peacefully, she would feel compassion for the earl.

Still, she couldn't help but wonder if Geoffrey would kiss her at the house party.

Sabrina wondered whether the early snowfall was an omen. Mrs. Dewberry, a poor elderly woman confined to her home in Tinbury whom Sabrina visited at least once every week, would have called it an omen. Then again, everything—the shapes of clouds, the spots on sows, the calls of birds—had begun to feel like an omen to her now that she was very likely on the brink of marriage.

Still, only little patches of snow remained, scattered across the green like abandoned lacy handkerchiefs. The wan early sunlight was gaining in strength, and the bare birch trees crowding the sides of the road shone nearly metallic in it, making Sabrina blink as they flew past in the carriage. She wondered, idly, why trees didn't become woolly in winter, like cats and cattle, but instead dropped all of their leaves and went bare.

She smiled to herself and tucked her chin into her muffler. It was the sort of thought she had grown accustomed to keeping to herself, and it was because of that furrow that ran the width of Vicar Fairleigh's forehead.

It had been dug there, no doubt, by decades of pious thoughts and an endless stream of little concerns—his parishioners, his next sermon, how he was going to feed his wife and five children—and every time Sabrina said fanciful things, or played a hymn on the pianoforte with an excess of feeling, his eyebrows dived, that furrow became a veritable trench, and his gaze became decidedly wary, as though it were only a matter of time before she sprouted wings like a fairy and flew out the window.

So she'd learned to lock such thoughts away in her mind, much the way she'd locked away her other small treasures: the small rock she'd found with the imprint of a leaf, the needle she'd first used when she'd learned to sew, a handkerchief given to her by Geoffrey, and of course, the miniature of her mother, a face so like her own that her heart squeezed each time she looked at it. She seldom looked at it, for in the household of five children, it made her feel strangely lonely, and it reminded her she did not truly belong. Vicar Fairleigh had in fact gently requested she keep the miniature safely tucked away, and she had obediently done so all her life.

She had nothing but one faint and frantic memory of her mother, and the Fairleighs had told her, quite gently, that they knew nothing at all about her. All Sabrina knew was that the Fairleighs had taken her in when she had been orphaned, and loved her and raised her as their own, along with their four other dark-haired, round-faced, well-behaved children: three boys and two girls.

But she knew that Vicar Fairleigh worried just a little bit more about her, was just a little more watchful of her than he was of his other children, as though he was prepared for her to do . . . *something*. She knew not what. Something disquieting, no doubt. Possibly because by the age of thirteen she'd gone and done the unthinkable and become what could only be described as . . . well, "pretty" was the word everyone in Tinbury used, but they used it gingerly, for it seemed unlikely—unnecessary, really—for a vicar's daughter to be pretty. She was fine-boned and creamy-skinned, with rich dark hair that fell in loose spirals to nearly her waist when she brushed it out at night. And then there were her eyes: large with a hint of a tilt to them, green as spring. In truth, the word "pretty" was very nearly a lie. Where Sabrina Fairleigh was concerned, the word "beautiful" begged for consideration.

Certainly, as Sabrina grew older, it became clear that many of the male members of the congregation had ceased pretending to listen to the sermons, and were instead admiring the vicar's daughter, and all of this was rather inconvenient for the vicar.

And of course, the handsome curate had no eyes for anyone other than Sabrina once he'd arrived in Tinbury. Sabrina rather suspected her father wouldn't mind at all seeing her safely married off, happily pursuing work for the poor on some other continent.

She peered out the coach window as the horses and carriage decisively took a curve in the drive. Here, suddenly, the trees grew more snugly together, evenly spaced and rigorously groomed and each equally as tall as the next, as though here the owner of the property had decided to show nature precisely who was in charge.

Her heartbeat accelerated, because she knew as the end of their journey approached . . . so did the beginning of the rest of her life.

She puffed out a breath: it hovered whitely about her face as surely as if she'd been smoking a cigar, which amused and scandalized her. She nudged her friend with the toe of her boot.

Lady Mary Capstraw opened an eye. "Mmm?"

"Mrs. Dewberry said the squirrels were gathering more nuts this year, and the bark was thicker on the north side of the trees."

Mary stared at Sabrina blankly.

"Winter," Sabrina explained impatiently. "She said it would be both early and hard this year because of the squirrels and the bark."

Mary stretched. "Oh, the snow has scarcely stuck to the ground," she scoffed cheerfully. "Winter might be early, perhaps, but I daresay this little dusting means nothing at all."

Sabrina said nothing.

Mary sighed. "It's not an omen, Sabrina,"

And then the house came into view.

Like a pair of birds hushed in deference to an approaching storm, both she and Mary went very quiet, and gaped.

Magnificent. She'd never before used such a word to describe any corporeal thing. She'd never before had cause.

It was less a house than a . . . than a . . . *range.* It dominated the landscape the way she imagined the Alps must. An edifice of tawny stone, easily four times as wide as it was tall. Its vast cobblestoned courtyard featured a large marble fountain: The Three Graces seemed to compete with each other to hold up a single urn, from which water Sabrina suspected would shoot up during warmer months. One of the Graces was loosing a glossy marble breast from her toga. Sabrina quickly averted her eyes from it.

It occurred to her that this was both a magnificent and stunningly . . . *arrogant* house. Who on earth would feel entitled to such a dwelling, or could live here without feeling dwarfed by it?

In silence, Sabrina and Mary allowed themselves to be helped from the carriage by a swarm of footmen, and watched as their trunks were deftly ferried into the house.

Sabrina glanced to the left of the entrance, and saw, on the snow-dusted green surrounding the courtyard, a man and woman standing close together, and something about their postures, the tension and intimacy of them, riveted Sabrina's gaze.

The man was very tall, and his greatcoat hung in graceful folds from his shoulders to his ankles—the way it fit him told her this was her first glimpse of truly fine clothing. His hair was dark, straight, gleaming with nearly a blue sheen; his head was lowered as though he was listening intently to whatever it was the woman was saying. The woman wore a scarlet pelisse, the furred collar of it cradling her delicate chin, and her hair was fair, bright as a coin in the sun. Her shoulders sloped elegantly; her long hands were bare and startlingly white against her pelisse. Everything about the two of them spoke of intimacy and tension.

Sabrina couldn't help it: she strained to hear, but could only make out a woman's voice, low, lilting, musical.

Suddenly then the man's head jerked back. He went utterly rigid and stared down at the woman.

Sabrina's breath suspended: She'd seen a fox look at a vole just like that. Right before it seized it in its jaws.

And then he abruptly pivoted and strode away from the woman in long strides.

The woman's laughter followed him, a thin silvery sound. Merry as sleigh bells.

Good heavens.

Such passions, she reminded herself. How uncomfortable it must be to be a slave to them. She wondered what on earth the woman had said to cause such a reaction from such a very large man.

She tried to force her interest and trepidation back into the clothes of compassion, but they wriggled back out again. She couldn't help but take a tiny involuntary step back toward the carriage, for the man's anger came with him as he approached the fountain.

And then seemed to truly notice them, and immediately his posture changed as though he'd thrown off a cloak.

And when Sabrina looked up into his face, her lungs ceased to draw in air.

This was the only sort of man who could possibly suit this house.

Much more imposing from a mere few feet away, he was lean and broad-shouldered, more than a head taller than Sabrina; she tilted her head up to look into his face. There was a hint of Geoffrey in the lean face and the deep-set eyes, but his jaw was angular, his cheekbones cut decisively higher, the planes and hollows of his face more starkly defined. And his eyes were startling: blue, pale, crystalline, glitteringly alive. His brows thick dark slashes over them.

The Libertine.

Absurdly, she thought: *Debauchery suits him.*

Clinging to him were the remnants of his anger, and also, beneath it, Sabrina sensed something else. Her eyes darted toward where the woman had been standing; she saw, in the distance, the scarlet pelisse retreating deeper into the front garden. Whatever the woman had said to him had been intended to cut, and Sabrina sensed that it had.

But in an instant he was all enveloping charm and elegance and command. She sensed it was all second nature, the grace and the manners, no more effort for him than breathing; she also sensed that he scarcely took note of her, had taken her and her friend in with a glance of those fiercely intelligent eyes, summed them up, silently dismissed them, had moved on to other far more interesting things in his head.

Compassion wasn't absent, but Sabrina knew that compassion was the least of what she felt for this man.

And she decided then and there that the Earl of Rawden would most definitely take note of her before his house party was over.

THE DISH

Where authors give you the inside scoop!

From the desks of

Julie Anne Long and Sarah McKerrigan

Dear Readers:

From fiery ballerinas to kidnapping hunks to marrying a rock star, Julie Anne Long and Sarah McKerrigan dish in this author-to-author interview.

JULIE: Hey, Sarah! What on earth are we going to do for our Dish thing? Do you want to talk about your book? Frankly, I want to talk about your book. Specifically, I'd like to know why your heroine is gripping a big dagger. And how do I get abs like hers? And who is that bestubbled hunk lurking in the shadows? What's their story?

SARAH: That buff and brazen blonde is Helena, one of the three warrior maids of Rivenloch, and there's a very good reason she's wielding that sword. See, this cocky Norman knight, Pagan Cameliard, is about to subject Helena's little sister to a fate worse than death: marriage. In order to save poor Miriel, Helena decides to kidnap Colin du Lac, bestubbled hunk and Pagan's right-hand man, to use him as a hostage. Thus the book's title, **CAPTIVE HEART** (on sale now). Speaking of titles, I *love* yours! How did you come up with **WAYS TO BE WICKED**? How many ways are there? And can we learn them by reading your book? Tell me more.

JULIE: Ah, so *that's* the secret to a toned body—kidnapping hunks! (But don't try this at home, boys and girls.) It sounds like your heroine, Helena, knows a thing or two about being wicked. And *speaking* of **WAYS TO BE WICKED** (how's that for a segue?): I found that title by riffling through my '80s record collection—it's the name of a great old Lone Justice song. And there are *infinite* ways to be wicked, by the way. (You can see my hero and heroine, Sylvie Lamoreux and Tom Shaughnessy, engaged in one of the more, ahem, *popular* ones on the cover of the book.) Sylvie is a fiery ballerina and the darling of the Paris Opera when a mysterious letter sends her across the English Channel in search of a past she never knew she had. She lands—literally—in the lap of London's most notorious man, the gorgeous Tom Shaughnessy, owner of the bawdy White Lily theater, and fireworks ensue.

WAYS TO BE WICKED (on sale now) is the second book in my Regency-set trilogy about the Holt sisters, three girls separated when they were very young when their mother, the mistress of a famous politician, was framed for his murder and forced to flee, leaving them behind. *Beauty and the Spy* is the first book in that trilogy. Isn't **CAPTIVE HEART** part of a series, too, Sarah? Can you talk a little bit about it? And speaking of secret pasts—don't you have a little secret past of your own?

SARAH: Wow, Julie, it looks like we have more than a few things in common! Yes, **CAPTIVE HEART** is also my second book in a trilogy about sisters, though mine are Scots warrior maids, twelfth-century damsels in shining armor. In my first novel, *Lady Danger*, that same doomed-to-be-wed Miriel is saved from the altar by the sacrifice of her oldest sister, Deirdre, who disguises herself as Pagan's bride. Unfortunately, all this happens unbeknownst to Helena, who is already escorting Colin away at swordpoint. But Colin deems wild Helena a rather captivating captor, and Helena's resolve to ransom him is somewhat compromised when she becomes, well, *compromised*. Still, it takes a return to the besieged Rivenloch castle, where they're forced to fight a common foe, to bring the lovers together at last.

As for *my* story, why yes, I *do* have a secret past! I started out as a singer in The Pinups, an all-girl rock-and-roll band, played drums once in a Tom Jones video, and married the current bass player of the classic rock band America. But I'm not the only one with a musical backstory. Hit it, Julie!

JULIE: OK, I confess: I wanted to be the female version of Bono when I grew up, so I played guitar, sang, and wrote songs in San Francisco bands for years. But you know, Sarah, when you think about it . . . now that we're romance authors, we still spend our days with passionate men who excel at, um, wielding their instruments. (Ha!) We just write stories about them.

Sincerely,

WAYS TO BE WICKED   CAPTIVE HEART
www.julieannelong.com   *www.sarahmckerrigan.com*